CONVICT'S GAME

SKELETON CREW - BOOK 1

Jolie Vines

WWW.JOLIEVINES.COM

Cover design (the model) – Natasha Snow

Cover model photography – Michelle Lancaster

Cover model – Anthony Patamisi

Cover design (the skull) – Qamber Design Emporium

Editing – Emmy Ellis at Studio ENP

Proofreading – Lori Parks

Interior formatting – Cleo Moran at Devoted Pages Design

Interior art (map, character art) – Amanda Desilets

SKELETON
CREW

READER NOTE

Dear reader,

Ever since Convict's introduction in my Body Count series, readers demanded more. Well strap in, because he's here to give you everything you asked for.

Be aware that this is a dark romance with boundary-pushing scenes. Check the triggers if you need to, but if you loved Arran's Obsession (Body Count, #1), you'll be on your knees for the broken crew member who got left behind.

If you haven't read Body Count yet, I recommend you do because it's awesome. You can also just dive straight in here if you prefer.

Adore audio? The audiobook is multicast duet and devilishly good, with Lucas Webley, Zara Hampton-Brown, Shane East, and Ella Lynch. There are sound effects! Listen along as you read - it's another level of incredible.

Are we good? Let's slip on our Skeleton Girls Detective Agency t-shirts and saunter into the dark streets of Deadwater together, back into the hands of our favourite skeleton crew.

Love, Jolie

TRIGGER WARNINGS

This dark romance features adult themes and explicit content that may be triggering for some readers (and a shopping list for others. We don't judge). Please proceed with care if you're sensitive to the following:

Sexual Content:

Inside of the relationship:

- Dubious consent
- Edging, denial, and orgasm control
- Free use elements
- Public claiming and rough handling
- Knife play
- Birth control removal
- Somnophilia
- Stalking and monitoring
- Power exchange, restraints, and public sexual display
- Emotionally loaded, possessive sex

Outside of the relationship:

- Threat of and attempted rape
- Threat of assault
- A predator-prey game
- Explicit sex club scenes

Dark Themes & Plot Elements:

- Amnesia and memory trauma
- Kidnap
- Human trafficking (referenced, not graphically shown)
- Torture during interrogations (low on gore,

medium on discomfort)

- Murder, death, and on-page violence
- Substance abuse and alcoholism (brief, not romanticised)
- Mental health challenges (PTSD, anxiety, emotional repression)
- Captivity and forced proximity
- Morally grey choices, criminal behaviour, and general gangland chaos
- This book is for 18+ readers who like their romance messy, their banter filthy, and their characters clawing their way toward love with bloodied nails. Feel free to email me with any specific questions or concerns, or ask in my reader group.

BLURB

Sequel to the #1 bestseller Body Count

I never planned to chain a gangster to my bed, but now, I'm not letting him go.

I was raised in boardrooms, not back alleys.

But when my grandfather died and our company fell into chaos, I uncovered something far worse than bad accounting: a connection to the city's darkest underworld.

I needed answers. I needed help.

So I made a deal with a devil in a skeleton mask. One with a body made for sin and a past that might destroy us both.

Convict is brutal, broken, beautiful, and claims he knows me, even if he's a stranger. Amnesia stole his memories, yet the way he touches me, looks at me, and possesses me, tells a different story.

Now I'm in too deep, with the man, with his skeleton crew, and with the secrets someone is killing to protect.

And the only way out is to bring it all crashing down.

Convict's Game is the first book in a high-heat, dark romance, murder mystery trilogy with a skeleton-masked crew, an obsessive-sweet gangster, the smart cookie he's insta-obsessed with, and a city where the shadows hide more than just sin.

This series picks up where the #1 bestselling Body Count series left off.

Tropes & Themes:

- Corporate Princess x Street King

- A deal with a delicious devil

- Dangerous games (the chasing kind plus more)

- Cute AF gangster hero with amnesia

- Obsessive love, rough play, and handcuff action

- Found family, secrets, and a deadly inheritance

- A murder mystery to solve (with clues)

Check the TWs in the front or on my website. Trust me, they're there for a reason, little gangster.

PLAYLIST

We're building this as we go with songs suggested by my
Facebook reader group. By book three, we'll have a whole set.

Circus Psycho by Diggy Graves
i'm yours by Isabel LaRosa
Just Keep Watching by Tate McRae
I hope you hate me by Dead Poet Society

WELCOME TO DEADWATER

1. SKELETON CREW WAREHOUSE
2. CHERRY'S CHURCH STEPS
3. GENEVIEVE'S APARTMENT
4. MAYOR'S MANSION
5. CONVERTED CHAPEL/BROTHEL
6. MONIQUA'S APARTMENT
7. FOUR MILERS TERRITORY
8. MILBURNE ALLEY
9. TOWN HALL
10. EMMELINE'S APARTMENT
11. MALACHI'S GYM
12. INDUSTRIAL ESTATE
13. TO THE BOATHOUSE
14. RIORDAN'S CLIFF

5
6
7
8
DEADWATER
HARBOUR
10
JOLIE VINES
BODY COUNT &
SKELETON CREW
SERIES
JOLIEVINES.COM

Prologue

Mila

Tonight, I'd girlbossed too close to the sun.

The disused office block where I waited was a holding cell. A place they kept women ahead of transporting them to their fate.

Somewhere I'd willingly walked into days ago, but had done so knowing I could walk out at any time, once I had what I'd come for.

I'd been so confident in my plan. Now, that confidence faded.

My hands trembled, and I hid them at my spine so the man in the doorway wouldn't see.

Salter pointed from my room to the hall, rings glinting on his fingers. "Go."

Shit. If he was kicking me out, everything I'd tried to do was over.

Shrinking in on myself, I crept into the corridor. Horror stalled my steps. A new moon had the city of Deadwater in a darkness so thick, only the neon purple glow from a window to the street lit the scene.

It couldn't hide how two of Salter's cronies held a man, gagged with cloth and on his knees with his hands and legs tied. He gave a muffled growl and fought his captors, bigger than them but outnumbered.

My brother. My backup plan. The one person who knew I was here and could get me out by force if needed.

Shock stole my breath. "What is this?"

From a sheath at his belt, Salter slid out a blade. Tested the edge of it against his nail. "This is checkmate, Miss Marchant. I'll make this short. We know who you are. Why you're on my fucking turf is the more interesting question, but I'm more inclined to consider what you can do for me. This is yours, correct?"

How did he know my name? I'd been so careful.

I didn't get a chance to ask. Salter hooked his knife under my brother's chin, stopping his struggles. A thin line of blood ran down the blade, the colour tinged strange by the light.

I clasped my hands to my mouth. "Stop. Don't hurt him."

The gangster gave a cold laugh and mimicked me. "Stop, don't. If you shut your bitch mouth and obey my every word, he lives."

At my frantic nod, he withdrew the knife.

"It just so happens I can use you. You've heard of the skeleton crew and the chase-fuck game they operate in their warehouse?"

"The...the what?"

He held his cruel gaze on me. "It's as it sounds. A group of men hunting women. Twenty versus five all locked in together. Cages, bloodshed, paying viewers. Each man fights the others to catch and fuck a woman, then to keep her as his property, her body under his ownership from then on. It's, shall we say, brutal."

It sounded terrifying. "What does this have to do with me?"

"One of the contestants is a man I need brought to heel. Guess which role you'll be playing?"

No, no! This had all gone wrong. I wasn't naïve, at least I didn't think I was. I'd grown up in this city of sin until fate elevated me from its dark side.

"I don't think—" I started.

Without warning, Salter grasped my throat then threw me to the floorboards. I landed hard and cried out. When I rolled up, I linked my gaze to their prisoner's furious one.

I loved my brother, even if we barely knew each other. Even if family politics had kept us apart for most of our lives until I'd corrected that mistake. He couldn't be hurt because of my decisions.

The knife was again at his throat, tight against his beating pulse.

Salter's lips curled in an ugly smile. "Choose wrong and he dies. Are you going to play, Miss Marchant? Yes or no?"

My brother's throat slit or accepting the terrible deal?

I had no choice but to enter the game.

1

Convict *– several weeks earlier*

Coming back from the dead was for heroes, not assholes like me.

The drip, drip, drip of my meds soaked into my dreams, mixing with flashes of flames and sirens, the only images in my otherwise empty head.

I was in a hospital bed, that much I'd worked out.

There had been a cop, then an ambulance crew, jostling my broken frame onto a stretcher. After that, a jumble of medics and needles and the numbing drug robbing me of the chance to recall who the fuck I was.

"Sharp scratch," they told me before stabbing me again, though I never felt a thing.

That must've been a couple of weeks ago. I'd woken enough to catalogue my injuries. A shattered leg. A burned arm. A crack in my skull that a nurse informed me left a scar.

Maybe that's what stole my memories. I couldn't summon a name, and the medical bracelet on my wrist gave me nothing. 'Roscoe Locke' it read. If I'd ever been that man, I had no recollection of him.

Unconsciousness sent my world to black once more. I woke to nurses changing the dressings on my arm.

"Prison tattoos," one hissed to her co-worker.

The second woman tutted. "Gang, more like."

A *gang*. That felt right. I was heavy on the inkwork, from the skin that wasn't under white bandages, including a snake that wound around my uninjured forearm, its head peeking onto my wrist. My body told my history with muscles, old scars, including on my knuckles, and so much black ink. No shit that I was bad news.

If I saw me coming down a dark alley, I'd run, too.

No wonder they were keeping me docile.

The first nurse eyed me. In her hands was a syringe of clear liquid, the shit that knocked me out each time they gave it.

"Hey," I tried. My first word in weeks was barely a rasp. "Lay off the KO juice."

The nurses exchanged a glance.

"Please?" I tried. "Doc said I could start making my own bad decisions again. I don't need it." A lie, but I had to get a clear head.

The second woman flattened her lips and spoke to her colleague. "Imagine what he'll be like off it. Screaming the place down in an hour."

I passed out the second the drug entered my system.

I couldn't tell the length of time until I surfaced next, maybe hours or days, but it was to a certainty that spiked my adrenaline and stirred my broken body. I had to get out of here. Even if I crawled and dragged my busted leg behind me. Except I needed clothes. The damn cast removed.

To be off their drugs.

Bribing a medic was out of the question with zero possessions to my name. Threats could work, but I didn't love the idea of hurting people who'd helped me, even with the side of judgement. Sweet-talking might be better.

My door swung open, and a cop entered my room, a big fucker with his hands in his pockets and a smug-as-fuck smirk on his miserable mug.

He inspected me. "Still alive, then."

Instinct shut me up. Whoever he was, he knew me. I'd been desperate for that recognition, for one person to walk into my hospital room and ugly cry over me or say my name. But not someone like him. I didn't know much, but I was certain cops and I weren't on bro-hug terms.

The officer picked up my chart and perused my injuries list. "That leg will keep you out of trouble, though the turf war appears to be over for a while. A skull injury? Possible amnesia? You're shitting me, Con—" He cut off his sentence and dropped the chart. "Amnesia. Just hilarious."

The bastard strolled away, laughing.

Desperation flooded my system. I tried to swing out of the bed but collapsed on the sheets, drugged up and weak as a kitten. A new fact became clear.

No one was looking for me.

That hollowed me out so badly that next time they stuck me, I didn't protest.

Instead, I plotted. Over the next week, I played nice with the medical staff while I watched their routine. I faked a lack of interest. I faked a headache so they didn't judge me as more of a threat. I lied about taking the meds they'd switched to providing in pill form rather than the IV.

My healing was going well and the heavy cast on my leg scheduled to be replaced with a walking boot.

The minute I was upright, I was gone.

The day dawned, and I was helped into a wheelchair and taken to a room where the cast got sliced away. A single nurse waited to escort me back to my room where I was due another dose of pain meds.

I wasn't going back. I'd tested my strength in private moments, and it had come back in spades. Outside the room, I was going to turn and stride in the other direction and not look back. They couldn't stop me.

Only one issue remained: I had nowhere to go.

After a month in that fucking bed, I still had no clue of the name I used on a daily basis. No phone, no TV in my room, no visitors besides the cop. Even the home address in my records felt like a stranger's.

Maybe I'd go there. Maybe I'd end up on the streets. Something about my scars and how ready I felt to use my fists told me I was a survivor.

The medic who'd removed my cast helped me up. My nurse steadied me on crutches, then together, we shuffled to the door, the weakness a pretence on my part. Sure, I wasn't at peak strength, but I could fucking run.

In Deadwater Hospital's bright corridor, I readied to go.

But down the hall, a woman stared at me like she'd seen a ghost. "Am I high, or is that really you?"

A stranger.

No.

Platinum hair, a banging body, kind eyes. I knew her, didn't I? Hell if I could recall her name.

Steadying myself on my crutches, and with the nurse hovering at my shoulder, I formed a half-smile, temporarily frozen in my plan. I hadn't expected that. A familiar face. "I guess so."

Blondie's gaze sank over me, taking in the boot. The bandages and healing scars.

"Oh, hun, I thought you were dead. We all did. Do you remember me? It's Dixie. Have you been here the whole time?"

The name resonated. She was a sex worker, my mind finally supplied. Or maybe an exotic dancer? I'd definitely seen her naked, but not in the touchy way.

She was a friend. Holy fuck.

At my nod, Dixie whipped out her phone and stabbed

at the screen with hot-pink nails. Her call connected, and she spoke in a rush, her other hand going to a bandage at her throat. "You'll never guess who I found. It's Convict. He's alive."

Convict.

Emotion lurched inside my chest. At long last, I had an identity, even if I was apparently named after a criminal record. Not only that, but someone was looking for me. My plans flexed and shifted.

"Dixie?" My tone still held a rasp after the smoke damage from the unknown fire that left the burn marks in my skin. "If I wanted to leave this place, do I have somewhere to go?"

Pity filled her eyes. "You don't remember the warehouse? The skeleton crew?"

At my side, my nurse clucked her tongue. "Mr Locke, without family to discharge you into the care of, you should remain here. The police recommend—"

Dixie returned the nurse's challenging glower and interrupted. "The police can suck it, hun. We're his family, and if you get in our way, I'll have the whole skeleton crew down here to take our boy home."

My need to run was no more. I was finally leaving. I wasn't alone after all.

I swallowed a lump in my throat. "I just want to go."

Dixie smiled. "Then it's settled. Damn, Convict. Risen from the dead. I'm going to start calling you a saint."

Everything moved so quickly my messed-up head spun.

Despite her words, my nurse had clear relief in her eye when I took the offered meds bag and walked away. A gangster was a liability to the hospital. No matter their protests, I was better off gone.

Then we were out into the night.

Rain drenched my face. The air bit into me. After fuck

knows how long, I threw my head back and let the city embrace me.

A man had joined us—Manny, the security chief for the skeleton crew who was there to escort Dixie. I knew him on sight. He guided us to a huge black car, muttering to himself about how Shade was going to shit a brick.

Shade. Another rush of relief nearly floored me. Shade was my friend? Or boss? Maybe both. Someone I cared about for sure.

We slid through Deadwater's mean streets in Manny's bulletproof ride, the city lights strobing over me. Exhaustion clawed at my senses, and the windscreen wipers and engine hum lulled me to rest. I fought it. Couldn't close my eyes. Not now I had friends again, and familiar faces after weeks of nothing.

I'd been in a coma so hadn't noticed how winter was giving way to spring. The weather didn't deter the crowd that formed outside a huge red-brick warehouse by the river, bright neon lights on the signs that read DIVIDE and DIVINE. The headquarters of the skeleton crew. A nightclub on one side and a strip club and brothel on the other.

Home.

I swung my crutches out of the car and gazed up at the building, music thumping from one of the clubs. 'Circus Psycho' by Diggy Graves.

A swell of emotion threatened my hardman exterior.

I knew every brick. I'd worked and played here. We got up to all kinds of twisted fun and games. A whole lot of sex.

I had no idea who the fuck I was, but I belonged in this hotbed of sin.

Across the car park, a crew member with a skeleton print black bandanna held open a staff door. He lifted his chin at my approach, Dixie and Manny either side of me.

"Good to see you again, Convict. Been a long time, and

we all thought… Doesn't matter. You're back."

"Thanks, man." I slapped his hand.

Manny powered on ahead to get the next door, and Dixie leaned in once we'd passed the unknown crew member.

"That was Mick. You weren't close but you liked him."

I slid her a glance, but there was no judgement in her eyes. She knew.

"You've been out of it a long time, and hospitals make you delulu with lack of sleep. Ask me how I know. That nurse said it could take a while to be back on your feet for more than just standing." She gently nudged me with her shoulder.

I found my voice. "What happened to your throat? Were you hurt when I was?"

Dixie's smile dimmed. She touched the white bandage and swallowed. "Separate incidents, and nothing I want to talk about, hun."

"Got it. Consider me shut up."

"After your return to the land of the living? A whole lotta folk are going to want the opposite, saint."

Deeper inside the warehouse's interior, people stared at me with open surprise. A half-naked dancer sticking jewels on her nipples gaped then hurried back into what appeared to be a changing room, whispers following.

I frowned inwardly. Her heavy, round tits had bounced as she'd moved. That was hot as fuck. But my dick? Not interested.

We arrived at an office, and a man swung out of the room with shock in his eyes. At about my age of twenty-eight, he had endless tattoos, piercing blue eyes, and black hair. Better still, I knew him, just like I had Dixie. Two for two.

Shade banded me in a hard hug, his arms crushing me. "Shite, did I hurt ye? That's a stupid question. You've never felt pain in your entire life. Not when we were kids in a fight club and not now." He palmed my jaw and examined me, his Scottish accent strong. "Do ye remember me?"

Shade was... I searched my mind. An enforcer? Yes, I'd seen him kill. He took out the assholes who crossed our crew. *Right*.

"Course I do," I muttered.

Like with the docs, I wasn't admitting my shite memory. It was bad enough that I was in hospital-issue t-shirt and trackies, cut to accommodate my walking boot, my dark hair overly long with a scar running back from my hairline from my skull injury. Coupled with the fact I needed a shower and a shave and to get off the fucking meds that were slowing my thoughts, I was a wreck.

Relief swept over his features. "Good. That's good. Don't worry, brother. We've got ye covered from here. Arran isnae home, but the minute he reads my message, he's going to fucking die."

He twisted to talk to Dixie, asking her about the hospital and what the nurses had said.

But the name Shade said gave me pause. Arran was the leader of our crew, my brain supplied an image of the man. I'd known him for years, and small details peppered my thoughts. He was as deadly as Shade and more ruthless. In that mental picture, Arran was enraged.

I'd done something bad to him.

Sickness crawled through my belly at the certainty. Somehow, I'd fucked over one of my closest friends and ended up broken in a hospital bed.

I swayed, either at the realisation or exhaustion.

Shade caught me. "Come on. Upstairs and to bed. You're dead on your feet."

He was wrong. I was alive.

We took the lift up to the fifth floor.

Shade led the way into a corridor with rooms opening to the left and right. "Thought it would be better for ye to stay here where we can take turns in checking on ye. I had someone prepare a bedroom right at the end, so ye shouldn't be disturbed too much."

Dixie whispered, "This is the cam girls' and boys' floor. Lots of faking orgasms for paying viewers."

As she spoke, a door opened to one of the rooms and a woman exited, buck naked aside from a barely there bra. She gave us a polite smile and sauntered to a bathroom opposite. Inside the space, another woman sprawled on a bed reached between her legs to slide out a double-ended dildo.

Fucking hell. That was fire. Or it should've been. Still, there was zero response in my body. No rush of heat. No reaction at all to the display of sex they'd just quit.

Either my brain was fried or my dick had gone on strike. And honestly, I wouldn't blame either of them.

Shade and Dixie directed me to the last room on the corridor and set me up with water, my oversized bag of medication, and promises for regular check-ins.

Shade held the doorframe. "Rest. Fuck knows ye need it."

Finally alone, I dropped down onto the cool white blanket and exhaled hard.

Somehow, I'd been gifted a second chance with people who cared about me. I didn't know what I'd done to deserve it, or to earn their rejection in the first place, but one thing was certain.

Whatever I did to get tossed in the fire, I wouldn't repeat it. I'd been burned once. Now I'd set the world ablaze for them.

I'd never fuck up again.

2

Convict

$\mathcal{A}$ wailing moan of pleasure pierced my consciousness, dragging me from sleep, and I sat up, blinking in the low light of my room.

There was no cast on my leg. No IV in my arm. No hospital beeps or the scent of antiseptic. Just the thudding bass of music and sex moans through the wall. Deadwater's version of a wellness retreat.

Fuck, I was free.

Swinging out of bed, I touched my booted foot to the floor then stood, testing my balance. Not bad. On the bedside table waited a white pharmacy bag, and I pulled out the only meds I'd be taking from now—the last of my antibiotics— swallowing them down with a gulp of water. My head hadn't felt this clear in forever, and I wasn't about to cloud it with drugs for pain I couldn't feel.

Someone tapped at my door. I stumbled over to open it.

With a bundle in her arms, Dixie gave me a once-over. "I brought you clean clothes from the wardrobe next to the strip club downstairs. Feel free to raid it if you don't like what I picked. Got to say, you're looking stronger already. I checked on you a few times throughout last night and today. You slept hard."

The clothes smelled clean and not of hospital. "If I'm a saint, you're an angel. What time is it?"

"Nine in the evening. Almost twenty-four hours after we brought you in. You ate?"

At some point in my rest, I'd spotted a packet of sandwiches left for me and had devoured them. "That was you?"

"No, Shade. Arran's going to call again soon, if you're fit to head downstairs? He tried once already, but we thought it better not to wake you." Something ticked over in her gaze. "Do you know who I'm talking about?"

I grabbed my crutch and threw a glance around the room to check I had all I needed. Except I didn't own anything. At least not here. No keys or phone to take.

"Yeah, I remember Arran." Just about. "Where is he anyway?"

"Honeymoon. Somewhere hot. I'm a little jelly over it so I'm choosing to space on the details."

Arran was married?

Dixie noticed. Tsked. "His wife is Genevieve. She's lovely."

The name summoned a face, though no other details. They'd come back. Piece by piece, the blanks were being filled in. "Fuck, right. I know her."

"That memory still troubling you?"

I purposefully eyed her throat bandage and returned her words from yesterday. "Nothing I want to talk about, hun."

She smirked in amusement, and we left my room and made our way down the hall.

Giving me a ten-minute warning, Dixie waited while I used the bathroom then cleaned myself up as best I could, changing my clothes for the replacement t-shirt and sweats, slicing them open for my boot, and the single shoe I needed to match.

I needed a shower, which I could do now I had the leg

cast off, but that meant removing the bandage covering the burns on my arm. I grimaced at it. In the hospital, the nurse had said it should be good, but I didn't want to stare down at that mess. Not yet. One demon at a time.

Back in the cloakroom, I called Dixie in.

"Can I use this?" I waved the razor I'd found in a row of toiletries baskets on the counter.

"Everything here is for the staff to use. Knock yourself out."

I fronted up to the sink, lathered up, and tackled weeks' worth of scruffy beard.

As I worked—fucking hell, did that feel good—Dixie hopped onto the counter and crossed her legs at the ankles, watching me as she continued her crew update.

"Shade's girlfriend is Everly, and she's pregnant. Cassie and Riot are paired off, but I don't think you've met him. He's a newer crew member, real name Riordan." She peered at me. "You saved Cassie from the fire that almost killed you. She came upstairs with me earlier to check on you. She's my boss now."

I scowled at my reflection, hating my broken memory. "Tell me about the fire."

Dixie launched into a story of how I'd been in the basement of a rival gang's brothel when someone torched the place. Cassie had been held prisoner and would've died if I hadn't boosted her out of a cellar door while the building burned around us.

"Several people burned to death that night. It's why everyone thought you were dead. But Arran kept the faith. No body, no mourning. They pulled out any number of charred corpses, but none were yours."

In the mirror, I finished my shave then ruffled my dark hair to cover the scar slicing back from my hairline. My brush with death was written right there on my face, but I was still the same guy from the wrong side of the tracks. Just one of my nine lives lost.

Out of the bathroom, we made for the lift, and I leaned on the wall while Dixie pressed the button.

"Why was I there? In the place that burned down."

"Beats me."

"Do the cops know I'm skeleton crew?"

"Everyone knows, hun. Why?"

Frustration twisted in my gut. I'd been a stranger to myself for weeks, but maybe I hadn't needed to be.

The lift arrived, and we descended to the ground floor, opening onto a busy corridor. Music thumped through the wall to the left that opened onto the nightclub, the scent of dry ice and beer battling perfume and aftershave. On the other side, two women lingered in the open doorway of the dressing room. It was for the strip club, my mind supplied.

In skimpy outfits, one a cowgirl and the other a bunny complete with fluffy round tail, both women snuck glances at me.

I checked them out in return, again, testing myself. I was reasonably certain I was hetero, but what the fuck was wrong with me if it didn't have even a flicker of interest? Not in them, not in last night's sex show, and not in Dixie who was clearly a friend but also knock-out hot.

"Am I gay?" I said in a rush.

Dixie blinked. "Don't think so."

"Do I have a girlfriend?"

Her shoulders sank. "Not that I know of, but you did have a thing with Alisha before she got killed." She winced. "Shit. Did you know that? She was a victim of the murderer haunting Deadwater. That case got solved, but it won't bring anyone back."

I stumbled, catching my step with my crutch. I had

known about Alisha. I'd heard about her when I was, where? A flash of recollection hit me. My first real one that wasn't putting a name to a face. A dank room with a crowd of people watching a gangster holding court. The smell of smoke had ghosted through the air. I'd been sad at Alisha's death, but not broken like a boyfriend would've been.

Dixie directed me to an office, the door opening on our approach and revealing Shade plus a second man I recognised as another of the skeleton crew's inner circle, a bear of a man with a thatch of dark-blond hair.

"Tyler," Dixie whispered.

I gave her a small smile of thanks.

Shade hugged me like he had yesterday, or maybe the day before, I'd lost track of time. Tyler carefully palmed my shoulder, murmuring a greeting with his serious gaze taking me in. For a beat, he lifted it to look over my shoulder.

Dixie peeked back at him, flushed pink, then closed herself out.

I was messed up, but I knew attraction when I saw it.

At the polished black desk, Shade collected a tablet and placed a call. While it connected, I took my fill of the room. I'd spent a lot of time in here, but on the other side of the desk. We had a bright spotlight that we'd shine on visitors to intimidate them. Against the red-brick wall at the back of the room was a filing cabinet with a stash of skeleton bandannas we'd use to cover our faces. There were knives concealed under the desk. A gun or two.

Fresh relief had me standing a little easier. Home sweet home.

"Arran, can ye hear me? He's awake." Shade held up the tablet, and on the screen, another familiar face resolved.

Fuck, my hard shell crumbled.

I hadn't dreamt last night. No hint of memory had returned over what I'd done to Arran. I knew it was bad. He had every reason to throw me out of the crew when I'd only just discovered it again.

But if I was shaken, he was, too.

Arran stared at me in amazement, his face white. He dug his fingers into his blond hair then swore. "You're a sight for sore eyes."

My heart thumped like it wanted out of my chest. "Good to be back."

He leaned in more, his gaze roaming over my features and lingering on my scar. "Shade tells me you were at death's door. What do you remember?"

I cobbled together the bits of the story Dixie had supplied. "Being in a cellar among people I didn't trust. Smelling smoke. Getting Cassie out. Then the hospital. I was out of it for weeks."

Arran inclined his head. "It was the Four Milers' cellar in an old church they'd converted to a brothel. You were undercover."

My mouth fell open. Not a betrayal, not if I had been working for my crew.

Arran continued, stress tightening his tone. "It was my fault you got hurt. I sent you in to spy on that gang and you nearly wound up dead. I could've got you out. You asked me if you could come home, and I said not yet. Your injuries, that scar, it's all on me. I'm so fucking sorry."

A rush of emotion threatened me again. I shoved my hands into my pockets. "Fuck off with that."

Arran laughed. It sounded like grief. "You should know the bastards who broke you are dead. Shade ended Bronson, then the fire killed Red. If it hadn't, I would've."

They were the Four Milers leadership, or had been. Every time I heard a name, it woke up a sleeping part of my mind.

"Good to know. The cop in the hospital mentioned a turf

war."

Shade stiffened. "Ye spoke to the police?"

"One visited me. I gave him nothing."

Both he and Arran stared.

Tyler leaned in. "Did you get a name, or can you describe the guy?"

I feature-listed the fifty-something cop, the big fucker who'd lurked at my bedside wearing a smug grin. Now I knew why.

Tyler twisted his lips and queried, "Kenney?"

"Got to be." Arran scowled.

The name jogged my thoughts. "Yeah, that was him."

Fury descended on Shade's expression, and his tattooed hand flexed over where I instinctively knew a knife was hidden in a holster at his side. "Chief Constable Kenney came here and told us ye were dead. He didn't have the DNA evidence to prove it, which makes me think he did it for his own sick pleasure."

"I'm going to fucking kill him." Arran braced his hands behind his head and tipped back in his hotel room chair, then came back with resolve in his eyes. "It's not enough, but I'm going to right all the wrongs you suffered because of my bad decisions. You saved Cassie in that cellar. You nearly lost your life as well. I can't change that, but I can make up for it as best I can. You have the run of the warehouse and any work you want, when you're ready. Shade, Tyler, take care of our boy. I'll be back next week."

I murmured my gratitude, because no way did he need to make up for anything, but the call was over, and I had two men to convince I was ready for work.

Still, I couldn't help the nagging sensation that Arran was wrong. I didn't deserve his respect. I just couldn't remember why.

It took another two days for Shade and Tyler to agree to discuss tasks with me. Time in which I met a grateful Cassie and her boyfriend, and familiarised myself with the warehouse again, putting more names to faces and sleeping long bouts in my sex-adjacent room. I even managed a shower, binding my arm in plastic so I didn't have to take off the bandage. The scar on my head was evidence enough of my history. I didn't want to see ruined tattoos and mangled skin from the burns.

The next afternoon, I was back in the skeleton crew's office and pleading my case. "I'm dying to get back to work. You've gotta give me something."

Shade sharpened a blade, the edge of it glinting in the light. He swapped a glance with Tyler. "We can't utilise most of your main skill set, not until that boot is off and you're fully mobile."

"What are my main skills?"

"Ye work well undercover, plus breaking and entering, stealing. Not so great at avoiding arrest."

Heh. That must've been how my nickname came about.

I steepled my hands. "I wouldn't be asking if I didn't have anything to offer. Let me earn my keep."

Shade grumbled but gave in. "I'm partway through organising the next game we're running. I have a couple of people left to interview."

I sat back, my heart thumping.

I'd assumed he was going to offer me guard duty with Manny's team, or something less...compelling.

The game. I remembered it, the dangerous fun we had in our basement. If things were murky going from the buzzing nightclub on one side of the skeleton crew's building across to the strip club on the other, then upstairs to the brothel with live performances and anything-goes sex, what happened in the basement turned up the dial to an extreme.

The game was a predator-prey chase where we caged men then released them on a siren to hunt women. Everyone who played did so voluntarily, and live cameras displayed the action to paying customers. It was violent, sex-fuelled carnage.

The description stirred my blood more than any naked bodies could've. Had I taken part? I wasn't sure. Perhaps I'd wanted to.

"I'll help."

Shade nodded then continued with a warning. "People apply for the wrong reasons sometimes. I'll let ye know when the next interviewee is coming in, and ye can be the judge. In the meantime, Tyler has something else he needs help with."

Shade left us, and Tyler took over.

"I lost two of my intercept crew recently."

I pulled my mind back from the game's dark reaches and gave him my attention. "Intercept?"

The bear of a man furrowed his brow. "That's my job. I intercept trafficking rings and bring them down. Did you forget?"

"Shite, no. Ignore that."

He bought my excuse and picked up the office tablet, logging on to a website. He handed it to me, and I squinted at the video footage of a run-down building in an alley somewhere in a suburb of Deadwater.

There were several feeds being captured, and Tyler tapped between them.

"We've been monitoring a property on Milburne Alley for months after it was reported that women had been brought in for unknown reasons. The caller thought it might be a brothel, but the cops don't give a fuck about those and passed it to us via a contact I have with them. They don't have the resources to investigate the degree of trafficking we know goes on. Nor can they take the kind of action that I can."

I got what he meant. The skeleton crew would kill if necessary. The cops had inconvenient laws to abide by.

"We know women are being trafficked into Scotland and Northern England. A year ago, we took down a team in transit and rescued two women and two teenage girls."

"What happened to the traffickers?"

"All dead. Unintentionally, in the case of the leader."

"Badass." I grinned.

Tyler's lips twitched. "I enjoyed it for the sake of the women we brought out of a container lorry, but it pissed me off that I couldn't interrogate their captors. I suspect this case could be connected. The one name we extracted from the traffickers before the last stopped breathing was 'Salter'. We think it's this guy."

On the screen, he opened one of the thumbnails of a rangy mutt of a man. Sallow cheeks, a patchy beard, dark clothing. Rings on his fingers caught the light.

"Jan Salter. Mean motherfucker. He's been seen at this building, as recently as last night when he met one of his lackeys. Since then, a woman showed up, too, apparently for a meeting. Lucky for us, we already had cameras up, as we believed this place is operating as a holding cell. What I need is for you to monitor the footage and see what you can learn."

I studied the live feed Tyler switched to. "What should I focus on?"

"Watch for Salter but also the woman. I want any clues to her identity. I don't think she's trafficked, she isn't behaving that way. Which makes me think she could be something to do with the organisational side of it. If so, she's possibly being coerced. I want to get to the truth."

He left me to start my task.

Getting comfortable behind the desk, I spooled through the cameras, counting off a view of the front of the building, one down the alley and catching the upper windows, and one inside the building which showed a darkened room where the alley's neon-purple lights fell over a bed. Holy fuck, he'd done a good job of setting up the spy kit.

I rolled the footage of the clip from yesterday.

On it, a curvy woman in an oversized hoodie and with blonde bobbed hair in loose waves crossed the screen. The camera captured a perfect view of her pert face, and my breathing stopped. Not because she was pretty—she was fucking beautiful—but because of something deeper. Attraction. Need. Recognition?

For the first time since I'd come back to life, my dick woke up and paid attention.

"Yup," I murmured. "You're coming home with me."

I knew her. I had to. Which meant maybe she knew me.

For several hours, I pored over the footage, streaming the street feed live so I didn't miss anyone showing up. There was no shot of the woman meeting Salter, if she had before she left. They hadn't appeared in the upstairs room which also had an active sound feed.

At last, after rain began pattering down on the alley, a taxi cruised into the camera's live scope and stopped by the building's entrance. A passenger exited.

It was our mystery woman. My pulse sped up.

With her head down against the rain, she cautiously stepped up to the building then went inside, disappearing from view. Instantly, I was overheating again. I switched to the interior camera, tracking her as she went out of sight.

It took a solid twenty minutes until she reappeared, this time in the upstairs room, visible to me on the wide lens. Alone, she perched on the bed, her legs bare under that same oversized hoodie, the picture of a vulnerable lass.

Was she waiting? The car dropping her off felt like she'd been delivered to this...whatever it was. I hadn't caught sight of who she'd met.

Dead certainty consumed me, and I wheeled my chair back to raid the desk. From a hidden drawer, I collected a knife, then a skeleton print bandanna from the cabinet. If I could get a phone and borrow a car, I knew exactly what I was doing this evening.

Leaping with both feet into my assignment.

I'd find out who she was, either by remembering or simply asking. The only way to be sure was to go to her, and if I was lucky, she might have something to say about me.

3

Nerves crawled through my stomach, still rising from my rush of panic at coming here. I'd nearly bottled it. Nearly turned around and run the other way.

But Mama didn't raise a quitter. I had to see this through, even if it meant being terrified for a few hours until it was all over.

From elsewhere in the run-down building, music buzzed, loud enough to pick out the track and concealing the sounds of any other people, though I knew someone had to be here besides the low-level grunt who'd shown me in. This was the time and the place. The organiser would arrive, tell me how this would go down, and I'd play the eager, naïve girl I was supposed to be.

After that, when I had what I needed, I'd run like the wind.

Perched on the bed, I ran my fingertips over the hem of my hoodie, clamped tight across my thighs. As instructed, I'd brought nothing. No phone, no ID. My only item of any value was a necklace I couldn't bear to be parted with— the initial 'E' in diamonds on gold. A twenty-first birthday present, gifted a few years ago by my grandfather.

Considering the reason I was here, it was only right to carry a token of him. I switched from worrying my hem to running the necklace charm back and forth at my throat.

There was nothing to do but wait.

Minutes passed, but no one came for me. Outside, an engine rumbled, so I peeked from the tall window, but a large air-conditioning unit blocked my view of the street door below. Instead, I took in the close-together buildings and the sparkling city beyond the far end of the dark alley, a rainbow of neon for different night-time offers. Opposite, there was a business of some sort, and though it appeared to be closed, its purple light cast a glow into my room, enough to create a shadow when I turned to pace away.

Unable to settle, I examined a broken dresser then the surprisingly clean bedding on the bed. I shuddered to think what secrets that mattress knew. What other poor women had been in my shoes, perhaps unwillingly.

Time ticked on. My heart rate didn't slow.

I was all but ready to despair when a whine of metal caught my attention. Except it came from outside. I faced the sound and jumped.

There was a dark figure outside my window.

A man. Perched on the air-conditioning unit, he squinted through the glass then waved to summon me and pointed at the catch.

What. The. Hell?

Warily, I crossed the room until I could see him better. He was a little older than me, maybe late twenties, with scruffy dark hair and a long-sleeved black t-shirt with no jacket, despite the cool evening. Across his lower face was a black bandanna with the print of the jaw of a skull.

For a strange moment, I was transported back to a childhood fantasy of Peter Pan. More specifically, of the lost boys turning up at my window to take me away. I'd found the idea compelling.

The lost boy in question ran his gaze over me then tugged down his bandanna to reveal a grin. "Let me in?"

"No," I mouthed.

I was freaking undercover, in a manner of speaking. Whatever he was up to was not going to help my plan.

The metal unit under him crunched, a bracket coming away from the brick, and the stranger jerked, his arms flying out for balance.

Involuntarily, I took a step closer.

He splayed a hand on the glass. "Seriously, help or I'm going to fall."

"Why are you even climbing up here?" I hissed.

"Breaking in, obviously. C'mon, open up."

"Why should I?"

"I'm charming, slightly concussed, and there's a fifty-fifty chance I'll fall off and die. It'll be character-building." His smirk faded. "I promise I won't hurt you, but they'll kill me if they catch me."

He braced his other hand to the exterior wall, and it was this change in position that allowed me a better view of him. Around his lower left leg was some kind of medical boot, strapped on, and with his dark jeans torn open to accommodate it.

This night was getting weirder and weirder.

That was my only explanation for why I muttered a swear word then flipped the window latch.

The man half fell into the room, landing lightly on his good leg and slithering down to sit on the bare floorboards with his back to the wall beneath the window.

He took a second to listen, presumably for any shouts of someone coming after him, then tilted his head at me. "Hey."

I pointed at the door to the hall. "Exit's that way."

"Don't need it. I came here to see you."

Like hell he had. "You don't know me."

"That's up for debate. What's your name? I'm Convict."

I blinked, entirely confused. "Is that a name or a job description?"

In the faint purple light, amusement flashed in his eyes. "Funny and beautiful. I like you. Let's just say I lost a reality competition in jail and the nickname stuck. Do me a favour and take a good look at me. Recognise my face?"

I stilled and did as he asked, not because I was all that obedient, but for another reason. Convict, as he called himself, was very easy to stare at. He was a big guy, over six feet tall, and with obvious muscles under a close-fitting shirt. Not that I was checking him out. I dragged my gaze from a snake tattoo around his wrist to his face, taking in an expressive mouth and regular features.

He was pretty. The strangest, most inappropriate bright swell of attraction took over me until heat flushed my cheeks. I forced my expression to neutral.

"Never seen you before in my life."

"How about my real name, Roscoe Locke. Familiar?"

"Nope."

His shoulders slumped, and he scrubbed a hand through his messy dark hair. "Damn. I was hoping for different. Never mind."

His movements revealed something else unexpected. Two things, in fact. A scar that led back from his hairline, and a flash of white bandage at his wrist.

I indicated from there to his leg. "Did you get hurt breaking into somewhere else? Is this a bad habit?" It explained his nickname, which had to be gang related, now I came to think about it.

"Wish I could tell you."

"But you won't?"

"Can't, beautiful."

I could've asked what he meant by that, but this was

already an unexpected and unwelcome interruption to my evening. If he was discovered in here with me, I risked being thrown out. There was a very tentative trust with the organisers based on me being a clueless girl, and if they got suspicious, this would all be over.

I had to take back control. "Not to be rude, but could you please go? I can't be found talking to a stranger."

Convict's focus lingered on me for a moment longer, then he eased up to peer out of the window. No shouts had followed his surprise entry, so I figured he was in the clear for whatever he was doing. The man passed me, heading to the door. After listening, he slowly twisted the handle and scanned the darkened hall outside.

But instead of leaving, he closed us in and flipped the lock.

Shit. I started forward, a hand out. "Seriously, you can't stay. I don't know what you're running from, but being in here is going to cause me problems."

He blocked the door. "What kind of problems?"

"None of your business."

He exhaled a breath of annoyance. "This is a very bad place owned by very bad people. There's no way someone like you is here of your own accord, unless you're a pretty little gangster. So help me out. Your name."

I pressed my lips together, irritated that he thought I was one of them. "Mila, and I'm not in a gang. You probably are, though."

He shrugged, those muscular shoulders rounding. "Something like that. Mila's cute. Got a surname to go with that?"

Cute? I ignored the flush of warmth and pointed to the door. "Leave. Please."

His gaze on me intensified. "Who's out there that you're scared of?"

"People. And I'm not scared."

"That's a lie."

"You don't know me to judge that."

"No, Mila, scared little gangster, I don't. My mistake in thinking I did. But tell me something. If you could leave this place right now and be free of whatever shit you're in, would you?"

He was giving me an out. It was kind of him, but misguided.

"No. I wouldn't. I know what I'm doing."

I tightened my jaw. He did, too. We glared at one another until a clatter came from beyond the door, audible over the distant music.

Footsteps at the bottom of the stairs.

My bravado slipped. "Someone's coming up. Please. Go, now. Don't make this harder for me."

He took a step closer until he loomed over me, frustration clear on his features. "What happens if I stay?"

I didn't answer.

He sighed and shook his head. "Got a phone?"

"No. I didn't bring one."

Convict slid a phone from his pocket and held it up to show me, then set it down on the dresser. Without another word, he strode away, not pausing as he climbed out of the window. The metal supports for the air-conditioning unit groaned, and I winced and quickly flipped the door lock open then darted after him.

But as I reached the glass, he was nowhere to be seen. My mystery man had vanished into the night.

That was fine with me. I shut the window and took a deep breath of relief.

Him being here could've ruined all I was striving to

achieve. No lost boy with a handsome face was worth that.

4

Convict

I sprawled across the back seat of my borrowed car, my leg up just as the doctor ordered, and with Mila on the tablet I'd brought with me from the warehouse.

I'd watched her for two hours. Not creepy if you had a surveillance excuse and a head wound. Probably.

Nothing had happened in that time. Whoever she was waiting for never showed. There was only a shady-as-fuck loser who skulked in a ground-floor room but did little else. Obviously a lackey or some kind of guard. At least he wasn't bothering her.

After a while, Mila curled up on the bed and didn't move. She'd fallen asleep, I guessed. The camera view stole her colour, but I knew enough to fill in the gaps. Red lips, blonde hair, pale eyes under the hood of her oversized hoodie.

The neon light that shone into her room cast over her bed in streaks, but it didn't touch her, like it was allowing her to hide from the light.

At length, it too went out.

When dawn streaked the sky overhead, I gave up and drove home.

Mila: 1. Excitement: 0. Boner: ...undecided.

I wasn't a fan of being out in daylight, and if my woman of interest wasn't doing anything, I could watch that from the comfort of my bed.

At the warehouse, the streets and car park were empty, the revellers gone home, but inside, Manny still watched the cameras in the guard room. He lifted his head at my arrival.

"Hey. Can I have a new phone?" I asked.

Manny tugged open a drawer and fished out a box. "Didn't Tyler give you one already?"

"He did. Someone else has it now." Luckily, I had the number memorised. With nothing much in my head, it had stuck. A thought sprang to mind. "I don't suppose we can track that one, can we?"

Life sparked in his tired eyes. "All our staff phones are traceable. Some of our people, too. Need me to do that now?"

"Not yet, but good to know for future reference."

I thanked him and asked after Tyler and Shade, but both were out. I went to leave, but Manny stalled me.

"Shade asked me to talk to you about your pay." On one of his screens, he brought up a form. "As you were undercover, we took you off the official books. I've been holding on to your pay, so the money's waiting, if you want it."

I peered at the screen which showed a payslip, and an odd feeling passed over me. A cursory glance at the address showed me the area was different to the one the hospital had for me, but I didn't want to note the street or any more details.

Remembering too much about my life at once would be an overload. At some point, I'd need to go home, wherever that was, but today was not that day.

I stuck my hands into my pockets. "Can I get a printout of that?"

"Sure thing. Do you need any cash?"

I stared at him. "For real?"

Manny rattled something under his desk then brought out an envelope. Inside was a wedge of notes. "I've kept this back for you, locked in the safe. You can have all of it, or I can transfer the same amount to your bank now you're officially back on the crew."

Fuck. If I had a bank account, I had no way of accessing it. Maybe the answer to that was at my home address, but that strange, cold feeling wouldn't budge.

"I'll take some now then leave the rest for later, if you're good with that?"

Manny inclined his head and passed me the envelope. I extracted a stack of twenties and handed the rest back.

The security chief regarded me. "Need a wallet, too?"

I choked on a laugh. "That would probably help."

The resourceful man located one in a stock cupboard. It had our crew logo of a skull wearing a bandanna across its lower face.

I thanked him for a second time and left, turning the wallet over in my hands. That image of the skull was me, in a way. A stripped-back, empty-headed version of what had previously been a man.

I still carried the worst feeling that if I did discover enough about my past, I wouldn't like what I found.

My next mission was food, and though the clubs were closed, there was still a kitchen in operation upstairs in the brothel part of the huge warehouse, where the clientele presumably built up an appetite after fucking their woman or man of choice.

I strode through the reception area where a few tired and mostly naked women waited on newcomers, sweet talked the cook into frying me up a burger, then retraced my steps with the food already devoured while I waited for the lift.

A lass in a see-through baby doll nightie, completely naked underneath with the front cut away to display her bare pussy, waved at me in greeting, her dark-haired friend leaning in to ask who I was. She whispered her answer, and

I picked up my name plus 'Arran's oldest friend'. Was I? Shit, who knew.

It didn't escape my notice that the naked skin all around still did nothing to stir my dick. Even when the doors opened and the brunette stripped her bra in a provocative display of welcome to two early-bird old gents. She ushered them in, and I stared as hard at her tits as they did, waiting for a kick of anything in my body. Nope. Not a smidge of interest.

The lift arrived, and I returned to my room, shutting myself away with a sigh. Tiredness dogged me, yet I couldn't help tuning back in to the Mila show.

There she was. My future emotional breakdown in a hoodie.

She hadn't woken, but she'd extended her bare legs. My heart thumped, and I travelled my gaze up her calf and to her thigh.

Lust kicked in a rolling wave that heated my blood and sent it straight to my dick. Not at the naked tits or ready-to-go pussy on display downstairs. No, just for this woman.

I knew Mila. Either because I'd seen her before, though I'd believed her when she'd said she didn't know me, or for a stranger reason. That, on first sight, my body had decided the lass was mine.

I passed out with my hand on my junk just to feel that it still worked, and the live feed running so we could sleep together.

When I woke, Mila was stirring, too.

I'd dreamt about her. Just talking as we'd lain in bed, then pulling her onto me for a slow morning fuck. Her mouth had mapped to mine, then she'd pushed me to lie on my back while she kissed down my body, on her way to toy with the ultra-hard dick that only seemed to like her.

Fuck it. I dialled the number of the phone I'd given her.

On the tablet screen, Mila jumped then snatched it from

under the mattress. She'd hidden it. Good girl.

The call connected, and she listened but didn't speak.

"If you aren't a sex worker, what are you?" I muted the camera feed in case of feedback.

Mila's posture relaxed, and her mouth curved. "Wouldn't you like to know? And what makes you think I'm not a sex worker?"

"Are you?"

"Fine, I'm not. Actually, I have questions of my own, stalker. How did you get hurt?"

She'd been thinking about me. I extended my free arm and the white bandage that really needed to come off. "I'll show you mine if you show me yours."

That smile of hers grew. "This turned dirty quickly."

She had no idea. I was hard again, just at the sound of her voice. Maybe my dick had never gone down. "Something about you does that to me, sweetheart."

She climbed from the bed and moved to the window, peering out into the rainy afternoon as if I might be perched on the rickety frame again. "Is that why you asked if I'd recognised you? Like some kind of cosmic connection?"

"Pretty much."

"Except you don't know me."

Her words gave me pause. And for no good reason, I found myself revealing the truth. "I didn't know for sure. Here's something real. I have amnesia. I can't remember anything past a few weeks ago."

Mila stilled, her hand to the window frame. "Honestly?"

"Entirely. And hardly anyone else knows."

"Why are you telling me?"

"Because of how I react to you. There has to be something that's familiar."

On slow steps, she made her way back to the bed. "React how, exactly? We met once, last night, for a minute."

I palmed my junk.

This was inappropriate. I should hang up, or at least apologise. But let's be real, neither of those things were happening. I wanted her involved. More, I just wanted to keep her talking.

Maybe I was an obsessive kind of man. But from first sight of Mila, I'd only wanted more, and now we'd spoken, that interest was turning into something else.

I had no idea if that was good or very, very bad.

5

Mila

"I'll leave it to your imagination over what my body does when I see you. Or, apparently, speak to you." Convict's voice was thick with sleep. Like he'd crashed out wherever he'd escaped to, then the first thing he did on waking was call me.

My mind leapt to a bed somewhere, and to the tall, dark-haired lost boy stripped down to his underwear.

What the hell was wrong with me?

I was suddenly, startlingly hot. So much I squeezed my thighs together in search of any small relief. "I want to know."

"Tit for tat, love."

Meaning if he was going to confess to me, I'd need to share something about myself. "I can't tell you much."

"You a cop?"

"No. Is it your heart that beats faster when you see me?"

"That's one very minor part of my reaction."

My breathing caught. "Your...?"

"Say it, and I'll confirm it."

I groaned but stifled the sound. There was no reason this should be so hot. So he was pretty? That didn't mean he was a nice guy.

I blurted my next question. "What are you? I mean what type of person?"

I heard the shrug in his voice. "No fucking clue. Amnesia, remember? I work for good people, though."

"I thought you were in a gang?"

"You assumed that. I never confirmed it. Does it automatically make me bad if I am?" At my lack of an answer, he continued. "What do you know about the gangs in Deadwater?"

"Not much, only their reputations. I grew up here, but that side of it isn't my world."

He snorted an unfunny laugh. "I know. Which makes no sense why you're there in that room waiting for fuck knows who. At best, it'll be some jackass gangbanger, which means you're risking your skin for what I hope to be a fucking solid reason."

I rubbed my forehead. Was I that transparent for him to have seen through me in two brief conversations? "Why did you leave your phone with me? Are you hunting these people? If so, that's not helpful to me."

"Figured that. Perhaps I just wanted to hear your voice again."

I closed my eyes and lay back on the bed. Throughout the conversation, I'd stayed alert for any other sound in the house, but the music had shut off at some point while I'd slept, and the place had been silent since. I hadn't meant to fall asleep, but no one had arrived yet, which meant I had to stay here until they did.

I should feel vulnerable. Yet strangely, the lifeline of this conversation was keeping my nerves under control. The stranger on the other end of the line was oddly more of a friend than any person I knew in real life right now.

"I'm not a bad person either," I breathed out in a rush.

"Good to know I'm not into a villain."

"Into?"

"We're back to the parts of me that are interested in you."

Damn it. Damn my heart for skipping a beat, and other parts of me for readying with need. It was unreasonable for him to have such an attractive voice, let alone say words that sparked fireworks in my belly.

My brain was broken. All I was certain of was that I wanted the call to continue, which considering my goal for being here, meant I really needed to hang up.

I pulled the phone from my ear and stared at the screen. The strange number gave me nothing. Yet I couldn't end the call. I wanted to see his expression while we spoke. Or if he really was on a bed and missing a shirt.

"Send me a photo for proof."

I was insane for this, but the distraction was helping.

Convict uttered a strangled laugh. "What kind?"

"Any that you're willing to send."

"You're asking for a dick pic?"

I couldn't reply.

He filled the space. "Going to need an answer if I'm putting my junk on the internet."

"Y-yes?"

The line went silent for so long, I checked the phone.

He'd disconnected. My heart sank.

But then, a video call landed on my screen. Breathless, I tapped to answer. His face came into view, and I exhaled stark attraction. He was in a bed, his messy dark hair against a white pillow. The glow of a lamp made him golden, even if there was menace in his eyes.

Convict watched me for a long moment. "Let's play a game. This hand is a claw machine. Direct my camera. Left, right, up, or all the way down."

Holy shit. I couldn't resist a game. "Down."

He panned the camera to his bare chest, over scrawls of dark inkwork. It stopped.

"Little to the left."

It centred over his sternum.

"Keep going down," I whispered.

Ridges of ab muscles were next. They flexed as he breathed.

A wave of heat swept through me. This was insanely hot. "Don't stop. Down."

Convict made an off sound, and the camera jolted still. "Sorry. You're out of credit."

I burst out with a laugh which I stifled.

"Kidding. You get a free go."

"Down, boy, down."

The camera view finally settled on his shorts that covered a thick bulge.

My heart pounded. I couldn't take my eyes off it. "Grab."

He palmed it with his free hand like I'd caught the prize in his game.

"This is what you do to me, sweetheart. Your voice, your pretty face, my imagination of what you're wearing under that oversized hoodie. I woke to thoughts of a cute girl locked away in that room, and instead of just doing this, I needed to ask permission first."

The camera returned to his face, but not before I caught another squeeze of his hand on his dick.

Electricity crackled under my skin. "I want to see what I won."

"Tell me I can claim the prize with your name on my lips."

A hasty little nod dipped my head, completely out of my control. The camera view stayed on Convict's face, but his lips parted, and he closed his eyes, giving me a burst of deep need at what he was doing to himself.

"Camera down," I ordered.

Convict shook his head. "First time since I came out of hospital. I thought it was broken. Then I see you and, fuck, I'm hard."

I knelt up on the bed. "This is the first time you've done...that? In how long?"

"At least a month. Keep talking to me."

"I will if you show me."

He paused, then I got my wish, the view sliding down him again to his shorts. He'd moved his hand away to give me a clear sight of the tent I'd apparently created.

"God," I uttered.

His hidden dick bobbed.

Convict groaned. "See? One word and my body reacts. I'm dying for you."

"How? I mean, why?" I spluttered.

"You're fuckin' beautiful, Mila. Besides that? No clue. I need more. Talk. Tell me anything."

"Like what?" I was fascinated. Hooked on the power I had over this man.

"What do you like for breakfast?"

I laughed quietly. "Tea and something sweet. Is my food order doing it for you as well?"

"Literally every word that comes out of those lips."

"Maybe it's my lips that are the problem."

I was never this brave with men. I was no virgin, but I'd never really played with my sexuality. Never teased anyone or had... This was phone sex. With a stranger. The realisation was shocking. I was turned on, too, though hell was I touching myself in a place like this.

Convict made a masculine sound of pleasure that made me regret my decision. Desperation edged his tone. "Put the camera back on your face."

Another noise broke through my haze of lust. A click in the hallway directly outside my room.

"Mila," Convict commanded.

In a rush, I killed the call and shoved the phone under my mattress. One second before my door flew open and a man appeared in the frame.

6

Convict

Jumping out of bed, I stumbled on the walking boot I hadn't taken off overnight and nearly fell. On the overhead cameras, a man was in the doorway of Mila's room. She'd almost been caught talking to me, which meant I'd put her in danger. I snatched up my shirt and tugged it on.

But by the time I locked eyes on the screen again, she had someone else in with her and the man was gone. The newcomer was a woman. No, a girl. If I was working the door of Divide, our nightclub, I'd ID her as she didn't even pass for eighteen, despite her makeup, tight black dress, and heels.

Mila approached her cautiously. I turned the sound back on the camera feed, my blood cooling rapidly and the strange moment we'd shared fading away.

"...said we weren't supposed to talk," the younger woman was saying.

"Fuck him. Will you tell me your name? I'm Mila," my lass said.

The girl gave a shaky response I couldn't hear.

The door behind them opened again, and a third woman entered. With her chin high, she smirked at Mila and waved with her fingertips.

Mila stared at her. "Esther?"

"Babe! No names, remember?"

"Right, God, why are you here?"

"I figured what the hell. You're doing it, and I could use the extra money. You only live once, right?" Her gaze slid over Mila. "Plus, maybe I wanted to see if you'd go through with it."

"But why—?"

"Joking! Chill out." Esther crossed the room to a cracked mirror on the far wall and checked her appearance, straightening her pigtails of brunette hair.

At a guess, I put her a little older than Mila, though from her getup, trying to appear younger.

The camera was positioned in the very top corner of the room, above the window I'd used to get inside. It used the light and gave an excellent view of this unexpected meet-up.

Esther started a conversation, a one-sided complaint about the price of rent in the city, with Mila and the girl barely getting a word in edgeways.

My phone buzzed with a message.

> **Tyler:** Manny said you were looking for me. I'm back but not for long. Come to the office for a catch-up?

I replied that I'd come down. For now, Mila was okay, even if taking my eyes off her felt like the worst decision in the world. I left the tablet on my bed. Oddly, I didn't want to share the video with Tyler, as if it was mine only to view, and regardless of the fact he'd set up the surveillance.

The skeleton crew's office door was open on my arrival.

At the desk, Tyler raised his head. "How are you feeling?"

I shrugged. "Never better."

It was true. Last night, I'd scaled a building. If I'd hurt myself in doing so, my body wouldn't be working today. It was doing all I asked of it, therefore I was good.

Without delay, I launched into the debrief Tyler wanted. "The woman's name is Mila. Nicely spoken, comes from money, though she's trying to hide it."

"What makes you think that?"

I thought about it. "Her clothes and her confidence. She has that self-assured vibe of someone from a privileged background."

"It's not an act? Money can come from many sources."

I caught his drift. "She's not a sex worker, and my gut tells me to believe her when she says she's not on the side of the people who own that place."

Tyler stared. "What do you mean, 'she says'?"

"I spoke to her."

"How?"

"I broke into her room. Well, technically, she let me in."

Tyler rubbed the spot between his eyes. "Fucking hell, Con. If I thought you were ready to go out into the field, I would have given you more warning. Backup as a minimum."

"Why? I didn't need it."

"You could have. The guy she's associated with, Salter, has history with the Four Milers. Since that gang blew up, nearly taking you with them, the stragglers and leftovers are scrabbling for new homes. Lesser collectives are forming and failing every week, blood spilled and grievances aired in that power vacuum. They are out there, and they know your face. It only takes for one of them to recognise you and game over."

I shrugged. "Or, I fake-join their new crew."

"No. Not happening. Enough people know you're back with us and have been welcomed in. They'll kill you for revenge." Tyler braced his hands behind his head of dark-blond hair as if I'd stressed him out, then he exhaled and rested his elbows on the desk. "I won't try to micromanage you, but I saw what Arran did to you when he was flipping out over Genevieve, and I fucking hated it."

"Did to me?" I repeated his words, veering dangerously close to revealing how little I knew.

"Aye. He regrets it. We all do for not stopping him. Let's not have you die before he can grovel to your face. Just be careful, okay?"

Odd emotion crawled through me, almost as unpleasant as the idea of finding out too much about my past. I didn't deserve their care.

"I'll keep watch and let you know if your man shows up," I promised Tyler.

I couldn't swear not to return.

In fact, I practically ran back upstairs, as much as my boot would allow, then I sat and watched the last ten minutes of Mila's conversation, split screening it with the live view so I didn't miss a thing.

I couldn't tear myself away from her. Just like I'd confessed, the sound of her voice alone did strange things to my heart. And elsewhere.

A fourth woman had shown up in the time I was away, her long, braided hair held in a high ponytail that swished when she moved.

Everyone in that room was dressed in some form of revealing clothing, though not overtly sexual like the women in the brothel. Mila's legs were bare with her hoodie long enough to make it appear like she had nothing on underneath. The one she'd named Esther had black shorts and a tight cropped top with her belly exposed, and the newer woman a long-sleeved minidress that skimmed her thighs. The youngster's black dress was the most revealing, something Esther kept side-eyeing with obvious irritation.

I couldn't work it out. If they were selling themselves,

why not go all out?

Getting comfortable on my bed, I listened in to their chat. Esther was talking, again, but a lull came in the conversation, and the teenager spoke up.

"How do you like your men?"

Mila tilted her head. "What do you mean?"

"It's why we're here," the girl practically whispered. "I've been thinking about the money we'll get and the fact they'll get to do whatever they please. If the guys want us to be in lingerie, what's the equivalent for them if the roles were reversed? What do you like your man to be in?"

Esther snorted. "Prison."

The woman with braids smirked. "Concrete shoes and the bottom of a lake."

Esther shoved her, and they both cackled.

The girl dropped her head.

Mila nudged her. "You mean what do I find attractive?"

The girl nodded.

Esther cut in again. "Men can wear lingerie. Like Tom Holland's lip-sync battle where he sang 'Umbrella'. That was hot as fuck, but if you're thinking we're going to meet sweet guys doing this shit, you're fucking deluded." She muttered something about dumb bitches her mother would slap sense into and rolled her eyes.

Mila ignored her and kept her focus on the girl, her expression kinder than Esther's. "Let me see, what do I like? A dark-grey shirt, rolled-up sleeves to show tattooed arms, and open a few buttons at the neck. Worn-over jeans to show he isn't flashy. Add a piece of rough jewellery like a leather bracelet and I'm deceased."

The girl brightened. "I like that. My boyfriend always, I mean, he..."

She clammed up, and though I could only see the side

of her face, I guessed her to have reddened. But it was Mila's reaction to her that intrigued me. Her expression turned serious as if she was worried about the kid. She should be, considering where they were and the people around them.

Yet another reason to believe my fantasy woman wasn't on Team Trafficker.

I watched for a while longer, texting Tyler so he was aware that this was ramping up. Four women, one with some kind of plan, one scared, one needing money, and something to do with men who'd have power over them. Nothing about this felt good.

A message dinged on my phone.

Shade: One of the last two applicants for the game is coming in for his interview this evening. Last minute, but better than nothing. He's all yours.

Shit. I had to carry out that interview. My crew came first, even if it meant spending more time away from watching Mila.

I replied that I'd be there, and Shade gave me a one-hour countdown. I made another choice.

I had to see Mila again.

If I didn't, I'd go crazy. But something slowed my steps. Not Tyler's warning to stay out of trouble. Not the fear of people I might run into, not now my strength was returning hard. It was a trip to the wardrobe Dixie had mentioned by the strip club.

I needed to change my shirt.

7

Mila

Something was wrong. First, the delay. I was supposed to have been picked up last night, yet they'd made me wait, and I was still here in the holding house but now with three other women.

Esther was a last-minute add-in, she'd told me.

Gloated, if I thought about it.

I'd been shocked to see her. Then again, she was the reason I'd found this place. I'd known her since school, and it was her I'd gone to for access. When she was sixteen, she'd bragged about how she'd been approached by Rhys Jacobs. He was a few years older and rumoured to run a sex auction where businessmen bought schoolgirls. A startling claim few of us believed.

Esther did. She had preened and boasted how she was obviously the prettiest girl in school because she'd been singled out, and how she'd make a bundle selling her body. I'd been fourteen and horrified.

Even worse was when she came back to class after the weekend with a new phone, jewellery, and bruises that she'd covered with makeup. That confidence? It had been replaced with a brash edge she still wore today.

I'd changed schools not long after, but her abuse had never left my mind. She'd acted like she was the winner, but someone had used her, and Rhys Jacobs had taken a cut of her pain.

A decade on, and it was him in my headlights. I needed to see him for reasons of my own, and he'd vanished from all but a few key places which assured me he was still around, just in hiding. Esther was my last chance of a way in.

She'd provided me with the details then obviously decided to enter the event once again herself—this auction being an anything-goes sale, rather than schoolgirls. A sense of worry dogged me that my question had led her back into this, but though her being here bothered me, it was nothing to my fear for Annabelle who'd arrived moments before her.

She was a kid. Though she wouldn't admit it, she couldn't be more than sixteen. Twice, she'd mentioned a boyfriend then clammed up. She was doing this for the money, but also because he was making her. I was almost certain. She had no idea what she was getting into.

I couldn't stand by and watch her go through with this. I might never have had a sister, but I'd stand in front of a vulnerable girl any day of the week.

All of which meant I now had two goals—to locate Rhys Jacobs and to get Annabelle out of here. They were completely at odds with each other.

While the women talked, and Annabelle played with a bracelet of plastic hearts, my mind raced over the problem. If she went out the window, like Convict had come in, she might be able to climb down. But then she faced the problem of walking the alley alone. If she was seen, she'd be, what, brought back up? Worse? That was if I could even persuade her. I needed to at least try.

"Hey, that's pretty. Did your boyfriend give it to you?" I tapped her knee and gestured to the jewellery.

Annabelle lifted her shy gaze to mine.

"Oh, I love it. Let me see." Esther reached across and snatched Annabelle's bracelet, sliding it onto her wrist and holding it out for admiration.

The door to the room flung open, and our guard appeared. He pointed in my direction. "Follow me."

I stood on shaky legs. "Just me?"

At his gruff nod, I trotted after him. I had no choice. At last, it was happening. I'd wanted this, but it meant my time to act on Annabelle was up.

Outside in the hall, the guard trudged the bare floorboards to another door. He pushed it open and gestured for me to go inside. At a table, an older man waited, some kind of medical kit laid out in front of him.

I stalled. "Who are you?"

The guard shoved me inside, and the medic inclined his head at the chair I'd grasped the back of.

"Sit. This won't take long."

I didn't move. There were needles. Tubes. Scissors. "To do what?"

"A simple blood test. If you don't do it, you'll have to leave." He picked up a strap and gave me an impatient glance.

Esther hadn't warned of this, but a fast check of his supplies reassured me a tiny amount. All the kit was packaged and appeared professional, the medical bag clean and new. I'd given blood once in the past, and being shown the door was out of the question.

Still, I thought of Annabelle. "What if I want to leave?"

He smiled, revealing stained teeth. "Too late for that. Are you going to do this voluntarily or do you need to be held down?"

Shaking, I sat and extended my arm.

The doctor took a vial of blood then withdrew his needle, giving me a piece of cotton wool to press to the tiny wound. Without another word to me, he called for the guard.

"Next. Have them form a queue. I have better places to

be."

The guard shoved me back into the bedroom and called the others out. It left me alone which offered a chance.

Diving for the bed, I found the phone Convict had left me and dialled a number. Not his, but one I'd memorised not all that long ago. My brother, there to play backup plan for if this all went wrong.

An answerphone played. I swore and switched to a message.

> **Mila:** It's me. There's a girl here who shouldn't be. She's just a kid. Can you come and take her? I can maybe send her out the window if you can pick her up outside?

I was foolish to ask for this. Annabelle wasn't my problem, except I couldn't ignore her presence. She had no one to protect her, and the auction would break her in two.

I stuffed the phone back into its hiding place then crossed to the window to stare out at the dusk. The lack of light made it harder to see, but the club sign blinked to life, slicing purple through the glass, right as a figure landed on the air-conditioning unit.

I squeaked in shock. It was my lost boy. Without thinking, I leapt to unfasten the window, and he dropped into the room, tall, dark, and just as handsome as I'd remembered.

Backing up, I stared wide-eyed at him. "You can't be here."

Convict prowled towards me. "Then why let me in?"

"At least hide."

Ignoring my gesture for him to duck into the corner where he'd be out of sight behind the dresser if the guard returned, the big man moved in on me and backed me to the wall.

My pulse sped, and I flattened myself to the cool plaster, momentarily lost on a surge of lust and something dangerously like happiness at seeing him again. Him being here flipped the balance in far too many ways. Just like our phone call had.

He dropped his lips to my ear. "I want you to tell me what's happening tonight. Why are the other women here? What are you going to do?"

How did he know about them? He hadn't been outside the window when they were in the room. I shook my head. "You shouldn't have come back."

"Your lips are saying the words, but every other part of you is screaming for me to stay."

My breathing came harder. His, too.

The world closed in around us. He was a magnet, and I registered the pull, the strongest urge to cling to him and claim his hot mouth in the middle of this terrible place.

Why was it that this complete stranger had such an effect on me, as apparently I did to him? I couldn't get the image of his body out of my head.

Another fact was just as clear, cooling my unwanted passion. The guard carried a weapon. I'd seen a holster on his belt. If he returned now, he'd kill Convict. Yet I didn't push him away. Instead, I got hooked on the strangest detail.

He had on a grey shirt, open at the collar, and with sleeves rolled up to display the white bandage still wrapped around his left arm. Tattoos decorated the other. God, that was attractive.

Lust might have taken over my senses, but that didn't stop my brain from filling in the picture. Slowly, I touched his collar, puzzle pieces fitting together.

"You know about the others. You've been watching. Are

there cameras on us?"

He didn't deny it.

I took a short breath. "You're monitoring the people who run this place. Why? No, wait, don't tell me. I don't want to know what interest your gang has in theirs. But if you act this evening, you'll mess up everything I'm trying to achieve."

His gaze skimmed my cheek and held on my mouth. "Which is what, exactly?"

"Why do you need to know? You're a stranger."

Convict caught my hand and flattened my palm to his chest. His heart thumped under my touch, the heat of him bleeding through. "Because that fast beat says otherwise. Why does my heart know you, Mila? Why can't I stop thinking about you? You say stranger, but I know you."

"No, you don't." I pushed past him to gain space. My panic returned like an old friend, but I wasn't scared of this man, only of the way he turned my head.

Convict tracked me. "Tell me why I shouldn't throw you over my shoulder and take you out of here."

For a terrible half-second, I almost agreed. Then I shrank back from the notion. This evening, I'd be leaving anyway, heading to the next destination where I'd find Jacobs, then I'd get out.

Yet even though that plan had been well thought through, I hadn't counted on feeling sorry for a misguided girl.

The solution was right here in front of me, and my backup plan had yet to reply.

I beseeched Convict with my eyes. "I can't go, not yet, but there's someone else who can. If you've been watching, you'll have seen Annabelle. She's just a child. She has no business being in a place like this. She's in real danger, and if you want to rescue someone, let it be her."

His dark eyebrows dove together, the movement tugging

the scar that led back from his temple. "How can she be in danger if you're not?"

"Because I'm not what you think I am, and I have resources she doesn't. Please, will you do it? She'll be back at any moment."

"I came here for you."

"I don't need a hero. Annabelle does."

Convict searched my gaze, his jaw tight. I had him. He wanted to do good, and I'd offered him the chance on a platter.

The door flew open, and Annabelle stumbled in, alone.

She clutched a piece of cotton wool against her tawny brown skin, tears lining her eyes. I went to her. Her gaze locked on me then behind me to the shadowed corner where Convict remained.

Annabelle took an intake of breath, her eyes rounding.

I held my hands out. "Stay quiet and listen. I know you're scared, and you should be, just not of us."

She shook her head, her focus never leaving the threat in the room, the unknown male.

I continued. "I don't know what you've been told, but this auction is no fairy tale where some gallant billionaire is going to pluck you from poverty and treat you well. That's a fantasy. The reality is you'll be sold to some old, gross, and maybe even violent man. A predator who won't see you as a person, only a purchase because that's exactly what he did. Bought you for no-holds-barred sex. There will be nothing to stop him once you're in his clutches. He'll fuck you as often as he likes with whatever he likes. If you refuse, it'll turn into rape. There are no rules. No one protecting you. The girls who go through this come out changed for the worse. Do you understand?"

As I spoke, Annabelle's focus came to me. Another tear leaked down her cheek. "I asked the guard if I could leave.

I said I'd changed my mind. He told me tough luck and laughed."

The bastard. I gritted my teeth. "My friend can get you out."

She swallowed. "I... I want to. I'm scared. But if I go home empty-handed..."

Fucking hell. I was right. She'd been put up to this.

"You need money?" Footsteps at my back told me Convict approached. Stopping directly behind me, he held something out to Annabelle. It was a wallet.

"What's this?" She took it, turning it over to reveal a logo of a skull with a bandanna over its lower face.

Convict's gang emblem, had to be. He'd worn it on a bandanna around his throat on his first visit.

His voice stayed low. "The cash inside is yours. The mark on it is for the skeleton crew, the people who'll vouch for me. Leave now, and I'll drive you wherever you want to go."

A moment of thick tension played out. The girl kept the wallet, peeking at Convict with a shift from fear to perhaps trust in her eyes. The gang name meant something to her.

At her tiny nod, I breathed a sigh of relief.

With gruff approval, Convict guided her to the window, talking her through how to get down. Annabelle slipped off her heels and perched on the sill. Left alone in the centre of the room, I held my ground, battling a sense of being abandoned. This was what I'd arranged. I didn't want to go with them.

Convict came to me. "I'm taking you both."

"No. I can't go."

Frustration played out in his features. "You can. You want that fate you spelled out?"

"It won't happen to me. Believe me."

"I won't leave without you."

"You don't have a choice."

Without a word, he palmed my jaw and gazed into my eyes. Then he pressed his lips to mine in a shocking, electrifying kiss. It was over before it began, and I swayed after him as if I wanted more.

"My heartbeat, my blood pressure, my dick. This is what you do to me. Tell me again how we're strangers." His lips curled at the edges.

At my back, the door opened, and I whipped around to see Esther. She froze, staring at us then at a disappearing Annabelle.

"What the hell are you doing?" Esther spat.

I made a gesture for her to stay silent, but she turned and fled into the hall.

I spun back to Convict. "Go! If she tells someone, they'll catch you outside." Then a lie fell from my lips. "Nothing will happen until midnight anyway. After that, I'll have what I want and can leave. Alone, stranger. I don't want or need your help."

There was calculation in his eyes. He was deciding he could do both, free Annabelle then return for me. It was clear in his pursed lips then eventual nod.

He went.

It was all I could do to stare after him with my fingertips pressed to my mouth. Convict disappeared from sight, and I darted to the window. Down the alley, I caught a glimpse of the two figures, escaping to a car. Taillights flashed, moved out, then they were gone.

I'd done it. Annabelle wouldn't get hurt.

I only had to ensure the same proved true for me.

8

Convict

Playing taxi service to a scared kid hadn't been on my bingo card tonight, and driving Mila's foundling out to a run-down suburb in the outskirts of Deadwater nearly cost me my ass. I was running out of time to get back for the interview.

I watched Annabelle to the door, eyed the woman who answered it, a two-decades-older replica of the kid, then burned rubber back to the warehouse.

The sliver of moon tonight darkened the shadows, and the city felt all the more menacing. I fitted in perfectly to the murky aesthetic. If there were people out here who wanted to kill me, they had to get in line.

Outside our headquarters, I had seconds to spare, but as I stepped from the car, I instinctively reached for the tablet so I could check in with Mila on the cameras.

Fuck, no. She'd told me nothing would happen for hours. I didn't trust that claim for shit, but for a more pressing point. She didn't want my interference.

Every part of this felt wrong. The urge to return to that room and throw her over my shoulder nearly floored me, but Mila had made her decision. Whatever the pull towards her, she didn't feel the same. We didn't know each other, and she didn't care.

My loyalty was to my crew. That deserved and demanded all my attention.

I left the fucking thing on the seat and forced myself inside the warehouse.

At the office, I greeted Shade with a bro hug and tugged on a skeleton bandanna to conceal my lower face.

Shade tapped the boss's seat. "You're leading the show. Confident with what you're asking? It's been a while."

Surprise hit me, but I took the big leather chair, more because he'd asked than I thought I had the right. A new memory hit, or a partial one, at least. I'd done this before, but standing where Shade was. The support guy, part of Arran's show of strength.

My blood rushed in my ears from a racing heart.

The doctor had told me if I had amnesia, it would lift by degrees. I'd told them it already had, so if anything, I should've felt better.

I didn't. I felt worse. Panicked and battling to hide it.

At my lack of an answer, Shade filled in the gap. "All we need to do tonight is size up the applicant and confirm his intent. He's committing to not just the game itself, and to making a claim, but to thirty days with his woman, if he's one of the lucky ones. He's passed all the checks. Finances, bloodwork, a home to take her to. I'll run through the specifics, but the point of the interview is to look for alarm bells. We had a guy a while back who went psycho after he lost. He stalked the woman he'd wanted, though she was happily paired off with someone else. He couldn't respect the rules of the game."

"What happened to him?"

Shade's face might've been covered by a matching bandanna, but I knew he'd formed a deadly smile.

"We manage the rules outside the game as much as inside. We took care of him."

I didn't ask if that meant he was dead. I didn't care.

The enforcer continued. "It's hard to assess that

dangerous edge, fuck, it's part of all of us and necessary once they're in that basement. But if ye pick up on anything ye don't like, we'll kick him out. There's always a long list of others waiting on their chance."

"Got it. Did you say there were two applicants needing an interview?"

"Aye. The second is a woman. If she can't make it in, I'll talk to her on the phone. In general, the lasses are safer to judge than men."

Someone knocked on the door.

"Come in." My voice rang clear, nothing like how fucked up I felt.

Shade palmed my shoulder and gave me a shake, stepping back to be my wingman.

One of the skeleton crew announced the visitor. "Rhys Jacobs. Applicant for the game."

He left us, and Jacobs took the chair beyond the desk. Our bright spotlight made his skin spectre-white against his charcoal suit. It also made it harder for him to see us. The man sat still. A deer in the headlights.

I stared him down. "Mr Jacobs. You kept us waiting."

He swallowed. "My apologies. I meant no disrespect."

On the desk was a clipboard of notes Shade had prepared. I picked it up and perused it. "You've fulfilled the basic requirements of entry, but we don't let any man in without getting his measure in person."

Jacobs forced a smile. "I wouldn't do business that way either."

At my side, Shade made a sound of derision. "Ye compare your corporate meetings with what happens in our basement?"

The applicant rolled his shoulders, nerves showing in his small, jerky movements. "In a manner of speaking.

Excelling at business requires the need to win at all costs. Just like hunting down the woman I intend to spend my life with."

I leaned in. "Then I guess you fuck over your business partners with the same ruthlessness. Save it. That doesn't impress us. Shade, the rules."

My friend rested his hip on my chair and counted off on his fingers. "On Friday night, if we accept ye, you'll be locked in a cage in the basement below this office. You'll be one of twenty men who will compete by any means necessary to claim one of the five women in our game. Ye can and will be hurt during this process. Men have been knocked out before the siren even sounds and left to bleed in the cage. Ye might die. How's this sounding so far?"

Jacobs blinked, his body held taut. "I wouldn't be here if I didn't agree to the risks. Tell me—"

Shade cut him off. "Don't try to lead this interview. If you're lucky enough and strong enough to claim a woman, ye need to fuck her on the basement floor. Once you're inside her, the claim is final. Cameras will be rolling with the action livestreamed to hundreds of people watching in the warehouse. They'll get off on the show but are also your witnesses. When the last woman is claimed, only then are the doors unlocked. After that, the winner takes his prize home and the losers limp away in defeat."

He took a breath while I lived in that moment, picturing it being me.

Even in the middle of that dark fantasy, my mind strayed back to Mila. The tension from our showdown in that run-down office building hadn't left me, and it altered to a ticking clock of wanting to get back to watching the pretty lass in the hoodie as I'd done for two days. Of kissing her again but properly. Thoroughly. My obsessive stalking had become an instant addiction.

Chasing her through the basement would be a fucking

trip.

Damn. I needed to stay in reality.

Shade was still working through the rules. "Ye share your lives for thirty days. You'll eat together, sleep together, and fuck daily. For the first week, ye cannae be apart for more than two hours. After that, it rises to four, with no exceptions. Hurt the girl and we'll come for ye. Break the rules and your reputation is ruined. We will publicly take down or even end the life of any man who crosses us. No cop will step in to protect ye. Likewise, we will protect ye from interference from outside sources."

Jacobs leaned in. The last part apparently interested him. "The skeleton crew guarantees that?"

"By whatever force necessary," Shade agreed.

He was done with his explanation, but I battled another wave of that same memory trying to reform. Of some previous game. What Shade described was so gripping, I got lost in the idea of me being in the frame. With my strength coming back, I was easily strong enough to take down the man in front of me, or far bigger men. If it was Jacobs standing between me and Mila, I'd happily tear him apart.

Hell. Maybe that's who I was at my core. An obsessive, violent man.

I let the memory fade and wrapped up the interview.

"Confirm if you're still asking to be considered," I said.

"Absolutely," Jacobs breathed.

I eyed my friend. I'd seen nothing disturbing in the man. As far as I was concerned, he was in. Shade shrugged.

I picked up the clipboard with the contract and handed it to the applicant. "Sign on the line and welcome to the game. See you on Friday."

Jacobs stared, his shoulders shrinking. He shook it off, scribbled his name, and left without another word.

Shade clapped my shoulder. "That was good. Ye did well."

"I barely spoke," I muttered.

"He was intimidated by us, which was the intent. That's the way we want them, scared and respectful."

Shade released me, and though I should've sought out Tyler and brought him up to speed with my concerns over what was happening at the Milburne Alley office, I didn't.

My feet found their way back to my car. I told myself it was to keep watch for Salter, the man Tyler asked me to locate on the feeds. But when I activated the tablet, I went straight to the view of Mila's room. Just to see her again.

It was empty. No one was there, not on any camera.

In the space of an hour, she'd gone.

9

Convict

With frantic swipes, I spooled back to when I'd left with Annabelle, then watched as Mila huddled in on herself and faced the door.

The other lass didn't return. Neither did the fourth. Mila was left alone for nearly an hour. Then right at the end, a figure burst in.

Salter. The man Tyler wanted. At last, he'd shown up.

I zoomed in to watch the bastard. Rings glinted on his fingers, and he indicated for Mila to go into the hall with a single word. Hunched down with obvious fear, she left. I couldn't see or hear any more of their interaction, no matter how hard I listened. Nothing happened until minutes later when at fucking last, she was marched out of the building and into a waiting vehicle.

Salter gripped the back of her neck.

He'd lose the fucking hand he'd touched her with, one ringed finger at a time.

A few moments on, and two men half carried out another person, a much bigger man, tied up and with his head covered. They shoved him into a second car. Both drove away, and with them went my last sight of Mila.

The only other event on the video was the final two women, picked up and driven away separately, but by that point, I was losing my mind.

She'd been taken, and I had no clue where.

A set of headlights fell over where I stood in the doorway of my car, and Tyler exited a big gunmetal grey 4X4, landing heavily on the tarmac.

He spotted me. "Problem?"

"All the problems."

The hulking intercept guy approached, exhaustion hanging over him like a cloud. While I'd been carrying out my surveillance, according to Shade, Tyler had travelled north to a Scottish port town, spending long nights trying to uncover another trafficking ring.

Tyler indicated to my car, and we used it as an office.

He regarded me from the passenger seat. "Talk."

I hauled in a breath. "Salter showed up. Mila is gone. I've fucked up."

He let me run through it all, giving me the space to explain what I'd done.

As I spoke, I realised my failure. "I should've called you. If I'd acted faster, we could've had people there."

"Aye, perhaps. But I only asked you to watch, not take action. I have no evidence on Salter yet. Only anecdotal. I can't prioritise the man without being sure he's up to something."

"Tonight changes that, doesn't it? He took Mila. She said herself that they were there to auction themselves to dirty old men."

Tyler scrubbed his cheek, his stubble thick with a couple of days of growth. "The point is that the women opted in. I don't like it, but my job is to protect those who are taken by force."

I stared at him with confusion. "You won't act based on what I saw and heard? Mila warned the kid that there could be violence."

"Could be versus undoubtedly has been. Compare that to a girl ripped from her bed in a foreign country, controlled by threat or pain, thrown on a boat, and transported here. No phone, no way to contact her loved ones. Or worse, the loved ones selling her into it as they're desperate. I repeat that I don't fucking like what you've told me, but if Salter is facilitating women selling themselves willingly, that pushes him down my list of men to take out, not up. And that list is fucking long."

"She asked to leave and was denied."

"The girl you got out, right? Leaving three willing victims."

He wasn't going to help me. I swore and glowered out of the front window. I was on my own.

I sensed Tyler's stare.

"What aren't you telling me?" He shoved my uninjured arm. "I just laid out my logic, and you're fighting a battle inside your head. Why? Is it the woman, Mila? Is there something about her?"

Bitterness flooded my tongue. "Nothing that would change your priorities."

Tyler gave a short, hard laugh. "My priorities are that way because of the scale of what I'm up against. I'd never turn my back on a woman in need. You should know that."

I gunned the engine. Somewhere, Mila was being held. I was sure of it. "Get out. I'm going to go find her."

"Then I'll go with you."

I gaped at him. "You're exhausted. You have other places to be."

Tyler closed his eyes and hunkered down in the seat. "I'd never leave a crew member to fend for himself. I can't pull a team to work on this, but you can have my time. I've got your back, always. Slight issue is I haven't slept in two days. If I pass out, then wake me when we get wherever we're going."

True to his word, he was almost instantly asleep, dropped like a tranquilised bear. I half expected snoring that registered on seismographs while suffering whiplash from feeling rejected to loved.

This was what it meant to have a crew. He'd given me a task with set parameters. I wanted to operate outside of those, and he was right there with me.

I pulled out of the warehouse car park to retrace my steps across the city, this time, with a sleeping Tyler in tow.

At Milburne Alley, I watched the building for a while, though the cameras showed no activity since all the vehicles had left. Then I shook Tyler awake and left him as lookout while I scoped out the place. In the darkness, I prowled from room to room, finding nothing. Not a trace of anyone having been here.

Except for the fucking phone Mila didn't have a chance to take.

When I returned to the car, Tyler was nowhere in sight. I spun on my heel, searching the shadows. A low whistle gave up his location.

I squinted, and he stepped out of a doorway, amusement bleeding through his exhaustion at how easily he'd hidden from me.

In a rush of memory, his skeleton crew name returned to me. "Just like a ghost," I muttered.

Tyler grinned, and we returned to the car.

"Where next?" He hunkered down once more.

"To the girl I drove away from here."

He slept again for the drive across the city then woke to play bodyguard while I knocked on Annabelle's door.

Her mother answered and summoned the kid.

"We're not here for anything bad. I just need to know everything you know about that place."

Annabelle hung her head. Since I'd brought her back, she'd changed into pyjamas with pug faces on them, and looked even more of the child she was. "My boyfriend arranged it. I mean my ex-boyfriend. You just missed him."

"Let me guess, he was angry that you didn't go through with it, and the money I gave you wasn't enough."

Annabelle toed the floor with a fluffy slipper boot. "He was angry, but I didn't get the chance to tell him about the cash. Mila made me realise what I'd been persuaded to do, and I told him I wouldn't agree to it again. He threw a fit and broke up with me. I'm glad he's gone."

Her tear-lined face said the opposite, but at least she was able to keep the cash. From the run-down street, the dirty house, and the recycling box filled with vodka bottles, the girl needed every bit of help she could get.

I took the ex-boyfriend's details and left her.

Tracking the jackass down was child's play, with Tyler having access to all manner of resources that gave us an address. But when we found him in a gaming session with his friends, all the ashen-faced lad could tell us was Salter had come to him at an amusement arcade. He didn't even have a phone number, only a time and date when he'd had to hand Annabelle over.

Another dead end.

Dawn shattered the sky when we returned to the warehouse. I'd failed. I had nowhere else to search. Even Tyler's efforts in getting a lead from his multiple contacts came to naught. No one could tell us where an auction might be happening.

I'd gone from complete access to Mila to none. She could be hurt right now, and I couldn't help her. She might even have been sold. All I could hope for was that she'd find a way out herself. She'd told me she could.

I hated that I'd probably never know.

A day later, and game night was upon us. The darkest night of the month.

On any average evening, the warehouse was busy. Weekends saw long queues outside the nightclub, but today, the crowd rushed the other side. For the rooms available to rent in the brothel where they could watch the fun happening in the basement below via livestreaming cameras.

I prowled the building, taking no joy from the party atmosphere.

With Shade, I'd prepped the basement, checking the cages, the locks, and the cameras, then I'd worked with the different teams in the building, making sure everyone had what they needed for the busy night.

Half the men and a couple of the women had arrived already, and I needed to prepare for the moment the siren sounded. I strode the busy corridor between Divine and Divide, passing sex workers and dancers who would make bank tonight, and entered the lift. Tyler was already inside and held the door for me.

The haunted exhaustion had gone from his eyes when he scanned me. "You okay?"

I shrugged. I'd been on an emotional roller coaster. High from the release from the hospital, low from the certainty that I'd been a bad person to my crew, then up and down again from meeting and losing Mila. Throwing myself into work had done nothing to ease my worry over her.

He let me brood, but when the doors opened for the fifth floor, he walked out with me, and his gaze stuck on a woman approaching down the corridor, her platinum-blonde hair bouncing.

"Dixie," he said in a low tone.

She did a double take at him, and her gaze jumped to me. She forced a smile. "Convict, just who I was looking for. Can we talk? In private?"

I shrugged, and she peeked again at Tyler, but then twirled away with a gesture for me to follow. Tyler gave her a long look but returned to the lift, travelling on to wherever he was going.

I trailed Dixie down to the opposite end of the hall to where I slept, following her into a bedroom. Like mine, it was lived-in, with clothes and makeup around. Not a room for use by the cam girls and boys.

I squinted at it. "Dixie, are you sleeping up here, too?"

She shrugged, her wide-necked top sliding over one slender shoulder. The bandage at her throat had been replaced with a smaller one, closer in colour to her skin. She touched the edge of it. "I feel safer here. Don't like to sleep alone at home."

I hadn't purposefully asked around for Dixie's story, but through conversations in the warehouse, I knew that the Deadwater serial killer had cut her throat and left her for dead. That murderer had been dealt with, in the permanent sense, but the scars left on my friend weren't just skin-deep.

Folding my arms, I rested against her wall. "What's the deal with Tyler?"

"There's no deal. Think he just feels sorry for me, hun. I don't need that."

"Or, he likes what he sees," I decided.

"Maybe once, he did. Not anymore."

I released a laugh. "Are you kidding? Dixie, you're hot as fuck."

She scowled at me.

I held my hands up. "I didn't mean it in that way. My dick literally only works for one woman, and it ain't you. I'm just saying that he admires you. I've seen it more than once."

She perked up. "Who's the mystery woman? Name, bra size, compelling facts. Spill the tea."

"Her name's Mila."

"Cute. Is that short for something?"

I frowned. Was it? Her name had got me nowhere in my search for her. Perhaps that was a clue, but not one I could obsess over this evening.

My phone chimed with an incoming message. Security had a new protocol for the contestants as they arrived for the game. Manny's team were responsible for the list, but a picture was taken of each then sent to management. Tonight, that was me. I checked the three photos. All men, all expected, the last being Rhys Jacobs. By now, they would've been escorted downstairs.

There was only one person I couldn't vouch for. A woman named E Marchant who Shade had spoken to. I'd check off her picture with him once I got it.

Something was bothering me about Jacobs. Since the interview, it had niggled at my mind though drowned out by my concerns over Mila. It was about his degree of interest in the protection the skeleton crew could offer him. There was no way that would be the primary thought for a guy who'd dreamt of hunting and fucking a woman, but he'd made a point of referencing it. At the time, I'd dismissed it, assuming he'd heard the story Shade told me about the loser who'd turned stalker. But what if I was wrong?

I lifted my gaze to Dixie. "Did you hear about a guy who lost the game and went after one of the women?"

She tilted her head in a thinking pose. "Vaguely? I think it was last year."

"How well known was it?"

"Outside of the warehouse? I'm not sure. Why?"

I exhaled and tried to dislodge the strange feeling. It was the type of dark gossip that would be shared between men. Some guy brought down by stronger men. I was overthinking.

"Never mind. I need to get ready. Are you done using me as a human shield against Tyler?"

Dixie rolled her eyes then pointed at the bandage on my arm. "That needs changing again."

A couple of days ago, I'd asked her to change my dressing while I kept my eyes closed. Sweetheart that she was, she'd obliged.

I wrinkled my nose at my arm, twisting it to display the lifting edges of the medical tape. "Probably."

"Still can't face it, huh? I'll do it for you."

I thanked her. She treated my arm while I watched the door, my focus anywhere but on the burn scar.

More contestants arrived, the pictures crowding my phone.

At last, the sense of excitement built inside me. I was still too pissed off to enjoy it, but it sped my pulse and warmed my blood.

In twenty minutes, the game would be underway. The fights would start. The fucking would follow.

Dixie spoke as she worked. "I'm glad that this is happening tonight, I mean that Arran has given you the management of it. After what happened last time, most of us feel he owes you."

"He owes me nothing," I said automatically. Then I hesitated. "What last time?"

"When you went into the game? You broke his rule that none of the crew can take part, and he retaliated horribly."

Shit, that's what I'd done? My stomach gutted out. I knew I'd broken faith in some way, but for Arran to give me a second chance that involved exactly the same risk to him made me nauseated.

He'd trusted me once and was showing me he trusted me again. Or that he felt so bad that I'd been injured he'd overridden his better judgement.

Another two photos landed on my phone. I checked and dismissed them. Only one left now. The last woman standing.

"I don't remember that," I confessed.

"Shit, bestie. It isn't right that your memory is still messed up." She taped down the fresh bandage on my arm. "You went into the game because you'd craved it, and Arran treated you like you were his worst enemy. None of what happened to you was right, but it started with Arran's delulu overreaction. That's when you were sent undercover, to make up for that plus some other minor things you'd done."

"Maybe it wasn't an overreaction. I broke his rule, like you said."

"I don't know. He's home in a couple of days. I want to watch him grovel. You're owed that."

Dixie was done, and I thanked her and tugged down my grey shirtsleeve, half covering the bandage.

I needed to get downstairs. I'd be the one to sound the siren. To unlock the cages.

But hearing how I'd broken the rules in the past summoned a flash of a memory, and I stared into space, trying to focus on it.

I'd been in the basement. I'd stalked a woman. I remembered the hunt and the feeling like no other. Why had I done it?

A wave of certainty followed, raising the hair on the back of my neck.

For the end result—the woman I'd get to claim and keep. I'd wanted someone to love who was mine and who'd love me back. A relationship I was sure I'd never had, though I didn't remember my history to know exactly how alone I'd been.

The realisation threatened something deep inside me.

Of a loneliness so acute it cut through me. Alone in the hospital. Alone before that.

I pushed it away. I couldn't indulge that kind of thinking, not after where it had got me last time, where rejection from my crew had nearly ended my life. I had a second chance. I was certain over my future. Over the home I'd found and the forgiveness I didn't deserve. The faith the skeleton crew had put in me couldn't be tested again.

A message titled 'Last contestant' arrived on my phone, and my pulse sped before I even checked it. They were all here. This was happening.

I could watch but never join in.

But the picture on my screen stole my breath and froze my heart. According to the text, the photo was for the final contestant on the list, no longer using her initial but giving her full name of Emilia Marchant.

New clothes, her hair up, but in every other way herself.

Mila had entered my game.

10

The sounds of a fight filtered through the basement to the brightly lit locker room where I waited with four other women. Three talked excitedly while a fourth sat on a bench and studied her hands, a mantra whispered on her lips.

"This will all be okay. I'll meet him. Whoever he is, he'll love me."

I couldn't share her reassurance.

My well-thought-through plan had been blown to pieces. It was all my fault. I'd texted the one person who'd been my get-out-of-jail-free. I'd asked my brother for help, and he'd arrived after Convict had already taken Annabelle away but walked straight into a trap. With the worst possible timing, Salter and his cronies had arrived. They'd captured him, and from somewhere, knew my name.

I wasn't sure how that happened, but I had my suspicions.

My plan had been straightforward. Put myself forward for auction, then when they took me to the boss, Rhys Jacobs, I'd get what I wanted then free myself. If my name hadn't been enough for them to let me walk away, my backup plan would've come for me.

Now that backup was in handcuffs and restraints, and I'd been forced into the skeleton crew's basement while his life hung in the balance.

I held myself taut, my mind spinning over what I'd been ordered to do. It was so strange. Salter's command this evening was for me to get to Jacobs.

He was in this same game.

My target all along, but also Salter's.

Except now, I had to let him fuck me in this basement where nineteen other men would be trying to do the same. My skin itched and crawled.

If I failed, Salter would make good on his threat and kill the man I should never have brought into this. The brother I'd fought to build a relationship with and now whose life was in my hands.

What a mess. What an absolute disaster I'd fallen into.

One of the women went to the doorway and peeked out, her white-blonde hair sliding over her shoulder. She was dressed to impress in pale lace that clung to her curves.

In contrast, I'd been thrown a bag of clothes by Salter and told to pick a tight dress. And not to bother with underwear. I hadn't cared about the option I'd chosen—a purple minidress that barely covered my ass. Especially not after Salter had crowed about how soon it would be torn off me.

The woman at the door shivered. "It won't be long. In another minute, the siren will go. Can you hear the men?"

The shouts of fighting were getting louder, perhaps at the sight of her as one of the cages was adjacent to the locker room door. I'd caught a glimpse when I'd scurried in.

Though the cage was unlit, the occupants had been outlined by the bright lights of the huge warehouse space that also revealed its concrete floor, gantry steps, pillars, and hidden doorways. Most of the men were bare-chested, but there was an added element that filled me with dread.

The skeleton masks.

All were wearing them.

How did I pick out Jacobs if I couldn't see his face? I'd

only ever met him across a meeting room table.

Another woman went to the door and stepped outside, her black hair twisted into a complex pattern. She adjusted her boobs in her bra top, earning a chorus of roars from the cage at her fingers on her ebony skin. "Get ready to run, ladies."

We all moved into the hall, and the others gazed up to the neon-pink light on the wall and the siren next to it. An air of excited anticipation ran over every woman but me. My stomach cramped from the rising adrenaline. My whole body trembled.

I was trapped in here. There was no way out. The doors had locked behind me, and no one could leave until it was all over. Every last woman fucked and owned.

The siren blared.

I burst out with a sob, shocking myself with the emotion. I'd held it in for days. There was no time for a breakdown— the cage doors grated and clanked. My heart thumped harder, and I ran, off to the left where the shadows were darkest.

A bellow came, and I peered over my shoulder to see the blonde woman sprinting straight down the centre of the wide-open space. A gang pursued her. One was in the lead, a huge beast of a man with black jeans and bare feet, a spray of blood on his olive skin. He gave an animalistic growl and swiped for her, catching her waist so the two tumbled to the floor.

Instantly, the rest of the pack set upon them, punches thrown at him while others grasped at her in a mass brawl.

That wasn't all the men, though. Maybe only half. Two pursued the quiet mantra woman up the metal steps to a suspended walkway. A third woman had set off in the opposite direction to me, with her own group stalking her. The fourth with the complex hairstyle, I couldn't see.

Not one of the men resembled Jacobs.

It had been only weeks since I last saw him at a corporate board meeting. He'd been in a suit and tie, smug and unspeaking. It was hard to place that man as one of these attackers.

He had to be here, though, which meant I needed to hunt the hunters. But in that came a problem.

Three men prowled in my direction.

One, in a black gym shirt which showed off too-thick muscles, pointed at me. "You're mine."

I backed away, matching their pace. None were Jacobs. They were too big. He was slighter than all of them.

At his statement, the man next to the gym bunny swore then hooked an arm around his throat and tossed him to the floor, a fight breaking out between them that tripped up the third man.

I took my chance and fled around a corner.

Hugging the wall, I stumbled in my footsteps and clung to a pillar, temporarily out of sight to anyone in the main space of the massive basement. I breathlessly searched the group still fighting over the woman with the sleek blonde hair. She was on all fours, trying to crawl away. With a rip, her dress tore away to reveal her underwear, one of her shoes already missing.

A man caught her ankle and dragged her back, and I winced. She'd be hurt. Her knees bloodied by the rough concrete and her flesh bruised.

None of them cared, and not a single member of the large group gave me any glimmer of recognition.

The man who had her in his grip crawled over her, changing his hold to the back of her neck while he wrestled with the opening to his jeans, freeing his dick. A second tore off his clothes and dove at the pair.

Oh God. One way or another, that woman's game was

almost up.

I couldn't watch.

On the far wall, the woman who'd run up the gantry had reached a metal walkway that bisected the wall, leading to what looked like an overseer's office with more steps heading down the other side. The men who'd chased her had been joined by others. I scoured the group, desperation filling me. Nope, not Rhys Jacobs.

Where was he?

I'd counted off, how many, twelve of the twenty? More?

A howl broke my thoughts. A man with a top knot of blond hair shoved another off the gantry. The victim dangled by an arm from the rail, high above the warehouse floor, his hands slipping dangerously on the metal.

No one helped him. The woman with the black hair appeared and kicked out at one of her pack with impressive poise. He stumbled away to be replaced instantly. The next man captured her, pulling her tight against his body.

He kissed her. Ran a hand down her body to yank up her dress and expose her bare ass, his fingers sliding between her legs. She laughed and slapped his face. He captured her hand and touched his forehead to hers, pure fury and lust holding his features tight.

Footsteps sounded closer to me, snapping me back to my own game. I spun to face a man prowling around the corner at the far end of the room, the way I'd come. He didn't run, and for too many heartbeats, neither did I. His focus fell on me like a spotlight.

A bolt of familiarity hit me.

In this place of depravity, he was the bright glimmer of recognition I'd so badly needed.

Except this wasn't Jacobs.

The man taking purposeful, slow steps in my direction wore faded jeans and a grey shirt, open a few buttons at his throat, and with his sleeves rolled up to show strong forearms. He was tall, with messy dark hair, and inkwork on his skin.

I couldn't see his lower face behind the mask, but I knew his shape. He was a lost boy, a gang member for whom this nightmare was any other day of the week. I'd touched the white bandage on his arm and wondered about the scar at his temple. The walking boot was missing, swapped out for running shoes.

My bottom lip trembled, and fresh tears threatened. I hated it here, and Convict offered safety and protection I couldn't take.

As much as I wanted to run to him, I turned and bolted the other way.

11

Convict

Fury guided my actions. I shouldn't be here. Arran was due home in days, and when he found out what I'd done, my home with the skeleton crew would be destroyed. I should've stayed on the other side of the locked doors, watching the outcome on the many cameras like every other envious asshole.

Then I'd seen the tears.

Mila had remained stony-faced in the dressing room, and I'd stared in shock, desperation, and with a thousand other emotions battering me. Whatever she was playing at, I couldn't work it out. Days ago, she'd been trying to get into an auction, only to vanish then resurface in our basement, a contestant in my game. Frying pan, fire.

At her sudden hit of emotion, I'd lost it. Every shred of my self-control splintered. This wasn't her choice. She was scared, and I couldn't stand by and let it happen.

Ignoring my team, I repeated the crime I'd once been sentenced for and entered the game. And as I prowled after Mila, I couldn't bring myself to care.

She scampered away, heating my blood all the more.

To my right, a man fucked into a blonde woman on the concrete. She screamed in pleasure, and he hauled her upright so everyone could see his dick thrust into her pussy, spreading her wide around him.

"Mine," he roared.

Groans of disappointment followed, along with the grunts of some whack job beating his dick to the side of them, his game over as he probably wouldn't get it up again.

My dick? Not interested.

I was a heat-seeking missile for one reckless woman only.

Ahead, Mila reached the second of the cages we kept the men in. She hesitated at the open doorway then stepped inside.

I jogged to catch up with her, throwing a look around to make sure no one else had noticed yet. Lucky for us, most were caught on the spectacle of the first couple's claim or lost in the hunt for the other women.

When I reached the bars, Mila stood over an unconscious man. She bent to remove his mask then stepped back in shock, her hands covering her mouth.

"You absolute bastard. You didn't even make it out of the cage? Wake up."

She kicked him in the ribs. I could've laughed, but other emotions had me in their grip. I braced myself in the doorway, fisting the metal bars.

She was attacking Rhys Jacobs. What the fuck was her interest in that guy? Some kind of business deal? Was he meant to protect her in here? I'd had that flash of suspicion about the man but dismissed it. Perhaps my instincts had been right.

Mila shoved Jacobs again, harder so his head lolled to one side. "You have to wake, you scheming con artist. What did you do, bribe, threaten, manipulate? Open your eyes or this is all over."

I tilted my head. "What's all over, Mila?"

Mila lifted her focus to me. Our gazes locked, and she took a shaky breath, fear and panic right there in her eyes. As well as something far more compelling. The recognition

I craved.

Men would move mountains for love. Or for the chance of it. I knew that for certain because at her distress, I was ready to face anything.

Whatever she had to say was lost to the fist that smacked into my head from the side and the rush of men into the cage.

12

Mila

Two men burst past Convict into the cell. I screamed and backed up, half falling in my haste. One snatched at me, snagging my dress in his creepily long fingers. He wrenched it, and the cheap material of the skirt ripped down the centre, exposing my naked lower body.

The second man snarled in lust and swung for him.

They landed on Jacobs's prone body.

I didn't waste the chance. Finding my feet, I skirted them and dove out of the gate. But I pulled up short. On the floor, Convict groaned and clutched his head at the site of his scar. He'd been badly hurt recently. He'd mentioned a head injury then had taken a hell of a hit.

Kneeling beside him, I took his hand. "Let me see."

He let me move it away, revealing a red mark but no blood. Gingerly, I traced over the skin.

"Doesn't hurt," he muttered.

"Because you don't feel pain or because the hit wasn't a bad one?" It had downed him. It had to have been hard.

Convict sat up, shook his head, then lurched to standing. He was so much taller than me, and his broad body filled my view. Something strange happened. It was the effects of the night, surely, but attraction slid over me in a warm rush. There was something in his shape and in the way he focused solely on me that woke a part of my brain. It tuned me in to him. It made me want to move in closer.

A yell came from behind us. The men in the cage were still brawling, but a pack had formed down the corridor, five or six strong. They'd spotted me.

My heart slammed into my chest.

"Don't run, Mila," Convict warned.

"Are you crazy?"

But his expression said something else. That I needed to stay. That he'd protect me. How could I trust that? My fear rushed back, and I turned and sprinted away across the width of the basement.

In the centre of the floor, the first couple was having frantic sex, their noises getting louder and louder. At least two unconscious men lay nearby. Above them, on the walkway, a second pair had just finished and were still entangled, the man speaking lovingly in the woman's ear while they panted.

A fully naked woman bolted past me with two men in hot pursuit. She spotted my pack and pointed at one of them. "You. You're who I want. Take me."

I spared a frantic glance to see her choice. If it was Convict...

But no, the leader of the group was in her sights, the musclebound gym bunny from earlier. He shoved away from the others and made a break for her, catching her as she circled to him. Others battled to separate them in a chaotic mess of limbs.

None were fast enough by the cries that followed, adding to the rhythmic sounds of sex. Then the fourth woman appeared, carried in the arms of her man, with her naked body pressed to his. They must've already paired off as no one troubled them.

It was almost over. Horrifyingly fast. I was the last woman standing.

On shaking limbs, I backed to the metal steps and climbed, but my breathing was coming hard, and panic had me quaking. The swarm of men followed, a mass of predators set on their prey. One laughed. I didn't share his fun.

Fucking Jacobs hadn't even made it out of the cage. I didn't want him in any way, but his failure meant I couldn't stop Salter from carrying out his threat. I'd failed. Emotion clogged my throat.

Laughing Man overtook me and snatched me up. I cried out, and he threw me over his shoulder then carried me up to the gantry. High above the warehouse floor, I hit out with my fists and thrashed to escape. If he dropped me and I fell, I'd die.

A bigger man crashed into him, and we all tumbled onto the hard grate. It couldn't end like this. If I didn't fight, I'd end up as the property of one of them.

I scuttled away, but Laughing Man grabbed for me and caught the remains of my skirt. The dress fell away with the cheap material disintegrating.

I was naked. Almost completely. Cameras were on me, and everyone watching would get an eyeful of my body. Humiliation crowded me.

But I couldn't wait around and cry. Footsteps rang out, and six or more men battled each other to ascend the stairs. I had to get up.

Turning on my knees, I faced down the gantry.

There was a second staircase. Evading the fighting men who temporarily blocked the way for the others, I lurched for it, only to pull up short. Another group gathered at the bottom and started climbing. All remaining men had targeted me. All of them were centred on one prey, pinned down with nowhere to run.

That was it. I was trapped. It was over.

Except I'd forgotten one.

With a yell of rage, Convict emerged from the shadows and grabbed the guy with the blond ponytail at the back of the line. He threw him to the concrete floor then punched the next in the face, downing him so the man cringed and dropped to his knees, blood dripping from a broken nose.

I whimpered, my strength low, beaten down by my absolute defeat, but also hooked on Convict's battle to reach me. He was beautiful and frightening. The kiss we'd shared had been more of a turn-on than any romantic encounter in the past. There was no way he could get to me in time.

Convict climbed the steps and wrenched a third man out of his way. A fourth, a thuggish, tattooed male, snarled and reared back to headbutt him, but he dodged and the asshole followed his own momentum and crashed to the bottom of the steps.

It left only one. The last man standing between us swung for him but missed, earning his fate in being tipped off the edge. Convict breathed hard and sprinted up to me, his bootsteps ringing out.

Instinctively, I knew if I rushed him, he'd let me pass.

What if I didn't?

What if I just let him catch me?

He cleared the last of the steps, reaching me before the others along the gantry who were blocked by the two still throwing fists.

My lost boy picked me up and clamped me against his heaving chest. "Little gangster. What battle are you fighting? Who put you in here?"

I couldn't answer. His gaze claimed and held mine. My heart thumped in a frantic beat.

One of the men ahead of us downed his opponent, clearing the way for the pack.

Convict swore. "New game. I caught you, I get to keep you. Just understand I need to do this to stop them."

He lifted me into his arms and reached between us to free his dick. My eyes closed of their own accord. My legs wrapped around his waist.

"I'd say I was sorry, but it would be a lie."

He fucked into me in one hard thrust that ended the game for all.

*E*verything that happened next came in flashes. The thickness of him pushing inside me, and my gasp of...what? Shock? Relief?

Certainly pleasure.

Yells of outrage and anger. The doors unlocking, then the jubilant victors carrying out their prizes.

In Convict's arms, I wilted. He pulled out of me and stripped his shirt, draped it around my shoulders and concealed my nudity. Outside the doors, we passed an exit where the cool air was filled by the cheers of a crowd. I kept my eyes closed tight.

Steps followed, going up. We were staying inside the warehouse. I was glad.

Someone shook Convict's shoulder. "Fucking hell, that was wild."

He didn't stop. Not for that guy, and not for the others who apparently knew him and wanted to give us both their well wishes. All I could do was huddle into him like a scared animal.

"Peachy," he muttered in a low rumble. "Just exercised my caveman right to claim a woman. Honestly, I feel enlightened."

Despite his words, he held me closer, like possessing me mattered.

A deep voice hailed Convict, this time causing us to stop. "Congratulations. That hit you took—"

Convict cut him off. "Probably knocked sense into me."

"Or cracked your head open again."

I peeked at his friend, blocking out all the other faces around. He was a huge man with dark-blond hair and a concerned expression. He palmed Convict's face to turn it, but the man who'd been inside me only a minute ago shoved him away.

"I said I'm fine."

His friend frowned and looked at me. "Watch him for signs of concussion, Mila. Double vision, sickness, dizziness."

He knew my name. I didn't have the presence of mind to question how.

Another man pushed through the crowd, meeting us at the entrance to a lift. He raised a tattooed hand to scrub through his dark hair, his expression troubled.

Convict centred on him but didn't put me down. "I'll leave if you order it."

The tattooed man shook his head. "I'm not asking that. Not after last time. But, Con…"

"But nothing. I'm taking Mila upstairs to bed."

A cheer rose from those nearby. I hid my face.

The lift doors opened, and we entered. Convict pressed a button then ran a hand down my back. He murmured something soft and soothing. I clung to him.

Out of the lift, down a corridor, into a room, at last, he set me down on a bed. He locked the door, and a new wave of panic hit me. I trembled.

Convict knelt beside me. "You're in shock. You weren't meant to be there, and it scared you."

I took a shuddering breath. There was no point concealing anything now. "I had no choice. They made me."

Slowly, he nodded. "What were you ordered to do?"

"Get to Rhys Jacobs."

"Why him?"

"I... I don't know for sure. All Salter told me was he needed to be brought to heel."

"Were you to kill him or fuck him, Mila?"

The simple conversation brought me out of my fright, and my thoughts returned in a rush. "We need to go back downstairs. We need to find Jacobs. Not just for Salter, but because he was the man I needed to reach. He's why I was trying to get into that auction."

Convict tilted his head. "You kicked him and called him a manipulator. Who did he influence? Wait, what does Salter have over you to make you obey him?"

I knelt on the bed. "Someone I care about who will die if I don't get Jacobs. Please. We have to go now."

As I spoke, I shifted my position, and the shirt draped over me slid off my shoulder. It bared my breasts. Convict's gaze followed it, then he swallowed and stood, backing to the wall. From his pocket, he found his phone then tapped out a message.

His voice came out thick. "I asked Tyler to send someone down. He's the man who told you to keep a watch over me."

"I'll go myself."

A gruff laugh was my answer. "No, you won't. Wait here."

With what appeared to be some effort, he left the room. The game might've been over, but I didn't feel safe, not now I was alone.

In fact, why was I sitting here?

I jumped up, right as Convict returned. In a flash, he claimed my arm, clicking something metal onto it, then he reached to connect it to the frame beside my leg.

"What are you doing?" I tugged at the constraint, a silver

bracelet that definitely was not jewellery.

He'd handcuffed me to the goddamned bed.

"You have a nasty habit of disappearing on me. I'll get your man, and I'll lock the door after myself so you'll be safe in here until I return. This is for my peace of mind."

I didn't have a chance to yell at him, as my saviour and captor left me tied up in his room.

13

Convict

No regrets bothered me. Mila would've run if I hadn't stopped her, and we had a lot to talk about.

The main one being that I'd been inside her.

I'd seen stars. Then Mila's face. Possibly the same thing.

I thundered down the back stairs to the ground floor, then strode through emptying corridors. Of the people still hanging around, I paid them no attention, though I registered their surprise.

I was bare-chested, bloodied from throwing fists, but I should be with my woman. The fact that I roamed the halls was shocking. Everyone knew the compelling nature of the game. It was one of the reasons I'd had to walk out. I could've left the manhunt to Tyler, but every single part of me demanded that I fuck the woman I'd claimed.

Particularly when her naked body was right there in front of me.

At the entrance to the basement, a team of cleaners wheeled in a trolley. One of the skeleton crew guarded the door.

"Tyler inside?" I asked.

The guard's eyes widened, and he gave me a single nod.

I strode into the space. It smelled of blood, sweat, and sex.

My body warmed in response. Mila running scared.

Mila naked. Mila taking me. I exhaled the weight of sheer need and tracked down the team leader in one of the cages. It was empty, and he was alone.

His forehead lined in a frown. "What the fuck are you doing down here?"

"Jacobs is important to Mila. I need to know why."

"And you didn't trust me to find him?"

I scowled back. "Of course I did. Where is he?"

"Not here. Looks like he woke up from his nap after the fun finished and the cameras cut out. I have people checking outside." Tyler tilted his head, carrying out a quick assessment of me in the way he did with everything. "I wish I knew what you were thinking, but this needs to be said. Arran gave us all the same rule. We don't take part in the game. We facilitate it, and the money it earns is used to help women."

"I didn't take part. I intervened."

"With your dick?"

I scowled, and he held up a hand.

"Mila wasn't supposed to be in there, was she? She slipped through the net, and if I'd have been here earlier, or had a chance to catch up with Shade on the work we're covering, this might not have happened. Same goes for you. But that isn't the point. Arran will possibly forgive you if you and Mila are endgame. The fact you're running around out here now suggests otherwise."

His phone beeped, and he read the screen then swore. "Jacobs's car is gone."

Shit. The guy had been unconscious. Asshole move to wake up and disappear after missing the entirety of the game.

I couldn't regret that part of it, though. If he'd been the one to catch Mila, for whatever reason, she would have given herself to him.

Absolute loathing closed off those thoughts. She was mine. Legitimately and fairly. The rules said I'd won. My brain said holy shit. My dick said finally.

I'd claimed her, and by every rule in the book, nothing could change that.

Well, except her.

Which meant I needed to convince her of the fact, and not only for the sake of my crew, even if Tyler was right.

Chaining her up might not have helped my case.

I turned back to Tyler. "On that point, I need your help. Come with me."

He stowed his phone, and we left the basement, returning upstairs.

Tyler spoke as we climbed the flights. "Something else I meant to mention. The cars that were seen on the CCTV taking Mila away from Milburne Alley had fake number plates which meant we couldn't ID them."

I knew that. It was another frustrating avenue exhausted in the past couple of days.

"One of those fake plates was picked up on a local highway plate recognition camera just this evening. I got the notification when you asked me to come down here."

"Where?"

"Leaving an industrial estate in the north of Deadwater. I can get a team out there. Do you know who they captured?"

"Not yet. But Mila wants whoever it is back."

"Then we take him alive?"

I left Tyler's question hanging and pushed through the doors for the fifth floor. At my bedroom, I asked him to hold back, then let myself in.

Mila scowled at me from the bed. "Unlock me."

I exhaled and knelt to unchain her. She'd reinstated my

shirt so her naked body was covered again, but I couldn't help my gaze travelling up her bare legs.

When the handcuffs fell away from the bedframe, she jumped up and made to circle me.

I blocked the door. "What is it with you and disappearing? I have information for you."

She tugged the shirt onto her now-free arm and rolled up the grey shirtsleeve, the shirt's hem coming to mid-thigh. "Lucky me that you're ready to share it without me being tied up."

I lowered my gaze at her, my body reacting yet again. "Don't tempt me."

Mila's eyes flared with unmistakable lust. But she gave up the fight and gestured for me to proceed.

"Rhys Jacobs has left the basement. He must've come to when the game finished, and his car is already gone from outside."

Mila deflated. "Then that's it. I've failed."

"Maybe not." I filled her in on what Tyler had told me. "We can send a team out on a search and rescue, but we need to know what you know. That means trusting me. I know that apparently goes against everything you believe, but I promise you if I can help, I will. My whole crew will."

Her gaze searched mine. "Why?"

I let every piece of my almost overwhelming need flood into my gaze. "You're mine. Whether you like it or not. I'm not above bargaining to keep you. Now, can I bring Tyler to the door to hear what you have to tell us?"

Mila's cheeks flooded pink. I reacted to her, but the same applied in reverse. She wanted me. She liked some part of the fact I'd caught her. It made me all the more certain I wasn't going to let her go.

She searched my gaze for a moment then apparently made a decision, returning to the bed to wrap herself in a blanket. "Chain me up again and I'll do the same to you."

I arched an eyebrow. "That a promise?"

An eyeroll gave me permission to proceed.

At the door, I beckoned Tyler in. "Mila's going to identify the man captured by Salter and his goons. He's our target."

Tyler nodded, keeping his gaze mostly elsewhere in the room. I appreciated the respect.

Mila swallowed and watched me. "Can I borrow your phone?"

From a shelf, I found my spare, the one she'd used in the holding cell. She brought up a browser and searched then located a picture, handing it back. Onscreen was a shot of a man about my age and fucking huge. "His name is Kane."

I passed the phone to Tyler.

He examined the photo. "Who does he work for?"

"I don't know. Not a gang, though."

"Can he handle himself?"

"In a fight? I'm pretty certain he can. I don't know him that well, but it was my fault he got jumped." In her fists, she mangled the blanket. "I was supposed to get Jacobs then call them, then they'd swap him out for Kane. By now, they must know I failed. You have to help him."

I hated the fear that laced her tone. "What is he to you?"

Mila went quiet. I swapped a glance with Tyler.

The team leader sent the picture from my phone to his. "We'll head out. You two stay safe in here, and I'll report back when I have news."

Mila's eyes shuttered closed. "Thank you."

"You're skeleton crew now. Convict, take care of your lass, aye? Remember what I said. Breaking the rules is worth it for the right reasons."

He left us, and I centred myself for what I needed to do

next, and the woman I had to tame.

14

Mila

Convict settled on the floor, his back against the wall and one leg extended.

It brought to mind when I'd last seen him in that position, back in the disused office space. I searched the room. "You're meant to be wearing a walking boot."

He blinked. "Couldn't show an obvious weakness in the game."

I spotted the black boot between the bed and the side table and picked it up, handing it across.

He took it and kicked off his shoe, fitting it into place. He didn't wince or move awkwardly, anything to suggest his actions in the basement had done him any damage.

"How much longer should you be wearing that?"

"A few more days. I'm pretty much healed."

I had such a problem with this man. Now my emotions had cooled, others had replaced them. Attraction was a big part of that, but also logic. On my own, I had no hope of getting Kane back. I couldn't go up against a gang of men. I didn't have a chance. Convict had jumped to find a solution when he didn't have to.

He'd also been inside me. I wanted more. Specifically to slide off the bed and crawl to his lap.

He watched me. "I have about a hundred questions to ask of you, but none of them are in my head right now."

"Why were you in the basement?" I blurted. "Your friend said about doing the wrong things for the right reasons. What did that mean?"

"It means I went in to fetch you because I knew you didn't go into that arena voluntarily."

A throb of something struck my heart. "Why would that be wrong?"

"Because crew members aren't allowed to take part."

Well, damn. There was me thinking it was a perk of the job.

Convict continued. "What Tyler meant was if I did it because of the thrill of the chase alone, I'll be out on my ass when Arran, the leader of our crew, returns. Kicked out of the only home I know."

I took a short breath. He'd just offered me leverage over him on a silver platter. Yet I didn't get a chance to turn this into a strategy because he pinned me with his stare.

"I also did it because I want you. I caught you in the game where the rules are clear, so every part of me believes that you're mine. So you weren't supposed to be there? Don't assume I'll be a good guy and give you an out."

"What are you saying?"

His heavy gaze intensified. "I'm proposing a deal. My help in whatever scheme you're working on in exchange for you obeying the rules. For you staying with me."

I knew some of the rules. The women had discussed them in hushed whispers in the locker room. "Those rules include sex. You're asking me to prostitute myself?"

"No. I'm asking you to fuck the guy you already want to fuck because you agreed to it."

A thrill buzzed through me. "Bold assumption."

Convict gave me an infuriating smirk. "Up on the gantry, you could've chosen any other of those assholes. They were fighting for you, Emilia. You turned and ran to me."

I had. And why did my insides liquify when he used my full first name?

I swallowed. Given another minute, I would've constructed this offer myself. I was dying for him. If he put me on my back now, I'd probably pull him closer.

But one rule of business my grandparents had taught me was never to follow emotion. Only facts.

"Be specific about what I give and what I get in return."

"The rules are that we're together for thirty days. We can't be apart for more than a couple of hours at a time. Yes, we fuck a lot, but we also eat, and talk, and enjoy each other's lives. I'm yours as much as you are mine, so whatever you need me to do, it's done."

"How sweet."

He arched a dark brow. "You get me and my terrifyingly competent criminal crew. It's a really aggressive honeymoon."

I fought an entirely unwarranted smile. "Why would your crew help me?"

"Because you're mine. The skeleton crew would show up for me, assuming I get to stay in it. My crew owns the night in this city. The police, politicians, all in our pocket. You get the same protection."

That...was appealing. Almost as much as getting to touch him.

His confidence faltered. "We're supposed to leave work behind and lock ourselves away. That's the only thing I can't do."

"Why?"

Convict's obvious hunger and determination dialled back to something more vulnerable. He made a circle around his head. "I've no fucking clue if I have a home anywhere. Whole amnesia thing."

"I have an apartment." I stopped my words and the offer that was about to fall from my lips, because the thought of hiding away with him in my lonely flat was disturbingly compelling. "When you get my... When you get Kane back, I'll give you an answer."

Something flared in his eyes. "I want more than that. I want everything."

"For thirty days only," I amended.

Convict watched me then jumped up, and I braced myself against a surge of something powerful that ordered me to reach for him. To throw off the shirt he'd given me.

He went for the door instead. "Hungry? Thirsty?"

I shook my head. I had no appetite. Salter's men had kept me fed over the past few days, but tonight, adrenaline had shrunk my stomach to a tight knot.

Convict left me with a promise to return soon. I curled up in a bed that smelled of him, and I must've fallen asleep, because I woke to the light dimmed low and one other reality I had to face.

The locked door I couldn't leave.

15

Convict

Emilia Marchant, twenty-four, granddaughter of Austin and Primrose Marchant, owners of quite the enterprise, according to my research. Mila worked for their business, a shipping and haulage company that operated out of major ports in Northern England and Scotland.

She was all over their social media after graduating university then officially joining the company a year or two ago. Even before that, she was photographed at every award ceremony or company event. There she was—champagne in one hand, granny on the other. Definitely not the kind of woman who'd shack up with a skeleton-masked maniac in a bloodstained basement. Yet here we were.

"Quite the golden child," I muttered to myself.

Except all wasn't well in Marchant Haulage.

Four weeks ago, Austin had died of a heart attack. Not a shocker for a man in his seventies with ruddy cheeks and the purple-veined nose of a heavy drinker, but the photographs of the funeral struck me in the chest.

Pictures showed a devastated Mila, crumpled and alone at the graveside. I got why the photographer had snapped the shot—she was beautiful, even in tears—but to plaster that all over the local news was low.

The story gave me a good dose of background to the lass. She was grieving for sure, and in that, had somehow been thrown into turmoil with the kind of men she should never have been around.

Assholes like the one who'd locked her up. Which now included me.

I checked the time and jumped up from the bed in the room where I'd hidden away. I had ten minutes until our maximum two hours of separation was up, and we needed supplies. Downstairs, I raided the wardrobe that I'd been dressing from then hit up the strip club's kitchen, scoring two hot chicken sandwiches.

While I waited to be served, Tyler called.

"Update for you. Target acquired. He's alive and well, also well-guarded. We'll wait and watch for an in."

Relief battled an odd sense of jealousy in my gut. Nothing in my research on Mila had thrown up a sibling or a boyfriend. If this guy was someone she'd been dating, I'd toss him straight back into Salter's hands.

I thanked Tyler. "I was thinking about what Mila said about whether they'd know or not if she'd succeeded. Unless they'd rented a bed in the warehouse during the game, they'd only be sure if they were waiting outside with the crowd to see the victors. I took Mila upstairs, and Jacobs slipped away unseen."

He made a sound of agreement. "You're thinking like me. Beds are booked out months in advance, but I already asked Manny to go over the list. He confirmed there has been no swaps or last-minute add-ins."

Those beds went for a premium. Old boys or groups of men booked their favourite sex workers and dicked down to the chase. Set that back over a month ago and it was too early for Mila's grandfather's death. I didn't know for sure, but that had to be the start of all her troubles.

We said goodbye, and I dialled Shade, something else bothering me.

"Did you speak to Mila to interview her for the game?" I

asked without preamble.

"Hello to ye, too. Yes and no. A lass dropped out a week ago, and I took the next on the list. Emilia Marchant. We had a phone chat, but I'm certain it wasnae the girl ye caught."

I swore. "How do you know?"

"I heard your Mila yell out during the game. Everything about her voice was different. She was set up, aye? That's why ye went in?"

Of course she was. I hung up on him, fucking furious yet again, and determined to find out who'd put her up to the task.

Mila woke on my entry to the room. "Where have you been?"

"Miss me?"

"No, asshole. You locked me up, again."

I furrowed my brow. "I locked the door for your safety."

She sat up and jingled the handcuffs still attached to the bedframe. "You might as well have tied me to the bed again."

I huffed a laugh and set down the provisions. "That can be arranged. Here, I brought food and clothes. Also news. Tyler has seen your man."

Her gaze clung to mine. "Alive?"

I nodded, that jealousy twinging again at her sigh. "They're waiting for an opportunity. If they think he's at risk, they'll act, but as things stand, we're guessing it isn't clear who you paired off with, so Salter isn't taking retaliatory action."

"Right. God. Thank you."

I gestured for Mila to take up one of the sandwiches, and I took the other, resuming my position on the floor. "When did you sign up for Salter's auction?"

Mila took a big bite of the food and moaned, the sound going straight to my dick.

"I didn't realise how hungry I was. Um, I went to Esther about a week ago. She's the one who burst into the room as you were taking Annabelle away."

I nodded, already halfway through my sandwich. "A week ago is the same time your name was given for the game and someone did a phone interview pretending to be you. Clearly not a coincidence."

"You think it was Esther?" She swore and stared off into the middle distance. "I never thought she was a trustworthy person. So that means Salter immediately made a plan to use me after Esther gave him my name. Then he recruited her. I thought it was strange how there was that delay in the holding cell. He kept me there overnight, maybe to make sure I didn't get cold feet and ruin his plans."

"Why not just use Esther to get to Jacobs? She could've gone into the game."

She took another bite and chewed for a minute, thinking. "When I went to her, I said I wanted to see Jacobs specifically, and it took some hours before I got an answer. When she called me, she said I'd only meet the organiser on the night the auction took place, and Salter would handle the preliminaries. She then made a comment that stuck in my head. She said I was exactly the clean type they wanted. When contestants apply to your game, are there specific criteria?"

"There are, including medical."

"Salter's people took my blood. I figured it was to do with the auction, but it must've been for your people. Maybe Esther wouldn't have passed that test."

A wave of protectiveness came over me. She'd been manipulated like a chess piece. Salter had sniffed out an opportunity, which meant he'd wanted Jacobs for something as well.

"Why exactly do you need Rhys Jacobs?" I asked. "I take it he's into some shady shit if the auctions were his idea but now Salter is running them."

She didn't give an answer right away, finishing her food then drinking from the water bottle beside my bed. When she was done, she offered it to me. I took it and drank, liking the little spark of intimacy at our sharing.

If she agreed to be with me, this would be my world for the next month. Sharing everything with her. Having someone of my own. If she turned me down, I'd have nothing.

Then Mila spoke, and my world faded to her.

"I first heard of Rhys Jacobs when I was fourteen. He'd gone to the same school as me but was older and had already left. The girls whispered rumours that he could hook them up with rich businessmen who would pay a lot of money for sex. No one used the term 'virginity auction' then, but that's what it was. Esther is a couple of years older than me, and she put herself into it and made a bundle. She never spoke about the experience, but I know she recruited other girls. I didn't stay at the school so lost touch with her, but she was easy to find again when I needed a last resort to get to Jacobs."

"Suggesting you exhausted all other avenues." I mapped that to the man I'd seen in the interview. "He's running scared of something. I met him, and his interest was in the skeleton crew's protection, which is probably why you couldn't reach him."

She pursed her lips, her food finished along with her sharing. I took the wrappers and binned them, resuming my sprawl. We were in a strange kind of holding pattern. I was already obeying the rules. I wouldn't leave her again. At the same point, I had to resist the urge to go to her and curl around her on the bed.

The same instincts that had battered me earlier returned in force, and my body warmed.

Mila gazed at me. "Why were you watching the auction

place?"

"Tyler suspected Salter of being a trafficker. Jury's still out on that."

She tilted her head. "Help me out with this. Are you the good guys or the bad guys? Would a rival trafficker be taking business from you?"

"Fuck, no. We stop people like that." I spread out my arms to gesture to the warehouse around us. "A lot of women work in this building on their backs. None of them are made to do it, and no one takes a cut of their pay. Arran set up this place to protect women. His mother was forced into the trade."

I blinked at the explanation that had so easily popped into my mind. I knew my friend's history better than I did my own.

Mila's eyebrows rose, her pretty expression registering her surprise. "Good guys after all. Except when you chain me up."

My focus slid down the shirt she still wore. It was open enough to expose her collarbone, and that glimpse was one of the sexiest things I'd ever seen. "I'm not all that good."

"You say that, but aside from a few shifty things, you've done nothing but good for me. I was thinking about it when you were gone. You didn't need to go into the game to pull me out. I reacted badly, but without you, I'd be in the hands of some stranger. Someone who probably wouldn't want to help. Or that I found...interesting."

Lust shot through me in a powerful wave. Of two things, I was certain. Mila wanted me. I'd caught her attention, either with my climbing in her window, my honesty in how I reacted to her, or with the darker side of chasing her down in the basement. If I could shake her out of her reserve, she might take what she needed.

My second surety was that if she agreed to the rules, Mila

wouldn't stay with me after the thirty days were up. If I was lucky, she'd be mine for a month but then she'd walk away.

Which meant we couldn't miss a minute.

Jumping to my feet, I locked the door then approached her on the bed. She sat up in alarm, but I caught the flash of something hot in her eyes.

Game on, little gangster.

16

Mila

Convict lurched over me, capturing my wrist. My heart thumped, and my body loosened in a predator-prey surrender response.

Except all he did was brush a kiss to my pulse point then boost himself to sit against the pillows beside me.

"What are you doing?" I asked.

"We've got a wait on our hands. I have ideas."

My cheeks warmed.

He grinned. "You took my virginity. Stop acting like you've never thought about my dick."

"You are not inexperienced."

He shrugged. "Actually, considering my amnesia, I'm technically a born-again virgin. Except for you, Mila, destroyer of my reset button."

"You don't remember sex?"

"Nope. Other than this evening. I know you want me as much as I want you. Admit it."

My exhale came out shaky. "I confess I'm curious about how much I affect you. But you make me nervous."

"You're scared of me? Same, same. But I have a solution. Here's me, shackled and shirtless, ready for your TED Talk. Or your thighs."

While I tripped up over the notion that the confident,

impulsive gang member could ever get panicky over me, he tossed his shirt then stretched back to the headboard.

A click followed, then a second.

I gaped at him. "You handcuffed yourself to the bed?"

He settled back, getting comfortable, all long body and bare, tattooed torso. Convict had so much ink work. I let my gaze wander from the snake around one wrist to a mixture of well-created pieces and rougher ones. Maybe prison tattoos, if movies had it right and that was a thing.

His other forearm was still bandaged, but it was his tight stomach my gaze snagged on. The way his muscles flexed when he breathed. The obvious tent in his jeans.

Oh God. The heat in my veins turned molten. I wanted to touch him, but that was terrifying.

"Eyes up here, Emilia."

I snapped my gaze to his face.

He smirked at me. "I'm teasing. Look your fill. You can do whatever you want to me. That's why I chained myself up, so you wouldn't feel scared. I can't hide my body's reaction to you, though. I don't want to try."

"Do you want me to... I mean, am I supposed to...?"

"Up to you. Torment me. Fuck me. You haven't agreed to be mine yet, but I'm one hundred percent yours."

That kind of power was dizzying.

A low moan sounded through the wall, and I lifted my head, startled.

Convict quirked an eyebrow. "This bedroom is on the cam girls' floor. You get used to the noises."

"Cam girls? You mean they're filming themselves?"

"For paying customers online, yes. Every kind of sex imaginable between consenting adults is sold in this building. Or given away."

His information was slotting into place with the glimpses I'd had when we'd moved through the corridors. Downstairs, women in very skimpy outfits had joined in congratulating us. Sex workers, I imagined.

I curled my lip. "I don't get it. Why do you want me when you could have sex with someone experienced?"

"I don't want anyone else. I'd rather have the smallest touch from you than any other woman on my dick."

I recoiled, hating that image. "Don't talk about other women on your dick."

"Jealous?" At whatever expression had settled on my face, he added, "Because I am over you. From first sight, I've only wanted you, and the thought of you pairing off with some other asshole in the game was enough to make me psycho."

A huff of breath left me. "You mean more psycho. And I'm not jealous. In fact, I was just thinking how I could walk out of this room now and you wouldn't be able to stop me."

He blinked, and his gaze jumped to the door. "Shit. You won't."

"But I could. Where's the key?"

He bucked his hips. "In my pocket."

I wanted that key. Lightly, I touched his waist.

Convict groaned. His dick moved in his jeans, and I stared, fascinated, losing my train of thought.

"How can you be so turned on by just being next to me?"

"Easy. Have you seen you?" He closed his eyes and shaped a teasing grin on his lips.

An idea came into mind, better even than snatching up the clothes he'd brought for me and walking out of here. I hadn't really meant that. I couldn't pretend I was only here because of his help. That would be a lie. From the first moment I'd seen Convict outside the window, I'd been all kinds of spellbound.

I slithered off the bed so he couldn't see me.

"Hey, where'd you go?"

"I want your dick to go down so I can test something."

His laugh was choked. "Not sure that's going to happen, sweetheart."

I scowled. "You mean my voice does it for you as well?"

"That, plus the image I have of you in my head."

"What image?"

"I have a series of favourites I'm currently running through. Your pretty eyes through the window. You asleep on the bed while I watched you on the cameras. My dick disappearing into your cunt."

A moan escaped my lips. I liked his dirty words. I liked his more romantic ones, too.

I knelt up to find his dick just as prominent as before.

"Try thinking of something less sexy. Your grandma, perhaps."

"Literally can't remember any relative."

I sighed, because the one thing I wanted to do just couldn't happen. I wasn't forward with men. Certainly not ones I'd only known a week, and despite the strange circumstances I was in with Convict, I'd been raised a certain way. Those manners balanced on a precipice when it came to a more pressing issue. Exactly how much I wanted him. I'd never felt anything like it.

Hesitantly, I returned to perch on the bed. "Do the couples who win the game really have sex all the time?"

"Pretty sure they spare a moment to shower and eat. But probably the rest of the time. Put your hand on my chest."

I obeyed. On my own, I couldn't do it. I was too conditioned to hold back. But Convict's instruction broke through that reserve. His skin was warm, and his light dusting of chest hair tickled my palm.

He shifted under my touch. "Good girl. Now explore me. Take your time."

I trailed down his belly. He let me play. His abs were solid, a rippling of muscle that was the opposite to my soft body. I got braver and touched his flat nipple.

He shivered. "Draw your fingertips lower to my waistband."

I did, running my fingertip under the material of his clothes.

"Open my jeans, Mila."

I held my breath but did it.

"Take them off me. In my chains, I can't touch you, so you lead the show. This is on your timetable. My words are just there to guide you."

I needed those words. They gave me the confidence to do what my body craved.

Convict shifted to help me, and I stripped him of all but his boxer shorts, discarding his clothes to the floor. Another first. I'd never done that to a man before in my life. His thick thigh muscles clenched when I touched a tattoo of a skull on his calf.

"Sit astride my legs. See how much harder I'll get for you."

I'd half forgotten that I was meant to be testing him.

"I'm naked under this shirt."

"As if that fact could leave my brain. I'm craving your skin on mine."

Carefully, I manoeuvred onto his thighs, my breathing coming faster at the contact of our bodies. Convict's lips curved into a wicked grin, and he lifted his knees so I slid onto his lap. I gasped. His dick was right underneath me, and the pulse of it hit between my legs.

Need flooded my system, my insides readying for sex and my body yearning for this to go further.

I braced myself on his chest. "No fair."

"I never said I'd play fair. In fact, count this as a lesson. If you say yes to me, I'll do everything to keep you. I'll push every limit you have. You like my dark side. You want more."

He bucked against me. I moaned without meaning to, and he made a similar sound of desire.

"Put me inside you."

"No!"

"The problem is, beautiful, that we started something in the basement that we haven't finished. You're going to have to see it through or we'll both go insane."

At my hesitation, he bucked again. "Ride me, woman. Or just use me as a tool and make yourself come. Finish what we started, and I promise you'll feel good. And you'll only want more."

Damn his mouth. I rose up on my knees, putting space between our bodies. But all other thinking had left the room. Maybe it was the low light, or the sex noises still coming through the walls, but I made a choice.

Climbing off him, I settled back on the bed and switched my gaze to his face.

Convict's desperation bled into his features.

"Just once, and we're not having sex," I breathed.

"Whatever you say. Use me."

I tugged down his shorts, revealing his hefty and very hard erection. I should've been terrified, but the shaking in my hands was purely from need.

I climbed back on, keeping clear of his dick and a little in love with his tight muscles and desperate restraint, his biceps taut either side of his face with his arms stretched.

"I've never done this."

"Good. It's new for me, too. Tease me. Press your pussy down on me. Make yourself feel good. If the ache in you is anything like mine, you're dying for this."

I inched forward until I made the contact I craved. His ultrahard dick notched to my entrance, overeager, but I shifted so I was against his shaft. Instant relief overwhelmed me. I'd been so tightly wound up.

Convict made a strangled sound of pleasure. "You're so wet. Grind on me."

With my hands to his chest, I rolled my hips, sliding along his length. God, that felt incredible, especially when the head of him nudged my clit. I repeated it, then again, trying another angle.

Deep pleasure broke over me. He'd been right. I needed this so badly, it was almost painful. I focused on my pace, going slower then fast. It built me up higher, generating power until I panted.

Yet Convict had gone quiet. He'd closed his eyes.

I slowed. "Are you okay?"

"Only terrified that you might stop. Keep going, I'm begging you. Think I might die if you don't."

I pressed my lips together to keep from smiling too big. His words brought a startling thought. It wasn't just my own pleasure I was seeking. I wanted his as well. I wanted him frantic underneath me. Begging me.

I ground on him again, so wet that I soaked his dick which made for an easier ride. This was wild. Sex had never been like this in the past. My other experiences had been led by the guy with my pleasure last on the priority list.

My lost boy encouraged me, moving slowly with my touch. "Sweetheart, if this is a torture method, I confess to everything. Keep doing that. Right there. Fuuuuck."

I needed more. I couldn't fuck him. Not fully. It was a

step too far on a confusing evening, but I absolutely needed to come. I ran my hand under the shirt that covered me and touched my clit.

Convict bucked, his chains clanking. There were no dirty words this time. Only an intense seeking of contact that I shared.

I rubbed myself, my hips working and my thighs clamped around him. My fingertips grazed the end of his dick, and at his moan, I slid my other hand down to touch his shaft. It was an instinct. I had no idea what I was doing. Only that it felt so, so good.

"You're going to make me come," he warned.

It didn't slow me any. In fact, my moves got faster, wilder. I needed that. I needed the release an orgasm would give. I had no choice in the matter because my body was barrelling towards that direction. I clamped him to me and jerked my hips a few more times, my eyes closing as the first wave of pleasure struck me down.

I moaned, and Convict gave a choked growl, the sound distant to my senses where I gasped then draped onto him, caught up in my own pleasure. A rush of sparkling happiness and relief had me reeling while I pulsed and clenched and almost wished he was inside me.

My body practically sang with good feeling. When I came back to earth, I lifted my head, my smile hard to hide.

"Fuck," the man under me drawled. He repeated the word, elongating the sound, then bucked between my legs. "That was the sexiest thing I've ever seen."

He hadn't come yet and was harder than ever. His steel-rigid dick surged in repeated hot slides. Unable to stop myself, I lifted the shirt out of the way so I could see him thrust against me.

My breath hitched. Convict swore again and arched to get a view down his body to where we touched. Every one of his muscles bunched. His thick thighs beneath me. His strong arms pinned above his head.

At the sight, he stilled then dropped back and came. Hot cum lashed my hand, my thighs, and the outside of my pussy, and I stared, mesmerised and still so turned on, even with my release.

He was beautiful. I'd thought so at first sight, but seeing him like this—vulnerable in his position below me—was something else.

Yet I couldn't keep the doubts at bay, along with a healthy dose of self-judgement at how I'd let myself be led by emotion.

With care, I climbed off him, my breathing slowing and embarrassment creeping in.

But my captor didn't let me slope off without a parting speech, spoken through a smile that almost made me want to jump on him again.

"That was fucking incredible. The image of you coming is now branded in my brain. I told you my body knows yours. Maybe not in real life, but in every other form of recognition. You're mine, Mila. Sooner you realise it, the better."

17

Dixie

Sex noises came from Convict's bedroom, the twin sounds of two people energetically fucking.

"Good for you, don't break anything off," I snarked, passing the door on my way to the lift.

I was happy for him. Okay, fine, I was Miss Jelly McJealouson. Not of the man himself. Just of what they'd done.

I hadn't been able to touch a man since the attack that ruined my body.

I had a new job which involved no dick for the first time in my life, and for a woman who'd lived by pussy power, I hadn't even touched myself since. My brain was fucked.

Nothing was right.

Including what I was supposed to be doing today. I headed downstairs to where Cassie had arranged to meet me. She was the best. When I told her I couldn't sell sex anymore, she gave me a new job. I was failing hard at that, too.

In the skeleton crew's office, she waited on the boss's chair behind the desk. She bounced up, all five-foot-nothing of her. "You're here! We're going to have so much fun. I have two new targets for you."

She rounded the desk to perch on the other side, a tablet held out. I took it and hid my wince at the names on the screen.

Cassie was a killer. A tiny, vicious pocket psychopath who was as deadly as she was adorable. The skeleton crew already had an enforcer in Shade, who took out the crew's enemies and also created a list of prison releases, picking off the ones who'd hurt women and children and didn't repent their sins.

Cassie liked their style. She'd decided that her role was to rid the city of rich men who were equally abusive but who'd never been caught for it. Or who'd paid their way out of trouble. I loved that. I loved that she'd wanted my help.

I'd wanted to love the work, but I didn't. The more I did of it, the more my skin crawled.

She gave me names, and my role was to research them to find addresses, work schedules, whatever I could get. If they were customers of the warehouse's brothel, I'd talk to the women who'd been booked by them to get any other feedback that could help Cassie's take-'em-out scheme.

She called it fun, but it meant hours of staring at the faces of rich businessmen and hearing stories about their dark deeds.

Cassie didn't know, but it triggered me so hard, sometimes I couldn't breathe.

These people were the worst. Entitled, wealthy sons of bitches who took what they wanted and didn't give a flying fuck about who they hurt. Girls like me. My inner teenager was a cold, wobbling jellyfish, on the edge of her nerves from bad memories and BS I didn't want to recall.

It had started creeping into my dreams. Even sleep wasn't safe.

It didn't help that half my job involved rattling around the internet, and I was shit with technology. My phone? No problem. Trying to manage files and piece together information to give to Cassie on the tablet? It gave me the panics. I'd made a friend who helped me learn the basics, but messaging her every time I couldn't remember which app was which or where a download disappeared off to was awkward as fuck.

Cassie chattered on, bright and excited. "This dickhole needs to die first, so see what you can discover about him. Does that sound okay?"

"Perfect, bestie," I lied.

No way I'd ever make her feel bad about my fucked-up head.

She left me to get to work, and I trotted back upstairs. My thinking place was a room off the brothel—I had barely left the nightclub after coming back from the hospital with my ruined throat—and I set my sights on my hideaway.

Across the brothel's receiving room, I waved to friends then ducked my head to avoid eye contact with clients. In the changing room, I threw compliments out like confetti for great tits and perfectly slutty costumes, then locked myself away, the familiar sounds of sex in nearby rooms creating the backdrop to my turmoil.

First, I messaged my helper, Lovelyn, a girl who'd come to the warehouse on business of the non-sexy variety, and with whom I'd struck up an unlikely friendship. She was the kindest person I'd ever met, and her instant reply softened my heart.

Lovelyn: Whatever you need, I'm here for you. Want me to stop by?

Dixie: I'll try myself first then let you know.

Lovelyn: You can do it! I believe in you.

Carefully, I typed the first name Cassie had given me into my browser. It brought back a sixty-something man in an expensive suit, some city banker rumoured to have a taste for preteens. I couldn't even look his photo in the eye. It was like my trauma had linked my attack to what had happened to me when I was a girl and resurfaced all my anxieties.

I moved on to the next, but the same thing happened. My hands began to shake, so I mistyped his name. This was hopeless. Panic inducing. I shut down the tablet and stared across the room to a mirror on the far wall. Shame crowded me. If I couldn't work for Cassie, what could I do?

Mirror-me had no answer. She never did, judgy cow.

I ran my gaze over my body. I used to do it by routine because I'd needed to make bank from my butt. I'd paid a lot of money to be perfect. My nose never had that cute turn up until a plastic surgeon added it. My tits were stunning and worth every penny I'd paid to make them round and weighty so much they even turned me on.

Except no man wanted a damaged sex doll.

The skin-coloured plaster across my throat hid the scar from my attack. I touched my fingers to it, ensuring the edges were stuck down. I didn't like seeing it and sure as shit couldn't wear it proudly.

Yet in the light of the room, the bandage was almost invisible. I twisted back and forth, checking how bad it appeared. I had on ripped jeans with a pair of red heels. A tight scarlet shirt with three-quarter-length sleeves and a scooped neck, the outline of my tits and a couple of inches of my belly showing.

I'd put on a little weight since getting hurt, but maybe I didn't look that bad?

My platinum hair was up in a ponytail that swished when I moved. I'd kept my makeup light, nothing like what I'd wear on the floor, but making the most of my features.

Perhaps I'd been too hasty in quitting sex work. It was the job I'd known and the work that had kept my head above water since I was fourteen and forced to endure what I'd eventually own and turn into a career.

My loyal clients asked after me all the time. The girls told me I was missed.

Sex work never made me feel shame.

Though it left a strangely sour taste in my mouth, there was only one way to find out if I had any kind of future with the skeleton crew. Because what I was trying definitely wasn't it.

18

Mila

My breathing slowed, and I relaxed on the blanket next to Convict. He had his lips parted and his eyes closed, his wrists still chained to the bedframe. I'd cleaned us up with his t-shirt, almost surprised at how I didn't instantly want to leave.

"Do you want me to untie you?"

"Up to you. You're safer this way. Now I know what an orgasm feels like, I'm going to be all over you."

A shiver ran through me at the promise, but I pursed my lips. "You are overegging the amnesia thing."

He grinned. "Probably. Or maybe I just don't want the old memories. The newer ones are better."

With freedom to stare at him, I took my time examining every feature. He was so pretty. Now he'd relaxed, he was back to the boy-next-door sweetness I'd first seen in him. My focus held on the white bandage that covered him from wrist to elbow. "Is the damage to your arm from the same accident that hurt your head?"

His eyes opened, and he followed my gaze, then lifted his chin in agreement. "I was undercover. The building caught on fire, and I was in the cellar. I barely got out with my life. Everyone here thought I was dead."

I swallowed and lightly touched my fingers to his temple where his fresh scar cut into his hair.

Convict nuzzled into my touch. "If you want, you can take the bandage off my arm. I don't need it anymore."

I peeled back the tape, slowly exposing the skin underneath as the bandage came away. His skin was healed but scarred far worse than the dent on his head, though it was hard to see with his arm still restrained.

Convict watched the wall. "I'm guessing my ink is fucked?"

"You haven't looked at it?"

"Can't bring myself to."

Climbing off the bed, I found the key, then knelt over him to unlock his handcuffs. Instantly, he held my waist then rolled us so he was looming over me, my legs wide around him.

His gaze searched mine. "Make me."

Make him look? I guided his arm to my chest, laying it across my body over the grey shirt. His gaze flicked down.

This was a strange trust exercise. There was something so vulnerable in his eyes, as if he was afraid of what he might see.

His tone returned tighter, reflecting the turmoil in his expression. "Like I suspected. It's fucked. The mashed-up tattoo is meant to be a skull with a bandanna."

I traced my fingertips up his arm like I had the right, though I kept my gaze on his. "To represent the skeleton crew."

"It was. Now it's a freak show. Hopefully not an indication of what happens when Arran returns."

I held my hand over the scarred flesh. "It isn't that bad."

"For real?"

"Considering you could've died, a few battle scars are a good trade-off."

A small part of his tension lifted. He'd been worried

about this. About how it appeared to others. It gave me another clue as to what made up this man.

"Do you remember much about the fire?"

"Next to nothing. And hardly anything about myself from before that. Other people, I'm better with."

I drew my eyebrows together. "You said earlier that you weren't sure where you lived."

"The hospital had one address for me. My payslip has another. I don't have any keys, so I'm not sure how I can test out which is right."

"What about your possessions? Your clothes and furniture?"

"No idea if I have any, though I don't need much. All I know for certain is that I was in hospital for weeks before my crew found me, then two days after coming out, I met you."

My heart hurt for him.

But the sadness didn't stay long in his expression, as Convict grinned. "At least I know my dick works. The final part of me finally woke from that coma and came out swinging."

He pressed our bodies together, hard again. I took a breath that was part fear and a bigger part turned on. Out of his chains, he could do anything to me.

I almost wanted him to.

But he jumped up, then searched for his shorts and pulled them on. "We smell like sin. Come shower with me and wash away the evidence."

We snuck from his room with the bundles of clothes he'd brought up with the food, and trotted down the hall to a shower block. Convict locked the door and set the water going in the stall so steam rose. A shelf held fluffy towels, and I picked one up and held it to my chest.

"You can go first."

"Together, little gangster. That's our life now."

I darted an anxious glance at him. "I haven't agreed yet."

He watched me for a moment then stripped his shorts and padded over, confidently naked and half hard. Taking my lapels, he undid the first button of my shirt. His voice came out low. "Then until you do, I won't fuck you. No matter how hard you beg."

His fingers kept going down the line of buttons until the shirt hung open. Then he backed away to the water and stepped under the spray.

I remained glued to the spot, nothing like the little gangster he'd nicknamed me. The shower soaked Convict's hair to an even darker black, flattening it to his head. Rivulets ran down his chest and drew lines down his long legs. His dick bobbed for attention, but he ignored it to beckon to me.

Joining him meant getting naked. I hadn't even done that in the game as, though the tattered dress had hung from me, Convict had covered me with his shirt before stripping the last of it over my head.

He closed his eyes. "I won't peek. I just want you here."

I really did need a shower. Slipping off the shirt, I scurried to get under the water. Convict's arms encircled me, and he hugged me, his cheek to the top of my head while warm water sluiced over us both. I liked him tender. I liked a lot about him, new discoveries happening by the minute.

"Good girl. Now kiss me while I wash you."

Too many sensations battled inside me. I gave a jerky laugh. "Prostitutes don't kiss on the mouth."

He caught my chin and laid his lips on mine.

The room disappeared. Time stopped.

He'd kissed me briefly days ago, and that touch had never left my mind. There were kisses, and then there were deep connections. His were in that category. His lips moved on mine like he was coaxing me back to life. Slow at first, then when I responded, he turned up the heat with a groan.

Deep presses, his head angled to better connect to mine, devastatingly perfect pressure.

Convict kissed me senseless. His tongue in my mouth. His fingers in my wet hair.

I clung to him, letting him lead. He glided one hand down to my lower back, caging my body against his and trapping his dick between us. But it was only as if he needed me closer. He kept to his word.

He kissed me for long minutes, only breaking to feel for the shower gel on a shelf. He cleaned my body and his, kissed me again, then told me to handle between my legs, because if he did it, he might break.

I almost wanted him to. I did as asked then picked up the shampoo and washed my hair. "Should I do yours?"

He ducked his head, and I ran my fingers through his messy strands, lathering him up while the conditioner worked on mine.

"This is the first decent shower I've had since I'd been out." He let me guide him under the water to rinse the suds. "I had a cast on my leg for a long time. Then the bandage on my arm stopped me."

"It must feel really good."

I'd set myself up for that one.

His grin spread, and he ran his hands down to cup my ass. "It feels unbelievably good. I'm glad I waited. Gonna kiss you again."

I nodded, not that he could see, and touched his face. Our mouths met once more. Kissing him should've been illegal. It was clearly addictive.

Against his lips, I said, "You should come with a warning label."

"Caution, may cause dizziness, obsession, and

spontaneous orgasms. And yet you keep reaching for me. What does that say about you?" He kissed me deeper. "What's more dangerous to you, Mila? My dick or something else?"

"To be decided."

"Say yes to what I'm asking."

Only the pattering of the shower water filled the air, tension rising with the stress laced in his tone. I knew what he wanted. My next thirty days. More of this. Much more.

"We had a deal," I murmured.

A phone buzzed in the room. Convict released a breath and pulled away from me. He left the shower to search the pile of clothes, extracting his phone.

I hustled to wrap myself in a towel, killing the water.

When he lifted his head, the lightness in his expression had gone. "Tyler says they're coming back."

I covered my mouth, the world rushing in where it had been held at bay. My fear for Kane hit doubly hard for having forgotten about him for a while.

"They have your guy. They're bringing him in unharmed."

Everything changed again, and I had to explain myself to the man I'd managed to get captured.

19

Convict

We dressed quickly, and though I found a hairdryer for Mila, her impatience to get downstairs meant we left my room with her fair hair still half damp.

In the stairwell, Cassie was coming up as we descended, her boyfriend behind her. She grinned big and paused on the landing, eyeing Mila. "We just heard about the game. Congratulations. Ye know, your boy saved my life. Nearly at the cost of his own."

Mila blinked at her. "It's nice to meet you, and that's good to know."

If she was impressed, I couldn't tell because we hurried on. I didn't like that she'd gone quiet. I especially didn't like the fact I had no clue who this Kane was to her. So far, everyone around her had been trying to hurt her. If he was some manipulative ex, I'd probably lose it.

On the main downstairs corridor between Divide and Divine, the crowd had thinned, and the clubs were closing, though the brothel upstairs never shut.

The office door was open ahead, with a woman peeking in the entrance, her jacket covered in embroidered flowers. Not a clubber. If she worked here, I couldn't place her.

She pushed her long hair behind her ear and stepped inside. "Are you available for a chat?"

Shade replied. "Your old man too scared to see us now?"

The stranger exhaled a soft laugh. "Something like that."

Her gaze settled on someone further inside, not yet visible to us on our approach to the doorway.

"Who's that?" she asked.

A darker voice I didn't recognise provided the answer, his accent Scottish. "No one ye want to mess with, flower girl."

At my side, Mila wilted in relief.

The woman reddened and turned, spotting us and making way. "I'll go find Dixie until you're free, Shade."

She left and we entered. Behind the desk, Shade was holding court, Tyler and the unknown male on the right-hand side of the room. He was a big fucker. At least six-five, and with his arms restrained behind him, presumably zip tied.

The man Mila had risked everything to save was here, and I was suddenly wondering how good he'd look with a black eye.

Mila took a short inhale and skittered over to him, throwing her arms around the restrained man's chest.

I watched like a hawk. On the phone, Tyler had asked if he should tell the prisoner who we were and who'd sent us to rescue him. I said no. I wanted to witness the moment he laid eyes on Mila.

"Who was that?" Tyler asked with a head tilt to the door.

I could've been relieved that someone else asked after the flower woman, as I'd assumed I'd forgotten her, but my focus was all on the fucking hug.

"Are you okay?" Mila asked in a whisper to the man.

He didn't lean into her. Though there was familiarity, he only appeared annoyed. "Fine. Thought ye were fucking dead."

Shade answered Tyler. "Lovelyn, Detective Dickhead's

daughter. He's avoiding us after his shite about Convict being dead. Apparently he sent her to do his dirty work tonight."

Mila stepped back and looked the prisoner over, tears lining her eyes. "The last I saw of you, Salter had a knife to your throat. I imagined all things. This is all my fault. I should have never asked for your help."

"They jumped me. I should've seen it coming but I was distracted. It is not your fault."

Mila shook her head and turned to Tyler. "Can you let him go?"

The team leader glanced at me, and I took the hint. We didn't know anything about this man. For all I knew, he could've orchestrated the mess Mila was in.

I moved to stand in front of him. "Who are you?"

He took me in, same as I was doing to him, his focus homing in on the skeleton crew skull on my t-shirt. "Someone more important to Mila than ye, arsehole."

I lifted an eyebrow. Already, he'd clocked my interest in Mila and was trying to use it against me. "Let's be clear. We extracted you because my woman asked it of me. Nothing more."

He snorted. "Your woman? That true, Mils?"

Fucking. Nickname.

She lifted her chin. "Don't be a jerk, Kane. Just tell him what he wants to know, then they'll set you free."

Kane returned his gaze to me. "I know of the skeleton crew. Never thought my sister would associate with your type, but it's her funeral."

Sister. He was her brother? They had nothing in common. The man was dark in all the ways she was fair. His skin tone a deep olive, his brown hair cropped to military short, his eyes grey to her pale green. Though Deadwater was on the border of Scotland and England, families didn't tend to be split in accents, and where she was short and curvy, he had thick muscles and was twice her size. I couldn't have picked them out of a lineup if I tried.

Something ticked over in his vision. "She didn't tell you that. No pillow talk on family history, then?"

He was so controlled in his manner. His posture, too. He stood tall but with his muscles loose and ready.

Did I believe him? For all I knew, 'sister' had been already agreed as a cover.

I folded my arms. "You're military?"

"Close but no cigar."

"Security?"

He lowered his gaze, not dignifying that with an answer.

"A merc," Tyler supplied. He said it like a dirty word.

Kane inclined his head.

"For who?" I asked.

"Whoever's paying."

"What was your role with Mila? Backup only?"

Kane didn't answer me. Clearly he had a share-little mentality.

Tyler continued. "Let's try this another way. How did a gun-for-hire get nabbed by a flesh merchant like Salter? Embarrassing, no?"

Kane exhaled, a small change in his upright stature telling me how little he liked the fact he'd been captured. "Like I said, I was distracted. Mila asked me to come in to extract some girl, and I was annoyed at the change in our plan. It made me sloppy, and I got jumped. They took me out with a Taser of all fucking things."

Mila covered her mouth. She'd drifted closer to me, and I had the urge to run my arm around her but resisted for fear of her shrugging me off.

She shook her head. "I hate that I got you caught because

of me."

A muscle in Kane's jaw ticked. "I never said that. It was my mistake." He gestured with his chin to the room. "That why you're with these fuckers?"

"Watch your mouth," I snapped.

Snake-like, Kane focused on me. "Watch yours, lover boy."

I stood taller. His gaze darkened.

To Mila, I said, "This guy always this charming or did he save all the dickhead for me?"

Mila sighed. "Can I have a minute to talk to my brother alone, please?"

Shade and Tyler watched me for their cue. They'd gone to any amount of trouble to get this man back, and though I wasn't convinced he was on Mila's side, I believed her when she named their relationship. Strange how strong that conviction was.

"We'll be outside." I gestured for my crew to follow.

We held up the walls of the corridor, a restock crew rattling through the open doors to the nightclub. I liked this time of night, when dawn was still a couple of hours off but most good people were tucked up in bed. It made me feel alive.

I tipped my head at the office door. "We're recording that conversation, right?"

Shade slid a blade from his belt and examined it. "Course. Wouldn't have called him for a brother."

Exactly as I'd thought. "Do me a favour and keep hold of him for a while."

"Think he's a threat?"

"I don't know what he is yet."

His blade flashed in the light. "Want me to disappear him?"

"Tempting, but let's play nice for now."

Tyler briefed me on the extraction, a simple enough smash and grab where they took out a lone guard while another two investigated a distraction. Our distraction, of course. A car blown up on the far side of their industrial building.

No one died to save Kane, which was a small tick in his favour.

Mila exited the office, her face pale. Shade and Tyler gave us space, and she came to me.

"Thank you for ordering his rescue. It scared me how easily he was taken. Which brings me to a conclusion. He and I can't do it alone. I need your help."

"Then accept the rules of the game."

"You're such a villain."

"Says the woman who so badly wants to fuck the villain, she crawled all over him earlier. Don't be mad that you tried to ride the devil and discovered he's no saint."

Her pupils dilated, and pink flushed her cheeks.

My dick instantly responded, and I pushed off the wall and doubled down on my offer. "I'll find Jacobs for you. I'll force him to say what you need to know. I'll even take out Salter if you want revenge for your kin. For the rest of the thirty days, I'll protect you, possess you, and fucking adore you as I fuck you senseless. Say yes. Put us both out of our misery."

"You won't stop me from walking away once the days are up?"

I wanted to say 'Trust me, you won't want to', but I didn't have that confidence. I was doing everything I could to keep the elusive woman I'd become hooked on, but I knew without doubt that she'd burn out on me.

I shrugged. "Without hesitation."

"Then we have a deal."

20

Mila

We left the skeleton crew's warehouse with a rucksack of Convict's scant possessions and in borrowed clothes. I wanted to go home. I wanted to take him with me. Luckily we were both on the same page.

He guided me to a car. "I'll get your door."

"We can walk. I don't live far. Only in the city centre."

"Is there parking?"

"An underground car park." I had a space but I hadn't used it in a while since surrendering my car.

"It's safer for you if we aren't out on the streets for any longer than necessary."

He opened the passenger-side door of the huge, black vehicle and helped me in, then we set out into the night. It was late, past four in the morning, but I wasn't tired.

Kane had been rescued. He wasn't hurt, or worse, as I'd imagined, and my overactive brain could settle on that score. It left all the space to think about the man driving me.

He casually spun the wheel to take us away from the river. "Direct me. Where are we going?"

"Harbour View Apartments on City Road."

"Fancy. There a doorman or something? You don't have a key."

I shifted in my seat. "I don't need one."

"How does that work?"

"You'll see."

He chuffed at my answer but let me lapse into gazing out of the window.

Deadwater was a city that never truly slept. Neon lights advertised clubs and services, and a group of drunks waved at us in the hope we were a late-night cab. Even so, traffic was light, and the drive was done in a matter of minutes. Convict entered the garage using a code I gave him. He backed the car into my spot, controlling the vehicle so easily, his actions accurate and somehow incredibly attractive. I liked how he moved. How he held the steering wheel with a light touch, sliding it through his fingers.

It was distracting. I had to keep reminding myself this wasn't a test drive with built-in orgasms.

Part of why I'd wanted to take him home was to process what I felt for him in my own space. A week ago, I'd first seen him through a window, and today, we'd had sex after a brutal evening. It was so far from my usual reality of responsible, cautious living that I couldn't understand myself. All I was sure about was that I wanted him closer.

He caught me staring. "Careful, Mila. Take me upstairs first, or any early waking neighbours are going to get an eyeful of you bent over this car."

I ducked my head and went to open my door. He stilled me with a touch, rounding to let me out.

"Such a gentleman."

"I'm really not."

Maybe that was what I liked. "Sure you are. You opened my door before mentally undressing me."

He kept my hand in his. I let him.

The coded lift took us up to the twelfth floor, and at my door, I pointed out the scanner.

"Biometrics."

"What are you, MI5?"

He whistled approval, but I saw how carefully he scanned the hall behind us. Trust didn't come easy to him, and I liked that.

The door popped open, and he held it to let me inside. I didn't know what I expected, probably for him to grab me the moment we were shut in, but instead, he toed off his running shoes and prowled through the rooms.

I followed, seeing it through fresh eyes. The pale wood floors. The high-end kitchen with the Miele appliances my grandmother approved of, and the living area to the other side, the white sofas arranged to take in the city view.

Décor-wise, it was practically unchanged from when I'd moved in. I'd never noticed that.

I hovered in the hall doorway. "My grandparents gifted me this place so I had somewhere to live outside of term at school and university. They liked me to come back to Deadwater."

"Not to live with them?"

I wrinkled my nose. That had never been on the table. "No."

Convict checked out the artwork that had always been on the walls then moved to the coffee table where I'd left a sprawl of paperwork, discarded when I'd come up with my auction plan. He picked up a thick file and read the first page.

"Last will and testament? If this is all about money, I'll be disappointed."

My heart sank unreasonably. To hide my reaction, I folded my arms. "Seriously?"

His grin returned, and he placed the file back down and slowly stalked over to me. "No. I'll still adore you. I am intrigued, though."

I stiffened, all too aware of how completely alone we were in this apartment. I wanted this. I wanted him. I couldn't be sure why it was so strong, but perhaps it was because he was so resourceful. Or maybe I needed the distraction of a dangerously sexy guy to balance out the mess my life had become.

Turning, I made for the hall, beckoning him to follow. "I'll show you the bedrooms."

In my bedroom doorway, I reached for the light switch, thankful that I'd left my bed neat and nothing embarrassing on display.

Convict's hand landed over mine and paused my action, leaving the room dark. He took in the space then gestured with his chin. "That fluffy white rug and the mirror."

"What about them?"

"If I let you take me into this bedroom, it's where I'll fuck you first."

I stared at him, shocked. Convict's eyes darkened.

"I'll drag that rug over so it's in front of the glass. Then I'll get you naked, put you on all fours, and fuck you from behind. You'll finally give in to the lust you're holding at bay, and you'll do anything I ask. You'll beg for more. When you're about to come, I'll pull you upright so we can watch my dick plunge in and out of you and witness the second you break apart."

I was lost for words, caught up in his fantasy. My body was so ready for him, heat pooling at my core and my skin on fire for his touch.

"Are we going in, then?" I finally managed.

He tipped up my chin, lowering his mouth until we were millimetres apart. Amusement danced in his eyes alongside deep, unhidden attraction. "Nope."

Disappointment pierced me. "Why not? Because you want me to beg?"

"Nah. That ship sailed. Let me remind you that when you agreed to the rules of the game, you gave your body over to me. I get free use of you whenever I want. I'll fuck you in your sleep, in the shower, I'll drive into you on those pristine sofas while the city watches us."

Damn his dirty mouth. I curled my lip. "I get the same rights."

"You do. I'll even trade in a safe word for a hydration break. But the flip side is what else you get from the deal. What should be the more important part from your point of view. If I'm to help you, I need your story. I want to know everything about your life. Every little detail to what makes up Emilia Marchant and why you're willing to go to dangerous lengths for your cause." He slanted his gaze to the room. "The moment we go in there, it's game over for talking."

Convict slapped my ass and moseyed back down the hall. "So get your story on. I'll make coffee."

Trailing after him, I had a choice to make. I'd done all of this solo, only bringing Kane in for one specific part which turned out to be nowhere near enough. But in tying myself to Convict for a month, I wasn't alone anymore. For the first time in my life, I had a partner in crime.

It might be time-bound, but my gut told me to follow this man. Honesty shone off him, as much as questionable morals and breathtaking heat.

I didn't trust him, not yet, but I felt...something.

I'd agreed to let him have sex with me whenever he wanted. In my sleep, as he'd pointed out. A shiver ran over me, the lust he generated just by existing ever present.

What would it be like to wake and find him inside me? Toying with me. Fucking me. For a dizzy moment, I couldn't breathe for wanting him.

Except he wouldn't go there without talking first.

The decision over sharing deeply personal parts of my life had been made. I just had to find the words.

In the living room, I gazed at Convict, busy in my kitchen, then drifted to the shelf and picked up two framed photos. I set them on the coffee table, tidying the paperwork I'd left in a mess.

The scent of coffee pricked my nose.

"No milk in your fridge. Tells me you're not ready to take care of more than a succulent." Convict joined me with two mugs.

I rolled my eyes, and we settled on the sofa. I took a sip of the hot drink, picking over where to start my story.

It helped that Convict had positioned himself to face me. He gave me his full attention. I needed it.

"A month ago, my grandfather died."

He wrinkled his nose. "I read about it while you slept. I'm sorry."

An all-too-familiar ache stole over my heart. I glanced at the first framed photo where my grandfather smiled back at me. I missed him so much. "It's hard to share this. I haven't talked to anyone. Even Kane doesn't know the full story. You might not be a stranger any more, but I still don't know you."

His gaze held mine. "Pop quiz. What's my name?"

"Roscoe Locke." He'd told me the first time we'd met, and I'd never forgotten it.

"Where do I work?"

"For the skeleton crew, in the warehouse by Deadwater river."

He inclined his head. "What do I like?"

The heat in his eyes was unmistakable.

"Me."

I was rewarded with a smile. "Then you know almost as

much about me as I do. If there's anything else, just ask."

This was easier than trying to make sense of my own story. "How old are you?"

"Twenty-eight. My birthday is the fourth of January, it says so on my hospital paperwork. Yours?"

"The first of June. How did they know if you were in a coma?"

"You used fancy biometrics to get into this multi-million-pound home. The hospital used mine to identify me. I have a criminal record. All my data is on file for the safety of the public."

Perhaps that should have alarmed me, but all I felt was intrigue. "What crimes have you committed?"

He raised an easy shoulder. "No idea, but you'll get the benefit of my dark side for all your scheming."

I took a steadying breath. At last, the words flowed.

"I didn't know my grandparents when I was growing up. I met them when I was fourteen. They put me through private school, bought me this place, and then paid for my degree in business management."

I collected the first framed photo from the table and held it out. "This is me with them when I was officially given the surname of Marchant."

Convict took the frame and examined it. "What were you before?"

"Emilia Gold. That's my stepfather's surname. My mother had me after a short fling with my bio father, my grandparents' eldest son. He's long dead."

He handed the picture back. "Is that why they didn't know about you, because he died and never told them?"

I stared down at the proud teenage version of me who'd been so enamoured with my newfound grandparents. Even then, my grandfather had a thatch of grey hair, and my grandmother her trademark blonde bob. "No, they knew about me. It was just complicated. But I'm digressing. I just want you to understand why this is so important to me."

"I'm listening. Share everything. I want to know it all."

My thoughts rushed. "They wanted an heir. That's the reason they took over my life so thoroughly, because of how vital it is for Marchant Haulage to survive. That's the company my grandfather built from the ground up. The one I studied hard to understand then worked at officially until a month ago."

I took the second picture, a landscape shot of two dozen people in a harbour scene, a huge red-and-white ship behind them, and a warehouse the other side of the water with the family logo proudly displayed.

"All the people in this picture are dependents of the company. They live off the profits and have done for decades in some cases."

I saw an argument form then fall away as his gaze travelled the picture. There was an entire seat cushion between us, and I knelt on it so I could point out what I needed him to see.

I pressed a finger to an elderly couple. "My grandfather's sister and her husband. Both are in their late seventies and had hard lives, so only have the state pension to live on." I tapped a woman with a baby in her arms. "Their oldest daughter with her firstborn. She has three kids, but her husband walked out on her. One of her sisters is also a single mother." I jumped one across to a man in a wheelchair. "My grandmother's nephew. I think he's in his forties now."

Convict gave a chuff of interest. "And all of them live off the company's payroll?"

"Exactly." I set the photo back on the glass coffee table, in our eyeline, just like I kept it on my shelf to remind me how important it was. "One of the first things my grandparents impressed upon me was how the company is a lifeline. I know in painstaking detail how my grandfather started out, operating a single boat with which he used to do the soft fruit route, as he called it. He would sail from Liverpool to Barcelona and back, bringing the produce into the country. From there, he scaled up and up, until he had a fleet of ships and lorries operating out of multiple ports to many countries. Alongside that expansion, his profits soared. He was smart. When consumer preferences changed, he'd talk to the fruit market owners and they'd adapt. When lawmakers got in his way, he dodged around them. At every stage, he innovated and he created an empire. I'm saying this as if he did it alone. He didn't. My grandmother also worked for the company and managed certain parts of it for years until she retired. For them, it was their life. And from age fourteen, it was mine, too."

"Impressive."

I took a breath. "Isn't it? It gets me in the throat when I think about what they achieved. I admire them so much. Even as a young teenager, I understood their importance."

He twisted his lips, his gaze never leaving me. "As did your parents if they were willing to trade you off."

"They didn't trade me off. They saw the opportunity of a lifetime for me and took it."

"What did they get out of it?"

I furrowed my brow. "You make it sound like they got a payout."

"Didn't they? It's hard to imagine giving up a kid to strangers, even if they're related."

Maybe that was fair, but he didn't understand my family. I shook off the insinuation and carried on. "That's the background. All these people and more rely on Marchant Haulage surviving. I feel the weight of that on my shoulders just like my grandfather described. He found it thrilling every time he made enough money to do something good. First, it was to give his sons a great life. Then, it was the extended family. By the time he reached his seventies, he'd created this institution. There are family trusts. There are dividend payments. There are people who wouldn't be alive without the money they get from the business."

"As the heir, your job was to continue what they started?"

"It was. But I failed at the first hurdle. When I finished my degree, my grandfather put me to work at the lowest rungs of the company. I moved between different sites and departments, learning what they do and getting to grips with all the moving parts. I loved it."

A darkness swarmed my heart.

"My final placement was to be back in the headquarters with him, but I put it off. Then he died. It just... I mean, I couldn't..."

My words stalled again, and tears pricked my eyes from exactly how badly I'd fucked up.

"My failure cost my grandfather his life."

21

Convict

Mila burst into tears. Not heaving sobs, but the heartbreak of long-held pain with her features crumpling, even as she fought it. I couldn't bear it. Just like when she'd been on the camera in the game, her tears did something strange to me. I didn't know physical pain, but I had the suspicion this was what the emotional variety felt like.

Reaching for her, I tugged her to my chest.

Mila scrubbed at her eyes with her sleeve. "If I'd only gone sooner, maybe he wouldn't have worked so hard. Not if he'd had someone to split the responsibility with. But I wanted to see every place we owned, so I begged him for more time in the field. While I was out enjoying the work, he was getting increasingly stressed until his heart couldn't take it anymore."

"Or he would have died anyway because his time was up and it was nothing to do with you. Can I ask some questions?"

She sniffed and sat up. "Yes. That might help. My thoughts are so scattered."

I kept her hand in mine, brushing my thumb over her knuckles. So far, I'd heard a lot about how two rich people had brainwashed a teenager into working for them and not a lot about why that girl then threw herself into harm's way.

"Where does Rhys Jacobs fit into this?"

"Right. Other than knowing about him from school, he's an associate of my grandparents who I saw at my grandfather's funeral. He was in my grandmother's ear, whispering to her. Then he was at the next board meeting which was held two weeks ago to discuss the future of the company." That stricken look tightened her features again. "Marchant Haulage has been suspended. There are legal complications over the company's operations, so the board announced it had to cease trading until those were resolved."

Things were starting to make sense in my head. I tapped her hand. "If the company isn't making money, those people don't get a payout."

"Exactly. That's their monthly income they've relied on for years, and it's just gone. They can't pay their bills. It's devastating. As of right now, they are cut off."

"Which you're trying to fix."

"I am. It's complicated, but by the next board meeting in a few weeks' time, all those with voting rights get to make the decision over whether the company folds or continues."

"How many people is that?"

"Four. My grandmother, her second son who is my Uncle Wallace, me, and Kane. Kane, who I'm not supposed to know about, thinks like me and would vote the same way. But let me play you this."

Mila leaned to the coffee table and picked up a phone, settling back at my side. Notifications filled her screen, but she dismissed them all to play a voicemail of a whiny male voice.

"Mila, this is Wallace. Mother wants out. We all need to vote with her. Do the right thing for the family and let's put the old girl to bed. Marchant Haulage is done."

She tossed the phone to the cushions. "Not in my wildest dreams would I believe that my grandmother would throw away everything she and my grandfather worked for. Sure, she wasn't the lead in every discussion, but she was always there in the background, guiding his decisions. She can't want the company to fall. I refuse to believe it."

"Have you spoken to her?" Her words in the cell in the basement returned to me. She'd raged at Jacobs and asked what he'd done.

Mila shook her head. "I've seen her once in the past month, and that was at the funeral where the single thing she said to me was what Wallace reiterated. That she's done with the business. She won't take my calls and she won't see me. When I go to her house, she isn't there. It's like she's disappeared off the face of the planet. Likewise, Wallace won't answer my messages. The only reason I know his intent is that voicemail."

I didn't like the sound of Wallace. "What's he to do with the business?"

"Nothing at all. I'll show you what he's about."

She grabbed the phone again and searched for a social media account, flicked through photos, then held it so I could see. Wallace, a forty-something man, in Speedos on a yacht. Wallace with his arms around much younger men and women in some beach location. Wallace at a party on a rooftop against the New York City skyline.

"He's a playboy." Mila's lip curled in disgust. "If the yachts got any bigger, I'd assume he was compensating for something."

I whistled. "I can't decide if I hate him or want to party with him."

"My grandparents despaired over both of their sons. My bio father took their money and went on drunken and drug-fuelled binges, one of which cost him his life when he overdosed aged just twenty-six. Wallace somehow escaped the same fate and is on a never-ending holiday."

"Isn't it in his interest to keep the money coming in?"

She reached for the stack of papers on the table. "You'd think so, but the will you found is an earlier draft of my grandfather's. I don't know what's different in the newer one, only that it exists, and I'm assuming some parts haven't changed. It is right here in black and white that Wallace gets a massive payout if the company is sold. Far more than his monthly dividend. It doesn't matter to him that everyone else might have to wait years for a settlement, if they are even entitled to a penny once it's all wrapped up. The reading of the new will is what we're waiting for. Once that has been held, the voting can happen and the future of the business can be decided."

"Tell me how Jacobs is between you and your grandmother."

"Since my grandfather died, he seems to have permeated their business. He is absolutely in contact with my grandmother, because the solicitors told me so. She's still talking to them, by the way. Just no one else besides Jacobs. That random businessman with a history of selling women for sex was at the funeral, in the company affairs, oh, and I forgot to mention this—if the family vote is split, from what I can tell, a thing called a trusted company panel casts the final vote. It's like a failsafe for circumstances like this, my grandfather explained once. There are three companies listed on that panel, with any of their multiple executives being able to take the vote, and guess who's involved with every single one? Rhys fucking Jacobs. The bastard has his fingers in all these pies and yet has vanished from sight. That's what I discovered. That's why I need to see him and why I was willing to go to any lengths to do so."

She sagged back into the cushions as if telling me all of this was a huge weight off her shoulders.

On the other hand, I felt bolstered. I knew nothing about her business or the payroll, but I cared that she did. That made it matter. I was immediately on her side. I cared that she was hurting over this. She was trying to do what was right for people she loved and those she felt she needed to protect. I fucking adored that about her.

I wrangled my phone from my pocket. Creating a chat with Tyler and Shade, I sent them a voice message. "I'm going to be searching for game candidate Rhys Jacobs. He's fucking over Mila's family. Can we make it a crew priority?"

I was pushing my luck after last night and the game. For all I knew, Arran could've already heard and sent them a message that I was out.

If that happened, I'd still deliver for Mila. Just on my own.

Reaching for her, I pulled her closer then kissed the mouth I'd been staring at while she'd laid her life bare for me. Mila's lips parted under mine, and her fingers slid into my hair.

I kept it light and ran my knuckles down her face, loving the wary expectation in her eyes. "All that talking earned you a reward."

She arched a brow. "You're deeply messed up if emotional vulnerability gets you going."

"Certified, probably."

"Is my reward you finding Jacobs?"

"No, but when I do, I'll force him to the ground in front of you to explain himself." I stood, catching her hand to keep her with me. "You earned the reward that had you all hot and bothered when I described it."

She breathed out, following me from the living room.

In her bedroom, I picked up the white rug from beside her bed and placed it exactly where I wanted, in front of the tall, silvered mirror. Then I smiled at my lass.

"Last chance to call for a safe word."

She didn't flinch. Brave little thing.

"Good," I murmured. "Now get over here, Mila."

Unmoving, she clung to the doorway, her cheeks flushed pink and her lips apart.

Damn. I loved the shy-girl look on her more than anything before.

"Scared?" I taunted.

A tightening of her jaw told me her thoughts, even if she still didn't speak. It brought an idea to my mind. An upping of the ante. Mila needed help not only in her family affairs but in how she and I worked each other out. We'd be having a lot of sex, after all.

From my pocket, I drew out a skeleton bandanna and tightened it between my fists. I had just the way to help her into this.

22

Mila

Convict prowled back over to me, a piece of material in his hands. I watched him in the way a rabbit would track a wolf. My heart hammered. I'd turned into a prey animal, and my muscles had locked so hard a tremble started deep inside me. It mixed with lust until I couldn't move.

My predator twisted the black cloth in his hands and closed in until he loomed over me. "Kiss me."

That, I could do. I raised my lips to meet his. I needed his guidance. I couldn't do this on my own.

He coaxed a hot kiss from me, and his arms moved around me until our bodies touched. My eyes closed, and I gave myself over to the rush of sensation and deepening need. This was chaste in comparison to everything else we'd done, but Convict carried menace like a weapon. It spilled over into everything he did, including in how he seduced me.

His knuckles came up to brush over the side of my cheek, then the material touched my face, covering my eyes. He tied it off at the back of my head, and I pulled back, raising a hand to touch what he'd done.

"You blindfolded me?"

"Don't take it off. Think of it as a trust fall, only with orgasms."

I sensed him stepping away. A click sounded like the lamp had come on.

Hyperawareness flooded my system at not knowing where he was. When he touched my shoulder, I jumped. His other hand landed on my hip, and a small push guided me to move. I obeyed, entering my bedroom, jumping again at the snick of the door closing at my back.

My bare feet touched the fluffy rug, and he murmured for me to stop. My breathing stuttered. I'd liked the scene he described, even if I'd locked up when presented with it. Somehow, he'd found a way to make this even hotter.

Convict spoke next to my ear. "You have no idea what you do to me. This first time is all for me. I'll take what I want and you'll love it. Nod that you understand."

I jerked my head frantically.

His fingertips slipped into my waistband, and he yanked down the yoga pants I'd borrowed from the warehouse. Underneath, I was naked, and cool air slid over my thighs and between my legs. Convict made a sound of hunger and dragged them off my feet then came back up me to grasp my t-shirt. He twisted it in his fist and drew it up my body. For a moment, I thought he was going to leave it in place, but he eased it over my head and removed it, leaving me completely bare except for the bandanna around my eyes and the gold-and-diamond necklace at my throat.

A careful finger plucked the jewellery from my chest, and Convict chuffed a laugh. "If only I'd seen this earlier, Miss E Marchant."

He released it.

My shudder took over me, and I resisted the urge to cover myself. I typically didn't stare at my body naked in the mirror. I didn't like my dimpled thighs. The groan of need from the man at my back almost persuaded me I was wrong.

Strong fingertips skimmed my sides until he cupped my breasts, his thumbs pressing onto my nipples. Fire trailed in his touch, lighting up my whole body. Overwhelmed, I tipped my head back to his shoulder.

Convict squeezed my flesh and laid a kiss to my cheek. "You're so fucking beautiful. Your body makes me weak. Get on your knees."

I sank down, a hand out to feel for the rug and my senses trained on whatever he was doing. A rustling of clothes told me he was undressing. I didn't have to wait long until his hands were back on me, his touch easing up my spine. Heat radiated off him. He held my shoulder and pulled me upright so he could play with my breasts, his body crowding mine from behind and his ultrahard dick against my ass.

His fingers trailed sparks over my skin. I was too alert to every touch.

"Fuck, you should see how you look. Your incredible body with me behind. Pristine girl and tattooed boy." He landed an open-mouthed kiss on my neck.

Even without seeing that image, I could imagine us in the mirror with his big hands moulding my breasts then tugging on my nipples. His much bigger form behind mine. All black ink and hard muscles.

Pleasure spilled through me. In a rush, I hated the bandanna, yet I couldn't ask him to take it off. I didn't want to get hooked up on my imperfections. It was bad enough that multiple people had seen me running scared and nude through the basement. This way, I could pretend I was perfect.

Convict splayed a hand over my sternum and drove the other down, over my soft belly to the apex of my thighs. He touched me between the legs, and I gasped at the hit of sensation. I needed more.

"You're fucking soaked, Mila. So here's the problem. I wanted to play, but if I don't fuck you right now, it'll kill me."

"Yes," I spluttered.

He gave a dark laugh and nudged my legs wider with his knees. "Wasn't asking permission. It was a warning. You're mine however I want you."

With no further pause, he placed his dick between my thighs. I thought he'd toy with me despite his words. But Convict notched himself to my entrance and thrust home.

Startled, I cried out and fell forward. He returned me upright, my back pressed to his chest, and his arm clamped around me. He swore and thrust again, going deeper.

All I knew was that point of contact. The stretch of him entering me.

Convict leaned back, taking me with him so my body was entirely exposed, the rolling of his hips continuing. "In the mirror, my dick is disappearing inside you. You're taking me so well, even if I'm not even halfway in yet."

My panic spiked. He was big, I knew that from almost riding him, but I could barely remember when he'd been inside me in the basement. Had he been all the way inside? I couldn't be sure. The whole event had turned into pieces of memory mostly made of terror and then relief.

I swallowed. "Go slow."

"No. I need to go deep. On all fours and relax for me."

I dropped my hands to the rug, bowing my head. Convict held my hips and circled his to open me. He worked in deeper, each thrust taking him in further and driving me more insane.

"Almost there. Breathe, baby. You're doing so good."

I exhaled, needing this as much as he did. I couldn't explain my attraction to the man, but our connection felt more vital than any I'd ever known.

He jacked his hips one last time then pulsed inside me. I cried out, my pussy throbbing around him in response. Our bodies were flush against each other. We'd done it. He was so thick and in so deep, he hit multiple pleasure points at the same time. I'd never felt anything like it.

My lost boy groaned and rolled his hips. "Fucking hell.

You're taking me. Good girl."

Pride suffused me. I gripped the soft rug. Everything narrowed to the point of where we touched. I needed to come, and fast. So much I barely knew my name. Only that I needed him to move.

He didn't keep me waiting. With his fingers indenting my hips, he withdrew and slammed back into me, right to the hilt. We gave up twin sounds of pleasure. Convict repeated the action, and I backed into the hit, charging up with electrifying need.

It was the fact he was bare. We hadn't even discussed it, only followed the need to fuck. I was never this reckless, but with the deal we'd made, it felt pointless. I liked giving myself over to him. I wanted to not be responsible for every little part of my life. God only knew how much I'd had on my shoulders, so this craziness with a beautiful boy pushed me so far from my comfort zone yet was exactly what I needed.

I'd lost my mind. I didn't care if I found it.

Each thrust got harder. Impossibly deeper. I dropped my head to my folded arms and just let myself feel the building desire, hearing his words about how beautiful I looked in the mirror. What should have been exposing was somehow freeing. I'd never known anything like the sensation of this man owning my body.

The pleasure coiling inside me intensified almost to the point of pain. He didn't slow. Didn't stop. Only kept up that frantic rhythm that was driving me towards a cliff.

Convict loosened his hold on my hip and eased his hand underneath me. Without losing pace, he touched where we joined then drew his fingers back to my clit. I was so primed for him that, at the barest of touches, I moaned. He tapped me right there on that sensitive bundle of nerves, still stretching me, still filling me.

I groaned and panted for breath, so close.

"Need to come?" he taunted.

"Y-yes."

"Maybe I'll let you. Or maybe I need you to admire my work."

Abruptly, he pulled me upright and yanked the bandanna up to clear my vision, no pause in his thrusts. I took a shocked inhale and stared at the mirror image of us. My curvy body being owned by him. His tattooed arm banded around to the base of my throat, the other hand between my legs. His dick spearing into me.

I'd never seen anything so hot.

It was his smirk that did it. A devilish smile that came as he tapped my clit again. I detonated. A surge of towering pleasure smacked me down. I draped back and throbbed around Convict's dick, my eyes closing, my body alive, and the sensation overwhelming in every way. Scorching waves of good feeling fizzed along every vein, dragging me under to a place I never wanted to leave.

Convict snarled and lowered the bandanna back into place.

My still-throbbing orgasm apparently triggered his, and with a few more ragged thrusts, he cried out and pulsed into me, spilling deep inside me.

I shuddered, high on what he'd done and barely attached to my body. It took long minutes to come back to earth.

Still half-hard inside me, he pressed a kiss to my shoulder.

"Don't move."

He pulled out. I mourned the loss of him. Footsteps sounded, then running water followed in the bathroom. He returned, and a wet cloth touched me between the legs. I jerked, and embarrassment flooded me. All of this was new. The animalistic sex, the after-care.

"Bed, now," were the last words spoken.

He picked me up and carried me to my sheets. The light clicked off. Then warmth, his body, his arms, his breath on the back of my neck.

We lay together in silence, skin to skin. The bandanna still covered my eyes. Not because he told me to keep it on, but because I wanted to.

I didn't want to see anything else right now. Just feel him.

23

Convict

When I'd been in the hospital, a medic of some kind had come to my room to talk about addiction. She gave me paperwork and spoke like I was already a junkie on the edge, though she'd admitted my test results were clean. At the time, I'd let it go. Now? Lying here with a naked Mila clinging to me like a fix, I got it.

They were right. I was a fucking addict. Just not the kind they'd meant.

Dawn had long cast the room in pale light, enough to see her by. The bandanna had fallen away so her pretty face was mine to itemise. The curve of her cheek. The bow of her lips.

Carefully, I rolled her onto her back and folded the quilt to the bottom of the bed, giving me free roam over her body. She was so fucking perfect. All curves and dips that had my mouth watering. And my dick hard. I palmed it and stroked myself, focusing on the head.

She'd been scared of me fucking her but also excited by it. I'd work out why soon. Right now, I needed more of her. We'd barely started to explore.

I knelt next to her and stooped to press a featherlight kiss between her tits, peering at her face for any sign she was waking. Mila slept on, a goddess outlined in soft light. I'd exhausted her.

Good.

With my tongue, I drew a line up her ribs and around her nipple, then blew on it. It hardened to a peak as if knowing I needed to suck.

Gently, I enclosed it in my mouth, not stopping my hand at my dick. I went slow. No point in coming before I was ready and I'd had my fill of her. If that was even possible.

Keeping the pressure light, I sucked her nipple, loving the feel of it in my mouth. I slid my tongue over it and onto the curve of her breast then back up to the tip. She hardened further. It sent a buzz through me. Even in her sleep, my woman responded to my actions.

I pulled away and gazed down at what I'd done, then climbed from the bed and rounded to the other side. Mila's bedroom was neat and tidy, like the rest of her place. All polished floorboards and white furniture. Gauzy curtains that did little to keep out the dawn. All the better for me to see her by.

Settled once again, I repeated my attentions to her other side until both nipples stood tall for me.

"Good girl," I muttered and knelt up to lean over her chest. Her tits would be the death of me. They were round and bouncy. More than a handful and mine to play with for twenty-nine more days. What a fucking gift.

The end of my dick was wet with pre-cum, so I touched it to the nearest nipple, my heart thumping.

She stirred in her sleep, her fingers flexing. Her eyelids fluttered as if a dream affected her, maybe about sex.

I inched back and waited, cooling myself. This was too much fun to stop. I'd fuck her again in the morning, but until then, I wanted her to wake up sorer than she expected.

When Mila's breathing slowed once more, I ran my teeth over my lip and gazed down at her. In my fist, I was rock-hard. Did I jerk off like a teenager? Or slide inside her and wake her with a moan? Mouth, cunt, ass, too many options and no bad ones.

Waking her felt like it would end the play. Decisions, decisions.

It was always a game. I was already two points up with playing with her tits.

How else could I score? I'd been fascinated at first sight, and now she was mine, I'd do anything and everything I wanted with her and to her. But that was for when she was awake.

My immediate need was to get inside her again, and to be in there for as long as I could without her knowing. If she woke, she won. If I came in her tight pussy first, I did.

No losers either way.

I considered her position. Flat on her back, the angle was no good for what I wanted. Had to move her.

The best way would be fast.

Lying alongside her, I pulled her into my arms and rolled us both so she was on her front. My pulse skipped as I waited for her to settle. She mumbled something and hugged my arm, her breathing quickly regulating once more.

For a long minute, I just held her. This, I liked as well. The feel of her in my arms did something strange to my heart. I wondered how much I'd been hugged before my accident. Something told me it wasn't enough.

I snuggled in and inhaled the scent of her hair. It only made me harder, and my dick throbbed against her ass.

Slow and steady won the race. I withdrew my arm from beneath her, ensuring she was comfortable with her head turned on the pillow. I couldn't play with her tits any more, but her ass was right there for me to admire.

Another wave of lust sank through me. I stifled a groan and beat my dick a couple of times to the sight. Damn, that was sexy. Not just her pert backside, but the gleam of her pussy in the light.

She was wet for me. Wet from my playing with her. Needy little woman, even in her sleep. And that just earned me one more point.

I shifted her knee out slightly to give me the perfect angle to take my dick to her entrance. With my actions slow and my weight off her, I dragged my cockhead up and down her, getting it soaked. My balls tightened to almost painful with the need to come.

Mila took a breath, like she was warning me not to push my luck. Too bad I had none left to shove.

I watched her. She didn't move, but I'd disturbed her. Fuck. It nearly killed me to hold still for the length of time it took to be sure she went back under. A lesson in what I needed to do next.

Almost certainly, if I pushed inside her, it would all be over.

I wasn't ready to lose.

New game rule: coming at the same time as her waking counted as a win.

Sitting up, I gripped my dick and jerked it, staring at her pussy, then I pressed her cheek to expose her asshole. My dick thickened. I fucked my fist harder. Both holes would be mine as well as her mouth and her tits. Every part of Mila was mine to play with.

Her words from earlier returned. She'd claimed the same rights. If I woke up with her riding me, I'd probably have a heart attack.

That final thought unexpectedly tipped me over the edge. Fever rushed, and I came onto her ass and pussy. Ropes of cum spilled onto her, and at last, I thrust inside her, finishing the job where I wanted to be.

Mila moaned, waking. I set my forehead to the back of her shoulder, shuddering with my release. She reached back and touched my dick where it spread her open.

"You made a mess," she said sleepily, need lacing her tone. Then she bucked against me, sliding up and down my length.

I wet two fingers in the cum then delivered it to her lips, my single word a breathless rush. "Suck."

Mila's mouth opened, and she did as I ordered, her hot tongue caressing my fingers and taking my cum into her throat.

She groaned and moved her fingers to her clit, rubbing in hard circles until she too tightened and fell into release, my happy dick absorbing every one of her throbs.

I sank down onto her, heavy with sleep and deep happiness. I was spent. Not just from the orgasms but from how she surprised me at every turn.

We were going to have so much fun together. Both awake and asleep.

End score? Convict: 1, Mila: 1, also.

Some hours later, I woke again, energised and refreshed. Now I was pretty much healed from my injuries, I figured I didn't need much sleep. Mila was still out cold.

I'd wake her in the best way, but first, I had a call to make.

Climbing out of bed, I found my boxers on the floor, tugged them on, then left the now-bright bedroom. In the living room, I collected my phone from the table where I'd left it.

Two messages already waited. Both from Shade and one an audio clip.

Shade: The recording from the office earlier.

Exactly what I was going to ask him for. I played the file on low, holding it up to my ear. Mila's brother was talking.

"Ye said you thought I was dead. I assumed the same. The man who fucking caught me, Salter, jeered about you being in the hands of the skeleton crew. Now that gang is somehow in your corner. What happened?"

"Salter said that he'd kill you if I didn't obey him."

"That why you're with this arsehole now?"

"Convict? It's more complicated than that. I already knew him."

Kane made a sound of disgust. "Don't tell me ye trust him."

She didn't answer. Why the fuck didn't we have a camera in the room so I could see her expression?

He continued. "Seriously. These men are criminals. You're biting off more than you can chew if you're getting involved with them. Don't do it on my behalf."

She made an off noise. "Funny way to say thank you for saving your ass."

That's what I'd wanted to hear. The sibling irritation in her tone. Though I believed their relationship, I was also acutely aware that I'd fucked up badly enough in my previous life to have wound up with a head injury and a tentative place in my crew. I needed to be smart.

"I'm not grateful. I would've got out by myself, and ye should've left me to find a way. No point two of us getting fucked over," he grouched back.

She sighed. "I should never have asked you to help in the first place. It's made me realise that we were never enough on our own. I underestimated what could happen. That's on me."

He scoffed. "On you. Heard from your darling grandmother recently?"

"She's your grandmother as well. Don't be a dick."

Kane said something I couldn't hear, then the audio clip ended. While we'd waited in the hall, they hadn't talked for long. This was why. There wasn't much to say. Mila had read the situation and made her decision.

She'd chosen me.

I didn't care that it was only because of what I could offer her. Weren't all relationships the same that way? I couldn't stop the burst of happiness it gave.

I replied to Shade with a thanks for sending it. He'd be sleeping now, I guessed, as any good night dweller should.

From Mila's kitchen, I fetched a glass of water then returned to the bedroom, snagging my hospital bag on the way. In her window with a view out over the sunlit city, I took my antibiotics and watched the traffic queueing below. I followed the street to a church spire in the distance which cut across the bright line of Deadwater River. In broad daylight, it was so different to the shadowed city I knew. From up here in Mila's pristine perch, all the grime and dark underbelly of Deadwater was kept at bay. She was safe and protected. I liked that for her.

I tossed the packet back in the bag. The paperwork inside caught my attention. My address was at the top of the first sheet: 14B Hazard Place. The payslip Manny had printed for me was below, and I flipped it over to show the alternative: 212 Linnet Road. Both addresses meant nothing. Like someone else's life scribbled on my file. What kind of man lived in two places and left no trace behind?

It bothered me how I didn't remember shit about either of those homes, especially after last night when Mila had laid out a whole life and history. In exchange, I had nothing.

What if I had family living in one of those homes? A strange feeling took over my gut. My crew had searched for me and had been told I was dead. If my family had done the same, I was clueless, but maybe they missed me, too. Maybe someone else out there, a mother, a sister, anyone, gave a fuck and would have something to say that would help fill the gaps in my mind.

I climbed back into bed and pulled Mila into my arms. This time, I didn't pretend it was about her. I needed the hug more than she did.

24

Mila

Waking in a man's arms was a brand-new experience and one I strangely liked. I'd never once had a boyfriend sleep over in this apartment, not that men had been high on my agenda. It belonged to my grandparents, even if only I used it, so it hadn't felt right to abuse their hospitality.

All the stops were off now.

I flexed against Convict's big body, shifting my knee over his thigh, the rough hair on his leg abrading my soft skin.

From last night, my body felt deliciously used. My limbs heavy, my pussy aching. Yet somehow, I wanted more. It was like a dam had been blown up. My sexuality had been unleashed, with only one target in sight.

Slowly, I shifted up onto my elbow and peeked at him. His face was slightly turned from me, his dark hair messy and his eyes closed. Sleep softened his rough edges, returning him to the lost boy I'd been instantly fascinated by. I let myself soak in the sight. So much had gone down in such a short time, I was in danger of believing that it hadn't truly happened.

The tall, dark, and dangerous man in my bed was very real.

With care, I tugged the blanket down to reveal his bare chest. Need sank through me at his hard body and expanse of tattoos. I never thought of myself being all that visual, yet I could spend hours just ogling him. If I only moved the blanket a few inches more, I'd get the money shot.

I sensed rather than saw his eyes cracking open.

Guilty, I jerked back.

He tightened his arm around me to keep me in place. "I'm not awake. I'm a coma patient, still. Any undressing is on you. Keep going."

I hid my face with my hand. "Oh God."

"I'm begging you to carry on."

"I'm so embarrassed."

Flustered, I tried to rise. Convict pulled me onto his body. Both of us were naked, the sheets twisted between us.

"What do you need, Mila? Tell me."

I buried my face in his chest. "To run away and hide. Then a cold shower."

Sure fingers stroked over my hair and down my face then tipped up my chin. "No, you don't. You're as needy as I am. Just like when I woke in the night and fucked you in your sleep."

Fresh desire tightened my insides. Coming to with him inside me had almost broken my brain. He'd even cleaned me up after. "I'm aware."

"But, all of that was yesterday, and the rules state that we need to fuck every day. Are you going to make me do all the work?"

I had to be bright red. "I can't just…"

"You did in my room in the warehouse." He released me to raise his hands behind his head, his wrists together and his biceps bulging. Then he gestured to the side of the bed. "Pick up my hospital bag."

I leaned to do as he asked and caught sight of the rug and mirror from last night. Thoughts of him railing me from behind while I wore the blindfold stole my breath.

Convict rumbled a laugh. "Get the handcuffs from inside. I brought them along. Chain me up and do what you want with me."

Shocked, I widened my eyes at him. "I can't do that."

"You can and you will. I don't even have to come. Just get yourself off."

My heart rate spiked. I was so hot for him it was burning me up. It wasn't that I only wanted sex. I wanted to be on him. To get under his skin. To have free use of him like he'd done of me.

Of their own accord, my fingers found the cuffs. I returned the bag to the floor. Then I spied the skeleton-print bandanna he'd used on me, down between the bed pillows. I fished it out.

Convict followed my actions. He flashed another grin and tipped his head forward, reading my intention like I was an open book. "Do it."

Autopilot had taken me over, because I folded the material and fastened it over his head then cuffed his wrists, all without conscious thought.

"You put a lot of trust in me. I could leave you here all day and no one would know."

His chains rattled. "Little gangster, your bedframe is no match for me if I wanted to get loose. But that isn't a threat. All I want is for you to get yours. So set aside whatever's holding you back and ride my fucking dick until you come."

Damn his dirty talk and the flood of liquid heat it generated.

It also made my hands shake. I unwrapped myself from the blanket and threw it to the end of the bed, leaving us both uncovered. Convict was hard, of course, his knees bent as if to offer me a good place to sit.

Still, I hesitated.

His lips moved. "I woke up ready to go and didn't think

twice about playing with you. I tried not to wake you, only partially for your sake because I wanted to have my fun while you slept. I wanted to use your body, Mila, just like you can use mine now. Touch yourself. I can't see you so you don't have to make a show of it. Consider me a human dildo."

I huffed a needy laugh. "Does my dildo have a mute button, or are you a deluxe model only?"

"Nah. You don't want that. You like my mouth."

He was right. Plus his words made me a little braver. On my knees, I considered what I wanted to do. I needed to come, but I had options.

With my fingertips to the centre of his chest, I drove them upwards, through his dusting of dark chest hair and to his throat.

His voice came out rough. "Need me to talk you through this?"

"No. Tell me what you did in the night."

He adjusted his position on the bed, his dick bobbing. "Favourite new subject. First, I just let myself look at you. Then I played with your tits and sucked your nipples, scoring points for not waking you."

Sitting back on my heels, I squeezed my nipple and tugged on it, a flash of pleasure echoing through my body. I did the same with the other side so I played with both in tandem.

"I knew I wanted to fuck you, but that would wake you up and I'd lose the game. So I turned you over to give me a better angle on your pussy." He exhaled. It became a groan. "I could've done so much to you. I wish I'd tasted you, but the need to come took over me once I saw your ass."

My heart thumped harder. I travelled my fingers down my body to pass over my centre. I was soaked.

"Open your mouth," I told him.

His lips parted, and I pressed my slick fingers to his

tongue.

Convict sucked me clean and groaned again. "Holy fuck, sweetheart."

This was oddly empowering.

If I was braver, I'd ask to ride his face, but for now, it was enough that I was leading this. Kind of.

I braced myself on his chest and threw my leg over him, settling onto his lap. Instantly, he adjusted his position to support me. Then I rose and fitted him to my entrance and sank down fast so I didn't lose my nerve.

Convict's groan answered my silent one, my lust peaking at how thick he was. Too thick to take in one go. I eased up and down him several times until I was fully seated, then held still, lost in the sensation of being so full. I wriggled, adjusting. No, *marvelling*.

I liked it far too much. It was an addiction I'd never worried about succumbing to because I'd never known this kind of perfect fit was a possibility.

"Move, baby," the gangster urged.

"Hush. Dildos don't talk."

I slid up and down him, my breathing shuddering and pleasure spilling out through me. When I circled my hips, his thick length lit up more places inside than I knew I had. At last, my brain shut off. In general in life, I overthought everything. Every decision. This was pure instinct.

With my palms flat to his chest, I rose and fell and worked myself on his dick. Tight heat pooled deep and low in my body, building up with every pass. It was electrifying, riding Convict. Not only from my feelings but by his sounds of pleasure.

This would take no time at all. If anything, I had to slow down to tease myself and build it up more so I didn't finish too soon.

My fingertip snagged on a line on his chest. No, multiple.

A scar? They were under a tattoo so I couldn't be sure, and I lost the pace in my fever to fuck him.

It returned quickly.

I peeked up at his face. With his jaw clenched, Convict had locked his muscles tight, his biceps bulging with how hard he held himself. I didn't know if he was trying to stay quiet or to stop himself from coming, but that image shattered my resolve. I reached for my clit, enraptured with him.

One pass, two. I arched my back and played with myself, getting faster and closer. Then I was falling and crashing into pleasure so intense, I cried out and slumped forward, clamping down on Convict's dick with each pulse of my climax.

Under me, he gasped out, so tense, and the moment I stopped moving, he took over. He bucked into me, driving his heels into the bed to fuck me half a dozen more times until he too stilled. Inside me, he came.

A laugh flew from my lips, made of relief and new pleasure from the way he thickened even more.

I propped up on his chest, breathing hard as I cooled. "Bad little dildo. You weren't supposed to come."

"As if I could stop it. You have no idea how incredible that was. And less of the little, thanks. I'm the XL edition, and you know it."

My lips curved. I pushed up the blindfold so I could see his eyes. They trained on me.

"Kiss me," he begged.

I pressed my lips to his. Convict kissed me with a fever, his hips working slowly even though we were sloppy. He kissed me like he didn't want to stop, slowing and deepening until I had my fingers in his hair and his half-hard dick had returned to full power once more.

Somehow, that had become almost romantic.

Confusion marred my happiness.

I sat up on him and touched the lines I'd discovered earlier. I squinted down. "You have a scar here."

"Fuckin' covered in them."

Except this was odd. It was crisscrossed in even marks. Three curved lines going one way, two bisecting them, half a centimetre apart like a fan pattern abandoned and incomplete.

I frowned at it. "This doesn't look accidental." I collected the key to the handcuffs and unlocked him, showing him what I'd found. "Like someone meant to leave a mark."

Convict's jaw worked for a second before he forced a smile. "Guess we'll find out who they were when we find out who I was."

He kissed my shoulder, his gaze slinking down to my bare breasts. "But I'm certain that if you don't run to the bathroom and lock me out, we are never leaving this bedroom today."

"You don't want to shower with me?"

"More than you can believe. But I also want to feed you and give your poor pussy a rest."

I climbed up and danced away. "So magnanimous."

"No clue what that word means." His amusement chased me and stayed with me while I washed myself clean of everything we'd done to each other since striking our deal.

When I was finished, Convict took his turn.

I hovered at the bathroom door. "Hungry?"

"I could go for tea and something sweet if you're making breakfast."

Those were my words from our very first phone sex conversation. He remembered.

"I'll order in. We're too late for any breakfast places, but we can get a late lunch from a sandwich shop nearby. I can get a selection plus coffee and pastries?"

"Best wifey ever," he called back.

I left him to it, carrying with me a warm little burst of happiness generated by his praise.

$\mathcal{C}$ross-legged on my floor, we fuelled up on the stack of sandwiches and coffee that had been delivered to the door. Had to love city living for the amount of food choices available at the press of a button.

Convict pointed at me with his coffee cup. "Why aren't you supposed to know about Kane? You said that last night. It's been bothering me."

I wrinkled my nose. "My grandparents only ever spoke about him once, and that was to explain why he had a vote. He was referred to as a distant relative and one I should steer clear of, but that only got me more interested."

He gave me space to speak, his interest plain. It encouraged me.

"For one of my placements around the company, I was with the Human Resources team. They have a digital system for all the staff but also a physical filing system called the family vault. Apparently my grandfather liked to have certain paperwork as a hard copy. But it was locked and coded. One night, I worked late, and when the last person left, I tried every code I could think of to unlock that damn vault. His and my grandmother's birth dates, when the company was formed, the numbers on the first cheque he ever received that was photographed and hanging on the wall. I tried my date of birth. Their sons'. Nothing. Then finally, I remembered my grandfather talking about his first date with my grandmother. It was the last day in a very hot July, so it stuck in my head. I had to guess the year, but at last, it worked. In the cabinet was a folder for every part of the family who got a dividend payout. Including Kane's side. It gave me enough information on him that I could contact him."

"So you did?"

"I did. Secretly, though. It was pretty obvious that it wouldn't please my grandparents. We met up for a drink one evening. He's the result of another short-term love affair our bio father had, but it's his mother who's on the company dividend list. She lives in Scotland, somewhere above Inverness."

"Not him? He doesn't get a payout?"

"Nope."

"So the reason he played backup with your scheme was for his ma's sake?"

"I think so. Which makes him sound dangerously noble. I'm pretty sure he'd deny it if asked."

Convict pondered that, throwing back two huge beef sandwiches before he spoke again. "Why isn't he the heir? He looks older than you."

"He is. Five years older. I assume our grandparents offered and he refused. He isn't...malleable, like I am. I would do anything to fit to their needs. He's like a brick. Solid and dependable but with no give. When we met, I was enthralled at having a brother. He was, not hostile exactly, but it took a long time for him to warm to me, and he refused point blank to discuss anything to do with the Marchant family. I chipped away at him like an ice block until he began to return my texts. I forced a relationship out of him. You know, after what happened yesterday, I should call him. Just to check in."

"He seems like the type who can take care of himself."

"True."

I side-eyed my phone. I'd skimmed my copious messages and emails last night to check what had come in while I'd been gone. My inboxes were overflowing. Relatives had been messaging me relentlessly after getting the same cold shoulder from my grandmother that I had. They'd drawn a blank with the company's board, and I was the next best bet.

I felt for them. With their income gone, they were in turmoil. I'd done all I could to help, but the only solution was to get the business up and running again, and I was breaking my back for that. I needed to send replies, but for one more day, they could wait.

I scanned the list of new messages. One caught my eye for the user name. I opened it.

Anonymous: Marchant was a despicable piece of shit. Enjoy Hell, Austin. You deserved to die.

It wasn't the first hate mail my grandfather had received. In fact, I had a folder titled exactly that, and I filed the new message away so I didn't have to look at it again.

It hurt, though. Austin Marchant was the greatest man who ever breathed. I missed him so much. How dare a stranger treat his memory like that?

Bothered, I wrote out a message to my grandmother, just like I'd done almost every day for the past month.

Mila: Are you available to meet today? I can come to you, wherever you are. I miss you. I need to know you're okay. Please call me.

I hovered over the 'Send' icon, thumb tapping the edge of the screen. Maybe it was pointless. Maybe she'd deleted every message I'd written. I sent it anyway.

Convict touched my knee and claimed my attention back to him. "All okay?"

"Just work nonsense. I need to get out of this inbox." I shut it down and tossed my phone.

"I meant to say I've heard nothing about Jacobs yet. Tyler has set up surveillance. Until he has news, I was thinking how I need to check out the places where I'm supposed to have lived. Want to come? I can be quick if you'd rather not. Maximum two hours apart."

There was hope in his expression, his hair still damp and falling in his eyes. It took him back to the cute, boyish side I liked so much in him. My heart softened.

"I'll come."

Just like that, the devil returned. A flash of humour and need in his dark eyes. "You'll come more if we stay here, but I'm down to see what we can manage in a quick outdoor fuck on our travels."

The weird thing? I didn't want him to be joking.

25

Into rush hour, we exited the underground parking, Convict pushing into the nose-to-tail traffic in a way I'd never have the confidence to do.

He raised an easy hand to thank the driver he'd cut up, earning the blare of a horn. "Can you drive?"

"Yes, but I don't have a car anymore." The sporty little Audi I'd driven from ports to office buildings all around the country was mine no longer.

"What happened to it?"

"It belongs to the business. Like everything else, it's unable to be used until the will is read. I'm lucky that the apartment is privately owned, though I've no idea if any bills are being paid. It's possible that the electricity will get cut off."

He twisted his lips. "All the more reason for me to find out if I have a place to live."

We stopped at traffic lights. I watched him slyly, using my hair as a shield. Convict in my home had been a devastating sight. A big man with ink and dark hair, barefoot on my white floorboards and with a coffee mug in his hand. Now we were in the car, I was back to ogling his confident sprawl in the driver's seat, two fingers guiding the steering wheel. I could get used to being a passenger princess.

His mouth curved into a smirk. "Keep staring at me like that and I'm going to get arrested."

"For what?"

"Indecent exposure."

I laughed softly. "Can I ask about your thing with pain? How does that work?"

He shrugged. "Wish I could tell you. All I know is how the nurses in the hospital talked to me about pain management, and I realised I felt nothing like what they suggested I should."

"You can feel touch, right?"

I reached out and ran a finger along his arm, from his wrist to the line of his black skeleton crew branded t-shirt. Then I trailed it back down but with a lighter touch.

He shivered and adjusted his position in the seat. "I feel that just fine."

"You're hard, aren't you?" I paused. "That's rhetorical. I can see it twitching."

"Check you out, all brave and talking about my dick when you think I'm too occupied to use it."

A thrill ran through me. God only knew how I could still be hot for him after all we'd done together. Yet my mind was right there in the gutter.

Convict slid a look my way. "To finish what I know, touch is fine, hard hits do nothing, and temperature is wacky. If you say it's warm or cold, I generally haven't noticed. Unless it's right before I go to sleep. Then I feel something. Fucked up, aren't I?"

I shook my head, making a mental note to ensure the blankets were over him when we went to bed.

Another thought occurred to me. "By the way, on health matters, I have a contraceptive implant, and I've never...been with anyone like we've done."

Something passed over his face. "I had every test known to man in the hospital, so you're safe with me. Well, safe-ish, because I'm having some pretty dark thoughts about your exes. Also, I'll be plotting ways to remove that implant, and searching up 'sneaky pregnancy hacks' like a man with a mission."

My jaw dropped. "You did not just say that."

"Which part? Removing the fingers and eyes of anyone who ever touched you or the part about knocking you up? Happy to repeat it or go into detail."

I hid my face and didn't answer, reasonably sure he was joking.

We journeyed through the city and crossed the river to the Scottish side of Deadwater, entering an area of the city my grandmother would've turned her nose up at. Convict used his phone's navigation to locate the Hazard Place address the hospital had given him, and we followed the directions deep into the suburbs and to a run-down street beside a flyover. He parked up adjacent to a terraced house.

The fact he'd needed directions to find somewhere he used to live hit me square in the feels.

I eyed the pebbledash building, noting how there were multiple bells for the different flats. "Anything familiar?"

"Nope."

He climbed out then rounded to open my door, claiming my hand in his to cross the road. At the house, he took a deep breath then pressed the bell for 14B.

We waited.

Nothing happened.

I tried this time, pressing it twice. The filthy net curtain in the bay window a few feet to the left of us twitched. I waved to indicate we were friendly, then the window cracked open.

"What do you want?" a man asked against a backdrop of loud chatter from a television. He was probably in his sixties or so and clutched a cigarette in his hand, the glowing end dangerously close to burning a hole in the curtains. But all of that faded behind the stench of unwashed body that eked from the opening.

Convict squinted at him but didn't speak.

"Is your flat 14B?" I asked.

"Might be. What of it?"

"My friend used to live here. Do you know if the landlord is around? We had a couple of questions."

"Fuck off. The TV was already here when I got this place. It's mine."

"We aren't interested in taking your television, only in knowing the dates my friend lived here."

"Ring the CHP, love. Don't fucking bother me."

He slammed the window shut.

Convict's eyebrows drew together. "I know what the CHP is. Community Housing Project. It's ex-prisoner accommodation. I must've stayed here after coming out of jail one time."

He said it casually, but his fingers curled around mine. Like he was trying to hold on to something solid while the rest of him slipped back into shadows.

"Not recently, judging on the new occupant."

He gave a short laugh. "Agreed. I think we can move on."

We returned to the car, and he plugged in the second address, Linnet Road, back on the English side.

"It stands to reason that my crew would have the up-to-date address. I just wanted to check both out anyway." He drove out of the suburb. When we came to a halt at lights, he darted a look my way. "Is it weird for you to be shacked up with an ex-con?"

"You introduced yourself to me by your nickname. It's not like this is new information."

He rolled his shoulders and tore his gaze to the road

instead of me. "There's a nickname and then there's seeing a guy like that. The alternative version of me in four decades' time."

I recoiled. "Why do you think you'd become like that?"

He shrugged. "He triggered a memory. Not of him specifically, but of broken men stuck in the same routine, day after day. I think I'm remembering my jail time."

"Then don't go back to jail again."

The glum expression lifted. "Thanks, heir-to-an-empire girl. I'll be sure to remember that."

He reached out for me, this time landing his warm hand on my knee. For the jaunt out, I'd chosen a plaid skirt and cream wide-necked jumper, overjoyed to have my wardrobe back.

Convict inched his fingers under the skirt's hem.

He didn't go any further, just stroking and indenting my thigh, but by the time he parked up at the second house, I was fixated on his touch.

Again, he climbed out and opened my door, that knowing gleam in his eye when he helped me out. It faded when he took in the building.

"What will be behind door number two?" he quipped.

The place was a block of flats, four storeys high. A long path to the front door crossed a concrete patio, and two old gents rested on a bench to one side, the cool early evening clearly not bothering them.

Convict raised a hand to them as we passed. Both stared back, then one gave a wheezing laugh.

"Convict. Thought you were dead, boy."

Convict blinked then forced a smile. "Rumours of my death are exaggerated. How's it going? All good around here?"

The man chuffed. "Aye, but I'm surprised to see you

back. Ma won't be pleased. The lass a human shield?"

'Ma' as in his mother? He hadn't been sure if he had family.

Convict stiffened. His hand tightened around mine. "Is Ma in now?"

The front door swung open, and a woman marched out. Aged probably in her forties, she had dark-red hair and ruddy cheeks. Anger marked her stomp down the path. "You've got some nerve."

We turned to face her. Convict didn't speak.

"Two months running. Then you show up like nothing's happened."

She didn't look anything like him, but genetics could be weird.

"He's been in hospital," I defended him.

The woman ignored me. "Explain yourself."

His gaze travelled over her features as if searching for the same recognition I had. "Sorry, Ma. I was in a coma. Hard to make a phone call when you're asleep."

"Don't 'Ma' me. That's reserved for my tenants. And you're not one anymore since I re-let your flat." She spun on her heel to walk away, calling back over her shoulder, "I kept your deposit. You still owe me a month in hand."

"She's not your mum," I whispered. "She was your landlady. Only that."

My words seemed to unlock him.

He stormed after her. "I nearly died, but sure, charge me for being unconscious. What happened to my stuff? My possessions?"

"I slung it all. It's in the terms and conditions of your tenancy. You never answered my messages, it was my right to do with it as I pleased."

She'd reached the door and went to slam it.

Convict grabbed it and planted one foot on the doormat. "All of it? When and where did you throw it away?"

He didn't believe her. I wasn't sure how I knew, but from her expression, he was right.

The landlady pouted. "There might be a few things hanging around in a storage cupboard. I'd have to check. Come back in five to ten business days."

"How about you check now and I'll make sure your rent is paid."

She glared at him. He stared back, not menacing her, but not moving either.

"The money first," she countered.

I lifted my chin. "You said you kept his deposit. He was only in hospital for a month. If you've already rented out his flat, you can't be out of pocket for more than a week or two."

"Yeah, but what about all the hassle of finding a new tenant and cleaning the space?" She curled her lip. "Fine." She spat a figure.

Convict nodded and found his phone. He dialled a number. "Manny? Can I ask a favour?"

He walked a few steps away, quietly requesting his friend put cash in an envelope and send it to this address via a cab.

The landlady listened with her arms folded. Her gaze slid over to me. "Pretty thing like you would do better to stay well away from a thug like that one."

"You don't know anything about him."

She sniffed. "Neither do you, I'd bet."

Convict returned to my side. "The cash is on its way. Now can I have my things?"

The woman would not be moved. She made us wait until the taxi arrived, then she counted every note, finally allowing us entry to the building when she was satisfied she'd been paid. In a dank ground-floor hallway, she unlocked a door and stood back to give us entry. "Take whatever you want then don't come back."

Convict waited until she'd gone then muttered, "Wouldn't if you paid me."

We entered the chilly space, a converted garage with a blinking strip light over metal shelving units holding cardboard boxes and other loose items. Lamps, crockery, bags of what appeared to be clothing. Some of it had to have been here for years, judging by the thick cobwebs and mould.

Convict tugged down the nearest box and leafed through a stack of papers. "When we were waiting for the money, I got a memory of that woman and this place. I don't think I lived here very long either, so there probably won't be much to find."

"Do you recognise anything on the shelves?"

He turned in a circle then raised a shoulder. "Not a fucking thing. I doubt I owned a vase, though. If I can find something with my name on it, that will be enough."

I took the opposite shelf and searched. The first box gave me nothing, but a second contained a sealed envelope with the name 'Mr R Locke'.

I held it out. "Bingo."

Convict took the box and sat on the floor while I searched the rest of the shelves. I turned back at his exhale.

"I have a bank account. Who knows if there's anything left in it, but at least I can access it now. Maybe see what I was doing in a past life." He read the next letter in the stack, one that had already been opened. "This tells me my final probation appointment. Three months' time. Good to know. It hadn't even occurred to me that the cops might be after me for recall to prison if I missed a date."

My heart skipped a beat at the thought of him being whisked away to jail. "They can't have you. You belong to me for twenty-nine more days."

He raised an eyebrow. Then he lifted from the floor in one easy move, picked me up in his arms, and walked me backwards until my spine met the nearest shelf. "How is it you're still into me now you've seen what a scumbag I am?"

Annoyance flashed through me alongside rising heat from him between my thighs. "You're no different to the man who appeared outside my window ten days ago."

"No? I guess even then I was breaking and entering. You must have a thing for bad boys."

He landed his mouth on mine. His lips moved surely, sliding into a devastating kiss. Oh fuck. I melted onto him, defenceless against his kisses.

It didn't matter that we were in a dank garage surrounded by other people's discarded property. My body knew only one thing: Need for this man.

Something vibrated between us, close to where our lower bodies touched.

"Oh hey, my dildo came with a surprise vibration setting."

Convict barked out a laugh, his eyes widening. "I love it when you dirty talk. It's so at odds with your good-girl exterior. Let me kill this call and we'll get back to what we were doing."

He checked his screen and frowned.

"If you need to take it, it's okay."

He nodded and accepted the call, dropping me to my feet. "Arran?"

As he listened, his expression shifted from confident and in control to that lost-boy worry. I knew Arran was the leader of the skeleton crew as well as his friend. He also held the power to kick Convict out of their crew altogether, if he chose.

"We'll be there. See you soon." He hung up and stared at the phone. "He's back. He wants me to come in this evening. You, too."

I took a deep breath. "It'll be okay."

From the floor, Convict snagged the single cardboard box we knew to be his and gave a hard laugh. "I'm homeless, probably barely staying within the law, and on a slippery slope to a shite future. If Arran kicks me out, I'll be unemployed, too. I'll have nothing to offer…"

He didn't finish the sentence.

"He won't. He's your friend. Friends care about you."

A tiny glimmer of hope returned to his eyes. I'd put it there. That felt powerful.

I stood taller, my mind racing over what Arran meant to him and what the man wanted to see. "Have we got time to stop in at my place?"

Convict tilted his head. "If you want me to fuck you, you just need to ask. In fact, I was halfway there. Lock the fuckin' door, baby."

I choked on a laugh. "I mean that we're going to the warehouse as a couple, right? When we came out of the game, people congratulated us. They celebrated the fact you'd done what you did."

"They'll do the same tonight."

"Right, so we put on a show to convince Arran that your actions were the right thing to do."

And if they didn't? Then I'd go down fighting for him, fake deal or not.

"Sweetheart, anyone looking at us would know it was right. I only have to think about you and he'll see it in my face."

We returned to the car, but that comment stayed with me. What was odd was how completely natural his statement felt, almost as if he meant it for real.

Back home, I dressed to impress in a thigh-skimming strapless purple dress—reminiscent of the one I'd worn in the game but a thousand times classier—and makeup that was on point for the hottest nightclub in the city. Armour against the man who owned it.

Convict was banned from the bedroom so we had a chance of making it out of the apartment. When I emerged, he was in a fresh black t-shirt and jeans from his stash.

He gave a low whistle. "Yep. I'm getting into a fight tonight."

My cheeks heated. "That was our deal. To show your friends that we're together."

"Just for the deal. Right." His eyes flashed dark, and he turned to leave.

And that countdown in my mind ticked on for when we'd come to a screeching end.

26

Convict

Pink neon lights strobed across the entrance to my crew's warehouse, filtering through Mila's blonde hair. Music thudded in time with my heartbeat. I fell back a few steps, running my gaze up her long legs from her high heels to the line of her short, sparkling dress. Outlined against the dark night, she was a fucking vision. An angel.

She twisted back to me and tilted her head, her fingers extending for me to take. Tight dress, pink lips, all mine.

For now.

I swallowed, and time caught up with me.

Catching her hand, I tugged her closer and ran an arm around her waist. The sound of the crowd rushed back in. From the line outside of Divide, people catcalled us. Men entering Divine's strip club on the other side of the rope watched her with lust in their eyes.

I glowered back until they dropped the gazes to the ground. Mila giggled and palmed my chest. At the front of the queue, one of the security team waved us inside, murmuring his congratulations, the sentiment echoed by those nearby.

"Good game. Way to fight for her. She knew she was yours," some suited arsehole commented.

The girl on his arm curved her lips into a knowing grin. "We re-enacted your claim. She got away then you found her again. It's our favourite."

Mila hid her face in my shirt and gave them a shy wave. Fucking sex tourists, though despite my annoyance at them seeing her naked, something about it was hot, too.

Inside the building, we passed through the dark nightclub, the music vibrating through the floor and stealing any chance of conversation. The DJ mixed a dance version of 'i'm yours' by Isabel LaRosa. Mila peered at the heaving dance floor where strobe lights flickered over the crowd. Her shoulders moved to the beat.

I wanted to hit up the VIP area and dance with her there. I wanted to do a lot of things with her. But I was here for one reason, and it wasn't good.

At the back of the lower floor, I tapped a code into the staff exit, and we entered the central corridor that ran between the two clubs. As always, it was buzzing with skeleton crew, dancers, and other employees, everyone busy on a Saturday night. Men shook my shoulder or slapped my hand. Women complimented Mila's hair, her fit, and her choice.

Forcing a smile took more energy than I had. At the office, I stuck my head inside, finding Shade behind the desk. "Arran around?"

The tattooed enforcer jumped his gaze between us, tension in his frame. "Upstairs in his apartment. He said for ye to go up. Hit the eight. Your pass has access."

In the lift, my pulse kept up the same thudding beat. A metronome of my impending doom.

Mila checked her makeup then watched me in the mirror. "Did I do okay as the bashful new bride?"

"You're perfect."

If Arran kicked me out, she'd have no reason to be with me. I stuck my hands into my pockets and tried to stop myself from spiralling.

The lift arrived on the eighth floor, and we stepped out into the hall. Other than the stairs and the lift, there were two doors, one ahead and one to the right. I hesitated, not knowing which apartment to choose. Knocking on the wrong door would be a dead giveaway.

Shade's words came back to me. He'd told me which floor to come to. Why would he do that? As far as he was concerned, my memory was fine.

The stairwell exit opened, and Cassie appeared. Her attention fell on us, all bright eyes and knowing smirk, like she already had gossip to collect. "Ohmigod. Hey, players. I'm surprised ye have the energy to walk around."

At the same moment, the apartment door ahead opened, and Arran appeared with the woman we'd seen in his office, Lovelyn, I recalled, plus another crew member who took to the stairs, leaving them behind.

There was no give in Arran's expression when he centred on Lovelyn. "I appreciate you coming in, but I don't like your father using you as his mouthpiece."

Lovelyn tucked her hair behind her ear with floral nails. "I'm grateful for your time all the same. Thank you for hearing me out."

Arran's attention fell on us like a dead weight. "Convict. You're here."

For better or worse, I was.

Lovelyn swung her gaze to us, her eyes widening. "Convict? That's wonderful timing. I came tonight with hope of seeing you as well as Arran. On my father's behalf, I'm truly sorry that he concealed your hospital stay from your friends."

Who the fuck was her father? My mind was slow to make the connection, though I was vaguely aware of Shade or Tyler saying something about it.

Cassie got there first. Her eyes bugged out. "Hold the phone. You're Detective Dickhead's daughter? Shite. I mean Chief Constable Kenney? No offence intended. Well, maybe some, but only to him."

Lovelyn grinned. "None taken. At least not personally. I've called him worse in my time." She turned back to me. "He offers no excuse. I believe it was done as a joke, though I can't see the funny side. I'm very glad to see you're back on your feet."

Right. Her father was the police officer who had known I was in hospital yet chose to tell my crew I was dead. "He sent you to do his dirty work?"

Lovelyn's smile slipped. "I think he knows he took it too far. Seems to me he had a personal beef with Arran or Shade and you were the victim. Again, I apologise."

"Rest assured he and I will be having words." Arran's sober tones drove away my wondering.

I laced my fingers with Mila's and drew her with me until we were in front of him. "Mila, this is Arran, the leader of the skeleton crew. Arran, this is Mila. She's...mine."

Arran's shrewd gaze took in my lass. "It's a pleasure."

When his attention came back to me, I wasn't sure what I could see in it. Shock. Some other high emotion. It cut through me.

He was so familiar. His dark-blond hair was swept back, his normally pale skin tanned from wherever he and Genevieve had been. He was in a black suit, looking every inch the mob boss, but my memory sparked other images. A younger version of him in a torn t-shirt with a bruised cheek. Him laughing with me as we entered a run-down building in another city.

My breathing stuttered. Remembering Arran was giving me parts of myself back. Something that had barely happened since I'd left the hospital.

Mila squeezed my hand. "If it's okay, I'll let the two of you catch up, and I'll go explore the nightclub. Maybe get a drink."

She'd picked up on the tension. It would be impossible not to.

Cassie arched a dark brow. "I'd step right out of that crossfire, too. Come with me. I'll bag us a table in the VIP suite so we skeleton girls can get to know each other. Lovelyn, you too. I want to hear all about how a nice girl like you is the progeny of your father." She shot a chin lift my way. "Don't worry. Riordan is working tonight. If he isn't watching over us, no doubt a dozen other skeleton crew will."

Mila waited on my word.

"Two hours maximum," I murmured.

She smiled. "Don't be late."

The three women entered the lift, and Mila kept my gaze right until the final second.

She didn't know it yet, but I was far from done fighting. Just because the battlefield could change didn't mean the war was over.

Their exit left me alone with Arran. He gestured for me to enter the apartment and closed the door after us.

Once inside, I knew the space. The red-brick walls, the engineered oak floorboards, and fancy fucking kitchen I was certain he never cooked in. There were new additions. Signs that a woman lived here and it wasn't just a bachelor pad. A cosy blanket on the back of the couch and a desk I didn't remember from before, presumably for Genevieve's use as the laptop case boasted a sticker declaring 'Won't work without caffeine'.

More telling was the fluffy brown cat with a pink collar that padded over to me and wound around my legs.

I stooped to stroke its soft head, near certain it hadn't lived here when I'd been on the scene. "Who's this?"

"Gen's cat, Rosie. Drink?"

"I'm good."

I wasn't. I was so far from good it was insane. I didn't know how to talk to Arran, whether to launch into an apology or just take the verbal beating I was due. He was so familiar. I loved this man. I knew him almost as well as I did myself, even if I couldn't recall exactly how.

He dropped heavily into a leather armchair and rested his elbows on his knees, waiting for me to settle on the opposite sofa. "I have no fucking clue how to start this conversation."

A laugh fell from my lips. "I was just thinking the same thing. I was debating grovelling—"

"Fuck. Don't do that. Just give me a second." He watched me for a long minute, his gaze soaking in every detail and lingering on the scar at my hairline.

The cat leapt on my lap and turned twice before sprawling on me and headbutting my belly for attention.

Arran's focus didn't flicker. He'd asked for a moment, and I understood why. He was looking at a ghost.

"After the fire at the Four Milers' chapel, you were declared dead. Not by us, but by the cop who was too cowardly to face us so sent his daughter instead. I never believed it. You're the hardiest motherfucker I've ever known. What right would a fire have to take you from this world?"

I couldn't smile. My stomach had compressed to a tight knot, and I balled my fists so my hands didn't shake. "I'm not dead, but I am a fucking idiot. I let you down. You gave me a second chance, and I'm very aware of how I'm back at the point of asking your forgiveness again. I don't expect you to give it. I don't expect anything. All I ask is the space to explain myself. Whatever you decide after that is good with me."

Arran tilted his head. "I'll hear you out, though you don't need to explain. Tyler and Shade told me exactly what happened with your woman. I have a question first, though."

"Ask it."

Something ticked over in his vision, the intensity sharpening. "I was thinking about when we were kids, fighting at the Borders club in Newcastle. Do you remember Big Al, the doorman?"

Vaguely, I remembered fighting. I remembered Arran as an angry teenager. The rest of it was a mystery I needed to lie my way out of. "Sure, huge guy, worked the door. What of him?"

He sat back and lifted his gaze to the ceiling. "Because you're full of shit. Tyler was right."

And now he'd caught me lying. I shifted uncomfortably, waiting for the judgement he was about to give. This was over. He was done with me. And rightly so.

On my lap, the damn cat purred, reading the room all wrong.

Arran's heavy focus landed back on me, full of exasperation. Not hate. Not loathing. "Big Al doesn't exist, nor does that club. You have amnesia, don't you?"

Oh fuck.

It hit like a punch. The falsehood, the failing memory, the fact I'd come here hoping to fake it through. I wasn't a ghost, I was a copy of a man everyone else remembered, except me.

I tried and failed to form an answer.

In all my preparation, I'd expected to blag my way through our shared history. I didn't want him to know what was wrong with me. In the same heartbeat, I was so damn relieved I had to pass a hand across my face to hide my emotion.

Arran stood and crossed to sit on the sofa next to me. He shoved my hand away from my face then tilted my jaw so he could see my scar. Lightly, he touched the edge of it.

"Is that cracked skull healed?"

"Mostly."

"Yet you can't remember anything?"

"It's coming back. Just slower than I'd like."

He swore again. "I'm to blame for what happened to you. You were undercover on my orders and because I was so fucked up that I was taking out my anger on one of the closest people to me. You were six months out of jail. I should've been more careful with you."

Six months. "What did I do to land the prison time?" There was no point pretending. At last, I could ask about myself and get real answers. Relief sank my shoulders. The cat purred louder.

"That time? Assault. You're handy with your fists. You got three years. They made you serve two. Is all of that a blank?"

I managed a small nod. "So what's my problem? Am I reckless or just really bad at not getting caught?"

Arran twisted his lips to one side. "Reckless is one word. I'd use relentless. I've known you for over a decade, and you haven't changed. When you have a task, you do anything to see it through. Nothing stops you. That tunnel vision carries the risk of not giving a fuck about the cops. A last-man-standing kind of deal."

"I'm boneheaded."

He shook his head. "You're loyal and determined."

"Am I?" I stared at him. "Because I can't handle the thought that I let you down. That I let my crew down. I know from Dixie that I entered the game against your orders. I earned your anger, and rightly so. What I don't know is the second part of it. Dixie told me I'd done something else except she didn't have the details. Can you tell me?"

Arran stood and crossed to the kitchen. From a shelf, he took glasses and a whisky bottle. He poured two shots and returned, handing one to me and staying on his feet.

He tossed his back and grimaced. "First, the game

incident. You broke the rules by going into it, but my reaction was unjustified. It centred on the fact it was Genevieve you hunted. Like you, she wasn't supposed to be in there. I was already fucked up over her, just as I'm even more fucked up over her now we're married. I'd kill for her. At that point in time, I didn't understand it."

"I get it. If anyone touched Mila, I'd find myself in prison again, this time for murder."

He snorted. "That's what Tyler told me. You and she were something, but she entered the game and needed rescuing. I understand the feeling. But back to the first time. After my bad reaction, I pushed you to the edge of the crew and gave you the task of monitoring the Four Milers. Not every part of it went to plan. I discovered you fronting for them and beat the living shit out of you. I didn't take the time to listen or even think about how my friend who'd spent years of his life behind bars was coping. No discussion, no reprieve. I hate myself for that."

I swallowed my drink, relishing the burn. What a fucking mess. "Don't. I no doubt deserved it. Is that when I went undercover?"

He explained how he'd publicly thrown me out of the gang, and fresh flashes of memory came of being snapped up by the Four Milers who'd thought me fair game.

Arran continued. "Know what haunts me? You asked to come home, and I said not yet. You have no idea how badly I've regretted that. I let down one of my oldest friends because of changes in my life I couldn't begin to get to grips with. That's on me, and it won't happen again. When I tell you I'm sorry, I mean it. I'll make it up to you. Whatever you need is yours."

I hadn't expected this. The emotions inside me surged, and I couldn't meet his eye. Only at the cat cuddled up to my chest and giving comfort I barely deserved. Arran wasn't kicking me out. It gutted me to think of the disconnect between us. I'd created that.

"The only thing I want is your friendship back. And maybe a little help remembering who I am."

Arran grasped my hand and pulled me to my feet and into a hard hug that felt so familiar it hurt. Rosie the cat slunk away, her work done.

"Consider it yours. Now, come with me. I want to walk around the club with you so people can see us together. They'll need to know we're both still breathing."

Together, we made our way out of the apartment.

"Any particular reason they're expecting bloodshed?" I asked.

Arran sighed. "After you arrived, I had a barrage of texts from various crew members, all offering encouragement to basically not be a dick."

He called the lift, and I lightly barged his shoulder with mine.

"What if we come out swinging? Give them something to stare at?"

He gave me an indulgent look. "This is why I love you. You have every right to despise me, yet here you are, your usual self."

"Love you, too, brother. That's one thing I never forgot."

We travelled down in the lift. At the ground floor, Arran slung a casual arm around my neck. I shoved him off me, grinning. Multiple people in skeleton crew t-shirts or the pink-and-black strip club uniform openly gawked then busied themselves at their tasks, stealing glimpses and poking others to take in the show.

At the entrance to the office, Shade and Tyler swapped a clearly relieved glance.

Arran gave a short laugh. "Put away the knives. We're good."

Shade cocked his head. "I was going with a straitjacket, actually."

Tyler's gaze stuck on me. "Why didn't you tell us?"

He meant my memory. No use hedging around it now. "And appear more of a fuck-up? No, thanks. Listen, if you're sticking around, I'll find you later with Mila."

Tyler nodded. "I'll be here."

Arran turned our steps to the nightclub. "You seem tight with Mila."

"We are."

"The game does that. I'm glad for you. You know, you were around when I originally came up with the concept. You had suggestions for others. If you still want to try them, have at it."

I hiked up my eyebrows. I enjoyed playing games with Mila. Looked like that was something I'd carried over from my past life. "Do you remember any of my ideas?"

"Sorry. Hopefully they'll come back as your memory returns. Seeing a doc for that, by the way?"

"I'm over hospitals. Not being dramatic, but I'm only going inside one again if I'm dead. Again."

We entered the club, the wall of sound stealing our conversation. At the steps to the VIP area, a bouncer in a black skeleton crew t-shirt hurried to unclip the rope and make way for us to climb to the next level. There, an exclusive bar and dance floor spread out with black-and-silver private booths to one side, club skull logos glowing in neon pink, and the noise level not so overpowering.

Instantly, I spotted Mila. She had her head close to Cassie's and Lovelyn's as the latter said something that had them laughing. Genevieve made up the fourth in their party. Fair hair, coffee cocktail on the table, I knew her straight away. Hated the pain that came with that memory.

I touched Arran's arm then gestured to his woman. I

needed to make amends. His lips flattened, but he nodded understanding.

On our approach, the four women glanced up, and the crew watching over them, Manny and Riordan, slunk back into the shadows. Mila eased out of the booth and came to me, melting into my arms like it was the most natural place for her to be. Her gaze took in mine, and she visibly relaxed at whatever she could see. I kissed her forehead in reassurance. Her fingers twisted in my shirt at the small of my back.

Damn if I loved having someone to hold on to.

Genevieve joined Arran, the same worried expression in her eyes.

I formed a polite smile for the woman I'd hurt. "Congratulations on the wedding. I'm sorry I missed it."

Genevieve tilted her head. At her throat, a jewelled choker sparkled. If I knew Arran, and I was starting to, that diamond band was bulletproof.

"I'm sorry you did, too. Can we talk for a moment?"

She directed me away a few feet. "I'm so glad to see you back. When we heard about you, I thought Arran was going to break down. He nearly did. A lot of what happened to you was because of me."

"You didn't do anything."

"He was trying to protect me. I feel guilt over it."

"If one more person apologises to me, I might quit the crew just to get some peace."

This made her laugh. "Okay. Friends, then?"

She stuck her hand out, and I shook it.

This evening felt like a reprieve. I could've lost everything yet I hadn't. I returned to Mila and walked her backwards to the silver barrier which overlooked the dance floor below. I stole a kiss, then another, and pressed her body to mine. A decision lodged inside me.

I'd wanted my position in my crew so badly it had overtaken how much I wanted her. Now that was settled, the need to keep Mila became my solitary goal.

She returned my kiss with an energy that matched mine. Publicly, barely decently, and hot as fuck. If it was fake, I didn't care.

I tore my lips from hers to speak in her ear. "Don't hate me."

"I don't."

"My job is secure. I can offer stability."

A line formed between Mila's eyebrows. "I wasn't going to leave you if tonight had a different outcome."

I clung to those words. Turned them over in my head. Then I laughed. "Holy shit. You like me."

She tried to pull away. "Stop."

"You do, though. For more than just my dick."

Mila batted at me, but I dove in and stole another soul-searching kiss, earning the same heat in return.

Maybe somewhere in that, I had options.

Arran had told me I'd dreamed up my own games. With Mila at the centre of them, if I fucked her and loved her enough, maybe, just maybe, I could make her fall for me in return. That was the point of spending thirty days together.

Arran had also warned me that I was relentless when it came to doing what needed to be done.

Mila wasn't just the prize. She was the whole damn playing field. And I was done playing by anyone else's rules.

27

Dixie

Reflected in my mirror in the brothel's dressing room, naked women crossed the space, but I stared at myself. Checked out my mostly see-through white bikini and the gauzy wrap I'd draped over my shoulders.

A gift, ready to be unwrapped.

As if they could sense my tension, the other girls were quiet, with only murmurs of conversation and shared glances. They worried about me, I knew that. I might not have been here the longest but I'd mentored many in our craft.

Where usually I'd be making suggestions for outfits and makeup, or in how to fuck a particular client to get him to come quicker, I was all up in my own head.

Tonight, I was back on the floor. I'd toyed with the idea of making myself available to just a few clients, but instead, I was going to walk out into the receiving room and have someone pick me. That's what I needed. For a new client to choose me above any of the other girls. That way, I'd know I still had a career in sex work.

I blew out a breath, straightened my tits in my bra, and left my station.

My hands shook on the short walk, but the sounds of the receiving room swallowed me whole, helping with its distraction. It was a busy night, and women draped over the furniture and groups clustered at the bar. Men waited for their friends or were deciding on who they wanted to take to a private room.

Act, bitch. I strutted, muscle memory giving me the pose, and all too aware of how many pairs of eyes locked on to me. This was my arena. Out here, I ruled.

Even if tonight I was the queen of delulu land.

A group of three men caught my attention. Even if my body wasn't in the zone, my business sense pinged for what I could charge them. Three on one. Three times the money for only a little longer, as one coming usually skipped to the good part for the others.

But it wasn't that which pressed my buttons. It was the girl they'd surrounded. Polly claimed to be twenty. If she was, I was the Virgin Mary. Girl was a lost lamb who'd wandered into the deep dark woods.

Or the wrong pool maybe, as they were sharks circling prey.

Not one of them had even a hint of kindness in his stare.

Smiling for them, I ignored how my skin crawled and beckoned, stealing them away from Polly in a way that had always been easy for me. A look. A promise in my eyes. Polly's fair eyebrows dove together, but I couldn't spare her any mind. In the past, I'd taken tougher clients from gentler girls and I'd do it again.

The men approached at a saunter. Their leader, a thirtysomething in a sharp suit, ran his critical gaze over me. With my shoulders back to present my tits, I tilted my head rather than lifting my chin so my almost invisible bandage didn't show.

"Available?" His tone was flat.

"Sure am. Going solo or did you want your boys in the room?"

Without acknowledging the others, he smiled without any emotion touching his eyes. "All of us together. If you can handle it."

This was a work outing, I was certain. A large portion of our clientele was made up of men on nights out with colleagues. They'd hit the bars for drinks, call the wives and kids to say goodnight and that they were heading to bed, then find their way to our club. I knew because they'd brag about it.

These boys were no exception. No doubt they were repeat customers. No one made it up here without membership. One of them leaned in to whisper to the leader, his gaze glued to the apex of my thighs.

I faked a provocative smile and twirled my finger in the air. "Follow this ass, honey."

I strutted down the darkened hall, heading for an available room, a low, rhythmic beat from hidden speakers marking my pace. Further on was the sex club where people openly went at it with partners or sex workers, or watched others in the act. Down there, anything went between consenting adults.

But up here, a closed door hid us from prying eyes.

At an open doorway, I stopped and gestured for my group then closed us into the space. I gave them the usual speech and pointed out where they needed to make payment, keeping my voice low and my moves provocative.

Something felt off with the vibe in the room, but I pushed on with it.

The leader paid with a tap of his card. "Get your clothes off."

He didn't even look at me as he spoke, shrugging off his jacket to hang it by the door. I didn't care. I was mostly naked anyway. Seducing a man with a strip show was second nature, and I arched my back then rolled my hips with my fingers twisting into the straps of my bikini bottoms.

"Fucking faster," the leader snapped.

That, I wasn't a fan of. I slipped the bikini off and tossed it, trying to keep my feelings off my face. Not easy when I was out of practice.

He ran his tongue over his teeth then flashed a look at his boys. "Hold the slut for me."

In the centre of the room, the others took my arms. Fear trickled through me. *No*, I told myself. It was fine. Groups often did this kind of shit. Impress each other with holding down a woman. Usually, I'd get the read on them first and lay down the ground rules.

"So we're doing role play—"

The leader cut me off. "Shut the fuck up. I chose you for your body, not your mouth."

His friend to the right of me brayed, gripping my wrist at the small of my back. "I can think of a few uses for her mouth that'll keep her quiet."

The two support guys whooped it up, laughing. They were drunk. More than I'd guessed.

The leader poked his tongue into his cheek and stepped up close. His hands landed on my breasts, and he squeezed, crowding into me so I felt his unimpressive erection.

That frisson of panic returned, and I dropped his gaze. I didn't like this. What had once been natural had changed. I wasn't in control of this encounter. At some point, I'd lost it, and I hadn't noticed early enough.

"She's scared of us." The leader gripped my chin, his eyes icy cold. "You should be, bitch. Whores like you take what we pay for. You'll earn your money tonight. Fuck knows I paid enough for your tight ass."

I didn't want this. My mind screamed at me to back out. There were panic buttons around the room, under the edge of the sofa and in hidden recesses. Easy to reach if you lurched for them. We also had cameras and the ability for security to listen in. The problem with that was interpreting role play from reality, but there were signs I could give. Repeated glances at the camera would bring someone running.

I slammed down on my wayward thoughts. If I couldn't do this with these specimens of mankind, I had no job here. I'd failed at what Cassie wanted me to do. I couldn't fail at this.

"Of course I'm scared. You're all so big," I faked a timid tone. "I don't know how I'll—"

"I said shut up. I don't want to hear you. Lay her out. Maybe I'll let one of you use her mouth while I ruin her cunt."

His friend to my right crowed. "Yeah, Sullivan. Get in there."

Sullivan's fingers went to the buttons of his shirt while his friends towed me backwards to the bed, holding me down. But when he moved into position, his purple-headed mushroom dick in his hand, the guy hadn't suited up.

"Condoms are on the shelf," I reminded him.

"Why, how diseased are you?"

He smiled. I didn't.

"Gotta use one."

"The fuck I do. This club doesn't hire dirty whores. We asked. So why should I pay for half the experience?"

He fisted his cock. I struggled against his friends, rising panic taking me from my place of no control to another time when I'd been in the same position. A long time ago, but the memories rushed fast. "Stop."

Sullivan ignored me and grasped my ankle, his fingers digging into my flesh. His friend held my neck, preventing me from angling my head to the camera.

He was going to rape me.

I couldn't stop them.

"What the fuck is that on your throat?" The friend released his grip on my neck like it was radioactive.

Sullivan reached out. Before I could flinch, he ripped the slim bandage from my skin. "Fucking hell. Look at that scar."

One of the men gripped my chin to extend my neck, peering even more closely. Disgust came quickly. Real, visceral revulsion.

I curled in on myself, horrified.

They inched away.

"Nah, man. I'm not sticking my cock in that. There's something wrong with her."

The leader shook his head. His erection wilted. Poor baby. No refunds for being a walking red flag.

"What the fuck are they trying here, pushing off damaged goods on us. I'm not paying for a fucking charity case."

I twisted away and pressed my fingers over the scar. Yet I couldn't find my words. Not a single one to tell them they were assholes.

Sullivan made it easy on me. "Get out. Send someone in who isn't ruined."

Naked, humiliated, and horribly close to tears, I opened the door and fled.

Dressing and packing my clothes in my room on the cam girls' floor happened in a dream. People spoke to me, I didn't answer. Nor could I reply to the single message I sent security, telling them to kick the guys out.

All I knew was that I had to go. I'd tried, I'd taken on new clients, and I'd lost. I'd *failed*. There was nothing for me here now.

I didn't just lose a job. I lost the last piece of who I used to be. The girl who could handle anything. Turned out, she bled out on that boathouse floor, and I was too slow to bury her.

In the reaches of my mind, I recognised how triggered I'd become, and how my trauma had mixed in with the guys' shitty words, but it was only when I reached the ground floor of the warehouse that my hold on my emotions cracked.

I'd intended to sneak out of the back, but Lovelyn was in the corridor. Her face fell when she saw me.

I really liked this girl. We hadn't known each other long—she'd only been on the scene working with Arran for a few months. She gave off sweetheart vibes, from her name down to the flower prints she always seemed to wear. Maybe it was the computer help she'd given me, or the fact that since my injury, she'd never poked her nose into my business. Just accepted me for what I was. Either way, one caring glance from her nearly had me bawling.

She swooped in on me with a hug. "What happened?"

I couldn't speak. I just shook my head.

Lovelyn peered at my face, concern written all over hers. "I can see you're upset. Whoever did that needs a stern talking-to. Should I fetch Arran or Shade?"

I shook my head sorrowfully.

"Is there anything I can do?"

Tears clogged my throat even more. "Talk at me?"

"Okay, if you're not ready to speak, I'll babble until you are."

I gave a tearful laugh, and Lovelyn continued.

"I made a new friend tonight. Someone I think you'll like. You know Convict? It's his woman. I was going to say girlfriend, but I know the game they operate here and how they don't like that term. Claimed woman? I don't know. Anyway, she's lovely. Her name is Emilia Marchant."

Marchant. No, oh hell no. My heart iced over.

I hadn't heard that name in a long time. I actively avoided reference to that family. I'd blocked out every memory.

"Emilia Marchant is Convict's girl?" The words were ashes in my mouth.

Lovelyn nodded, the concern in her eyes growing.

Further down the corridor, a door swung open, and Tyler emerged with another man behind. I could barely focus on how huge, beautiful Tyler instantly locked on me, or the fact the second guy wore fury that simmered.

In another life, Tyler could have been mine. Never in this one.

He still looked at me like I was his. That's what made it worse.

Folding Lovelyn into one last hug, I squeezed her hands, whispered my goodbye, then fled.

"Dixie, wait," she called.

I disappeared into the dark night.

It was better for everyone this way.

28

Mila

The throbbing club beat sank through my body, and on the dance floor, Convict moved against me, his mouth on mine. He was okay with his friends. The relief it gave me was bigger than it should've been.

Possibly because I was a little drunk.

When I'd sat down at the booth with Cassie, Lovelyn, and Genevieve, a round of Espresso martini cocktails had magically appeared. I'd knocked mine back in a few gulps, then welcomed a second. I rarely drank so was a lightweight. The alcohol loosened me up nicely.

Convict put his mouth to my ear. "As much as I want to bend you over that rail and fuck you for all the club to see, there are better places to do that. Can I show you the rest of the warehouse? Maybe reward you for your unspoken confession somewhere along the way?"

Need surged in me, and I nodded. He caught my hand and led me out of the VIP area. I waved goodbye to the women to follow him out of the nightclub and through a corridor, a padded door opening into a darkened hallway with private rooms either side.

My heels sank into the plush carpet. Even the walls were velvet. This was part of the strip club, I guessed, though I wasn't tempted to peer into any of the rooms.

I squeezed Convict's hand. "Are those rooms used for... extras?"

"Men who aren't brave enough to go up to the brothel? Yep."

We emerged into a wide club with a busy bar and booths and seats facing a stage that extended out onto a catwalk.

Every seat was filled, almost exclusively with men. On the lit-up stage, barely dressed women performed, one either side of the main stage and a third at the end of the catwalk that split the room. All of them were knockout beautiful with bodies that had me staring.

When I glanced up at Convict, his gaze was on me.

"Many of the lasses who work here only dance. They make decent money from stripping, and that's enough for them."

I watched the nearest woman slide to the catwalk floor with a sexy bump that had the nearby men drooling.

The music changed to 'Just Keep Watching' by Tate McRae, the sultry beat indicating a switch up of the performance. The three dancers strutted off the stage, and the lights dimmed further.

Convict pressed a kiss to the side of my cheek. "Want to watch?"

I pulled his arms around me, not budging. At least for a minute, we could stay, just to satisfy my curiosity about the club. Plus there was an energy in the room I wanted to follow. An expectation of what was coming.

A new woman crossed the stage from the wings, whoops and hollers from the crowd marking her appearance. All eyes were on her, and with good reason. From the six-inch heels of her thigh-high boots up to her cascade of dark hair, she was captivating. Her breasts overspilled a silver bodysuit which played peekaboo with the curves of her ass, and long gloves covered her arms.

On her saunter down the stage, she perused the avid audience like she was stalking prey, ensuring she had everyone's attention locked on. She had nothing to worry about. The men were caught on every roll of her perfect hips.

At the end of the catwalk was a pole. The dancer circled it, her fingers trailing on the gleaming metal. Then at the beat, she gripped the pole and lifted herself effortlessly, spinning high in the air until she flipped upside down, one slow arm at a time peeling off the bodysuit to reveal glittering black lingerie and skin laced with ink.

Holy hell, that was impressive.

Convict didn't look at her. While his fingers slid over my sides and caressed my waist, grazing under my breasts, his focus stayed on me. Steady and hungry, like my reaction was part of the show. And God, I reacted. When she dropped into the splits and rolled her hips on the floor, I nearly whimpered.

His other hand eased under my dress from behind. He was close enough to me that anyone nearby wouldn't get an eyeful, but my heart hammered.

Even as I inched my legs apart.

"Are you playing a game with me?" I whispered.

"Always, little gangster. I like you crazy."

The dancer crawled across the stage, the crowd clamouring to get closer with their fistfuls of cash. Convict ghosted his fingers over my thigh then up to my ass, a light touch over my skin.

His breath ghosted over my ear. "The dancers sell an illusion. A tease that they are available and down to fuck. They allow access to parts of themselves that are otherwise tightly controlled and hook in the weak-minded men who think it's just for them."

A chair appeared. The dancer straddled it backwards, knees wide, chest arched high. She unhooked her bra with a teasing slowness. It hit the floor. She cupped her heavy breasts, shameless, confident, beautiful.

I was overheating. I didn't know if it was the dancer, or the smirk curving Convict's mouth when I peeked back, but I was wet and flustered.

"I could never do it," I confessed. "I mean, I don't have the body for it—"

"Yes, you do. They'd be lucky to watch you. Then unlucky as I'd burn their fucking eyes out for daring to see what's mine."

My heart thumped harder. If he touched me now, I'd melt for him right here in the shadows of the strip club.

I arched up to speak into his ear. "Can we go upstairs?"

A spark of mischief shone in his eyes. Convict led me to a lift and hit the button for the third floor.

Third, not fifth and the cam girls' floor. "We're not going to your room?"

"We aren't done with the tour yet."

We emerged halfway along a corridor, and he tipped his head to the right.

"Down there is the sex club. You say you couldn't strip, but a lot of the people in this building have already seen you mostly naked and got off to the image."

Heat painted my cheeks. "I'm aware."

He watched my reaction then gestured to a series of doors either side of us. "We can give them another show, or we can pick any one of these private rooms. Just tell me what you need."

Either his challenge or the martinis bolstered me. I linked my fingers through his and drew him in the direction of the club. Turning a corner revealed a big room, painted black and with neon-pink low lights. The beat in the air mimicked my fast pulse.

In here, all pretence of civility had gone.

Three gold cages hung from the rafters, each holding

a naked woman or man engaged in some kind of physical act. Then there were sofas, tables, and stations with people sprawled across them. Bare breasts, bodies, hands everywhere.

They were having sex. Openly, and with an audience of at least a couple of hundred people around the wide-open space.

On a padded mat beneath a wall apparatus, a man pulled a chained and blindfolded woman down onto his waiting cock, his head tipped back in ecstasy. Standing over him, another guy fed his dick into her mouth.

A muscular blond man tied an older man onto a stand-up cross, both of them completely naked and hard, then picked up a sex toy from a table.

I didn't know where to look first. Or when to stop staring. I turned into Convict's embrace and hid my eyes.

"Too much?" he asked.

"I... I don't know."

He took something from his pocket then brushed back my hair. Material landed over my eyes, and I touched my face to the blindfold he tied on.

"You make good use of the skeleton bandannas I always carry. Listen up. I know this place is a lot to take in. I also know you're wound up so tight that if I touch you, you're going to come so hard. So tell me, should I take you home, or do you want to play?"

Need laced his tone. I squirmed on the spot.

"Tell me what you want," I asked.

"To find the nearest open place and fuck you in it. People will see. I won't let anyone touch you."

The thrill that had been building under my skin cascaded through me in an electric rush. I reached for him, but he caught my hands and linked them at the small of my back.

"Choose, Mila."

"Here."

"Good girl."

He guided me deeper into the club, through the sounds of people fucking. Moans and gasps passed us, people coming or getting close, others encouraging them. Then we stopped.

A dizzying rush of hyperawareness chased my need as I waited to be touched. Anyone could be watching me. After so many years of playing the perfect granddaughter, I couldn't have done this without the blindfold. I didn't kid myself that it truly disguised me, but it stopped me from seeing others, and somehow that made it okay.

Convict stroked into my hairline at the back of my neck and angled my head to receive his kiss. "Hold the bar."

He brought my hands down to a waist-height padded barrier. Then he wrenched at the front of my dress so my breasts spilled free. I gasped in shock, but it soon turned into a moan when his hands and mouth played and sucked. He teased my nipples until both hardened, then kissed my lips again.

"How does it feel to know every man and woman in this room is staring at your perfect tits, Mila?"

I shook my head, unable to answer. I didn't even try to imagine myself, bare boobs out and my strapless dress around my waist.

"They wish they could get their hands on you. Should I let them?"

"No!"

"Damn right."

With gentle pressure, Convict guided me to bend forward then shifted something over me. It clicked beside my head, and I flexed against a restraining bar, locked over my hands and neck.

I was in the stocks, a frame with a gap for head and hands. I was otherwise trapped and entirely at the mercy of whoever wanted to touch me.

Blindfolded, I'd never know.

Convict's satisfied laugh told me he was behind me. Slowly, he inched the hem of my dress up over my backside. "I hope you aren't attached to this underwear."

He snapped the straps then kicked my feet apart. Cool air touched me between my thighs, and I gripped the padded bar, loving and hating the fact I couldn't see in equal measures. But I could feel and I could hear. The rustle of his clothing. The graze of his touch over my bare cheeks.

I waited for humiliation to creep in. It didn't. Only a growing need for him to fuck me.

He didn't keep me waiting to start playing. Yet the first touch to my core wasn't his dick. It was his tongue. With his fingers, he spread me open and lapped me from behind, his hot tongue sliding into me.

I made an ungodly sound of pleasure and backed into the touch, though the stocks restricted my movement. Convict rumbled approval against my body and thrust his tongue again, pressing on somewhere inside me that caused a gush of wetness.

"Can't believe I haven't done this until now," he groaned.

While he ate me out, he toyed with my clit, and I whimpered, so wound up from the events of the night. The strip show, the way he'd kissed me when he came back from his meeting, the visual of people having sex around us, and my exposure.

He gave me no peace. Each lick and suck perfectly timed to drive me insane. So much I could hardly bear it.

"I need you," I begged.

"Then have me. I was going to play for longer but I can't resist." Lifting, he slid his dick over me then thrust inside.

I cried out and went up on my tiptoes, full and alive. He eased out then bucked again, going in deep.

His taunting words stopped. He was so thick and hard, he had to be going as crazy as I felt. Convict bent over me and reached for my clit, his thrusts never stopping.

My whole world centred on the way he fucked me. Publicly, relentlessly, and making his ownership clear. Maybe I liked being seen. Not by them. By him. Maybe I needed this to believe I was more than a means to an end.

My body knew his like it had been waiting for him. Crowd or no crowd, I just needed more. Of everything. More of the way he stretched me. More of his sounds of pleasure and how he used me hard and rough.

Desire spiked, and I cried out.

The man between my thighs kept his pace exact. He didn't speed up or slow down. Just the same demanding pressure until my knees shook and I was unable to control my moans.

"Mine," Convict gritted out.

Was he telling me or an audience watching us? The possession blew through my last tendril of reserve.

Through ragged breaths, I came hard, gripping the bar then draping over it, endless waves of pleasure following my spasms.

Nothing felt as good as what he did to me. It permeated every cell until all I knew was deep satisfaction.

Convict growled then held my hips to fuck me harder. Now I'd come, he needed to get there as well.

"Let me fuck her mouth," someone said.

"Try it and I'll slice off your balls," Convict snarled.

I surged at his protective words, backing into him as much as I could in my restraints. Something in the knowledge that he'd hurt others to protect me lit up my brain like he was doing to my insides.

In a minute, I was wound up and on the edge of another climax.

I tightened around him, and Convict jacked into me a few more times then came, holding his dick deep inside while he throbbed. A new rush of sensation filled me, spilling over into another mind-blowing orgasm. The lack of a barrier between us pushed me over the edge. I cried out and shook.

Then reality kicked in. This had been shocking and fast, even if my buildup was slow. We were messy. People would be watching.

I shivered and tried to stand, but the stocks prevented it.

Soft words reassured me. "Hold on, baby."

Convict unlocked the bar, straightened my clothes, and lifted me into his arms. He carried me across the club, and I tucked my head against his chest and blocked out everything but the strong beat of his heart.

In a room, he locked the door then put me on a counter and eased up my blindfold.

I blinked in the bright light. We were in a bathroom. Oh shit, and my breasts were still out of my dress. I flushed hot and wrestled them back in place. Standing between my legs, Convict caught my chin and kissed me.

My embarrassment faded. I adored his kisses. I was such an addict for him.

One last lingering peck had him inching back to regard my face. "The image of you spread out for me like that is never leaving my brain. You are perfect."

My pussy leaked more cum. I pointed to the door. "Out."

His eyebrows dove together, adorably quizzical.

I flapped a hand. "I need to clean up."

A devilish smirk spread over his face. Convict hooked

under my legs and tugged me to rest against the mirror at the back of the wide marble counter. He drove two fingers inside me, and all reason fled my brain. I set my heels to the counter edge, bucking into his touch.

"What if I clean you up with my mouth?"

I didn't get a chance to answer, as his lips were parting my lower ones and he licked me then sucked on my clit like he hadn't just destroyed me in his sex club. He slowly thrust his fingers in and out of me, adding a third that had me panting.

Shamelessly, I linked my ankles behind his neck to keep him close. I didn't dare look at him, though. That would be too much. It was far easier to just feel everything he did to me.

Convict worked me until he'd kindled that heat all over again, then he sent me over the edge with a growl of pleasure at how quickly I fell.

I breathed through a spinning mind, not all that much cleaner but a whole lot more relaxed.

He kissed my thigh. "I want you to wear my cum when we go back downstairs."

"I don't have any underwear. What if we see people?"

"Then they'll understand your wet thighs and blissed-out expression. Everyone is expecting this. They'll welcome the sight of a claimed couple getting down and dirty at every opportunity."

I glowered at him and grabbed a handful of paper towels from a dispenser then wiped myself partially clean. "I'll play your game and meet you fifty-fifty but I'm not dripping all the way home."

He smirked. "Bargaining with me. Wouldn't have you any other way."

Then his mouth was back on mine, and it took long minutes until we left the room and the club behind us. I didn't dare make eye contact with anyone.

We travelled back down in the lift, Convict's eyes flaring when I adjusted my hem to ensure I was covered. The lack of underwear felt more exposing out here than being half-naked in the club.

The doors opened on the main ground floor corridor, and Convict directed me to the office.

"I asked Tyler for a catch-up."

"I'll be sure to sit with my legs crossed," I grouched, but my heart rate picked up again and for a different reason.

Convict's side of our deal had neatly taken the burden of finding Jacobs off my shoulders. The worry about it had never left me, though. Not with dozens of messages from hard-up relatives and the fact my grandmother still hadn't called.

Yet it was tempered by another fact.

Convict told me he'd stay with me and he had. He assured me no one else would touch me when I was vulnerable and he'd delivered. I trusted my lost boy. Not just to help me but in everything he said. That was a startling and happy realisation. One I let myself accept.

29

Convict

Behind the huge desk, and with a bandanna around his throat, Tyler waited for us to settle. I fixed the bright light so it wasn't in my eyes and collected Mila's hand in mine then gave it a squeeze.

"Do you have news?" she asked.

Tyler's gaze carried a weight. He had something to say, and I suspected it wasn't good.

"Jacobs is still missing. If he went home after the game, he hasn't come or gone since, or switched the lights on at night. Nor is he at his workplace, which is a single rented office in a municipal block where no one can tell us anything. He also isn't staying with the woman he was known to be dating. According to her, they were never a true couple and he'd stopped returning her calls weeks ago. We can't find that he had any family, and there's no one checking on his place. He's a loner."

Mila's exhale told me of her disappointment.

I grumbled. "I assume you have cameras up all over?"

"I installed them myself. Here."

He handed over a tablet displaying an array of CCTV panels. I passed it to Mila, and she tapped through the different views of Jacobs's house and his office building, lingering on the view of the front of his property.

"I've been to this house numerous times since seeing

him at my grandfather's funeral. He never once came to the door, even when there was a car outside. It isn't there now."

Tyler nodded. "I have an alert set up for it, so if it's picked up on a numberplate camera, we'll know. Our guess that he's in some kind of trouble makes me assume he's done a runner. He failed in his strategy to gain skeleton crew protection so he moved on to another option, a secondary plan he'd already decided on and utilising a route without cameras so he can't be traced."

"Suggesting not a major motorway," I observed. "Maybe a boat, or a taxi to an airport. Do we have any clues on the shite he found himself in?"

Tyler drummed his fingers on the desk. "Not directly. On the surface, he's a finance guy, so it's possible he lent or borrowed money from the wrong people. I'm checking any gang affiliation, but my gut feel is it's to do with his more secretive trade in the flesh market. Which puts him squarely on my radar, especially if he's caused problems. If there's upheaval among the established traffickers, that's an opportunity I won't overlook."

Mila's eyes rounded. "Wait. How did we get from the auctions he ran to people trafficking?"

"Hard to imagine that once he'd made money from willing victims, he'd ignore the cash from the darkest side of the marketplace, particularly when coupled with everything we've found out about him since."

She shivered, and I slipped an arm around her, picking up on the same thoughts I guessed she was having. She'd walked into that arena and skirted a potentially devastating situation.

"I hate the fact I was closing in on him but couldn't find anything out, but at the same point horrified at how close I came to disappearing into that hell he's involved with. But what could he possibly be doing with my grandmother?" she wondered.

Tyler's eyes darkened, but Mila's mind was clearly racing ahead.

She exhaled an unhappy laugh. "I'm working it out. We have ships. Established routes in and out of the country. My grandfather did trade throughout Europe, the Americas, and even further afield. Is that what Jacobs is after? A shipping route he can use for trafficking now my grandfather isn't there to protect the business? But then why abandon it and run scared?"

"We'll know more when we find him. But there's something else we need to talk about. Something that happened closer to home."

Her gaze had distanced, and she shook her head, appearing lost in her thoughts. "It must be to do with Salter. Perhaps he's a middleman in this."

Tyler's focus came to me. "Regarding Salter, did you read my message from earlier?"

I drew my eyebrows in and fished out my phone. A message waited, informing me that he'd made a job offer to an interesting individual.

I curled my lip. "Odd choice, but you said you needed boots on the ground."

"Exactly. He has the skills and is available to hire. But if it will cause you any problems, I'll back out."

I shrugged. "No problems here. Do what you need."

Tyler wrote out a quick message. Almost immediately, a knock came at the door, and Tyler called out for the person to enter.

Kane strolled into the room.

Mila's attention snapped up, and she stared at her brother. "What are you doing here?"

His serious expression didn't shift. "Never left."

"You... They kept you here?" At his nod, she whirled

around to me. "Did you know about this?"

"Of course. He's an unknown quantity. We were hardly going to let him walk out the door."

Outrage crossed her features. Mila snatched her hand from mine, an expression of betrayal replacing her shock. She stifled it and regarded Kane. "Did they hurt you?"

"No. I accepted their need to manage a threat and I was treated fine."

"But locked up?"

His jaw flexed. "I said I'm fine. If I wasn't, I'd never have agreed to a temporary contract with your crew."

She scoffed. "My crew. You're in voluntarily? They aren't making you?"

Kane shook his head once. "I don't do anything I don't want to. Hunting down those who captured me will be a piece of cake."

"You're going after Salter?" Mila confirmed.

Kane agreed. "There's something else you need to know."

She swallowed whatever retort she wanted to give. And she wouldn't meet my eye. She was angry at me. I didn't get it, but worry tightened my gut.

Tyler took over. "The woman who arranged your access to the auction was found dead this evening."

Oh shit. Of all the information he could've given, I hadn't expected that.

The colour drained from Mila's face. "Esther's dead?"

He nodded. "I'm sorry if she was a friend of yours."

She tried and failed to start a sentence, then managed, "How did she die?"

"She was discovered in Deadwater Harbour. Drowned."

Tyler told us what else he knew, which was only the very basics, and promised more when he had it. We filtered outside, Kane coming with us.

In the corridor, Mila stepped closer to him. "Seriously, if you're doing this for me, don't bother."

"I'm not. It was my choice. I saw an opportunity with your boyfriend's people. Probably with more sense than you did."

Irritation rose in me. "Watch your mouth."

Kane shrugged. "Calling it as I see it."

I got in his face. I was a big guy, but he was fucking huge, yet that intimidated me none. "At least in part, I blame you for Mila going into that auction. You're her brother. What the fuck were you thinking?"

"I don't coddle anyone. Emilia isn't a kid. She said she knew what she was doing, and I played the role she asked."

"And if she got hurt?"

"All she had to do was pull her last name card and she'd walk. Her grandfather's reputation would save her."

"Except it didn't, right? Meanwhile, you were all too happy to throw her to the wolves. Why? To keep the money rolling in like all the other relatives harassing her?"

He looked past me to Mila. "How much do you like this guy, because he's starting to piss me off."

Mila's tone was tight. "Kane never took the money. It goes elsewhere in his part of the family."

Her brother held his steady gaze on me. I got the sense that if I punched him, it would be like hitting a wall of solid rock.

"Not that it's any of your business, lover boy. We might be colleagues, but I don't have to like you." He slanted a final glance at his sister. "I've got work to do. See you around."

He strolled away as casually as he'd appeared, and Mila watched him go. I reached for her hand, but she pulled away.

"I want to go home."

Heaving a sigh, I followed her out of the warehouse and to the car then got us on the road.

The frostiness from the office descended over us like an icy fog. I peeled out of a junction, still confused over her upset.

"Sorry about Esther."

"So am I, but how about my brother? I can't believe you did that."

I exhaled exasperation. "You thought I'd just release him?"

"Yes! Did you think I lied to you about who he was to me? Unbelievable."

"No, I just didn't trust him. The man who'd already thrown you into harm's way and who could do it again."

"He'd spent days as a captive already. Can you imagine how that would've affected him? I asked you to rescue him and you just swapped out his cage."

"Seemed fine to me."

"That's not the point. I'm so... You lied to me," she spluttered.

"How? You never asked about him."

Mila balled her hands into fists on her knees, slices of streetlight cutting over her. "A lie by omission is still a lie. What else are you keeping from me? I can't believe I started to trust you."

My stomach gutted out. Everything was wrong. What I'd done was perfectly reasonable. I didn't understand why she couldn't see that. "Let's make one thing clear. I'll do anything, lie, steal, kill, to keep you and keep you safe. I won't apologise for that."

"Great. Then this conversation is over."

The short drive took us into the underground car park, and inside the apartment, Mila kicked off her shoes.

"It's after midnight. I get my two hours away from you and I'm taking them now. I'm going to bed. Don't follow until you have to."

She disappeared into her bedroom and slammed the door. The sound of running water followed. I trudged to the guest bedroom and showered alone. Then I sat on the floor outside her room, lonely with my thoughts and waiting out the two hours.

If I'd ever been a boyfriend before, which I doubted, I didn't remember it. I had no clue on how to be a good one. Messing with relatives didn't hit.

I'd fucked up.

When my phone buzzed to tell me the time was up, I entered her room and climbed into bed. She slept in full pyjamas, facing away, and with her brow still lined. I curled around her. Mila shifted away from me.

The tight ache in my chest didn't budge even in my sleep.

Nor did it the next afternoon, when Mila got up early and didn't wake me. She spent most of the day on the phone and with her nose buried in her laptop or talking to needy relatives who seemed set on guilt tripping her, and giving me yes or no answers.

A couple of times, I noticed her checking the news, presumably for an update on Esther. From my own cursory check, the story hadn't broken.

I ordered us food. Borrowed a pad and pen and started designing games for the warehouse. I had all kinds of ideas. Dark and twisted ways for people to connect. But that disconnect between Mila and me was a weight on my chest I couldn't shift.

Except in the night when she let me fuck her. She wouldn't meet my eye, but she came so prettily on my tongue and my dick that it gave me something to cling to.

The pattern continued for several days.

Mila could hold a grudge, that was for sure. Luckily, I was a stubborn fuck who could wait her out. It gave me a chance to play a new game with her.

At her laptop, she'd pointedly ignore me. Unless I worked out on the floor and stripped my shirt. If I scrubbed down the kitchen in just my shorts, her gaze would scald my skin.

I'd purposefully catch her staring. Each time I did, I'd win a point. If I got her to sigh, it was five. A hand to her lips, chest, or thighs gave me ten. Then in the night, I'd reward her with her points winning prizes by way of orgasms.

She could be as pissed off as she liked, but that didn't stop me adoring her.

In between my game, I searched through the box of possessions I'd got back from the Linnet Road address, finding no phone or wallet but enough information so I could order a new driver's licence, thank fuck I had one of those, and get a form of ID back.

Arran sent photos of younger versions of us, triggering small flares of memory. Mila listened when I told her, as I never stopped sharing, even if she gave little reply.

At last, near the end of the week, she broke the stand-off.

"I promised some of the family that I would see them face to face. They want me to know how much they're struggling, and I can't say no anymore. Will you drive me?"

"I will do literally anything for you."

She rolled her eyes. "Including scoring points off me. Can we stop with the games?"

"Never."

Her sigh of defeat lit me up as if I'd hit the jackpot.

Over-fucking-joyed to have her attention again, I drove her across the England-Scotland border and up to the small town of Selkirk.

We passed through the pretty town buzzing with shops, and I parked up outside her first set of relatives' place, a big detached house with views across the valley, and with two nice cars outside, a silver Mercedes and a dark-blue BMW.

I whistled. "They're doing well for themselves."

Mila shielded her eyes to regard the house, stiffened her shoulders, and went to the door. She didn't ask me to wait outside, which worked for me as I didn't want her out of my sight.

We were ushered inside by a fifty-something man with greying hair. In the kitchen, his wife received us, her mouth pinched. On the other side of the room, a man about my age played a videogame on a big-screen TV, a girl under his arm. The mother asked him to put on headphones, but he tossed the controller, gave us a dirty look, and the two vanished upstairs.

They were the Marchant-Smythes, Mila had told me. Philip and Phylis. Freaking weird.

The husband and wife tag-teamed in persuading Mila they were hard up with the money no longer coming in from Marchant Haulage. Mila had only introduced me by my real first name and nothing more, and I peered around the place, not minding my own business.

Nice TV, everything clean. On the relatives' countertop were packets of food from a high-end supermarket, presumably left out by the son making himself and his girl a snack. It summoned the image of a home I'd once lived in, black mould growing in the corners of the rooms, the cupboards empty of food and my stomach twisted with hunger. Like fuck were these people in real financial trouble.

Mila listened and reassured, but she cut them off after fifteen minutes and stood. "Like I said, I'm doing all I can. After the will reading, I'll have more answers."

The woman gripped the arms of her chair. "Your grandfather promised security. He died. And now we're all paying the price. You don't understand the stress me and Philip are under. Our worries for Presley. He's our priority, and your grandfather left us high and dry."

Mila's mouth popped open.

"Show some respect," I said for her as she didn't seem able.

The woman pouted. "Or you could respect our suffering."

Mila muttered another platitude then turned and left. Outside, she flung herself into the car.

I gunned the engine. "I take it none of them have jobs? Four adults in that huge house. The heating on in every room and their overgrown kid playing a subscription video game. They aren't suffering. They're just greedy and used to their slice of the pie being handed to them."

If she agreed with me, she didn't say.

I drove us on to the next, an elderly couple who needed carers so had reason to worry about their cashflow, but the last visit was more of the same. A family in a smart house with zero signs of true poverty. Mila's expression got stonier the more they griped.

We set tracks for home.

"Maybe they were just the loudest people, rather than the neediest," she murmured, half to herself.

This time, I didn't give an opinion.

At the outskirts of Deadwater, she spoke. "Can we take a diversion? It isn't far."

I followed her directions to a country lane, gated driveways announcing a series of what had to be very large, very private properties.

"The next on the right," she told me.

I pulled over at a pair of white stone gateposts. For a moment, Mila just stared at them then climbed from the car. At the intercom, she pressed a button.

Nothing happened.

Then she tapped in the code. The light turned red, the gates unmoving. She tried her phone next. No answer.

My heart ached at the slump in her shoulders.

"Your grandparents' place," I guessed.

Through the gates, I glimpsed a huge modern mansion down a tree-lined drive. Holy fuck, but these people were rich. If I thought the relatives lived in luxury, this took the biscuit, the cake, and the whole damn bakery.

The spiked fence protecting the property went deep into the woods, so I guessed security was high. Sure enough, cameras watched us from corners. If her grandmother was here, she didn't want to see anyone.

Without another word, Mila sighed and returned to the car.

When we were back in the apartment, my phone dinged with another photo from Arran, along with an offer. The picture was of me and him, bloodied and shirtless, both grinning. We were in some kind of cellar, like we'd just come out of a fight.

I showed it to Mila. "As of tomorrow, we can spend more than two hours apart."

Her gaze traced over the photo. "Suits me."

Sadness hung over her like a grey cloud. I hated that I'd caused it.

"Arran offered to take me to the place we met, a fight club, to jog my memory and fill in some gaps. You can come, I'd like that, or he says Genevieve and Cassie would love to see you in Divide."

"Option B. Don't get lost on your trip."

I watched her, my heart thumping. "Would it help if I said I'm sorry?"

Mila gave a sorrowful shake of her head and returned to

the desk where she'd been putting in long hours for people I was increasingly sure weren't worth it.

"If I thought you were doing it genuinely, then perhaps, and if you were honest about all you'd done. But you aren't and you haven't been. I can't reward control dressed up as care. You said you'd do anything to keep me. An apology would fall into that category, no?"

It would. Except this time, I didn't want to lie.

As the evening went on, an overwhelming panic rose in me about separating from her. Leaving her and being over an hour away scared the fuck out of me. She'd told me not to get lost, but how would I find her again if she did? If someone grabbed her when I wasn't there to protect her?

Mila wanted honesty from me, and if I gave it, I only had one chance of gaining forgiveness. That meant any further fuck-ups had to happen now.

I locked myself away in the bedroom and made a quick call. "Manny, you know we track phones, is there a way to track people?"

The chief of security chuckled. "Shade's your man for that."

I hung up and dialled the tattooed enforcer, asking the same question.

"You've been together for a week. How has it taken this long to ask?" he griped. "I'll have someone bring you a delivery."

An hour later, a text alerted me to go fetch said delivery from downstairs. I jogged back up and used the code Mila had given me to bypass her door security, 2566, and had the benefit of her stubbornness in not asking what I was up to, even if curiosity ticked over in her gaze.

Later in the night, in our darkened bedroom, after I'd fucked my lass into a heavy sleep, spending all her points for the day, I slipped into the bathroom with the small case I'd been sent and texted Shade to talk me through the process.

Shade: It's already set up. Put it against a fleshy part of her skin and pull the trigger.

Shade: Arse is good.

Convict: Thanks, bro.

Shade: She might not like it once you tell her. Not all lasses do.

Convict: Asking for forgiveness is better than asking for permission, no?

Shade: You're in deep, my friend.

He wasn't wrong. Back in the bedroom, I discarded the phone and readied the gun. Then I slowly inched down the blanket to reveal Mila's perfect backside, her ugly pyjamas lost from when I'd fucked her earlier. Ignoring my dick's eager rise, I held my nerve, pressed the device to her skin, and shot the tracker into her with a low click.

She flinched. I buried the device under my pillow and spread her legs, kneeling between them then rubbing my dick up and down her centre. She relaxed with a sigh that I took to be a welcome.

Thank fuck that even with how she felt about me, we still had this.

Slowly, I pushed inside, breathing hard at my victory then grinning when her internal walls clamped down tight. Perhaps I was wrong in what I did, but if it kept her safe, I'd take her hatred over her getting hurt every time.

She was mine. I'd never lose her again.

30

Mila

My clothes hangers rattled on my leaf through my wardrobe, and I plucked out a dress for the evening. Purple again, with a halterneck, silver studded gems around the neckline, and a floaty short skirt.

I paired it with silver heels then finished my makeup, my stomach tight when I glanced in the tall mirror that still gave me shivers. For the first time in over a week, Convict and I would be apart for hours.

I didn't like it. No matter how I felt about him imprisoning my brother, not that Kane seemed to give a damn in his one-word answers to me since, but Convict didn't get why that was an issue.

Kane was claustrophobic, one of the few things I knew about him that wasn't easily seen. I'd guessed it after seeing how he always drove with the window open, even in the rain, and how he could never sit in a booth at a café. He saw it as a weakness, and I'd never reveal his secret, but I didn't have to. Convict should never have ridden roughshod over my family.

Even with that hanging over us, I still couldn't shake a strange sense of loss and apprehension.

I'd also received another shitty email.

Anonymous: All those boats sitting in the dock. What a legacy you left, Marchant. Fuck you for everything you've done.

Fuck the sender. Tonight, I had my own worries, and they were all shaped like a man I'd obsessed over.

Outside the bedroom, Convict leaned on the opposite wall in the hallway, the grey shirt I liked so much open at his throat and rolled up on his forearms. I stopped and stared, more than a little stuck on how badly I wanted him. Holding back had been an exercise in pain. Every night, he showed me what I was missing, spending hours between my thighs. He never resisted the pull. That was all me.

I let him fuck me and showed him nothing in return.

I didn't recognise my stubbornness. I didn't know how to stop it either.

Convict's gaze travelled up my legs, heat in his eyes along with concern, urgency, and a dozen other emotions. That heavy focus sent a crackle of electricity over my skin, alerting me to the danger he presented.

We'd barely been apart in a week, and now he was leaving on a road trip for hours that suddenly felt like days.

I wanted him so badly I couldn't breathe.

"Fuck it." He shoved off the wall and caught me up in his arms. His mouth landed on mine in a bruising kiss.

I returned it. If he expected me to push away, both of us were failing.

We crashed into a hot and wet attack. Our teeth clashed, but we didn't slow, only built and built into a fever. I wound my legs around his waist, and Convict turned me to the wall and reached between us, cupping me through my underwear.

He didn't speak. No taunting me about how wet I was

already. Nothing but a return of his mouth to mine and the opening of his jeans.

I tucked my head to his shoulder, needing this more than I could say. He freed his dick then pulled my lacy underwear aside and pushed inside.

I gasped open-mouthed.

Without any kind of foreplay besides the kiss, it burned where he stretched me open. It was like being back in the basement again, with the roughness and the spiking emotions, but that was where the similarities ended.

He held still. Supporting me one-handed, he used the other to wedge between us and tease my clit.

"I'm going to miss you tonight." He spoke against my temple. "As much as I need to learn about myself, I'll be thinking of you the whole time. Understand?"

His fingers kept moving until desire rushed in and the burn turned to pleasure.

He jacked his hips to fuck deeper into me, beginning a rhythm in time with the circles he made with his hand. Waves of delicious friction centred on where he touched me. In his arms, I rocked, chasing that need.

"You might not like me right now, but I'll make it up to you. Give you what you need. Do whatever it takes. Feel how much I need it? How badly I want you to look at me again?"

Inside me, he thickened, thrilling multiple pleasure centres at once.

It boosted my scattered state to the stratosphere. Usually, he held back until the very last minute, ensuring I got mine repeatedly first. I was deep in lust with him being out of control.

I crushed him with my arms and legs, wanting nothing more than to keep him in place. Convict's strokes sped up until he was hammering into me.

"Only you, Mila. I've only ever wanted you, and that is

never going to change."

It triggered the approach of a fast climax. Abruptly, I came, and with such sweet relief I could've sobbed.

Convict groaned, tucked his head beside mine, and thrust hard for three more beats. He stilled and pulsed into me.

Both of us gasped for air, clutching the other. For a long minute, I didn't want him to let go. But by degrees, he set me down on my heels and stepped away. The lust in his gaze shuttered.

"Go clean up. I know you won't want to wear me all evening."

I did as ordered, but with the strangest sense of regret.

When we arrived at the warehouse, Convict led me to the central corridor outside the office and made a public display of kissing me stupid.

In my ear, he whispered, "Thank you for playing your part."

If he meant with the kiss, nothing on my part was an act, but all too quickly, he was leaving with Arran, and Cassie had hooked her arm through mine to lead me into the lift.

Him walking away felt like my heart was separating from my body.

It took a long moment for me to realise we weren't heading into the nightclub. "Where are we going?"

"Genevieve's place. She's made cocktails and mocktails, and Everly baked something."

I hadn't met Everly, though knew she was Shade's girlfriend. She was also lovely, welcoming me with a hug and apologising for the fact she wasn't drinking due to her pregnancy, one hand to the oversized hoodie that covered her stomach.

I congratulated her and concealed my shock. Surely

babies didn't mix with gangs and sex clubs, but then again, it felt like a different world up here at the top of the building.

On the eighth floor, the red-brick apartment had polished floorboards, arched windows with a view over the glittering city, and a gleaming kitchen. A fluffy brown cat wound around everyone's legs, purring up a storm.

Cassie got behind the kitchen counter where Genevieve had bottles, a shiny cocktail shaker, and fruit on a chopping board. Pendant lights lit their station.

Cassie took frosted glasses from a silver freezer and dipped the rims in a liquid and then into salt. "Margaritas," she explained.

I tilted my head at her, or more specifically at the t-shirt she wore over a red microskirt. "Skeleton Girls Detective Agency," I read.

Cassie grinned. "Last year, there was a spate of murders in Deadwater. We investigated them. I had shirts made."

"Those are too cute."

"Aren't they? Pertinent for tonight as well."

Genevieve rattled the cocktail shaker then tipped the contents into four glasses, while Cassie prepared a fifth, sans the alcohol, and handed it to Everly.

"Are we expecting anyone else?" I asked. There were four of us but five glasses.

I took a deep sip of mine, the sourness of the lime exploding over my tongue, followed by the burn of the tequila.

"Lovelyn. With her access to police information, she's my new best friend."

A knock came at the door.

Cassie hopped in glee. "That's her. The fun can begin."

She trotted over to answer it, giving a hug to Lovelyn, then lingered to talk to the man who'd escorted her. It was

Riordan, Cassie's boyfriend. He snaked an arm around her, muttered something about her being a wild girl, then drew her in for a hot kiss that had me exchanging a look with the other women.

Lovelyn giggled and greeted the rest of us, taking a seat at the kitchen counter next to me. The pendant lights lit the blonde highlights in her waterfall of sleek light-brown hair, and her dove-grey sweaterdress had tiny purple flowers stitched onto it. "Got to hate being single. I feel like the odd one out. All of you are matched up."

I pulled a face. "If it helps, I'm barely talking to Convict right now."

Genevieve uttered a laugh.

My mistake slammed into me. In all my thoughts on the evening, I'd settled on the positive of spending time with the women here. But in that, I'd forgotten that I was supposed to be a convincing partner to Convict.

I'd agreed to play a role and had betrayed him with one sentence.

But the wife of the mob boss only handed me a glass with a sympathetic smile. "Equally if it helps, for the first two weeks of being with Arran, I wanted to strangle him."

I widened my eyes. "What did he do?"

"Everything. He was overbearing, controlling, hostile, I could go on. But also, it was a two-way thing. We didn't trust each other. Luckily, the game rules have a way of fixing that."

"They do?"

Cassie bounced back over, her energy infectious. "Now we're all here, I officially commence a meeting of the Skeleton Girls Detective Agency, welcoming two new members in Mila and Lovelyn. Ladies, do you accept the invitation?"

Lovelyn and I exchanged a bemused glance then nodded in unison.

Cassie beamed. "Excellent. Solid choice. On tonight's

agenda is the recent murder of a young woman named Esther Eavis."

I choked on my drink. "Did you say murder? I knew her. I thought she drowned."

Cassie's eyes rounded. "Tyler said you knew her, but I thought he told you the details. I didn't mean for that to be a shock."

All week, I'd waited for a news report to come out regarding Esther, but all I'd found was a line in the local press that had stated the facts I already knew in short sentences. *Woman drowned, no suspicious circumstances.*

"We went to school together," I explained. "Then I saw her again recently. If she was murdered, why isn't there more of an outcry?"

Cassie spread out her arms. "Exactly. Which is why I wanted this meeting. No one else but us seems to care."

Lovelyn set down her glass. "I can tell you why she's not being treated as a priority. Sex workers never are. It's common practice for police to overlook or even ignore those they consider to be on the lowest rung of society. Mostly because everyone else does, too. If my father came across a prostitute lying in the street, he'd more likely step over her than offer help."

The set of her jaw told me exactly how she felt about that.

I was stuck on the sex worker label. It made sense, yet it made me feel even worse for Esther.

I asked, "Why do you think she was murdered? Couldn't she have just fallen into the water and drowned?"

Cassie's eyes flashed with intrigue. "Would you strip off every piece of clothing and go for a swim in Deadwater Harbour on a cold spring night? I find it hard to believe that Esther did."

My mouth fell open. "She was naked?"

Cassie nodded. "Lovelyn told me on the phone earlier. Isn't that right?"

Lovelyn confirmed it. "Naked aside from a bracelet of plastic beads. My father is not a fan of paperwork, and he often gives it to me to manage. Therefore, I have access to all the systems, so I can do some digging." She winced and peeked my way. "It could be difficult to hear when it's about someone you were friends with."

The bracelet sounded like the one Esther had taken from Annabelle when we were in the holding cell. "No, it's fine. We weren't friends. I don't want to speak ill of the dead, but I'm not sure she liked me all that much."

The half a cocktail I'd consumed loosened my tongue, and I found myself spilling the history I had with Esther, from teenage years until when I'd gone to her to find Jacobs. Then onto the auction, and her presumed role in what happened to me after.

Genevieve held her hand over the jewelled choker at her throat, her only embellishment to a little black dress, aside from a huge diamond engagement ring and a shiny wedding band. "She helped them use you? To what end?"

I couldn't talk about going into the game, so I hedged the question. "I'm not sure, and now, I'll never know."

What I really wanted to talk about was how Convict rescued me, but I was already deep into oversharing and risked messing up. Instead, I gave them the link to my family concerns, explaining that I'd been in turmoil after the funeral and how I knew Esther.

"I asked for her help in finding a man called Rhys Jacobs who's manipulating my grandmother. She led me to trouble instead. Convict's now helping to find Jacobs, and once we have him, I'll finally be able to work out why he's messing with my family. I'll never be able to ask Esther why she did what she did."

With the words said, I felt...lighter. No one judged me

for the crazy actions I'd taken in my desperation and grief. They only seemed intrigued, even if they only knew half of it.

At school, I'd had a good group of girlfriends but had lost touch when I'd moved to private school under my grandparents' guiding hands. There, they'd encouraged me to befriend specific girls whose families they approved of, but those relationships hadn't lasted.

I wanted a friendship group. I didn't know if it could be these women, but for another three weeks, I was tied to a member of their crew. Maybe this was another way to make the best of it.

We'd moved to the sofas mid-chat, and Everly handed out a tray of pizza bites. The curvy brunette stared at the food with one hand to her belly then leapt up and bolted across the room.

Genevieve stared after her. "Morning sickness. She's suffered it for months. It should be stopping soon, but any child of Shade's is going to be trouble." She arched an eyebrow at me. "Talking of difficult men, Mila, come help me mix the next round of drinks."

I joined her in the kitchen area. Genevieve set me up at a chopping board and handed me a bowl of limes.

She fetched ice from a tall freezer and cracked it into the shaker. "You asked about the game rules and how they bring you closer. No one else here, but you and I have been through it, so I wanted to share the wisdom I've gained."

I swallowed and nodded.

She picked up the bottle of tequila. "I didn't love Arran when we were first tied together. Like I said, he drove me crazy, but the feelings hit hard as the weeks passed. It's to do with the closeness and the bond that gets forged by the experience. If two people are together every day for a period of time, and by together I mean intimate, not just work colleagues or friends, they connect. Thirty days is how long it takes to fall in love with that kind of intensity, and by all accounts, the game does that job very successfully."

"It does?"

"No couple has ever broken up."

I blinked, stalling in my task of juicing the limes. Her words rang louder than the party chatter. I wasn't sure if it was a promise or a threat.

"There are so many women who sign up for it and who are willing to do whatever it takes. Some don't like the man who catches them at first, but that changes. I'm explaining this to you because, like me, I'm guessing you didn't opt into the experience."

I closed my eyes. She'd read between the lines so easily. "I…"

"It's okay. Arran already knows. Tyler had been updating him daily on Convict's health and the work he was doing, then he stopped short once the game had taken place. It was no surprise that you were the woman he emerged with. Arran predicted it."

"He won't kick him out for it?"

"He loves him. When we were on our honeymoon, he opened up about when they met at a fight club in Edinburgh, down by the docks."

I gave a weak laugh. "We have a warehouse there. Maybe we crossed paths."

"Maybe you did. Like with the game, Arran and Convict fought and bled together. I'm pretty sure your man could do anything right now and Arran would forgive it. Let's just say he's come a long way in managing his very big and very strong emotions. So back to you. I'm not prying, but I know exactly what you've been through and I'm walking proof that it all comes good."

"I don't hate Convict. He's just…"

"Infuriating?"

"An excellent word."

Everly returned from the bathroom and settled on the sofa. Lovelyn rubbed her arm.

I twisted my lips and told Genevieve, "He kept my brother here without me knowing. How am I supposed to forgive that? I know he's in a gang, but I'm not. I've never been near this world."

"Neither had I before Arran, and he and Shade did something very similar to Riordan. He's my brother, if you didn't know. They didn't hurt him, and I got over it because he did and because it's part of the life. You get addicted to the gang shit, believe me."

I finished with the limes, and Genevieve added the juice to the tequila and triple sec. She shook the shaker then poured. "I'm telling you this because one, I can see that you're struggling, and two, if you really don't want this world and the man you're tied to, you should get out now. Before more time progresses and the love comes."

My shoulders dropped. "I don't want to leave him."

"Right. Then piss him off in exchange and you'll feel better."

I laughed in surprise, and Cassie joined us, taking two of the glasses. "Is that Convict? If he's driving you around the bend, do the same to him. Let him wonder where the hell you're going so he flies into a panic."

I angled my head in question. "Where am I going?"

"We've established that Esther died in suspicious circumstances and that you know some of her history. Do you know where she lived?"

I nodded. She'd mentioned a block of flats when I'd asked to meet up, though we'd ended up making the arrangements over the phone.

"Excellent. That plus a chat with the other women who were in the auction with you is a must to give us intelligence.

Who bought them, what did they know of the deceased, and what rumours have they heard since? I feel a field trip coming on. Charge your glasses, ladies."

A clamour of answers started, Everly crying off at leaving the warehouse, Lovelyn excited about investigating the police angle, and Cassie narrating the text she was sending her boyfriend who'd act as our security.

She winked at me. "If Convict freaks out, tell him it's part of the Skeleton Girls curriculum: Field Trips and Fuck Yous."

I stared between them. "Wait. How will Convict know that I've left?"

Cassie snickered, and Genevieve covered her mouth. Even a queasy-looking Everly smiled.

Cassie gave me the answer. "If he isn't tracking your every move, then he doesn't deserve the title of skeleton crew. Trust me, he'll know."

31

Convict

The drive to Edinburgh took us through dark countryside and lonely roads. Arran had to take a call for the first stretch but was done by the time the route spat us out in the suburbs. We skirted the city and followed the signs for Leith.

Arran tapped the steering wheel. "I spent time pulling my memories together to help you get back yours. A lot of it I'd blocked out. It wasn't the best time for me."

I wanted to ask why, but I kept my mouth closed. I needed everything he could give me, and if I spoke, I might break the spell.

"Do you know where you're from?"

Slowly, I shook my head. This evening, I carried a blade. We both did. I toyed with mine.

"Here, but you moved around with most of your time in foster care in England, hence the lack of a strong accent, but you were born in and came back to Leith more than anywhere else."

He turned onto Salamander Street, and I peered out at the mixture of modern blocks of flats and old stone industrial buildings with deep yards on the other side of the road. A memory flickered. Of being a kid and sneaking under the gates at night, or climbing walls. Probably up to no good.

"It's changed," I mumbled.

"The whole area is booming. Gentrification," he said like a dirty word. Arran eyed me. "Is it coming back?"

"A little."

A car swung out of a junction without pause. Arran laid on the horn, and the driver of the blue BMW gave an answering angry blare before shooting off.

"We met here as teenagers, but you shared candid stories of your upbringing. I think because I was so obviously fucked up, you did it to show me there was life on the other side of everything breaking apart."

I couldn't smile. "Trauma bonding."

"Something like that. What you told me isn't great, so you have the choice over hearing it all, or a basic version so you don't have to relive it."

"For fuck's sake. All of it."

Arran inclined his head, and after a couple more turns, parked up on a junction with Ocean Drive. We climbed from the car.

Wind whipped us, carrying with it the salt of the sea and trying to steal his words.

He pointed to a block of flats on the corner of the street. "The Glasshouse pub was here. I didn't know it had been razed and built on. Fuck developers for taking this memory from us both."

I heaved a breath. "Can't stab a planning committee, but I'd give it a go."

He dragged his gaze off the ugly block and back to me. "The first night you came, you were dropped off by your probation officer. You were seventeen and had done a stretch in a youth offending centre, then for the last couple of months, they'd housed you in an adult jail in order to deter you from offending again. Such a fucking joke. I was sat in my car and saw the guy arrive with you. He told you with your track record, you'd never get a job. Your best bet was to earn money with your fists. You had nothing. Not even a bag of clothes."

"Shit. At seventeen, I bet I thought I'd live forever. Just didn't think I'd suck so badly at it. Did I have a home to go to?" I regretted the words, even as I asked them.

Arran's shoulders rose and fell on a sigh. "No, though your mother was still alive at that point."

"She's dead?"

He winced.

I did, too. "I don't remember her, so don't apologise. I just...hoped. Did you ever meet her?"

"Once. You did as the probation officer suggested and fought your way into a pocketful of cash for the night, then came back for more. I was made of anger and resentment, but you took pity on me and made a point of talking to me when most others turned their backs. After a while, we became friends, and one day, you asked me to go somewhere with you. You didn't say why, but it was to see your mother."

I shoved my icy hands into my pockets. There was no good reason for me needing moral support to visit the one person who should've loved me.

"On the way, you told me how you were an only child, born to a mother who'd never had the help she needed, and coped by relying on abusing various substances."

Another recollection battered me. Of opening a bedroom door and finding a woman sprawled on the carpet with blood on her arm and a crust of saliva and vomit around her mouth. Of relief that she wasn't dead.

"She was unhappy, so whatever you're remembering, bear in mind you were never the cause. Just another victim, like she was."

"Do you know her name?"

"Dorothea."

RIP, Ma. Dead before I even knew her name. "What happened to her?"

"Earlier in life? I'm not sure. If you knew, you never said. But she overdosed when you were away on another stint in jail. You found out on release, and it sent you spiralling for a while. Landed you back in jail three weeks later."

I hadn't been with her in the end. I turned my face to the sea breeze and started walking, if only to have movement to calm my brain.

Arran kept pace.

He let me process my thoughts without interruption. When my heart stopped thumping so hard, I braced myself against an iron railing that overlooked the docks, waves rippling on the harbour wall below. Boats were moored next to warehouses and industrial sites, lorry parking, and a rail connection waiting to take the goods inland.

Then I yelled. Loud, once, and done.

I hung my head until I was ready to move on. "So we met here and beat up people for cash and feelings management. How did we get to you running the skeleton crew and owning a warehouse?"

"Do you remember much of my history?"

I shook my head.

Arran shoved the hair from his eyes and watched the water. "My father was Lord Kendrick and a police chief here in Scotland. A corrupt son of a bitch who murdered my mother in front of me. Many people hated me for being his son and didn't give a fuck about the life I'd led or how much I'd despised and suffered under him as well. Along with you and Shade, I practically lived at the fight club and developed a reputation for talking with my fists, wearing that like a protective shield. I was targeted, not only for who I was, but for what I started to realise I needed to be. My mother was a sex worker, too. She was murdered in cold blood by the bastard who thought himself so much better than her when the opposite was true."

My jaw unhinged. "We used to beat up kerb crawlers. We'd wait and lay into them after they'd paid their money."

Arran's lips curved almost to a smile. "I was out of control, but you were right there, supporting me regardless. It became my vow to bring terror to men who hurt women. But then the sex workers got angry at us for driving away their trade. It made me realise they needed a safe place and I could provide that. My father left me an inheritance. Forming a crew was a natural step, and we had to get out of Leith, so Deadwater felt like a good solution. Right on the border. The tidal river to wash away the bodies we handled along the way. You weren't around when I found the warehouse, but you spent months helping with the renovations before being recalled to prison for yet another bullshit reason."

"Sounds like I've spent more time in jail than out."

"Want to know the strangest thing? Until the warehouse was established, you didn't seem to care. You told me that jail was not that different to the foster care homes you'd mostly been raised in, except you were guaranteed your own bed and three meals a day. I'd argue that you were institutionalised."

I didn't know the word, but I got the gist.

"Guess I didn't have much to live for."

"That's different now. This time, you'll stay out. You're on parole. Did you know that?"

I nodded, not bothering to ask how he knew.

Arran's gaze held mine. "I've spent time working on the cops so every fucker knows your name and won't touch you if they find you. I can't promise that it's enough, but it's a start."

Small pieces of memories slid together like a puzzle. Facing off against a teenager with dark-blond hair and bloodied knuckles. Brawling and landing punches which made us laugh. Sitting in a tattoo chair...

I lurched for him. Wrenched up his t-shirt to reveal his side and a tattoo of a skull wearing a bandanna. Same as the one that had been on my arm.

Arran let me look then shoved me away. "We were skeleton crew before we even had the name."

My heart sank, but I tore up my sleeve to brandish my disfigured arm, waiting for the disgust in his face. "Not anymore. Mine was burned away on the night of the fire. Guess I deserved that."

Anger came swift to his features. "No you didn't."

I had no reason for my instant fury with Arran. He was my friend. The one person who had consistently been there for me. Until he hadn't. I battled with the hurt that came from his rejection.

He grabbed me by the shoulders and held me steady in front of him. Meaning flashed in his eyes. "I've said it already, but I'm so fucking sorry for what I did to you. I can't change the past but I can ask for forgiveness, and I can make life as easy for you as possible now."

I couldn't speak. He hugged me, too hard, then thumped me on the back and pushed me away.

Neither of us spoke for a long minute. Only continued our walk down the edge of the water, slowly frosting over in the freezing North Sea wind.

As soon as I could manage it, I gave him the truth. "I think Mila will leave me when our time is up. We made a deal that she'd honour the rules of the game in exchange for me helping with her family problems."

I was a thug, I thought with my fists, but I didn't want to be a liar right now.

Arran swallowed but inclined his head. "Have you told her you love her?"

"No."

"But you do." He didn't ask it as a question. "It isn't a rule, but some contestants make a point of saying it from day one. Some from the moment they make their claim. It's powerful. Having someone love you is," he searched for the words, "fucking everything."

I knocked down the surges of emotion that wouldn't stop coming. From his revelations, from his promises, from thoughts of Mila.

"That's the only thing I want besides my place in the skeleton crew. Her. I need her."

"I know exactly how you feel."

I watched the black sea, my head thick with stories and half-formed memories. My need to have Mila in the forefront of my life, even as I was miles away from her.

It was then that I realised what I was looking at.

I stopped dead and stared at the ship across the water, a huge vessel painted red and white with cargo containers on the back. Across the side read 'MARCHANT HAULAGE' then the ship's name, *EDEN*, further along.

"That's one of Mila's family's ships."

Arran said something, but it was lost to my mind summoning a more recent occurrence. I knew that boat. I'd seen it before. Maybe within the past few months.

I focused hard, but the recollection slipped and fractured. Fuck my broken brain. I didn't know if that was real or if I was hallucinating from the night I'd researched her while she'd slept in my cam girls' room.

From my pocket, I found my phone and went to search the same thing I had that night, checking if this ship appeared as a picture.

A notification pinged on my screen at the same moment. My tracker, set up according to Shade's instructions. Mila was moving through the city, fast. My gut dropped like I'd been punched.

"Mila's left the warehouse."

Arran swore and brought out his own phone. "Genevieve, too."

I slapped him on the shoulder, urging him to go. Right as a crack rang out and the Marchant ship exploded in a rain of fire, bright in the pitch-black night.

Her name, her family, her fucking inheritance. Going up in flames.

32

Mila

A convoy travelled with us through the streets of Deadwater, Manny in a car ahead with a skeleton crew member whose name I didn't catch, Riordan driving our vehicle which I was pretty sure was bulletproof, and another crew member in a car behind. Additionally, Tyler was watching us, though I hadn't seen him since we'd set out from the warehouse.

It was for Genevieve's benefit, I gathered. Arran would flay them alive if anything happened to his woman.

Cassie pulled her phone from her ear, her pretty features wreathed in worry. "Has anyone spoken to Dixie recently? I can't get hold of her and I haven't seen her in the warehouse."

Lovelyn put up a hand like she was in class. "I did a few days ago. She was upset about something and left the warehouse in a hurry. I'm sure she'll come back when she's ready."

Cassie sighed. "I hope so."

I hadn't met the woman in question so focused on our task. We'd already tried Esther's flat, and my knock had been answered by a woman who had to be her mother. She'd stumbled and slurred, screamed at us to piss off, then slammed the door so hard the echo rattled down the sparse corridor. I felt so bad for her, but obviously now wasn't a good time to talk.

Tyler had been able to give us an address for Annabelle,

so we switched our approach to the two other women who'd been in the auction with me. Perhaps they would have clues.

We pulled up at Annabelle's street, and I hopped out, Cassie and Riordan coming with me. The rest of the crew held back. We'd agreed not to go mob-handed and for Genevieve to stay in the safety of the car.

Annabelle opened the door. She blinked at me. "Oh, hi."

I got straight to the point. "Did you know Esther died?"

She gave a wide-eyed and fast nod. "I heard about it. It's terrifying. I never thanked you…"

"You don't have to. Did you ever meet her before that night?"

"Never."

"When we were in the cell for the auction, you went out in the hall with her and the other woman. Did she say anything?"

"She spoke to the guy out there who was shit talking us. He grouched about not taking long like you had, and she said you were a nice girl and too good for that place. You had people who cared about you. He laughed and said what a great friend she was with all she was doing to you."

I held in my hurt. That pretty much confirmed she'd set me up. "The other woman who was there, I didn't get her name. Did you?"

The youngster jerked her head. "I've seen her before. She works at the Burger Barn. Pretty sure her name's Becky."

I thanked her, extracting a promise that she'd never do anything like that again.

Annabelle gazed at the skeleton crew cars blocking her street. "Your boyfriend already made me swear that when he was hunting for you. I'm glad you found each other again."

We drove away, and my heart thumped at the thought of Convict searching for me in the days Salter had held me before the game. The two margaritas must've heightened my emotions as I felt the weight of him being so far away as a band constricting my chest.

A quarter of an hour on, we'd arrived at the fast-food chain restaurant Annabelle had named. It was past eleven p.m., and the place was empty though the lights were still on, and people moved at the back of the kitchen area.

I rapped on the door, but none of them approached.

Manny, escorting me this time, made a dismissive sound and booted it. It flew open, and heads popped up in the kitchen.

A manager stepped forward, her gaze darting from us to the crew and the cars. "I don't want any trouble."

Manny shrugged. "You won't get any. We need to talk to Becky. It won't take long."

The manager peered over her shoulder and flapped a hand, then the woman with braids I remembered from the holding cell crept up to the counter. In her blue-and-yellow uniform, she darted anxious looks at me.

"Did you hear about Esther?" I asked.

Becky sucked in a deep breath and circled out of the counter opening, catching my arm to guide me across the floor, all the way beyond the doors and to an outside eating area.

In the cool night, she shoved her hands into her armpits. "I heard. I don't know anything about it."

I leaned on a low wall to a children's play area and took in the woman I'd so briefly met in that holding cell. Going by her expression, Becky was wary and afraid. Almost hostile.

"You know she was a sex worker?"

She leaned in and dropped her voice down low. "That isn't news. She has been for years. She tried to target wealthier clientele, but her habit set her back."

"She used drugs?"

"Obviously."

"Did she go through with the auction?"

Becky darted a glance into the nearest Burger Barn window then up at a camera. "I don't know what you're talking about."

"Please? Esther died. Someone needs to care."

She worked her jaw then swore and walked away, out of the perimeter of the building and into the car park. I followed, Manny tracking me.

In the open space, she whirled around. "I can't lose this job. I have a kid. I need the money."

I formed a sympathetic smile. "Then you went through with it, too."

Brittle tension rolled off her. "I can't tell you anything useful. She was sold first. There were other girls there who I heard, one was crying nonstop, but we were kept blindfolded until they took us out front."

"Do you know who bought Esther?"

"No."

"Did you see any of the other handlers?"

"Only the two men who had been at the place I saw you. They didn't speak often."

"Did anyone say a name?"

"Like I said, they weren't chatty. One called another Dumbo, but that's got to be a nickname, right?"

I lodged that fact away, though she was probably correct.

"Then someone bought you. You must've been so scared." At her tiny nod, my heart broke for her. I gentled my tone. "I'm sorry for what you went through."

She snorted, not meeting my gaze. "I made it out. Figured you for dead, but here you are, backed by fancy men with fancy cars. Looks like we both did okay."

"This next bit is important. I need to know who bought you."

"Why should I tell you shit? You didn't go through it. You come to my place of work and cause drama. All those nosy bitches are going to have a field day over this."

"You should help me because someone needs to be held accountable for what they did to Esther."

Becky's gaze flew to mine. "Maybe she deserved it. I only know her because she would come in here and other places to try to recruit girls. She was a fucked-up user. I'm not sad. Only shaken that it could've been me. Whoever bought her must've been a real bastard. No one in the auctions will be safe if he's on the scene. To think, he could've bought me."

She wasn't wrong. The mystery buyer was more than likely Esther's murderer.

"Exactly. Which is why I want to work out who he is. Your buyer might be able to tell us."

"Fuck. Fine. I didn't see him when I was being sold. Not until I was escorted to his car and locked in the back. He didn't tell me his name, not when he was inviting his friends to run train on me and not when he did the most degrading shit a prissy princess like you can even imagine. The auction was for no-holds-barred sex, you know that? I put up with what he..." She gazed to the dark skies and took a steadying breath. "I would do anything to give my son a better life. The money paid for his school uniform, new, not secondhand, shoes that didn't have a previous owner, day trips he'd otherwise miss out on. Don't you dare judge me."

I kept silent. I wasn't judging. I'd been in a place where I'd have done anything for my family.

Becky centred herself. "When the bastard was asleep in the rented apartment, after everything was over, I went through his bag. There was no wallet, but in a side compartment I found a gym membership card with RS Yelland on it."

My mind spun. I recognised the name. Richard Yelland was a Deadwater businessman who had occasionally attended events I'd been to with my grandparents.

"Man in his sixties, bad teeth, stinks of cigars?"

Her shoulders rose and fell. "I'm so ashamed. Fuck you for making me feel it all again tonight. Are we done?"

I nodded, and Becky stormed away. I didn't follow, for a moment, standing with my thoughts in the desolated retail estate where shadows wrapped around the edges, all the other businesses dark. It was a dead end. Men like Yelland would keep secrets to avoid implicating themselves.

The cold crept in around me. All of a sudden, I felt vulnerable, though Manny was close and the cars only twenty feet away. The hair on the back of my neck rose, and I peered around, searching the gloom beyond the Burger Barn's slices of light. A litter-strewn hedgerow, a couple of cars and pushbikes further away on the expanse of tarmac. Nothing obviously wrong to explain my intuition.

Something shifted in the dark. Not a sound, not a shape, just a presence. Like the night itself had taken interest in me.

"Mila, call for you." Manny approached and handed over his phone.

I raised it to my ear. If mine had rung, I hadn't noticed.

"Don't leave me," Convict said down the line.

I turned away and clutched the phone tighter. "I'm not."

"I'm on my way back. We'll be there as fast as we can. Just hear me out. Let me make it up to you. I promise to be better."

A faint noise reached me. A chill slid down my spine. The yellow patches of light from the restaurant cut out, plunging us into darkness.

"Mila," Convict said again.

"I'm here. It's just... Something's off. I don't know how to explain it."

"Get back in the car. Please, listen to me."

A scream stopped my chance of a response.

From the shadows, a figure lurched and ran full pelt at me.

I didn't spot the knife they threw until pain bloomed and blood flowed.

33

Convict

A woman's howl of anger came down the phone line, and Mila cried out in fear.

My heart stopped beating. "Mila? What just happened?"

"I'll kill you for what you did to my Esther," the other woman screamed. "You were supposed to be her golden ticket but you screwed her over, and now she's dead. It's all your fault. You deserve to die with her."

A clatter sounded followed by the stranger yowling out like a deranged cat.

"Put your fucking foot down," I ordered Arran and stabbed the call onto loudspeaker.

He slammed on the accelerator so we bombed into the dark night along the coastal road towards Deadwater. "What's going on?"

"No clue. Mila, can you hear me?"

Gasps and wrestling made it down the line, then Manny's voice returned. "Mila's safe. I've put her back in the car and the threat has been neutralised by Tyler."

"What threat? Who was it?"

"Where the fuck is my wife?" Arran snarled over the top of my words.

"Genevieve never left the vehicle and is perfectly safe. As per my message, the womenfolk were interviewing people as part of their investigations. The mother of the deceased launched an attack as we were leaving a venue. There are no major injuries, and the attacker and blade are secured."

A blade. The attacker had a blade. There were too many questions I needed answers to but I crushed it all under the knowledge that Mila was okay. My hands balled into fists.

"Get back to the warehouse," Arran ordered Manny.

"Already moving. I'll keep an open line until we're there," he replied.

We travelled on in silence, any chance of conversation over. After the explosion, and the realisation that Mila and Genevieve were out of the warehouse, we'd already turned tracks for home, giving us only a thirty-minute race to reach them.

While Arran drove, I watched the tracker on my screen return Mila to safety.

Outside the warehouse, Arran skidded into his parking space and stormed out of the car, snarling at the guard for taking too long to open the rear exit door. I was right there with him, my heart in my mouth, visions of the devastating future taking the place of my recollections of the past.

What if the attacker had hit her mark? What if Mila had bled out in some godforsaken part of the city?

We burst into the corridor and to the management office. Inside, Mila sat in a circle of chairs with Cassie, Genevieve, Everly, and Lovelyn. Without hesitation, Arran picked up his wife and carried her from the room. She didn't argue, just banded her arms around him and held him close.

It was then that I saw the bandage on Mila's arm. Red mist descended. I'd intended to treat her gently, but in a heartbeat, I was more animal than man.

Scooping her up, I threw her over my shoulder with an arm wrapped around her thighs. Then I stalked from the office.

"Talk later," Cassie called after us with a cackle.

Mila didn't say a word. She let me put her in the passenger seat of my car and strap her in. Then I drove to her apartment block and parked badly, scooping her up again to carry her upstairs.

"I can walk," she complained.

"Let me do this."

She didn't argue any further. Inside her apartment, I carried her into the bedroom and locked the door. When I placed her on the bed, Mila peered up at me.

"Genevieve said Arran would do this so not to be surprised if you did, too. I'm fine."

I paced the rug in front of her and dug my hands into my hair. "You're hurt. Someone came at you with a knife."

"She did. She threw it at me."

I stilled and stared at the bandage. "I'm so fucking furious right now. The minute I'm away, someone tries to hurt you. I should never have left you alone."

She gave a soft laugh. "I was never alone. We had a full complement of guards, and the cut is shallow. There was no harm done."

I muttered her last three words like a madman.

Mila watched me. The hostility that had lingered in her gaze throughout the last week had gone. She'd been afraid. I didn't know why, but that last realisation broke my final semblance of control.

I centred my gaze on her, showing her every bit of how I felt. "Listen up. I need you to know that I don't blame you for this. It wasn't your fault. But I'm going to punish you all the same. Lose the dress. Hands above your head."

Her focus held mine, unreadable at first. But then her gaze flared. It wasn't defiance. It was need, and lust, and high emotion I couldn't identify but felt like a bullet to the chest.

Mila stripped her dress and bra then stretched out her

stunning, mostly naked body, and lifted her arms. "Show me what it does to you. Show me how much I matter."

Pride inflated my chest, and I collected the handcuffs then quickly restrained her wrists to the bedframe. Instinct led me, and my breathing spiked. Kneeling on the bed, I spread her legs to accommodate me. I tore away her underwear, revealing her pussy.

"You'll take it, every bit of me, because I need to remind myself that you're here. You're alive. Mine."

"You talking to me or my vagina?"

I curled my lip and switched my gaze to her face. "Run that mouth and see what better use I can make of it. In fact..."

I stripped my clothes and knelt over her head, facing down her body in the sixty-nine position. On all fours, I fisted my rock-hard dick and took it to her lips. "Suck. Ground me before I go insane."

Mila enclosed me in her mouth, her heat surrounding me. It dialled back about one percent of my panic. This was what I needed. To be on her. In her.

I stroked in and out of her lips in shallow thrusts, watching her take me. Her tongue curled around me, and I groaned and dropped my face to her cunt, sliding my tongue into her liquid heat then kissing those pretty lips hello.

She stopped sucking and bucked against my face.

I reared back and slapped her between the legs. "You don't get to come. Not until I've worked through everything that happened tonight. Remember, I still don't blame you."

My dick in her mouth prevented a response, but I sensed her annoyance.

It gave me free rein to do what I wanted to her. I returned my attentions to her centre and licked and sucked until I sensed she was close, her heels driving into the mattress and her body surging against me faster and harder. Only then did I back away, letting her cool off.

I did it again. Getting her close to the edge but denying her the orgasm. There was no rewarding almost getting killed. No way she should enjoy her near exit from my life.

It wasn't fair, but I was fucked up over this woman. Therefore, she needed to feel it.

I didn't hold back my own pleasure.

At the third denial, I was dying for her, my cock so thick between her lips that I saw stars. It was the line of tears down her cheeks that pushed me over the edge. I paused to fuck her face until I came on her tongue. My groan of pleasure nearly triggered hers, but I denied her even the slightest touch in time to keep her hanging.

Just like always with her, one time wasn't enough.

I never went completely soft anyway, so I let her swallow me down then build me up again.

Mila tolerated my torture until she was a panting, sweating mess, her thighs clenched where she arched against the air in desperation for any relief. She made me come again, this time with me withdrawing from her mouth to finish on her tits.

I switched position to regard the mess I'd made. Driving my fingers into it, I spread my cum over her tits and up her throat, then down her belly and between her legs, over her swollen clit, painting her with it.

Red-faced, she breathed through her nose, hands fisted beyond the cuffs.

"You're mine," I told her. "I claim you in every way. No one can take you from me."

Mila swore, and her eyelids closed, her head falling back on the pillow.

"Eyes on me," I demanded. "You like me like this. You're enjoying my suffering because it shows you how feral I am for you. How badly you affect me."

She didn't deny it, just watched me, her lips parted and

her body gleaming with my cum.

I collected more on my fingers and thrust it into her, her tight walls clamping down on my fingers. "Your pussy is greedy for my cum. You want me inside and out."

Mila moaned and worked her hips so she slid up and down the hand inside her. I let her until she panted then pulled away, denying her again.

I trailed a hand up her so-tense body, a new idea sending blood to my dick so it hardened again. "If I put a baby in you, you'd remember you don't walk into danger like that. Where's the implant you told me about?"

"My left arm. Why?" Her mouth formed a shocked O as she caught my drift. "You wouldn't."

"I absolutely would." I stroked her arm, finding a tiny bump on the outside.

"Convict!"

"Emilia. Consider tonight a reset. I'll get this out of my system and tell you all the fucked-up things I've done to you then beg for forgiveness. I can't promise I won't do anything else, but you'll hear me out and forgive me all the same. There's a reason for it. We'll get to that at the end."

It was then that I reached for two things. A skeleton crew bandanna and my blade.

34

Kneeling between my thighs, Convict brandished a savage-looking black-handled knife. "I'm taking the implant out of you."

Heat flooded my veins, rage following. "You're insane."

"For you, completely."

He dropped the knife to the sheet and took up a bandanna. I expected him to blindfold me, but instead, he forced it between my teeth and tied it off behind my head.

Oh, fuck! I growled around the material, trying to show him with my eyes how pissed off he'd made me.

Convict's lips twitched. "You're so fucking beautiful when you're angry. You don't fear me at all, and I love that. Even when I have you completely at my mercy. Even doing this."

On all fours over me, his head above mine, he picked up the knife and drew the dull side of the blade over my belly and to my breast. He stroked it up and down against my nipple, the savage edge glinting in the light from the lamp my grandmother chose for me.

"I stopped your mouth so you have no way of saying what you think should be said. You're such a good girl, you ought to tell the bad boy no. That all the things I want to do to you are wrong. This way, you can just enjoy them."

I had no excuse for the surge of relief that came with

his words. I was wound so tight from his torment. A pulse beat in my clit, and I rode an edge of need so powerful it overwhelmed me.

Convict shifted the pillows under my head so I had a better view down the bed, then drew a line up my leg with the tip of his blade indenting my skin.

I froze. One slip and he could kill me.

That cool tip crossed my hip and eased over my clit. I closed my eyes, my heart racing.

"Watch, Mila."

I did, trying to calm my breathing through my nose. If I could speak, I'd beg him. Either to stop or for more. I couldn't tell which.

He used the dull side to press down on my clit, then flipped the knife so he pitched the bladed tip. I took a shuddering breath through my nose.

He notched the blunt handle to my clit and ground it into my flesh, then he parted my lower lips until it met my entrance. "Relax. I'm way thicker than this, and you take me."

But my body wouldn't give.

"Too swollen." Convict clucked his tongue then reached for a spare pillow and lifted my backside to place it under me.

He teased me with his fingers, drawing the arousal lower. I flinched when his fingertip touched my ass.

The bastard smiled. "No one ever fucked you here? Good."

I cursed him silently, nearly dying with shame when the strange sensation turned pleasurable and my body throbbed. He smirked and pushed that finger inside my ass, continuing the pressure with the knife handle.

"Back when I first saw you, it was on the cameras we had

set up on the holding cell for the sex auction. You knew about the cameras, but what you don't know is that I watched for hours. I watched you sleep. I thought you were the prettiest thing I'd ever seen."

I moaned at the thought. The handle slipped past my resistance, penetrating me an inch.

Convict's tattooed chest rose and fell. "Good girl. If you like that first confession, you'll love the rest. Every obsessive and possessive thing I do turns you on."

Holding the finger still, he circled the knife, the light catching it on each turn as it went deeper into me. The blade terrified me, but he didn't. Somehow, the danger curled around my desire instead of smothering it. I wasn't sure I liked it, but my pussy did. I needed to come so badly, just like how the ass play went from strange to pleasurable so fast.

"Next, once I found you in the game, I could've extracted you without fucking you. I could've stripped my shirt and hidden our bodies so I could've faked it and saved you the honourable way, but no. I needed to claim you, even if just that once. You were my claimed woman, and everyone saw my dick disappear into you. All those men wanted you, and you were mine."

Of course he'd done that, and I wasn't mad about it.

The knife handle was halfway inside me now. The spiralling warmth of my desperately approaching orgasm had never gone away, but the urgency kicked up a notch.

Still, he moved slow and with unerring precision, never letting the edge stray close. His confession continued. "After that, I had the chance to help you because you needed it, but I chose to trap you in a deal that meant I could keep you. I also spent time internet stalking you to go with the physical stalking. To be clear, I'd do all of these things again."

Arrogant bastard.

He tilted his head and regarded my face, spotting the

challenge in my eyes. "My apology is for the part you found wrong. The lie by omission about your family member who I won't name as there's no one in this bedroom but us. For that, I'm sorry. Also for listening in on your conversation with him when you were in the office. I know with both those things, I crossed a line, even if protecting you didn't feel like a mistake."

God, he was such a jerk.

The handle bottomed out, only the sharp edge sticking out of me. Convict fucked me slowly with it, rapture in his eyes. All I knew was the dangerous thrill it generated. Not the same as his dick, but any relief was welcome.

When I rolled my hips to take another thrust, he pulled it out of me, the finger leaving my ass, too. I whimpered around the gag, a tear leaking from my eye with how badly I needed to come. But then his dick filled me, and his body pressed down on mine.

Convict speared me open. I could've cried with how my relief flowed. He filled me so perfectly, and it felt so good to finally get what I craved. What I needed.

He tapped my ass cheek then reached for my restrained arms. With a click, the cuffs fell away. I clutched on to him hard, trembling, desperate.

"I shot a tracker into you. Not sorry for that either, but you should know. No one can ever take you from me. I'll always find you. Always."

I barely cared, so caught up on his increasing tempo, but also on the powerful sense of completeness that stole through me. Cassie and the girls had implied as much, and I loved it. I wanted him so gone for me, so unhinged he went to extremes.

He fucked me harder, driving me into the bed and kindling the heat inside me into an inferno. I burned for him. A white-hot blaze.

"Do you want to come, Mila?"

He tugged the gag from between my teeth.

"Yes," I cried.

"Then give me what I need. Give me that forgiveness for everything from this night and before. I don't care how fucking twisted it is to take it from you like this."

I didn't care either. "Don't lie to me again."

"Okay."

"Forgiven."

He shuddered in obvious relief. "Lastly, I'm sorry if this hurts."

My orgasm crested, and I cried out. A shallow slice of pain registered in my arm, but it was barely a blip on my overwhelming rush of pleasure and happiness. My body sang, pure satisfaction rolling through me until my legs shook.

Thank God. Thank all the angels and devils and whatever gave him his power over my body. I lost myself to the stunning climax, my ecstasy extending when I clamped down on him enough that he thickened and came for a third time.

His laugh pulled me from the depths of my stupor. With bloodied fingers, he daubed red onto his cheeks then held up a small plastic stick.

My contraceptive.

"I'm so fucking in love with you."

We alternated fucking and sleeping hard in a mess of sweat, blood, cum, and scattered pillows. Convict was relentless in his need to be inside me, and when he slowed,

I took over.

I loved the frenzy. I didn't feel the pain.

Not until late morning when I woke with him sleeping on my belly, one hand still on my breast.

Impossibly, I still felt needy.

Probably due to the fact the asshole had sliced my arm and removed my contraceptive. The cut was shallower than the one delivered by Esther's mother, and he'd patched me up with antiseptic and a bandage. I was insane for finding it the hottest experience of my life.

The cold light of day was always my friend.

I held my arm up and twisted it to regard the two beige strips. Then I reached for my phone. Ignoring all the notifications, I searched for an appointment slot at my doctor's office, finding one for late afternoon. One tap and it was mine.

Convict shifted in his sleep and blindly groped for my breast, fitting his mouth to my nipple. He stroked me with his tongue and sucked. Done with my task, I dropped the phone and threaded my fingers into his hair, arching my shoulders to push into his mouth and enjoying the zing of pleasure.

His hand drifted up my legs, that snake tattoo between my thighs. As he sucked, he got his fingers wet and played, still not entirely awake.

I didn't know what round of sex this was. I'd lost count long ago. All I knew was the easy path of following my body's need which never seemed to end. I let my knees fall wide open and closed my eyes so the sensation took me over, an easy climax coming with a cry of desire on my lips and a whisper of love on his.

We slept again.

When I next woke, it was the handcuffs I reached for, along with Convict's wrist.

35

At around four in the afternoon, I showered the night from my skin, ignoring the flares of pleasure when I passed my fingers over sensitive areas, and replaced the bandages on my cuts. Then I dried my hair and returned to the bedroom to dress.

With his head resting on his biceps, Convict watched me, his arm outstretched where I'd chained it to the bedframe.

I had a gangster tied to my bed. I didn't know myself anymore.

He took in my brisk movements around the bedroom, his relaxation dialling back to concern. "What are you doing?"

I straightened my dusky lilac blouse, the sleeves long enough to cover my injuries but loose enough to reveal my whole arm if needed. "I'm going to the doctors to talk contraceptives."

Any vestige of sleep fled his face. "Without me?"

"Obviously. Considering it's your fault I need to go at all."

"Don't. I'm begging you."

I gave an easy shrug and left the room. "And have you intimidate the doctor into giving me sugar pills? Or to try to persuade me not to go at all? Hell, no. I'm not ready to be a mother. Don't let me coming at your stabby action suggest otherwise."

His voice chased me down the hall. "Shit. I didn't. I don't want to be a father either. It was heat of the moment. Mila, come back."

I slipped my feet into the kitten heels I'd usually wear to the office. Donning my workwear was purposeful. I needed to get back into my professional mindset and not the lunatic version I'd fallen into.

"Damn it, Emilia. Don't make me break your bed after we spent all night wrecking your sheets. You were attacked last night. You need protection."

"I'll look after myself. No one else is coming after me."

"Yes, they could be. Fuck. I forgot to tell you about the explosion at the docks."

I stilled my hand on the door lock and reversed my steps to the entrance to my room. "The what?"

"Last night, Arran and I were at the harbour in Leith. I saw one of your boats moored up. It had the name *Eden* on the side. Right as I got the notification that you were out of the warehouse, the fucking thing blew up."

My jaw dropped. In my haste to get ready, I'd ignored the messages pinging into my phone, assuming they were more of the usual from relatives. I snatched the device from my handbag and scrolled. Multiple people had sent me the same news headlines. He was right. The *Eden* had been destroyed.

The lead photo showed a fireboat in the harbour, tackling the blaze. Orange flames scaled the black night. I knew the deck they devoured. I could picture my grandfather standing there, his smile broad over white bristles, his arms out ready for a hug.

Shock and pain pierced me. "I don't believe it. I mean, I do, but... Shit."

"Sweetheart, come here."

I kicked off my shoes and padded over to the bed, sinking

down next to Convict. He banded his arms around me, and I sank into the hug.

"*Eden* was the pride of my grandfather's fleet. One of the biggest we owned."

"What does the news say?"

"An explosion of unknown origins tore through her then fire broke out. At two a.m., she sank." I set down my phone and stared into space. "You probably think it's ridiculous me being upset about a ship."

"I don't."

"It's just that my grandfather loved that vessel. Of all the inventory and routing work he gave me, he always reserved any task on the *Eden* for himself. It's like the sea has stolen one more piece of him."

I earned a squeeze for my explanation.

"It reminded you of how much you miss him. I get it."

For a long moment, he just held me, lending me his strength until I regained my own.

"Will you need to talk to the cops?"

"No, though I'll try. There's a temporary management of all business assets in place by a caretaker function. They'll handle it. The relatives will still come to me, though. I'll have to draft a statement." I checked the time. "Later, though. I've got fifteen minutes until my appointment. It's only around the corner, but I hate being late."

He lifted his arm. Rattled the handcuffs.

With a sigh, I grabbed the key and unlocked him. "You're lucky I didn't tattoo that warning label on your dick while you slept."

He leapt up and kissed me. "Like you need the reminder."

Convict took a one-minute shower and was dressed more quickly than was reasonable. Men had it so easy.

At the door, he linked his fingers in mine. "Swear to God

I won't interfere with your appointment. I'll sit in the waiting room like a good boy."

I twisted my lips but didn't have it in me to glower at him. Even if he deserved it. "You really think I'm in danger?"

"A woman tried to stab you last night, someone used explosives to make a point, your grandmother is being manipulated by criminals, and there's a huge amount of money at stake. Yes, I do."

I didn't argue when he put me in his car for the two-street trip.

After my appointment, during which I informed the medic my implant had been removed and I wanted a new one immediately, and convincing them I wasn't crazy, I exited the office to find Convict waiting in the hall, one booted foot up against the wall.

"They've got worse magazines than prison," he grouched then raised his phone. "Esther's mother is awake. Tyler said she was drunk out of her mind last night but is now ready to talk. Want to head to the warehouse?"

In no way was I surprised that they'd captured the poor woman, though I hadn't been aware of it last night. I nodded, and we made tracks for the skeleton crew's headquarters.

Once we were inside the warehouse, the crew member at the entrance opening the door with a nod of respect, I paused Convict. "Just so you know, I'm investigating Esther's death with help from the women in your crew."

He stroked his thumb over my knuckles. "Anything I can do, let me know."

"You're not going to tell me to stop?"

His lips twisted in a patient expression. "I love you. I won't stop you doing anything. I'll just make sure you're protected while you do it."

There was that love declaration again. So it wasn't a heat-of-passion thing. I wasn't touching that with a barge pole. I dropped his gaze and found my phone.

Last night, Cassie had added Lovelyn and me to a chat group titled 'Skeleton Girls Detective Agency'. I messaged the group.

> **Mila:** Esther's mother is awake. Does anyone remember what she shouted at me in her attack last night?

> **Lovelyn:** She said you were supposed to be a golden ticket. That has been bugging me all night.

> **Cassie:** Me, too! My mind started pinging off with connections between Esther and Salter. Considering we can't find the rat bastard, maybe she can help. Wait, are you here?

> **Mila:** About to go into the management office.

> **Cassie:** I'll get out of bed and come down! Don't let anyone else talk to her. We'll do it ourselves.

We arrived at the office, and I smiled at the image of her still being tucked up under her blankets. Convict's crew were night dwellers. Come to think of it, he'd seemed uncomfortable at being out in the daylight.

He nudged me. "What are you grinning at?"

"Are you a secret vampire?"

He rolled his eyes. "As much as I love your blood, baby, I'd rather feast on your pussy than your throat."

The door swung open, Tyler in the frame. His expression told us that he'd heard the last words said, but he did a stand-up job of not reacting.

My cheeks flamed when we followed him into the room.

"Cassie's on her way down," I told them.

Tyler lifted his chin. "Figured she'd have an interest in this. I'm waiting on someone as well."

He showed us the live feed on his tablet. Esther's mother sat on the edge of the bed, her mouth open and her fists tangled in the blanket beneath her.

"She followed the cars from her flat. I was wrong to disregard her as an unlikely threat," Tyler said.

He'd been the one to take her down, arriving out of nowhere only half a second behind her, though not fast enough to stop her from throwing the blade.

He tapped the sound icon, and wailing filled the room. He tapped it again to silence her. "She's been like that ever since she woke. Screaming her head off."

I traced my gaze over her features, recognising Esther's rounded cheekbones and querulous mouth. "I hate what she did, but being locked up must be horrible for her."

"She's calling out for a drink more than freedom."

"You didn't give her water? Isn't that a basic right for prisoners?"

"Not that kind of drink. She has bottled water and food in the room but trashed both. That alcohol dependency will be useful for getting her to talk."

Convict tugged me against him, and I guessed his thoughts. Her attack could've ended so differently. I hugged his arm around me. All the drama of last night had brought us closer.

A minute later, and Cassie bounded into the room, her thick curls tied back in a barely contained ponytail and a skeleton crew bandanna around her throat. Then the door opened again and my brother entered.

His gaze flicked to me, lingering on Convict's arm around my waist. "Mila."

I smiled to see him. It faltered at what I had to say. "Did you hear about the *Eden*?"

"That a boat?"

"A ship. Our grandfather's favourite of the fleet."

Kane's gaze shuttered in a way it always did when I referenced the family. "What about it?"

"It was blown up last night. Convict saw it happen."

He switched his focus to the man beside me. "Have a temper tantrum, did ye?"

Convict curled his lip. "Still sore that you failed to protect Mila?"

Kane's knuckles tightened. "If protecting her is important, try doing it without treating her like property."

Convict's laugh was razor-edged. "Better than treating her like she's disposable, hey, brother?"

Cassie perched on the huge black desk. "Boys, I swear to God. Whip them out and measure. It'll be faster."

Both glowered, and she snickered a laugh.

Then she picked up the tablet. "Mother Eavis has some explaining to do. Tyler, I assume there's still nothing on Salter?"

He regarded Kane who gave a single and frustrated shake of his head.

Cassie inclined hers. "Then that's our objective. Mila, are ye ready?"

I recoiled. "You want me to help with an interrogation?"

"Don't you? We aren't going to beat her up. Only persuade her to give us the information we need. Think of it as a business meeting. You're dressed for it."

I swallowed bile. In my preparation for the auction, I'd considered how far I was willing to go to protect what I cared for. I'd spent the year going into new situations with new people, many of them viewing me with hostility as a management plant they didn't trust. I'd grown thick skin, but extracting information from prisoners pushed my limits.

Then Convict's touch on my spine grounded me.

I flashed a look at him. "Will you come?"

"I'll be right there with you."

Strangely, that was all I needed. "Let's do this thing."

The three of us journeyed to the basement, and to a hall of rooms outside of the main floor where Convict and I had sealed our fate just a couple of weeks ago.

In a small, locked room, Tracey Eavis, Esther's mother, rose from her bed. Her hands were cuffed together and linked to a chain on the wall. It rattled when she moved, giving a macabre addition to the stench of vomit and sweat. "It's about time. I've been calling and calling and nobody—" She spotted me, and her complaint shifted to a snarl. "You."

I held up the vodka bottle we'd taken from the nightclub's stockroom. "My arm is feeling fine, thanks for asking. We have some questions for you."

Her gaze followed the bottle. She lurched for me, the chains holding her back. "Give that to me, you stupid bitch."

Cassie tutted and extended a hand. I passed her the bottle, and she stepped over to the corner where a bucket sat next to a drain. Then she unscrewed the lid and upended the bottle so the clear liquid poured out.

That wail we'd heard over the CCTV filled our ears.

"What did Jan Salter promise Esther for selling me out?" I shouted over the noise.

Tracey spluttered. "Don't do it. Don't do it!"

Cassie righted the bottle, and I repeated the question, gaining Tracey's attention this time.

She blinked with reddened eyes. "Why the fuck should I tell you anything? You're the reason she's dead."

Cassie tipped the bottle again, the alcohol glugging away down the pipes.

"Stop. I'm begging you. Just give it over."

"Then answer me."

"He offered her a job," she spluttered. "A good one. Decent, honest work in managing the girls at the auction."

That's what she meant by me being a golden ticket. "Girls they were selling?"

She gave a shaky nod.

"Why did he want Rhys Jacobs?"

"Who?"

Damn. I tried another approach.

"Did Salter come to your flat?"

She kept her gaze glued to the vodka. "Esther always went to his place."

"And where is that?"

She extended a hand. Her fingers shook. "The drink first."

Cassie laughed and flicked the bottle to spill a couple of shots' worth. "You have to be kidding."

"Fuck you, you stupid slut. You're a nasty bitch. Okay, okay. He does business from his office in Stanholm Yard. You'll never get him, though. Esther said there were so many escape routes. It's a rabbit warren. She never liked to stay long."

I swapped a glance with Cassie and Convict, and both nodded. We were done.

But Cassie gave one last parting word. "We've gone easy on ye today. I am not above ending the life of an old drunk because you've pissed me off. Say a word about being here or what we asked, and I'll drown ye in a fucking vat of the alcohol ye find so precious. Understand me?"

Tracey nodded frantically and snatched for the bottle. She sucked down the vodka like she'd die without it.

"Thanks for the information. I'm sorry about Esther," I murmured, my instinct to close out the meeting in the way I would at work, but she wasn't listening anymore.

Outside, I breathed in a lungful of clean air.

To Cassie, I said, "You're scary. I'm glad we're on the same team."

The woman preened. "I aim to please."

"In a way, you're right. That was like a board meeting. Just with more honest emotions. We got what we needed, right? Or as much as we could."

Convict pressed a kiss to my hair. "You did good, little gangster."

I had no excuse for the burst of pride his words gave me.

Back at the office, Tyler and Kane had clearly listened in and had been joined by Arran, Shade, and Riordan. Someone had pulled up a map on a screen. They scrutinised it, phones in hands.

"Can't find it on any of the industrial estates." My brother's usual scowl deepened.

Arran swore. "I know this city like the back of my hand. But that name rings no bells."

Cassie cleared her throat, plucked out her phone, and dialled a number, putting the call on loudspeaker.

Lovelyn answered. "Hey!"

"I'm calling in an official capacity of the Skeleton Girls Detective Agency."

Lovelyn laughed. "Are you assigning us roles? Can I be the sassy hacker type? I make a mean spreadsheet."

"Deal! Love that for us. How about starting by locating Stanholm Yard in Deadwater?" Cassie asked.

Lovelyn made a sound of interest. "I've heard that name somewhere. Hold, please, caller."

All gazes fell on Cassie's phone, then Lovelyn spoke again.

"It came up in an informant interview about six months ago. I knew it was familiar. The location is the Scotsdale Trading Estate, the last plot. It used to be a pet food warehouse. Is that helpful?"

Kane stared at the phone, Shade slapped Arran's chest, then they commenced a frantic discussion, all the men leaning in. Weapons appeared then vanished under clothes.

Cassie tipped an imaginary hat. "You're literally the best researcher I ever met. Want to come by for breakfast?"

Still on the line, Lovelyn laughed. "It's closer to dinnertime, but yes, why not."

Cassie hung up and linked her arm through mine. "While the boys play, want to come up to mine? I can catch ye and Lovelyn up on Richard Yelland."

I'd put the disgusting pervert who'd bought Becky in the auction to the back of my mind having passed all I'd learned over to the skeleton girls. "I'd love that. I have some work to do, though. Is that okay? The exploding ship needs to be handled."

Cassie cocked her head. "Are you thinking it's somehow linked?"

"I wasn't until this very second. Surely not." Yet Convict's words about all the threats around me circled back. I frowned and went to him.

Convict took in his crew mobilising, his expression tortured. A dark light shone in his eyes.

I touched his arm. "Are you going with them?"

A muscle ticked in his jaw. "I won't leave you alone. Not after last night."

I took his hand and led him down the corridor so we had privacy. Then I made him look at me. "My plan for the next few hours is to hang out with the girls and try to unpick some mysteries. I won't leave the warehouse, not because you've commanded it as I won't be treated like property, but because I choose to give you peace of mind while you work."

His lips quirked. "You like it when I treat you as belonging to me."

"Or maybe I need time away from you," I countered. "You want to join your crew and be useful. I can see it in how tightly you've clenched your jaw. Go. Trust that I'm good for my word."

He studied me for a long minute, maybe reaching the same realisation I had. Without trust, we had nothing. And if we kept repeating the pinnacle we'd reached last night, we wouldn't survive it. Whether 'it' was fake or not.

"How about a compromise? I'll work on the remote camera feeds and be the eyes in the sky for my crew. That'll take all my attention but I'll stay in the building, in the ops room down the hall."

I was still annoyed, though much of it was an act. "So long as it gets you out of my hair, it's perfect."

He reached for me. Palmed my cheek and kissed me hard. Then he joined the mission planning while Cassie and I got to work.

36

Mila

Cassie's apartment was a floor down from Genevieve's but almost identical in the red-brick walls, oak floors, and arched windows overlooking the sunset city. Near the entrance, a shelving unit held motorbike helmets, one with cat ears, and a bookshelf thick with romance novels.

Cassie breezed into the kitchen and searched the cupboards, pulling out packets and raiding the fridge. "Gen is studying today, so we won't see her for a while, and Everly had a rough night, so ditto. It'll just be us three."

I settled on a stool the other side of the kitchen counter. "Mind if I check my email while we wait for Lovelyn?"

Scowling at a box of eggs, she flapped a hand for me to continue.

I opened the app and sighed at the sheer number of messages that flooded in, several familiar names scrolling by. But the message at the very top pulled me up short.

Anonymous: Shame his shiny gold coffin wasn't on that ship. Would've been a fitting sendoff.

A chill slid down my spine, something not adding up.

A rap sounded at the door, and Cassie opened it to Lovelyn, escorted by a member of the skeleton crew.

"I'm attempting pancakes," Cassie informed her. "If they turn out edible, I'm claiming witchcraft. Otherwise, it's just violence with eggs."

"I'm sure they'll be wonderful." Lovelyn joined me at the counter and set down a huge handbag, the handle boasting the floral print I'd started associating with her.

I greeted her but struggled to keep my smile.

Lovelyn eyed me. "Are you okay?"

"Not really. Can I talk to you both about something? I haven't shared this with anyone else but I could use your detective agency thoughts."

The women gave me their full attention, and I read out the message. Then told them what was bothering me most about it. "My grandfather's funeral was closed to all but the family, and there are a lot of us. But no press. No photographers inside the building. The pictures that were shared online of the funeral procession and of me at the graveside didn't show the gold referenced in that message."

Cassie caught my drift. Pouring batter into her hot pan, she said, "Suggesting someone who'd been at the funeral sent this hate mail?"

I cringed at the description, even though it was correct. "And several more since he died."

I showed them the email folder.

Lovelyn scanned the list. "Explain to me the significance of the gold?"

"He had an open casket. The gold was inside. Gold satin, gold studs. The outside of his casket was plain wood which reflected the kind of straightforward man he was, but my grandmother wanted to bury him with a little luxury."

Her gaze returned to me. "Has anyone from the family been obviously hostile to you or your grandfather? At any point, not just at the funeral."

I swallowed. "They're all frustrated at the money not

coming in, but that doesn't lend itself to taunting me or spitting venom about my grandfather. He was beloved."

"So that's a no? I ask because in cases such as these, nine times out of ten, the answer is the most obvious one. It's in plain sight. Do any of the messages make demands or threaten you directly?"

"No. It's just jabs at my grandfather. He really was the best of men. He built up Marchant Haulage from nothing to an international behemoth of a company. All the money he made from it, he split between the family, expanding out his reach as he went."

"He put his relatives on the payroll?"

"Not even that. He gave them monthly dividend payouts. Like a salary, I suppose, but with no work required. Just support for those who needed it."

As I said the words, I doubted the last part. Like Convict had pointed out, not everybody had a real need. A generation had grown up used to having that money with no effort or even a recognition of the privilege on their part.

Lovelyn's tone was careful. "What did he ask in return?"

I opened and closed my mouth. I'd never considered that. "Nothing as far as I know. Why do you ask?"

"Purely from an outsider perspective, and with no shade thrown at your frankly wonderful-sounding grandfather, all of those people were put into a position of obligation to him. He made them dependant, whether purposefully or not. It meant he could ask them for favours and they would jump to give them. I'm not saying he did, but we are looking at messages from someone who hated him, despite all the great things he did. I'd try to understand why they need you to know this so badly."

My shoulders rose. "You don't think it's jealousy?"

"If they were just making snide remarks about him, then sure. But making the effort to create an anonymous account and repeatedly send messages from it suggests something more pressing."

Cassie pointed a whisk at her, the pile of pancakes growing. "Reckon they'd escalate to blowing up a boat?"

Lovelyn blinked.

I filled her in on what happened to the *Eden*. Then I drew my eyebrows in and opened a previous message from the hate mail stack, showing it to Lovelyn.

She read aloud. "'All those boats sitting in the dock.' They said that right before the boat blew up?"

"They did. Just a couple of hours."

My phone rang with the number for the Marchant legal team. I excused myself and answered it. I'd left them a message when driving back from the clinic, not expecting a reply until morning as it was after hours now.

Cochran, the lawyer handling my grandfather's affairs, spoke down the line. "Miss Marchant. Thank you for your message. How can I help you?"

"What can you tell me about the *Eden's* destruction?"

"Very little, I'm afraid. The police have not yet commented, and the caretaker company has not reported their immediate next steps."

I grimaced. That wouldn't help me update the relatives. "Do we know if there was any loss of life? Any cargo that's been destroyed?"

"We have no information to share at all. May I recommend speaking with your uncle?"

"My uncle? Why would Wallace know anything?"

As far as I knew, my playboy uncle was sunning himself somewhere tropical. He'd never attended a business meeting or showed any interest in the company, nor had my grandfather trusted him to make a single decision. After the funeral, he'd hopped straight back on a plane.

"Then you haven't heard. Mr Wallace Marchant returned to these shores a few days ago, I believe to prepare for next week's meeting and to support your grandmother. She told me herself."

"When did you speak to her?" I squeaked.

The lawyer cleared his throat. "I'm not at liberty to discuss individual client's activities."

Meaning she'd told him not to. Yet she was fine and still in contact with others, just not me. I didn't get it. Wallace was the last person she would turn to for support.

At the funeral, he'd worn his sunglasses and a bored expression. But now I thought of it, he had been at his mother's side once or twice. Presumably poisoned by the same venom that was hurting her.

A problem I still had no solution for.

"About that meeting, would there be any possibility of extending the date?" I asked.

"I'm sorry, but no. Mr Wallace already requested it be brought forward and was refused as there is no justification. Assuming all voting parties will be in attendance, it will go ahead as planned next Friday."

Thanking Cochran, I hung up and dialled Wallace. The call rang out, and his answerphone kicked in. I killed the call and stared at my phone.

"Food's ready," Cassie said.

I returned to the counter and accepted a plate of pancakes with lemon and sugar plus strawberries.

Next to me, Lovelyn touched my arm. "I'm sorry if I was mercenary in my questions. I should've been gentler. I didn't think about how much you must be suffering."

"It's okay. I asked for your help."

"Are you sure? I have big emotional reactions sometimes, and it hit me when I saw your face fall on the phone. Did I cause that?"

"No! Not at all." I squeezed her shoulder.

She exhaled shakily. "Right. I need to chill and stop being ridiculous. I get all up in my feels, and it's like a tap I can't turn off. I try to ignore it for as long as I can. A set-and-forget timer, until it explodes. I just don't want you to think I was being careless."

"You weren't. I was broken up when my grandfather died, but it's settled into a background sadness now. It doesn't keep me awake at night anymore, if you know what I mean."

She gave me a wobbly smile that somehow told me she did.

We ate, and I sorted through my thoughts. Lovelyn's tap she couldn't turn off sounded like how I felt for Convict. Except he was a torrent falling all around me and sweeping me away. Being with him hadn't pushed aside my feverish energy for protecting my family, but he used it up in better ways that gave me a clearer head.

I devoured the sweet breakfast food and the coffee Cassie poured, working out what I needed to do next.

"Lovelyn, I don't suppose you have access to the Scottish police as well as the English?"

"I do. My father's role spans both. Why?"

"The lawyers can't give me any intelligence on the explosion. Would you be able to access the investigation? If that won't get you into trouble."

"I'd love to help. I can take a look without it causing any problems."

"Are you sure? I don't want to take advantage."

"Consider it a debt my father owes your boyfriend. Besides, Arran pays me well if he needs me to do some data digging. It's nice to do it for a different purpose."

She reached for a tablet from her bag and started typing.

As she worked, she darted a glance between me and Cassie. "I like feeling useful in our club. I haven't had Esther's post-mortem results yet, by the way, but that's coming. I'll pull my weight."

"Detective agency," Cassie corrected. "And I didn't just ask ye to join for what I can get. I'm not from Deadwater so I need more friends. I chose ye both because I like ye."

The three of us shot each other grins.

"Does that mean we get shirts, too?" I asked.

"Already ordered and on their way." Cassie took a deep swig of her coffee. "Which brings me onto my update on my scheme. Richard Yelland is our businessman friend who purchased Becky from Burger Barn. Heh. Love that alliteration. Anyway, because he's so friendly, he spends a lot of time sharing the love around different brothels in the country. According to my stalking, he should be back in Deadwater in a few days. Riordan and I will pick him up and do a little interrogation to crack that bad egg." She winked at me. "Ye may not want to be in the room for that one."

I wrinkled my nose. "Deal. I'll happily let you handle him. My money is on Esther's buyer being her killer, who Yelland can name, or it was Jan Salter, but in either case, I have no idea why. As a minimum, Salter will know what happened to her, I'm certain of it. He planned to give her a job, so if it wasn't him, he'll be pissed off that someone ended the life of one of his people."

Cassie hummed. She collected a pad of paper, her plate cleared, and wrote 'Victim' and Esther's name at the top of one page, then 'Suspects' on a second, listing Salter and her unknown buyer.

"I'll make notes of the evidence as we discover it," she commented.

Under Esther, she added a bullet point: 'Discovered dead in the harbour'.

"Add the bracelet," I suggested. "It's our clue to the timeline. My guess is she was killed directly after the auction, otherwise why would she still have it on?"

We added what else we knew. Her name, her role. I liked the feeling of creating a record. Then above the suspects, Cassie wrote: 'Means, motive, and opportunity', but we could only populate her buyer having her after the auction as an opportunity. After that, we were stuck.

Lovelyn made a sound of success. "I've found the case file for the explosion. There are no witness statements yet, but a detective has been assigned." She read, drumming her fingers on the counter. "Oh, that's interesting. An initial review of CCTV shows the busy road nearby but also two figures on the outer harbour wall at some point before the explosion. The timestamp isn't noted. The operator records that they appear to be all in black."

My mind raced over the report. What couple would want the *Eden* destroyed and also have the capacity to do it? "Wait, could that be Convict and Arran? They watched it explode."

"Damn. Yes, possibly."

A knock came at the door. Cassie went to answer it.

"Mila? It's for ye."

I jogged over to find Convict waiting in the hall.

My heart swelled.

He didn't come in, instead giving me an unsure look. From obsessed maniac to lost boy. I was falling for the whole range he covered.

"I don't want to interrupt, but I'm done. We found Salter. It's the right place, and he's barricaded up tight. Kane's watching for an opening, but it'll take strategy. This won't be a smash-and-grab." His gaze soaked me in. "I'm going to hang around downstairs and make myself useful until you're ready."

"Are you checking up on me?"

"Nah, just loitering like a very handsome stalker." His lips curved. "I'm missing having CCTV to watch you on."

I'd missed him, too. It had been under an hour, and I wanted to jump into his arms.

"I'll let you know when I'm done," I forced out. If I obeyed my instincts, I'd fly at him, and that wasn't healthy at all.

He turned to go.

"Con?"

He came back around, and a slow smile tipped up his lips. "First time you've used that nickname for me. Any, if I think about it."

Why did that tug at my heartstrings? "Give me thirty minutes then I'm all yours."

"There's nothing I want more, beautiful."

He left, and I closed the door and leaned on it. Cassie was clearing up the kitchen, a tablet on her countertop displaying a live feed of downstairs in the warehouse.

She caught me staring. "I'm watching Riordan at work. I get withdrawal symptoms if I can't ogle him for a while."

I smiled, considering how Convict would do the same if we had cameras in here, and grabbed a cloth to help. "I take it you've been together for a while."

"Nope, but I knew the second I saw him and I've been obsessed since. It took longer and some minor kidnapping to convince him he was mine." She breathed out happily.

She was joking, surely.

Side by side, we cleaned up, then I returned to my task and wrote a very bland statement for the relatives, sending it to all of their emails.

The whole time, the ticking clock of returning to Convict gained increasing urgency. I'd always believed relationships had to follow a certain path or they weren't right. Knowing someone didn't happen overnight. You had to see them happy, sad, stressed, and that took time.

That didn't explain the feeling in my chest. The draw to him that was so strong it was overpowering, and the connection a rope, towing me back to his side.

Cassie hadn't denied herself the same feeling for Riordan. From what she'd described, she'd embraced it and ran with the ball.

I had a whole lot to rethink.

For a moment, I sat back in my seat and just let myself enjoy the rush, and it felt so, so good.

37

Days passed of calm. Convict's crew had apparently settled on a strategy to grab Jan Salter, but not the chance to do it. I only became more distracted and lost to my thoughts. As if he could sense my distress, Convict stuck close.

I needed him near.

On the sofa, with the sunset painting blood-red streaks across the sky, I picked up the family photograph my grandfather had given me years ago. The one with the first group of relatives Marchant Haulage supported and the ship behind them.

To myself, I muttered, "How many of you were ever in real need? How many just took advantage of a good man?"

Convict moved to the back of the sofa and dropped a kiss to the top of my head. "Is that the *Eden* they're in front of?"

I linked my fingers through his, anchoring us together. "It is. There's still no police report available, according to Lovelyn, which is so freaking frustrating. The meeting is coming up in just a few days, and I have more questions than answers."

"What's the most pressing?"

With my head back on the sofa, I gazed up at him, my stomach tightening with anxiety and a building sense of dread. "Exactly how much I don't know about my family."

On the coffee table, my phone rang, and I set the photo

aside and picked it up, blinking in surprise at the name on the screen. "It's my mother."

I loved my mother and stepfather, but we weren't close. My stepfather had brought two young children to the relationship, and they'd kept my folks busy enough not to worry about me.

I hadn't talked to them at all about the Marchant family business. I'd invited them to the funeral, but only out of courtesy. They hadn't been able to make it, which was fine. I hadn't needed their support.

I swiped to answer but kept hold of Convict's hand. "Hey. This is unexpected. How are you?"

"Emilia, how are things with your grandmother?" Mum's familiar voice was strained.

"It's nice of you to take an interest. She's...as you might expect after her loss. Keeping to herself, though I'm doing all I can to support her. How are you? Are Jeff and the boys okay?"

"When you say 'support her', are you sure you're doing all you can?"

"I... What do you mean?"

Mum took a breath. "I don't mean to interfere, but your Uncle Wallace popped by and asked me to speak to you. He's deeply concerned."

My jaw dropped, and from Convict's matching expression, I knew he could hear the other side of the conversation. Wallace hadn't answered any of my calls or texts. I'd invited him over for dinner. I'd asked for a quick chat whenever he had time. Nothing.

"Wallace visited you?"

Mum continued. "We had a lovely cup of tea. I always said I'd have nothing to do with Marchant family affairs, none of my business, but I'm worried about you. I don't want you to throw away the opportunities your grandparents gave you."

"What exactly did my uncle say?"

"He encouraged you to do everything you could to make this transition easier on your grandmother. I have to say I'm surprised to have seen him. He had a lovely tan. The family meeting is soon, I believe?"

I released a breath of pure surprise. There was no reason for my mother to know about the meeting. I probably should have phrased my next sentence carefully, but I was rattled. "Did Wallace by any chance come bearing gifts?"

"As a matter of fact, he did, though it wasn't planned. That sweet man asked all about Jude and Mitch then made a very generous offer to support their clubs for the next year. It was completely out of the blue."

I sighed. "No, it wasn't. He was trying to bribe you to have this conversation with me."

"Surely not. Why on earth would he? He was just being nice."

My mother's world was so far apart from the Marchant life. There were no deals, no business manoeuvres. She lived in a nice three-bed semi, just down the road from the hairdresser's where she worked, with Jeff right next door in an estate agent's office. The boys went to a well-rated school nearby. The four of them played family tennis together on weekends.

Explaining the situation I was in suddenly felt exhausting.

I closed my eyes. "No, you're right. Sorry. Did Wallace say anything else?"

"Only that he's worried about his mum and he wants all the business drama to be over and done with soon."

"Of course he does. We all do."

With a few more platitudes, I got off the call.

Convict circled the couch to sit next to me. "Are Wallace's actions a threat?"

"I don't think so. He isn't vicious in any way. If you met him, you'd see what I mean. I just don't understand why he won't pick up my calls yet he'll set my mum on me."

"Cowardly."

An idea sprang into my mind.

Two, in fact. I needed more information to work with. There was no point in me complaining about being in the dark when I hadn't tried all the ways to turn on a light.

Throwing my leg over Convict, I settled on his lap and rested my elbows lightly on his shoulders, drifting my fingers through his too-long hair.

"Will you come with me to do something illegal?"

"Always. When are we leaving?"

I loved that. I loved his instant readiness to be whatever I needed him to be. If I needed space, he gave it to me. When we hadn't been talking, he'd made sure I was fed. Even before we were together, when I was out on a limb and doing dangerous things for questionable reasons, he'd been watching over me.

Since his confession of all the bad things he'd done, I'd only started seeing the good, and it was building up to a conclusion I wasn't ready to accept. I could, however, give in to the urge to start taking care of him in the way he did me.

"After nightfall. Maybe in a few hours."

His dark gaze held mine. "Whatever will we do with ourselves until then?"

I leaned in and kissed him softly. "You need a haircut."

"Can you do it while riding my dick?"

I was pretty sure that was inevitable for us.

We set up in the bathroom with a kitchen stool and an old towel. The scissors made a soft snick as I clipped a lock of Convict's dark hair. With his shoulders relaxed and chin tipped down, he kept one hand on me when I moved around him. Always touching me somehow. The bathroom mirror reflected us in golden light. Him, shirtless and calm, and me, trying not to fall apart while my priorities battled and changed.

"Let me fuck you while you work."

I tutted. "Not yet."

"We'll make it a game. You give me a haircut, I give you an orgasm. First one to mess up loses."

I rolled my eyes and moved on.

His hair had grown out silky and thick, curling slightly at the ends. I combed it with my fingers and worked carefully to crop it back, shorter at the sides and blending it to longer on top. It was strange how familiar he'd become. The faint freckle behind his left ear, his ink, the raised scar on his shoulder he couldn't explain, and the exact spot on his neck where I could drop a kiss that would make him shiver.

I landed my lips there.

He hissed and tugged me around to the front to claim my lips. I let him, just once, then pulled back and continued my task. I took my time over getting it right, and dusting the loose hair away so it didn't tickle his skin.

It was a journey of discovery, of sorts. I was seeing him differently. Not just as the lost boy who'd made me a deal, but as more. More than thirty days. More than temporary in my life.

When I came around the front, his gaze filled with hunger and longing. "On my lap. I'll hold you. Just let me warm my dick inside you."

Heat surged in me.

My hesitation condemned me. Convict seized the chance and ran his hands under my skirt to wrangle my underwear off me in a move than had me gasping. Then his jeans were wrenched down, and he picked me up, settling me over his lap.

He pushed inside me in slow, torturous inches. "So wet for me. Your cunt is my happy place, know that? You feel so good."

My heart pounded. I draped against him, my eyes closed and the scissors held at bay. I tightened my legs around his waist, the way he filled me lighting up pleasure centres that stole my thoughts.

Yet he didn't take it further.

"Just keep trimming. I'll stay right here, balls-deep in my emotional support girlfriend."

"You expect me to work like this?"

"Come on, businesswoman of the year. Let's see you handle a hostile takeover."

The haircut was close to being finished, but continuing while being filled with his considerable length took every ounce of presence I could summon. Yet he'd made it a challenge, and I could leave him a mess.

Opening my eyes, I fought through the lust and continued cutting.

Minutes passed, and my heart calmed, my focus returning to me. I liked simply warming his cock. There was an intimacy to it I hadn't anticipated. Far from the frantic, clawing sex that was more of our norm.

When I was done, I traced my fingertip over the pale scar that led back from his temple. It was the visible reminder of his amnesia which had mostly been hidden beneath the longer strands. That scar worried me, more than I let on.

One of his hands cupped my ass while the other flirted with the hem of my thin, strappy top. "What is it?"

"What if one day you remember something about your old life that changes you?"

He shrugged a bulky shoulder. "Pretty sure I know all the important things. Anything else is just background detail."

"What if you had a girlfriend?"

"I didn't. Kind of love the direction of your concerns, though. Keep going on your trip down insecure alley."

I scowled and tried to lift off him, but he grabbed my thigh and held me down. Inside me, his cock throbbed. Heat flared in his expression.

"You're worried about me falling out of love with you."

I made an off sound, pretending to focus on his hair again, though I'd already set down the scissors. "You are not in love with me."

He tipped my head down to link his gaze to mine. Nothing but sincerity shone in his dark eyes. "After coming out of hospital, there were very few things I could be certain of, but from first sight, I knew you."

He took my hand and placed it on his chest so I could feel the fast beat.

"My heart was yours from that moment. No hesitation, no doubt. Remember how sure I was that we'd met?"

I slowly inclined my head.

"Nothing from my old life could ever change that connection. I've been regaining memories every day, but this thing? It's only getting deeper."

I kissed him. Not hard or fast but the kind of kiss that held meaning, because everything he'd said had shaken me up and settled me down exactly as I'd needed.

In the midst of chaos, he was the one person I could rely on. The eye in my storm.

Convict stood and lifted me onto the counter, my thighs wide around him so my skirt rode up. His mouth landed on mine again, then my neck, his hands finding my breasts.

I matched his urgency.

When we moved together, it was as much relief as desperation. The slow grind of his body, the way he filled me, owned me, erased the noise in my head until I came with his name on my lips.

When he finished, his forehead pressed to mine, breath heavy and his words on repeat, I didn't say it. I couldn't.

But I was certain I was falling in love with him, too.

38

Convict

Metal clanked, and I winced and shushed it. Ahead of me in the dark yard, Mila snickered a laugh, and I jogged from the gate to catch up with her, both of us keeping our torches off on our break-in shenanigans.

Marchant Haulage's office block rose above Deadwater's harbourside. A brownstone block with several storeys of vacant space since all the staff had been put on indefinite leave.

We'd snuck in around an alley where Mila had remembered a gate being broken but hadn't made it inside yet.

"Hopefully they haven't changed the codes in the past few months."

Her fingers trembled slightly as she tapped at the keypad, and the glow lit her face, casting her in blue. The lock remained firmly closed. She tried again. Nothing.

She pouted in annoyance then widened her eyes. "Wait. There's an old master override."

An engine roared nearby, and I tensed, scanning the shadowed alley, my hand brushing the knife at my hip.

A low beep sounded, and with a soft click, the door creaked open. Mila grasped my hand, and we slipped through it and shut out the night.

Inside, the air was dead. Too still, like the building

had gone to sleep and never intended to wake. Our boots whispered on the polished concrete, and I swept my phone's torchlight around. On the reception's ceiling, the high rafters and exposed pipes cast long shadows like reaching fingers, and the company name stood tall on the front desk in bold red letters.

The overhead fluorescents buzzed to life in a slow flicker, and I jumped, whipping around with my blade palmed.

Mila exhaled a shaky laugh. "The lights are motion-sensitive. They won't go off unless we stand still. I know that from late nights spent working here."

"That's going to be noticeable from outside."

"I was hoping we could sneak in and out unseen."

I shrugged, undaunted. This was second nature to me, even if I couldn't remember any other time of doing it when I wasn't in her company. "We'll move fast. If anyone comes investigating, we'll run."

She gave me a dubious once-over. "I'm suddenly realising that bringing you with me could be a bad idea. Probation and all. What if someone calls the police?"

"If they catch us, I'll deal with it. Arran told me he'd handled the cops."

"What does that mean?"

"It means you have nothing to worry about. Now move that cute ass. Clock's a-ticking."

Mila relented, and we jogged across the floor with echoing footsteps to the staircase then climbed. At the third-floor landing, the motion sensors didn't trigger. Mila activated her torch, her light sliding over the old family pictures that lined the walls. More of what I'd seen in her apartment. The family members gathered near boats or in a transport yard. All smiles. All feeling more like a front the better I understood the Marchants.

"The family vault is just down here."

Mila crept on until we reached a door halfway down the hall. The lock was gone, and from the smashed wood, it had been ripped out.

"Oh my God," she whispered.

A warning played out in my head. "Someone else has been here. With a crowbar, if I had to guess."

She shivered. "Unless they guessed the code, they can't have got into the cabinets we need."

"Wait here while I go in and check."

I pushed the door open, treading on the splinters of wood underfoot, and entered the space. The shadowed office was narrow with a large table in the middle of the room taking up most of the space, and cabinets around the walls, many of which were opened with their contents strewn.

Not many places to hide.

I scoped the corners and stooped to peer under the table then gave Mila the all clear to follow. Whoever had been here was long gone, leaving a flurry of paperwork in their wake.

Prowling in deeper revealed a map on the wall, or what was left of it. It was torn down the middle, the left and right sides hanging from where they were tacked to a board and the rest of it shredded.

Mila stared at it. "That used to show all our trading locations. Why would someone vandalise that?"

She shook her head and continued to a cabinet in the corner. It was identical to all the others, but the drawers remained shut. Kneeling, Mila poked at the dial lock built into the mechanism then yanked at the top drawer.

It didn't budge.

"They've had a go at trashing this, too. The code's in, but I can't get it open. I think it's broken."

I dropped down beside her and gave it a sharp tug.

Something cracked, and the drawer slid out.

I fake-polished my nails. "Or you just ask your big strong boyfriend to do it for you."

Mila gave a soft laugh, kissed my cheek, then dove in to bring out an armful of folders. She handed each stack to me as she gathered them. This was what we'd come for. The vault her grandfather had created. Why we needed it was a mystery.

In the dark, the file covers gave me nothing. "What are we looking for?"

Mila giggled. "You ask that now?"

"What? I'd follow you anywhere. There doesn't have to be a good reason."

She continued loading me with paperwork, moving on to the second drawer and emptying it. "I'm not entirely sure, but my gut tells me I need to understand why my grandfather decided to support all these people. He wouldn't just throw money away. He was shrewd. He made good decisions."

Mila brandished a file and activated her torch, holding it low. She ran a finger on the name on the front of the cover then flipped it open. "This is one of the families we went to see, the Marchant-Smythes. It lists their basic details and also their previous employment. They ran a taxi service thirty years ago. No sign of them doing so now."

"Does it include their son?"

She traced down the page. "It lists their child, Presley, with his birthday, so yes."

"Meaning your grandfather was in the habit of updating his vault." I set the stack on my lap and leafed through it. "They're colour coded."

She swung the light across to my files. My top one had a green tab on the cover, while hers had an orange one. I opened mine. The single page listed an elderly couple, both with the words 'Deceased' underneath their names.

Mila regarded it then checked through the other folders, sorting them between us. "Some have an orange tab, some are green, and some are yellow. I need to work out what that code means."

"We're taking them, right? Better to do that detective work in the safety of your apartment."

She hesitated. "I can't just steal them. Can I?"

A rattle came through the open door, a distant sound from somewhere deep in the bowels of the building.

Both of us stiffened.

Mila's eyes met mine in the dim glow of the torch. "Please tell me that was the pipes."

I shook my head once in silent disagreement. Someone was down there.

Leaping up, I snatched a box from on top of another cabinet, dumped the contents, then stacked the files inside. Mila did the same with hers, her stealing question neatly answered.

She clutched the file box tight to her chest, and I reached for my knife, holding it low to my thigh.

"Mask up," I ordered.

Both of us covered our lower faces with the skeleton crew bandannas we'd already tied around our necks. We moved to the door then checked the empty hallway before scurrying out, the sound of our steps muffled by the cheap office carpet.

Behind us, the clank came again, closer this time, metal on metal. A dragging sound. Instinct told me it came from the floor below.

The air changed. Heavy. Electric.

Mila made a small sound of fear.

"Don't run," I whispered. "Not yet. Am I right that there's a fire exit this way?"

Like any good thief, I'd noted it from outside when we'd approached the place.

Her reply was barely audible. "It runs down the east side of the building."

"Get us there."

She led me down the hall in the opposite direction from where we'd come in. If someone had entered behind us, they'd likely expect us to double back. My bet was Mila knew the building better than anyone.

Another sound chased us. Footsteps. Not rushed. Steady. As if the owner knew they didn't need to hurry.

Mila's breath caught. "Can we run now?"

I reached back and threaded my fingers through hers, pulling her into a jog. Down the corridor, we slipped past abandoned cubicles and a toppled desk chair, my grip tight around the knife hilt.

"Stairs." She pointed.

We rounded a corner and burst through a door into the stairwell, the light above flickering once before dying.

A soft click chased us. The unmistakable sound of someone entering from the floor beneath us.

I didn't hesitate to peer into the dark. I dragged Mila up. Higher, towards the roof.

The footsteps followed. Not stopping. Getting closer.

We burst onto the roof with a slam of metal on brick. Wind caught Mila's hair, and she let out a shuddering breath. Behind us, the door slapped closed.

"There." She pointed to a caged ladder on the side.

We sprinted over, and I hauled open the cage door and peered down. Just a zigzag of ladders and platforms that dropped down the side of the building. Easy.

I helped Mila onto it, holding the file box under one arm so she could climb more easily. I followed, fast, grasping the wet metal rung, and just in time to see the figure emerge from the roof stairwell. Black-clad, material hiding their face. Not all that tall, but it could've been the angle.

As I stared at them, they didn't follow. Just watched.

Whatever, weirdo.

We descended in a hurry, rattling down each floor then fleeing to the alley behind the building, our breath fogging in the cold.

Mila took back the files and held them tight, her eyes wild on our jog back to the car. "Did you see them? They just stood and stared. Was it security?"

I scanned the dark street for backup or any signs of pursuit. "Security wouldn't cover their faces. I don't know who it was, but they weren't trying to catch us. Just scare us."

"Creepy bastard."

I didn't answer. But the way my skin crawled told me one thing for sure. Whatever we just took, someone else had been after it.

At the car, I closed Mila in then got us on the road fast. "We're going to the warehouse. Whoever that was wants those files, and if they recognised this," I tapped the bandanna once more around my neck, "they'll know the skeleton crew has them. Safer to visibly carry them inside and lock them up there than take them to your place."

Mila didn't argue.

In slowing heartbeats, I drove us across town, then at the warehouse, we entered purposefully through the front, Cassie meeting us to take the box.

We returned to the car.

In the seats, Mila mangled her fingers together. "Are you sure you want to go out for part two of my investigating? I already feel like I've put us in danger tonight."

"I live for this. Besides, it's important, right?"

She shook out her hands as if trying to rid herself of tension. "It is."

"Then that's all that matters."

I pulled the wheel and set tracks for location number two. Granny's house. The place that had sparked my curiosity and featured in any number of my idle daydreams about how I'd break into the gated mansion.

Looked like I'd get to use that imagined practice after all.

The dark countryside swallowed us whole, and a couple of hundred metres out from the house, I killed the headlights, burying the car in an off-road field entrance.

I hopped out and tried the gate. It gave, and I drove across the grass, leaving the car under the cover of trees.

Through the woods, we approached the property, "house" being too humble a word. Visible through the fence, the place was a Bond villain's retreat. Stark white render. Geometric lines. I'd caught a glimpse on our previous visit, but soaked in how the huge glass panels swallowed moonlight and how the boxy edges cut across the rugged Scottish countryside.

There were lights on. Someone was home.

Which meant I needed to find us a way in. A cable ran along the high fence, a clear sign of power going to a security system. Any neighbours were far enough away so there was no chance we'd be seen. Until we stalked out across the open ground.

The wind picked up, uncaring that we were about to commit yet another crime.

Beside me, Mila folded her arms tight. Her expression was calm, but her foot tapped the woodland floor.

"Nice place," I murmured. "Totally pictured your gran as a minimalist ice queen, so it tracks."

"She always was, though when my grandfather was alive, it felt warmer here. His office is the one room in the place that's done out in his style. All wood panelling like a ship and old records everywhere. I've only been inside once since he died. His office had been cleared out and felt like a mausoleum."

I squeezed her hand, sensing the sadness hanging over her.

Together, we stalked down the perimeter towards the entrance. Cameras in every corner. Motion sensors by the front gate. High-tech. Discreet. Expensive. "She's paranoid."

"She's wealthy. Same thing."

I grinned. "Come on. If she has any kind of staff, there'll be a service entrance. Gardeners don't use retina scanners."

We cut across the front and into the hedgerow on the other side. Twigs snapped underfoot, the night air damp. Along the edge, I found what I was hunting for, a lane leading to an outhouse of some kind that bisected the fence. No digital lock on the entrance. Just two motion lights and an old-fashioned deadbolt. Someone on the security design team had missed a spot.

I pulled my skeleton crew bandanna from my throat. "Give me yours. The motion lights love to ruin the mood."

She handed it over. "These are endlessly useful."

"I planned for this. I plan for everything. Except you. You're the chaos variable."

She snorted. "Flatter me more."

"I will. Later. When we're not about to be arrested on the grounds of a billionaire fortress."

I wrapped the material around the lights and dropped to a crouch, examining the lock. It was then that I spotted what I'd missed.

The outhouse wasn't just bolted. It had a camera hidden at the top of the doorframe and staring right down at us. Fuck it. If anyone was monitoring that, they'd be calling the cops faster than we could escape. More, there wouldn't just be this single, breakable lock.

I dropped it. A sound broke over the stillness, tyres on gravel.

I yanked Mila down, my heart thumping. Through the fence, a white car skidded down the drive, headlights slicing up the dark on its way to the road. The vehicle moved too fast to be sure of the occupant.

"Did you get a look at them?" I asked.

"Nope. Speedy driver was too busy burning holes in the driveway."

The gates clanked, opening, and I gave a short laugh. This was our chance, handed to us on a silver platter.

Still grasping Mila's hand, I said, "Run."

We belted down the tree line and to the edge of the road. The car bombed past us without slowing, and we waited a beat then sprinted on through the open gates, just as they began to slide shut.

We kept going, down the grass and all the way to the house. Pressed against the smooth white render, I exhaled. Mila laughed softly beside me, her eyes wide but alive.

"That was slick," she breathed.

I smirked. "Told you. I'm Bond. If Bond had a record and unresolved mother issues."

She gave me a side-eye. "You're more like Bond's evil twin who got banned from spy club and started a sex cult."

I grinned. "Still got the girl, though, didn't I?"

She didn't answer.

Didn't need to. Her fingers hadn't let go of mine.

There was nothing for it other than to enter the property. Mila indicated a side door. I could have gone with stealth, but we were there to be seen, not to steal this time. Pulling her clear, I reared back and barged the door.

It gave. I fell through and rolled to my feet at the end of a wide, white corridor.

Lining the walls on both sides were black-and-white pictures of a beautiful woman, tastefully draped over furniture or posing on a bed, and very, very naked.

Every single one was of Mila.

39

Convict stopped dead and stared at the portraits. "That is fucked up."

I shrugged and walked on. "They've been there all my life. I'm used to them."

He caught up. "They aren't of you?"

I swung back and gawked at him, open-mouthed. "That's my grandmother when she was a young woman. You thought it was me? Ew."

He blinked then scrubbed his face. "I need an eyebath, stat."

A laugh flew from between my lips, and I peered up at the nearest photo. As a teenager, the bare breasts had felt awkward but I'd stopped seeing them. "I guess we do look alike. My grandfather loved her so much. See how he put her on a pedestal? He adored her above all things, and the pictures were taken at the point he fell in love with her. That's how he explained this to me."

A sound came from somewhere in the house, directing us both to face down the hall. Adrenaline spiked my heartbeat, reminding me of my task. At last, I was here. They couldn't block me out if I was right in front of them.

Still, I was scared as hell.

"Hello?" I called out.

No answer came. The first room, a little-used cinema,

was empty and dark. Prowling further down the corridor brought us to a formal dining area, bathed in moonlight and vacant.

Convict walked a step ahead of me, his hand wrapped around mine and his focus sharp.

The hall opened out to a vestibule, and I pushed open the kitchen door. It made no sense that a visitor had just left, but no one was around to see him go. I called out again, but no reply followed.

In the kitchen, my gaze locked on to a barometer on the wall. It had come from a ship, and my grandfather would tap it to check the rising or falling pressure and predict the weather.

A wave of sadness captured me.

On almost every other occasion visiting here, he'd been alive. I'd hear him before I'd see him. That's what was so odd. The silence that came after death. The lack of a man who'd been so larger than life that his energy had filled the space around him.

As if he sensed my turmoil, Convict ran an arm around me from behind to hold me with my back to his chest.

I turned to face him. "It's so weird. I miss him in the oddest moments."

He brushed a stray lock of hair from my eyes. "I'm sorry."

I rested my head on his chest and let the unhappiness well and fade in the tiny moment of peace in a fraught evening.

A figure loomed at us from across the kitchen, something flashing in their hands.

I screamed. The sound erupted from me and cut through the still air. It was a repeat of the burger place where Esther's mother had tried to stab me. Except this time, in a heartbeat, I was behind Convict and he'd palmed his blade, his stance protective.

But our assailant uttered a matching scream and tumbled to the floor, a cereal bowl dropping from his hands and shattering. The shiny spoon he'd been holding clattered across the tile, and milk and frosted flakes pooled at the feet of a man I knew well.

"Wallace," I gasped.

In a blue satin dressing gown, and with headphones dislodged from his ears, my uncle scurried back until his spine hit the cabinets. His focus stayed fully on the man guarding me.

I exhaled my panic and squeezed Convict's arm. "It's okay."

Wallace's terrified gaze jumped from the knife to me. "Emilia? What the hell?"

At last I'd get to speak to him, but with his expression souring by the second, Wallace was not so happy to see me.

Ten minutes later, with the mess cleared up, we'd relocated to the den.

Wallace regarded me with a baleful expression which sank to fear each time he snuck a look at Convict. Every word since our shock encounter had been a gripe.

"You should have let me know you were coming." He took a sip of the hot drink he'd made himself, a swig of something stronger added.

I huffed an unfunny laugh. "I've been trying to speak to you for a month and you never replied to a single message."

He wafted a hand. "What can I say? I've been busy."

Busy sunning himself, from the deep tan. "You managed to go see my family."

"I was in the area. I thought your mother might make you see sense."

Yeah, right. "You were paying her off to talk to me."

"It worked in the past. She took my parents' money to

have you."

I fought to keep my expression clear. Convict had once guessed that little fact. I hated that it could be true. "Is my grandmother here?"

"No. She doesn't want to see you either, so I don't know why you're harassing her. Let the poor woman grieve."

Pain pierced my frustration with him. "I'm grieving, too. The company is in turmoil. It's important that I see her before the meeting on Friday."

Wallace rolled his eyes. "There's nothing to say. In fact, maybe it's a good thing that you broke into the house in the middle of the night because we get to have this talk. Listen, Emilia. It's better for the whole family if you vote with us. Mother might be grieving, but she isn't acting in grief. She knows exactly what she wants. Give up this champion role. You don't need to do it anymore. We should respect the choice of the remaining founder of the business."

I clamped down on the urge to yell at him. "What about all the people dependent on it? What about the work that just stopped? What about the boats left to rot in the harbour? Do you know what happened to the *Eden*?"

He heaved a sigh. "I heard. My money is on one of the greedy parasites doing it out of spite." He sniffed and leaned forward, resting his elbows on his knees. "Money is always an issue, but if you're concerned about that, you should know there's a huge payout coming your way. Father told me it would be in his will."

"I don't care about money. Why does your mother want the company shut down?"

"It's none of my business, and it isn't yours either."

"Is she being influenced by Rhys Jacobs?"

"Never heard of him in my life, and you sound delusional." His gaze held mine. "Stop it. Now. Don't hurt her by voting against her."

"I'm not trying to hurt her. I'm trying to do what's best for everyone."

"Why? You're free from it all. Get on a plane. Get some sun. At last, go live your own life."

I had no answer to that. Marchant Haulage was my life. It had been all I'd known for years, just the same as for my grandfather. In the face of Wallace's complete apathy, my arguments dried up on my tongue.

Wallace climbed to his feet, bundling himself tighter in his dressing gown. "If you're done whining, I'm going to bed."

I stared after him. "Will you at least ask her to call me?"

"I won't. You need to learn when to leave well enough alone. Oh, and by the way, next time? Just knock at the door, and leave the scary minder at the gate."

He shuffled from the room, leaving Convict and me to stare at each other. Convict lifted a single questioning eyebrow.

Crestfallen, I stood. If my grandmother was here, she would've come out. I didn't doubt that for a second. Even so, I poked my nose into the other rooms, including her bedroom. All empty. My grandfather's office was soulless and cold.

There was nothing for it but for us to leave.

On the drive back, my thoughts tumbled together. I'd been fighting a battle I was so sure was worth winning, yet at each challenge, more doubt trickled in. Over and over in my mind, I replayed the talks I'd had with my grandfather. How he'd impressed on me the scale of what he'd built and how much good it did. There were needy people depending on the business, but that had been at a point in time and needs had changed.

My thoughts flipped to Wallace's challenge. I didn't want to act against my family. I'd spent my life acting *for* them.

Was this all still worthwhile?

Or was I wholly acting in grief as I'd accused my grandmother of doing?

Back at the warehouse, Convict led me inside, and in the central corridor, I lifted my gaze to find my brother approaching.

"Can I talk to you?" I blurted.

Kane followed me into an office.

Convict hesitated at the door. "No, I'm not listening in," he said low before shutting himself out to give us privacy.

I faced Kane. "Why did you take this job?"

He folded his thick arms but didn't answer.

"For the money, right? Because Marchant Haulage stopped paying out?"

Something ticked over in his vision. "Correct."

I managed a shaky nod. "Is it enough?"

I had no idea what the skeleton crew paid, but my grandfather's handouts had been generous.

Kane tightened his jaw. "It never could be."

I already knew he wouldn't tell me what the money was used for, I'd asked before and been shot down in flames.

I had one final question to ask. "We need to fight for this business, don't we?"

The pain in his eyes spoke volumes. "I'll never stop."

Certainty settled my writhing belly.

That's all I needed. A reason.

If not for my grandmother, and if not for all the relatives I thought needed it, I had to stick to my guns for the sake of my grandfather's legacy, and for whoever Kane was protecting. What was I if I didn't have this?

40

It took until Thursday for me to face the family vault. Seeing Wallace and hearing his challenges had cut me to the bone, and I couldn't shake the sense of wrongness. That if I went digging any further, I wouldn't like what I found.

I used my down time in better ways, taking Convict shopping and buying him things I knew he needed. Clothes including cargo pants that looked so good slung low on his hips. A hoodie so he'd be cosy in the cool spring weather, even if he didn't feel the cold.

Later, in the bathroom, I caught him staring at the toothbrush I'd picked out. He'd been using a spare from a multipack in my cupboard.

Bare-chested, and under the warm lights of the mirror, he glanced up at me. "I don't think anyone ever bought me one of these before. Not one just for me. I've no idea how I know that." He dropped my gaze. "Thank you. It means something."

That tiny confession hurt my heart and confused me further.

A message from Cassie finally spurred me into action. She and her boyfriend were at last heading out this evening to capture Yelland. She suggested Lovelyn, Genevieve, and I meet at the warehouse, and I doubled down, asking Lovelyn to meet me earlier. Convict had work to do there anyway, and Cassie gave us the run of her apartment where the files

I'd stolen had been locked in a safe.

Cross-legged on the floorboards, I stared at the stack I'd sorted.

Adjacent to me, Lovelyn made a note on the pad. "Fourteen green-coded files, six orange, and three yellow."

I blew out a breath that stirred the lock of blonde hair falling in my eyes. "Now the hard part. What on earth did he mean by it?"

"People make lists for all kinds of reasons, but it usually comes down to a practical purpose such as treating the groups differently. Either communicating with them separately, or perhaps in the way he paid them."

This was why I'd wanted her help. Not only was she smart, but she exuded calm methodology in her thinking.

I nodded. "Such as the green group might be higher needs or more important than the orange?"

"Perhaps. Does that resonate with what you know about the people?"

I pondered this. "No. I haven't met all of them, so some I only know from my grandfather's stories, but recently, I went to visit three families, one from the green files and two from orange."

She twisted her lips. "Was there a clear pattern? I'm guessing not from your frown."

"Nope. In the orange corner, the Marchant-Smythes, a family of three, are not hard up, though they grouch that they are, and the Kingleys are more arguably in need as they're elderly and have carers. The green-coded family, the Grants, seemed to be living pretty well."

"Then it's something else. Mysteries are meant to be solved. Let's engage our brains."

We considered the positions on the family tree, geographical area, the date they were brought into the fold, and whether their file appeared to have been updated. All non-starters.

Lovelyn was undaunted. "Perhaps another approach. The yellow group appears to be an outlier with so few in it."

I picked up the stack, though I'd already pieced through it. My file was first, then Kane's, and lastly an unidentified one. The third was empty, no name on the front and no paperwork inside. "Let's assume yellow means close family. My brother and me plus probably our dad."

She tapped her pen. "If so, we're missing a file for your Uncle Wallace, suggesting the family vault is incomplete."

I thought about the person who'd been sneaking around the office when we'd raided it. All signs pointed to them being the one who'd broken into the room before us. It stood to reason that they might also have stolen files. Perhaps we'd disturbed them doing it.

All of which gave me nothing.

Exasperated, I tossed the yellow files down. "This is hopeless."

Lovelyn watched me, hesitancy on her pretty features. "There is something else I considered, but I feel I need to couch it with a warning. Though your grandfather started this beneficiary role, he may not have been the one to set up the coding, so this might not be on him."

My gut twisted with the same sense of wrongness. "What are you thinking?"

"I mean, I'm probably way off base."

"Out with it."

The air seemed to tighten around us.

"Those in the know and those not."

A knock came at the door, a message arriving simultaneously on my phone to tell me it was Tyler and Kane. I informed Lovelyn, and she grabbed a blazer from the back of the chair and slid it on over the cropped top that bared her waist.

I arched an eyebrow, glad for a break in the tension rising in me. "You're fine."

She shook out her sheet of long hair. "I don't want to appear unprofessional."

"There's a nightclub of barely dressed people downstairs."

She didn't meet my gaze. "Not many of them are bigger girls, though."

"Are you kidding? You're gorgeous."

Lovelyn flashed a quick smile that didn't convince me she agreed. Someone had clearly done a number on her self-esteem.

I went to the door and let in the two men. Earlier, I'd asked Convict if there was any update, and he'd replied that Tyler would tell me himself. I hadn't expected my brother to come with him, and when Kane took in the piles of paper on the floor, then pointedly retreated to play sentinel against the kitchen wall, a small flare of irritation rose in me.

At the counter, Tyler walked through an update on the hunt for Jacobs. There wasn't much to say. No return home. No licence plate registered.

"In my experience, men like that don't abandon all they've worked for without exceptional reason. If you believe he's influencing your grandmother, our next play will be to stake out the meeting tomorrow."

Strange relief had me breathing easier to know the skeleton crew would be around. Convict had assured me he wouldn't leave my side. I needed that more than I understood.

Tyler looked at Kane. "Anything to add?"

My brother curled his lip. "My guess is he's dead at the hands of whoever he crossed."

I snorted. "Which helps us none."

Kane inclined his head. "Agreed. If that proves true, we'll take it out on that miserable sewer rat, Salter."

"Any closer to driving said rat out of his sewer?"

Grouchy emotion flickered in his eyes. "I'll tell ye when there's something to say."

Tyler's phone buzzed, and he turned away to take the call. I directed my cool gaze back onto my brother. My feelings were all over the place, and for some reason, he appeared like an excellent target.

"Ready for tomorrow?"

A muscle ticked in his jaw. "We have no fucking clue how this vote will resolve. It's pissing me off."

The looming meeting had me so nauseated I could barely think about it. It was still a draw, two votes for, two against. Nothing I'd done in the past several weeks had made a difference, and the hope I'd held of finding and blackmailing Jacobs shrank by the hour. "I think the trusted company panel gets a vote in the event of a deadlock."

"Ye think or ye know?"

"I'm not certain. The will reading has to happen first. That's the clincher."

"It's bullshit that this is left to an unknown fate."

"Don't you think I know that? I'm doing my best," I snapped.

He stood to his full height, easily a foot taller than me. "As am I."

"Really? Want to come help with the family research? Want to go digging around in dark corners of the people you share DNA with? Didn't think so."

Kane's file listed his only relative as his mother. He had to be helping her, but if so, why not talk about it? Why not trust me when I'd gone all out to build a connection with him?

Tyler ended his call. "Lovelyn, do you have a second?"

My friend, who'd been doing a very good job of faking interest in her phone, scuttled away. They went to the end of the kitchen area, but the distance didn't disguise the conversation.

Or Tyler's cautiously neutral tone. "I haven't seen Dixie around."

Lovelyn exhaled, and her eyes crinkled at the edges with concern. "She hasn't been back since when you saw us in the corridor. I've texted her a few times and no reply. I was considering paying her a visit." She paused. "If you want, you can come."

I glanced back at my brother to see something interesting. Kane's attention had followed Lovelyn. The oversized oaf soaked in the sight of the woman, lingering on her curves and the tiny flash of exposed flesh still visible at her waist. Just as quickly, he shut down his reaction.

I tilted my head, curious. Never once had he mentioned a love interest.

"Are you seeing anyone?" I asked.

His focus slammed back to me, his annoyance obvious that I'd caught him checking her out. "Aren't we a little old for girlfriend and boyfriend talks?"

"I'm only asking."

"Don't. I don't date."

I heaved a sigh. "Probably better for the majority of womankind."

He was so closed off, any girlfriend would need the patience of a saint.

Kane muttered something about me being a brat, which was probably fair as I was sinking into the worst mood ever.

My phone buzzed with an incoming call from Convict. I answered it, scooting away to an arched window overlooking the city.

"Are you busy?"

Damn, his voice made me melt. "We've heard nothing from Cassie yet, and Lovelyn and I have read every one of these files a hundred times and got nothing to show for it, so not really."

"Want to play a game?"

My insides liquified. I stared out of the glass into the night, unseeing, and with heat rising through me. "Always."

"In twenty minutes, head down to the wardrobe and borrow an outfit."

"You want me to change?"

"Put on something you don't mind being torn off you."

The heat inside me turned into an inferno. "Why do I get the feeling you're up to no good?"

"Always, little gangster. Don't keep me waiting."

41

Convict

Manny clicked the next magazine into place and lined it up with the rest on the steel table. "Are you sure about tonight?"

"I am." I racked a weapon. The weight in my palm was solid and real. Better than the storm brewing in my gut. I couldn't shake the edge of it. Mila had been rattled for days, and tomorrow was the meeting everything had been leading up to.

So far, I'd failed in my promises to help her.

I wanted to solve the Jacobs problem for her and had the chance of going out with my crew on a raid of Salter's HQ.

She'd told me to go. That she'd be safe here.

I would, if they stopped trying to babysit me.

I also wanted her under me where she belonged. In minutes, we were meeting in the club. I'd planned to mess with her, but the way I was feeling demanded something darker and more twisted than a satisfying fuck while strangers watched.

Bootsteps sounded in the corridor. Past the open door to our weapons room, Shade plus two crew members dragged a man, the prisoner's hands zip tied and his face a mess of bruises. Though a bandanna covered his eyes, from the loll of his head, he was out cold.

"Sit his arse down," Shade ordered.

I went to the door. "Who's that?"

The enforcer glanced over. "A small-time runner we leaned on for intel on Salter. Your woman got the name Dumbo but figured it was code. Turns out everyone calls him that, and he's been in and out of every gang in the city. He took our money, blabbing on Salter's warehouse and the part he knew about the auction, which was pretty much nothing, but my guess was he'd turn tail and run, so we picked him up early. Save spoiling the evening's fun."

They hauled the guy to a chair in an adjacent room. His shirt rode up, revealing a tangled scar low on his side. The skin was puckered and white, shaped like a spiderweb with jagged edges.

My breath caught. On my own side, hidden under my crew t-shirt, was an identical scar. The same shape. The same mark.

"What the fuck is that scar on him?" My voice came out rough.

Shade answered without looking up. "That's a Four Milers mark. They'd brand new recruits with a tattoo or cut the skin if they thought you were at risk of doing them dirty. Sometimes both."

I stared at the prisoner. My pulse spiked, and my vision swam. A flash of memory hit, me strapped down, breathless. The sizzle of heat followed, then a knife and the stink of burning skin. A punch to my gut. Someone laughing.

I didn't give a fuck about being scarred on the job or the fact the Four Milers had done it. My skin was a mess of ink, welts, and jagged lines. But the sense that I was missing something major glimmered at the edge of my brain. It was infuriating that I couldn't remember. It was so close yet so far. And it felt vital.

Manny and Shade discussed something in low tones that my heartbeat drowned out. Manny took over managing the prisoner, and Shade gestured for me to follow him into the corridor.

"Are ye sure about coming on the raid?"

I rolled my eyes. "For fuck's sake. Look at me. I'm healed, my head works, why the hell wouldn't I?"

"We lost ye once. Don't want to risk it again."

My annoyance fled. "I don't want that either. I also can't stand the thought of being left behind."

The enforcer heaved a sigh. "I get that. Ye always were at the front of any fight we went into. Arran said the two of you went back to Leith. He asked me to try to come up with any memories of our time there."

With the way my head was reeling, I almost didn't want to know, but maybe it would help. I recalled Shade in pieces of splintered memory. A dark-haired furious teenage version, obsessed with some girl he would never talk about and a stepfather he intended to one day kill. Pure savage boy. No wonder I'd liked him. "And did you?"

"Aye, it was about your nickname. How Convict came about."

I should've stopped him. There was no way this was going to end well, and I was clinging to the edge of my sanity. Yet I needed to know. I lifted my chin, and Shade scratched his cheek with a hand tattooed with the Scottish flag.

"We never used real names at the club, only numbers or nicknames. Ye fought dirty and would take any fight going so long as ye were still standing. Ye didn't care about the prestige, only the money. One night, some guy paid ye to take a dive so his kid would be the victor. The club didnae give a fuck. The problem was your reputation. No one believed some golden boy got the jump on ye. After hours, you'd vanished, and Arran and I discovered a group of arseholes surrounding ye. They called ye a conman and claimed to have lost money in bets. Does any of this sound familiar?"

I shook my head. Complete blank.

"We pulled ye out. A few nights on, when ye next took to the ring and some of those bastards booed and yelled out 'Con', we changed the chant to 'Convict'. Ye won every fight that evening and the nickname took."

Manny stuck his head into the hall and said something to Shade. I stared into space. I'd assumed my repeated jail time had been the source of my name, and I'd been wrong. Like everything else in my life, it was rooted in shit.

I swallowed. "I'm going to the club with Mila for an hour. I'll be back down in time for the fun."

Shade didn't stop me. "Play nice."

Fat chance. My chest burned. I needed Mila, for her to look at me like I was more than this broken piece of shit.

And God help her if she didn't.

42

Mila

The rhythmic thud of music marked my slow stroll down the sex club's corridor. I'd been escorted to the wardrobe by Tyler, who'd played bodyguard for the short walk through the warehouse. He'd handed me over to Clem, a woman who ran the bar staff and who'd promised to stick with me until I was safely in Convict's clutches.

Clem guided me with a light touch until the music swelled and the room opened up, a vast space, dense with bodies and heat. With a blindfold on, I couldn't see anything, but my other senses worked overtime. The scent of perfume and sex mixed with expensive alcohol and leather.

The pulse between my thighs was impossible to ignore.

Convict's presence closed in behind me. Heat at my back. A familiar, grounding scent that had become an addiction.

A cool, small object pressed under the blindfold and into my ear. A headphone.

His voice poured in, low and rough. "You'll hear me now. Even when I'm not touching you."

I swayed towards him, the only solid thing in this overwhelming sea of sound and sensation.

He directed me through the room then stopped me. Metal creaked.

"Kneel on the platform."

Bars pressed against my outstretched hands, and I

ducked my head and crawled onto a lightly padded, raised stage.

No. My brain filled in the picture. A cage.

My pulse thudded faster. It had to be one of the gilded ones I'd seen women suspended in, people touching and even fucking them through the gold bars. Desperately, I tried to work out where I was in the room. In the centre or off to the side? How many people watched me right now?

"Hands up."

I flinched at the soft clang of chains but obeyed, raising my arms. Leather cuffs snapped around my wrists, binding them to opposite sides of the gilded frame. I was spread open, exposed and vulnerable in a way that sent another wave of heat pooling low in my belly.

The room buzzed around us. Footsteps nearby. Laughter. Moans.

Then hands slid up my thighs, taking my borrowed dress with them. I'd chosen skimpy black lace to match the underwear beneath it. Underwear that was in danger of being revealed when the dress inched higher.

"What are you doing?" I whispered.

His voice came low through the earpiece. "The game starts off as an obedience test. The better you do, the more I reward you."

I shivered, automatically on board with whatever this game was. My emotions needed burning up, and doing something dirty and public would push me to an extreme. One rewarded by orgasms.

"Widen your knees."

I obeyed.

"Good girl. Now stay very still."

Something touched me between the legs, and I jumped. Convict shifted my underwear aside and eased a cool and slick toy into my wet centre. He seated the curved end perfectly against my already swollen clit so it cupped me on the outside as it filled me inside.

Shocked at the sudden fullness, I gritted my teeth and adjusted my position. My pussy fluttered around the intrusion. Being on display was so strange. Particularly when I wasn't sure he'd be part of the show. I stifled my reaction, though my skin had to be mottled and flushed.

Convict placed my underwear back over the toy. "You're beautiful like this."

A hum started, soft and teasing and right there inside me. Maddening.

He retreated. I couldn't see or hear him but I sensed him moving away.

I swallowed hard, tugging uselessly at the cuffs. I rode a wave of pleasure from the vibrations, exhaling when they died back. God. It was remote controlled. I pictured him through the crowd, leaning back against a pillar, eyes on me and my every reaction.

Another boost of the toy had me drop my head back and flex my thighs.

It made me want to perform for him. To drive him so wild he climbed in with me or even just dragged me to the bars to fuck me. My nervous system zinged wide awake, and my skin begged for touch, my nipples hard and desperate for his mouth.

Then a new sound reached me. Deep male voices, too close. Heavy boots on the floor.

"Check out that one. Fuck, she's fit."

My pulse spiked in panic.

"Convict, there's people."

"I know." His voice was a soothing caress. "They're all around you, admiring what they can't have. Anyone can look. No one touches."

The vibrator surged, the pressure stronger. I bit my lip. At least he could hear me like I could him.

"Can they tell what you've done to me?" I didn't know how obvious the toy inside me was or whether my clothes hid it.

"Yes, baby. They can see."

I whimpered. It was so exposing to be on display like this, caged, and with a sex toy inside me and my dress rucked up. Yet at the same time, the bandanna hid my identity, and I knew Convict would tear into anyone who got too close. "You're going to make me come in front of them?"

The torment eased, the sensation dying back.

I hung from my restraints, sweating under the lace and the tension. It rose again with the vibrator activating, speeding up, then right when I caught the edge of a spiralling pleasure I couldn't stop, he slowed it.

"You'll come when I'm ready. Until then, fuck the floor."

I wanted to snarl at him but I had no idea where he was in the room, and worse, with the toy activating, my body was primed to obey him. My hips worked the air, my suspended arms holding me an inch away from being able to apply pressure myself.

If only I could touch the cage floor, I could grind on it to make myself come, but he had all the power. Frustration rose in a jagged arc.

"This is infuriating."

"You're doing so well, little gangster. You should know how perfectly fuckable you look in that black dress flirting with your ass and the glimpse of the toy through the lace. I like you with your hands tied up. In fact, you passed the obedience level. We're moving on to a loyalty test." His voice darkened. "You can crawl to the edge of the cage, beg someone else to finish you. There are men and women who will happily put you out of your misery. Or..."

The vibration cut out entirely. I whimpered at the sudden loss.

"Or you can give me the three little words you know I want. Then I'll come in and finish you myself."

"W-what?"

"You heard. I'll play with your ass then fuck you there with the vibrator in place."

Tears pricked beneath the blindfold. "Why would you do that?" I meant the words. He knew.

"Because I need them."

My voice shook. "You arranged this deal. We're temporary."

Silence. Then the vibrator resumed, stronger than before. My hips jerked involuntarily.

"We never were. Not from the first time I saw you."

My body shook. Need blurred my thoughts.

"Convict..."

"Say it." His voice held a plea. "Or anyone here will see how desperate you are for me. I'll make you scream for as long as it takes."

A sob caught in my throat. "Love is earned. Not demanded."

"Not for me. Not now. I need it."

My mind raced, my emotions spilling over themselves. In a flurry, the events of the past few weeks battered me with a barrage of hits. Of suddenly being alone, no job, no grandparents. Of being at a loss of how to fix a terrible situation and at the centre of everyone's blame. Of slowly realising all was not as it seemed in the life I'd been swept up in then abandoned to.

"I asked you not to lie to me," I bit out, focusing on that last point above all others. Others had lied to me repeatedly. Convict had, too. "On the night of your big confession, I asked it and you said you wouldn't anymore. Have you kept that promise?"

He hesitated. "I think so. Fuck. I'm not sure. Lying comes as easily to me as breathing. Same as stealing, hurting, and every other crime there is. It's second fucking nature."

Tears spilled hot down my cheeks, soaked up by the skeleton crew bandanna. "Then how am I supposed to trust you? I need that from you. I need you to be honest. Never to lie to me."

A ragged breath sounded through the earpiece.

"I'm trying, Mila. I'm trying to be what you need. You keep putting barriers between us."

"By making demands like this? Do you know how messed up that is?"

"Yes, because I'm messed up. I'm the king of red flags. Yet still you want me."

I opened my mouth to answer.

A harsh crackle cut through the earpiece. "Convict. Salter's in play. We're mobilising. Five minutes."

Convict swore a bitter stream.

The vibrator stopped abruptly. Rushed footsteps followed. Hands on my wrists, undoing the cuffs. The toy removed and discarded.

I sagged forward, only for his arms to catch me.

His tone was harsh. "I have to go. You'll be guarded all night. Unless you ask me to stay."

I wasn't going to ask it. I needed the space. But his mouth was on mine, hot, desperate, unfinished.

Then he was gone.

I knelt alone in the cage entrance, my blindfold slipping askew.

Around me, the club throbbed with life. Strangers' eyes

burned across my skin, but a quiet enquiry from Clem told me he hadn't left me unprotected.

I wiped my face, my chest rising and falling.

I'd nearly said words I couldn't take back. And now, I wasn't sure if he'd return.

43

Convict

My crew's convoy of night-black vehicles crept through Deadwater's industrial quarter. Hidden in the back of the lead truck with Shade, Arran, Manny, and Tyler, I touched the gun at my hip, every one of us armed to the teeth with the weapons glinting in the dim red light.

Kane drove another vehicle, the stubborn fucker refusing to wear a skeleton mask over his face like he didn't care if he was identified. He'd have no choice over the masks we'd wear once inside. Gas masks dangled from straps around our necks, ready to deploy.

I sat with my elbows on my knees, my head pounding a fast beat.

I couldn't stop thinking about her. Mila in that cage. Mila saying, *Love is earned, not demanded.*

It had gutted me worse than any blade to the ribs.

I'd thought I could handle tonight. Thought I could lock my shit down and give the crew my all. But her voice kept looping, a taunt and a truth in equal measure.

And underneath that, something worse.

Memories clawing for the surface.

Her face. Perfect, beautiful Mila in the time I couldn't remember. Why did I know her? If it was real and not some trick of my amnesia, why didn't she remember me?

Or was that the biggest lie between us?

"Stay on the planet," Shade muttered.

I blinked. He'd caught me zoning out. "I'm fine."

"Do that when an asshole with a machine gun is running at ye then tell me everything's grand."

Arran leaned forwards and commanded everyone's attention.

"Listen up. Salter's rabbit warren has multiple choke points. We've got no reliable blueprints, but from intel, we know it's underground. There are two main air shafts leading to the back of the complex, plus one central staircase that feeds the sublevels."

Shade tapped a chunky black briefcase. "We'll drop gas through the shafts. The chemical mix I've rigged is a fast-acting, temporary KO agent. That'll give us five to seven minutes of free movement before it starts wearing off."

Arran grinned dangerously. "Salter will be running scared. Bastard has a habit of using his people as human shields. But this time, we bottleneck the fucker."

Shade looked at me. "Convict, you're with Manny and me. No solo hero shit. Arran's leading the main breach with the others."

I flexed my fists. "Understood."

Liar. I didn't agree. I wanted blood. I wanted answers. I wanted to rip something apart just to quiet the screaming in my skull.

But orders were orders.

Arran gave the final rundown: three teams, one to secure the main floor, the others to lock down the tunnels.

"If we funnel him, we can push Salter towards the old maintenance tunnels on the west side. No cameras. No exits. That's where we take him."

The vehicle jerked to a halt.

"We're on."

We jumped out, weapons ready.

I jammed the mask over my face and followed them out into the dark.

The complex sprawled low and wide, an old pet food factory converted into a fortress. Steel walls gleamed with damp under the streetlights.

Tyler's crew peeled off first, heading for the air shafts. A rope drop had been pre-set earlier by a scout team. I followed Shade and Manny around the side. We reached a narrow service entrance with a keypad.

Arran's voice buzzed in our earpieces. "On my mark. Hold until gas is deployed."

I crouched, my breath misting the mask.

And in the space of waiting, everything unspooled.

Mila's eyes, wide and wet with unshed tears. Her mouth gasping when I upped the speed of the vibrator. *I need you to be honest. Not lie to me.*

The name *Convict*, spat at me by a faceless crowd, teenage fists flying in the blood-slicked basement of that Leith fight club.

The spiderweb scar. The scared face of a girl. The feeling that everything I knew was a lie I'd built to survive.

"Deploying gas," Shade reported.

I forced my mind to the present. Listened as his crew dropped two canisters down into the vents. A hiss. Faint green mist coiling up.

Seven minutes, Shade had said.

He readied the override for the service door. "Go."

The door clicked open, and we slipped inside.

The interior was decay and rot. Forklifts abandoned mid-run. Pallets stacked floor to ceiling. Faint alarms buzzed, but nothing else stirred. The gas had worked. Bodies lay slumped already, guards in masks, collapsed where they stood.

We moved fast, hugging walls, eyes on every side passage.

Arran's voice crackled. "Main floor secured. Tunnel teams on the move. Salter unaccounted for."

Manny returned, "Copy. Stay sharp."

My headache spiked. I stumbled and caught myself on a rail.

Shade stopped. "All good?"

"Fine," I lied. The sense of déjà vu was unbearable. The smell of damp and the dim lighting. The way the tunnels forked.

The sense of something deadly lurking around a corner.

I'd been here before.

Not this exact place. But a place like this. A warehouse, as a recruit. Or something worse. My hand went back to the scar on my side, feeling it pulse.

I pictured Mila, and fear ghosted over me.

Something shifted ahead.

Arran's announcement crackled over the line. "Salter's on the run. We flushed him out of the sublevel tunnels."

Manny cursed. "Fucker's smarter than he looks."

Shade gestured sharply for me to cut left. We took a side passage, angling to intercept. The gas was thinning. Ahead, faint shouting echoed, panicked voices, gunshots.

"Go. Now!" Shade barked.

We sprinted.

The tunnels narrowed, and we passed cages stacked against the walls. Old, rusted things. Memories blurred with reality, me hating a place like this. But not with my fists raw, but something else. A need to act and hide my emotions.

I barely heard Shade's shout from far ahead.

I'd fallen behind.

Between me and them, a door burst open. Salter fell out, gaunt, wild-eyed, and gasping. He clutched a gun with his silver rings glinting.

He froze when he saw me.

I didn't.

With a yell, I surged forward, gun up. I didn't pause but fired a round to his thigh. The bastard crumpled and screamed. I was on him in seconds, yanking the weapon from his limp fingers, driving a knee into his back.

Blood smeared the floor.

His voice came high and shaking. "You don't...fucking... know who I am."

I grabbed a handful of his greasy hair and slammed his head to the concrete. "You wish that were true." To my crew, I reported, "Got him."

Arran's team piled in behind me.

He knelt at my side. "Nice work. Are you okay?"

"Fucking fine." Why the worry about me when I'd caught the guy? I hauled Salter upright, shoving him into a limping walk while he screamed.

As we moved, my skull nearly split in two. The scar burned. Memories tried to flood in, too fast, too much.

Blood on the blade. My blood. A brand, not a scar. *Convict.*

And Mila. Always Mila.

Somewhere, somehow, before all of this, I'd known her. The truth danced just out of reach.

We got to the van. Manny threw the back doors open, and we dumped Salter inside. To my right, Tyler threw his mask off like it burned him.

Arran clapped my shoulder. "You did good tonight."

But I barely heard him.

Because every beat of my pulse screamed one thing. Mila wasn't a stranger. I'd been right about knowing her. This whole time, we'd been known to each other all along.

At an off-site nondescript trading estate, we drove into the cover of the building and offloaded Salter to an interrogation room. Safer not to take him to the warehouse when we were unsure if we'd be pursued.

The extraction operation had gone nicely to plan, thanks to the intel given up by the grunt Mila had gotten the name for.

The underground room was concrete with no windows. A bright light fell over a steel chair above a drain, and the single camera feed went to the crew who watched from outside.

Salter had been stripped to his boxers and duct taped to the seat, his wrists behind the backrest, and ankles locked to the floor bolts. Blood oozed from the gunshot wound to his thigh.

He woke to a jolt from an electrode pressed to his bare side. A muscle stimulator had been wired to a portable battery. Shade's handiwork.

Salter hissed in pain, jerking in the seat. "What the fuck is this?"

Shade stepped back and gestured for me to proceed.

I brushed my fingers over the skeleton mask hiding my face. "Jan Salter. Answer our questions and you might live to see sunrise. Lie, and you'll die in this room and no one will ever know how your miserable life ended."

"Fuck you. What do you want?"

I crouched to eye level with him. "Where is Rhys Jacobs?"

Salter laughed a wheezing hack. "That piece of shit? You're out of luck. He's long dead."

My stomach gutted. "How?"

He flexed on the seat, grimacing. "No idea. I was told it but I never saw the body."

"Then how are you sure?"

"Because I would've found the miserable son of a bitch by now. He came out of your goddamned game, and my guess is he got jumped and eradicated that night. Now you know as much as I do, let me the fuck out of here."

I chuffed a laugh. "You're in no position to make demands."

"I'll see both of you hanging from the rafters of the base you raided and let your blood decorate my floor."

How descriptive.

Shade tutted. "How did you know he was going into our game?"

Salter clamped his jaw.

Shade handed me a pair of black metal pliers. "Your choice."

I took them without flinching.

Salter's eyes widened. I gripped the pliers around his smallest finger and squeezed, enough to crush the nail, break the bone, and pulp the flesh beneath.

He screamed, the sound bouncing off the walls. "One of my girls gets the names from her boyfriend."

"Who is?"

He gave up the name of one of the guys who worked the bar in Divide. He'd be fired by the time we got back.

I moved on. "Why did you need Jacobs?"

"He was trying to quit his part in our chain." Salter's breath came in ragged gasps. "He couldn't walk away. My goddamn livelihood, and he was fucking around with it."

"He was selling the women you supply in his auctions? That's why you took over?"

Salter's mouth stayed closed. Wrong choice.

I picked up his next finger. Crushed it. Then a third.

Silver rings tinkled to the floor and rolled, one by one.

His anguish filled the room. "Fuck, okay! You're wrong. He brought the women in, not me. He had a reputation with clients and could earn top dollar. I couldn't replicate it and I couldn't let him just walk away."

Mila had said the auctions were run by Jacobs when he was fresh out of school. "If he sourced the flesh and ran the auctions, what was your role?"

"Vendor for rejected stock."

Disgust coated my tongue. We'd suspected Jacobs could've moved on from virginity auctions of willing women to being a people trafficker, but Salter was claiming he was more. The kingpin in the trade that disintegrated with his departure.

None of this gelled to the image of the man I'd met in the interview. The grandma-fiddling contestant who'd wanted skeleton crew protection. Who'd been knocked out only minutes into the game.

"Why did he quit?"

Salter breathed through his nose. Stubborn fuck.

I nodded to Shade, who clipped a jumper cable to Salter's broken hand. A zap of current and Salter convulsed, howling. Sweat poured down his face.

"No idea!" His spit flew. "Something scared him off. He stopped showing up. Pulled his money. Wouldn't answer calls."

"You expect us to believe that's all you know?"

"I swear it. Something changed. Someone bigger than

me spooked him. I just wanted him to man the fuck up and keep the business going for all our sakes."

And for that, he'd forced Mila into the game.

I leaned in, my voice low. "You're going to give us more than that, Salter. You're going to tell us everything you know about who he worked with, when and where it took place. And if you don't..."

Shade reached for a scalpel with a steady hand.

"Then we'll open you up and find the truth ourselves."

44

Mila

Genevieve lifted her head from her phone. "They're coming back."

Cold relief rippled through me. As mixed up as I was over Convict, I'd hated him going. Even though he'd given me the choice to have him stay.

At least the Skeleton Girls Detective Agency had used the time well.

Cassie and Riordan had caught Yelland and chained him up in a boathouse of some kind. Then they livestreamed his question-and-answer session to us, sitting watching from the safety of Genevieve's sofa. Gen and Lovelyn sat either side of me. Everly had refused point blank to be in the room while the torture went on. I didn't blame her.

Yelland was exactly as I remembered. Brown-stained teeth. Ugliness to him that no amount of money could hide. I almost enjoyed spotting the bruises that must've come from his capture.

With his features tight in terror, he'd readily admitted buying Becky but said he didn't know anything about the other buyers.

Cassie didn't believe him. Her persuasion had Genevieve muting the feed.

I typed a text message to Cassie, knowing Riordan would whisper it into her ear.

> **Mila:** Ask about the format of the night. We know enough from Becky to tell if he's lying.

Riordan gave a thumbs-up to the camera. Genevieve activated the sound again, and Yelland's spluttering voice filled the room.

"The attendees were all separated in booths. I never saw the others. Even transport was arranged at separate entrances. They had a car pick me up and take me back to where I parked."

He coughed up blood. I winced but didn't look away.

"Who told you about it?" Cassie asked.

"A fellow at the Greystone club."

Genevieve glanced at me. "Any clue?"

"It's an old boy's club. Privately owned, whisky and cigars, that kind of thing."

My grandfather had been offered membership but hadn't taken it. He considered networking a waste of time and would just seek out those he needed information from.

On the video feed, Cassie demanded a name.

Yelland answered more readily. "I don't know him. We were at the bar, and he was telling someone else about it. They called him Sulli, that's all I know."

"Describe this Sulli."

"Brown hair, younger than me. It was a short conversation. What do you expect me to say?"

"Did he attend the auction, too?"

"I don't know."

His whiny voice had me cringing.

Cassie was unfazed. "Based on this short chat, you decided to prey on women?"

Anger flashed through his fear. "Rhys Jacobs was

supposed to be running it, and it was his name that sold it to me. I was told they'd be willing to do anything. It was a waste of money."

"You trusted that name because you've bought from Jacobs before," she decided.

"Once or twice, but there's nothing wrong with what he does. Everyone is consenting adults, so I don't know why I'm here. The bitch I purchased griped and complained. I was glad to see her go when her friend came."

"What friend?" Cassie asked.

"She called her Esther. They aren't allowed phones, so someone had to pick her up."

All of us stilled.

I exchanged a look with Genevieve and Lovelyn. Becky never told us about seeing Esther the next day.

A grinding sound came down the phone, then Cassie spoke.

"Esther's dead. As far as I can tell, you're one of the last people to see her alive. Did you go after her because the woman ye bought wasn't what ye wanted?"

Yelland sobbed. "I don't know anything about her friend. There's a pawnbroker two doors down on Strathmore Road. She got into the car right outside of that. They'll have cameras. You can watch them drive away together."

The phone shifted, and Cassie's face filled the screen. She stomped away from Yelland and exited a door into the night. "Annoyingly, I don't think he's lying. Either way, we can test it. Riordan is arranging for someone to go to that pawnbroker's now."

"We should also pick up Becky," Genevieve suggested.

Cassie nodded. "We'll get someone on that as well. So, what am I doing with this arsehole? In the river or let him go home to lick his wounds?"

I stared in horror. "We should release him."

She sighed in disappointment. "Fine. I'll give him a little warning about treating women with respect. Talk later when we have any more news."

The line disconnected.

I slumped. The mystery of Esther's death still wasn't solved. I had to hope that Convict returned with news from Salter.

It wasn't long until he was back, the smell of blood, gunpowder, and the night clinging to him. He grabbed my hand and led me down through the warehouse and to our car, driving me home without a word.

A dark storm of energy crackled over him.

It bothered me. His obvious impatience. How he white-knuckled the steering wheel.

Worse, I was keyed up and still on edge from his game. Like hell was I asking him to solve that problem.

In my apartment, he locked the door, kicked off his shoes, and stormed into the living room. Then he wheeled around on me.

"Salter believes that Jacobs is dead, though has no evidence. He claims Jacobs supplied women and ran the auctions as a trafficker, giving Salter any he couldn't sell. His urgency and blackmail of you came from the fact his supply of bodies would dry up without Jacobs. But where was Jacobs getting his supply? Why opt out from what was making him a fortune, according to Salter? Something changed. Some unexpected event took place that tumbled their house of cards."

I fought the urge to shrink in on myself, his words leading to one conclusion. "You're implying it's to do with my grandfather's death."

He watched me, his muscles locked tight and wariness in his eyes.

"You do. You really think it."

Convict held up a finger. "The boats." Another finger. "The routes in and out of Europe." A third. "Secrets he kept from you. Relatives who aren't what they seem. The trafficker haunting your grandmother then vanishing." His fourth and fifth fingers added to the damning list of evidence.

I shook my head, unable and unwilling to believe it. Outrage consumed my need and every other emotion. How *dare* he? My grandfather would never have anything to do with a world like that. Yet even as I knew that to my bones, all the other factors crowded in.

"There has to be another explanation. This is way off base. Marchant Haulage isn't a front for people traffickers. My grandfather was a good man. It doesn't make sense. There's nobody else who could have fulfilled that role. There's no way it would be a woman, and you've met Wallace. He couldn't organise his way out of a paper bag."

He just kept that judging stare on me.

My blood heated further. "Plus, what about me? I've been in every part of that business. I've seen how it works. It's a well-oiled and highly profitable machine that has operated for decades. Don't you think I'd know if there was something else going on?"

Convict went to speak, but I was so hurt, so livid by even the suggestion of the picture he painted. I held up my hand. "Don't say another word. I don't want to hear it."

He breathed through his nose, that tension in him clearly building. "You asked for my help. Now I've given it, you won't let me speak?"

I planted my hands on my hips. "You've done enough."

"What does that mean?"

"I'd say our deal is over."

Emotion flickered in his gaze, then he poked his tongue into his cheek. "If we're so temporary, all you are is a hole to fill, is that right?"

I jutted out my jaw, in pain but defiant.

His eyes gleamed. "You're forgetting the thirty days. It isn't over yet."

"I have no idea what I was ever doing with you. Taming a monster or slowly being devoured by one."

"That's bullshit." Convict stepped up to me, his fingers curving under my chin to hold me still. "You want me to own you. You need my insane degree of obsession and my loyalty. Want to hear my theory why?"

If he expected a response, I wasn't giving it. I glowered up at him, infuriated and messed up beyond belief.

"Because your world is falling apart and it's happened before. You were given away by parents and swept up by grandparents you barely knew. But they used you and cast you aside, too."

Fresh pain welled. His fingers gripped tighter, pinching so I couldn't tear my gaze away to hide it.

"A house you never got to live in. All the responsibilities and hard work but never in the heart of the family. Only the job. They rejected you after being your everything and left you with this shitstorm to handle. Your grandfather dead and your grandmother retreating into a life she refused to take you with her. I would never do that. Even if you walk away from me, even if the world stops fucking turning, I'll always be yours."

My frustration rose in a hot wave. "Stop talking."

"Never. I belong to you just as you belong to me."

He stole a savage kiss. I shoved him. He didn't budge.

"Don't fight me, Mila."

"Don't pretend you know me after barely a month."

His laugh was cold. "It's been a lot longer than that."

"It hasn't."

"No? Then why can I see your face in my past? Why am I so certain I knew you before my amnesia? If I'm a liar, you are, too."

He was insane. I pushed him again to loosen his hold. Convict snarled and spun me around, pinning me with my back to his chest. He marched me to the edge of the couch that overlooked the city view, and kicked my feet apart. Reaching under my dress, he shredded my underwear and undid his jeans.

"Mine since I don't know when. Mine forever."

I wrenched to get free, but he brought his dick to my core and punched into me, so hard I saw stars. Pulling his hips back, he wrapped my hair around his fist and fucked into me again, his rough treatment and actions holding me in place as much as my body wouldn't let me give him up.

Fury mixed with rising heat. If he was insane, so was I in how much this turned me on.

"I will never give you up. I'll toy with you and play games because you love it. Because you love me, even if you won't say it. That denial fucking kills me because it's the one thing I want. The only thing. But still, I'll never leave you. The sooner you accept that you belong to me, the better. You're mine, Mila. Mine until I die. Mine in every hell that comes after."

With my cheek to the cushion, I gripped the material, so tense I could break.

Each statement was marked with a jerk of his hips and his thick fullness thrilling my body. The orgasm he'd denied me in the game in the sex club rushed back, and I couldn't stop the flood of need and desperation.

Yet it was his ragged breaths that drove me over the edge. Or his demanding words or the fact he'd claimed my silence hurt. He told me over and over that I was his until I cried out and shattered into a million pieces.

I wasn't sure if I'd ever be put back together the same again.

45

Convict

Sleep wouldn't come. Though Mila had curled up on the couch and passed out, dawn found me borderline frantic.

I was wrong. She wasn't lying.

Or, I was right and she was.

My head was so fucked, I was going insane.

Alongside that was the weight of partial memories I still couldn't reclaim. Every time I tried, they slipped around and moved.

My phone buzzed in my pocket, and I slid it out to dismiss it, but it was a message from my bank. At last, I'd gained access to my account, having supplied the driver's licence I'd needed as evidence. Piece by piece, I was becoming real again.

The notification allowed me to log on to their app, and I scrolled through the transactions, hope stirring in my chest that the familiar spending pattern of my old life would trigger memories.

My pay. Endless pizza takeaways. Some bills. I scrolled back to the date when I was supposed to be working for the rival gang.

A ten grand payment stood bold on the page. I stared at it. There was no way the Four Milers would have paid that to a new recruit. Nor did it come from the skeleton crew because Manny told me they'd switched to cash. Unless I'd had a surprise lottery win, logic gave me only one solution.

I'd been paid off for something.

Sickness swirled in my belly.

When I'd come out of the hospital, I'd been certain that I'd betrayed my crew. Even when I got to the bottom of entering the game and my breaking of Arran's rules, my gut had told me there was something else.

Fucking hell. If the money was a bribe, I was the worst. Maybe it was better that Mila didn't feel what I wanted her to. Her family's meeting was in a matter of hours, and even with Salter brought in, I'd failed to deliver Jacobs which meant Mila couldn't swing his influence.

We'd run out of time.

She wanted to leave me. If that was true and not the heat of the moment, after the deal we'd made, I'd be the worst man alive if I didn't let her walk away, and I was already toeing that line. Besides, what was I supposed to do, handcuff her to the bed for the rest of her life?

I couldn't even joke at how the thought was compelling.

A strange and entirely new sensation spread through my chest. A kind of spasm, but it broke my mood and edged me into desperation, my fingers gripping the edge of the sofa as the crush of it worsened. What the fuck was wrong with me? Was I having a heart attack?

I held my gaze on Mila.

The answer came slowly.

This was pain. I'd never felt it before, but the knowledge that she would walk out of my life *hurt*. The more I considered living without her, the more I descended into agony. My body felt like it was dying, except it was all in my head.

For the first time in my life, real pain became known to me.

I got why others did anything to avoid it, because this fucking sucked.

Climbing to my feet, and careful not to disturb the exhausted woman, I stumbled to the kitchen in search of water.

An image hit me so hard it nearly knocked me out. A recent memory formed from fragments that had troubled me for days.

A woman's face. Maybe even a girl because she was young. I'd picked her up from somewhere. I was the driver.

Breathless, I jammed my fingers into my hair and tried to push the scene out. Nighttime, yes. Late enough that the streets were dead. Salt air. Holy shit. Leith? The scenery filled in. It was a dockside building. I knew the street.

That was enough.

The sickness inside me spread. What if the money was worse than a bribe? What if it was a payout for fucking trafficking?

I had to fill in the gaps, the importance of it overriding every other sense. A quick glance at the time told me I had three hours before I needed to be back for the meeting. Just enough time to make the trip and force the rest of the damning scene to the fore.

I pocketed my keys. Stooped to kiss Mila on the forehead.

The notepad I'd used was on the coffee table, and I scrawled a quick message.

Be back soon. I won't miss the meeting.

Then I was gone.

A little over an hour later, and I rolled into the town of my birth, my manic rush and the early morning giving me a clear run up the coast. I passed Ocean Drive where Arran and I had walked, and drove onto Dock Place, crossing a bridge that led to where the *Eden* had been moored.

Outside a huge warehouse, I exited the car and stared up at the white letters on the red frontage. *Marchant Haulage.*

The memory blurred then gripped me once again.

It was here I'd come to pick up the woman, her dark hair half hiding her terrified eyes.

Horror chilled me, and I stumbled closer, gaining more slivers of a picture as I moved. It was a job for the Four Milers. They'd sent me.

I swallowed. Maybe this wasn't on me. I'd been undercover for Arran. But fucking trafficking?

She'd trembled in the cold, so I'd stayed gentle and calm, offering her a coat that she refused. I couldn't identify the grim-faced man who'd escorted her out, but I'd delivered her to the Four Milers' brothel, assuming she was a sex worker.

Wait.

Something had happened before that.

I crossed the yard and approached the brick building, setting my hand to the cold wall, just like I'd done in the not-too-distant past.

While waiting for the woman to come out, I'd searched for the warehouse's name, typing Marchant Haulage into my browser. It brought back Mila's face. Not the sad funeral shot as she hadn't been bereaved at that point, but a happy one with her grandfather. I'd flipped through more, instantly hooked on the beautiful woman.

Holy shit, I was wrong in thinking I knew her. Nor had she lied to me.

Hers was just one of the last faces I'd seen as that was probably the evening where everything had gone to hell.

My elation curled in my gut and soured, the cold light of day exposing a damning fact. Last night, I'd implied that her grandfather might be a people trafficker. Now, I was ninety-nine percent certain it was true.

How the hell did I tell her?

She'd hate me for it. She'd hate me more if I lied.

She'd despise me if that money I'd been given was for more than the undercover work.

"If you're here to steal, you're out of luck."

A voice cut through my thoughts, and I jerked around to see a man approach. I squinted in recognition. He was the son of the Marchant-Smythes, the one who'd been playing video games in the daytime like a fucking teenager when Mila and I visited his parents. Preston? Wesley? Fuck if I could remember his name.

"Everything is locked down tight," he continued. "Protected from thieving chavs like you."

At whatever my expression had shifted into, he gave a mocking laugh, his fingers moving over his phone. "You didn't think I recognised you when you showed up with Mila? What are you, muscle to protect her? Definitely not a boyfriend. Not for someone like her with a stick so far up her ass she can sweep the floor. Does she know what kind of scum you really are?"

I'd missed something with this guy.

Staring hard, I worked out what I knew. He lived with his parents. He had a girlfriend and no job. One of the cars outside their luxury home was probably his.

The cars.

My mind leapt back to the night I was here with Arran and the blue BMW that had cut us up in town. His. Fucking. Car.

I lurched to a conclusion. "Fine words for a man who blew up a boat in the world's biggest tantrum. What, did Mummy and Daddy cut your allowance?"

"The *Eden*? Why the fuck would I do that? It was worth a fortune. Maybe I'm just here to see if the old man lined his cabin in gold like his fucking coffin." Mini Marchant-Smythe stepped up to me, inches shorter, and giving me a close-up of his mid-brown hair cut straight across his forehead. "And fuck you for that attitude. I owe you for knocking me out. I don't give a crap if it was ten years ago."

Ten years?

"What are you talking about?"

His features tightened. "Piss off. I don't buy it that you don't remember me. I split your lip."

No memory served me, but I took a guess.

"You visited the Glass House for fights. So did a lot of people. I floored a whole lot of boys like you. Congrats on the lucky shot."

Anger flickered in his eyes.

I'd pissed him off. Good. I wanted him rattled, because him being here was no coincidence. His family were among those shouting loudest about being cut off. He knew the area and had clearly hung out here when he was a teenager. Then he was back on the very night the boat blew up.

What else had he done?

I lifted my chin. "What's your name?"

He didn't answer. Only held his gaze on me then snuck a look at his phone.

I tried again. "You're working for the company. Was that off the books? Carrying out dark deeds for old man Marchant?"

It wasn't him I'd pictured in my memory of the trafficked woman, but that didn't mean he wasn't involved. Why else would he be here? Not just today but often.

Mini Marchant-Smythe curled his lip. "Work? This fucking family is a joke. Did you know my girlfriend's mother is a police officer?"

I squinted, not following his train of thought. What difference did that make?

It was then I picked up the siren, wailing in the sea air and coming in fast.

He'd called the cops on me.

Shit, I was on probation. And trespassing. Arran might have paid off the police in Deadwater, but I had no idea if that applied here.

His mocking continued as I backed away. "She was so interested when I said your name. I remembered you as Convict, but Mila called you Roscoe. No confusing the identity of a man like you."

I exited the yard, rounding the tall stone wall onto the road and the bridge over the water to the mainland. The police car screamed to a stop, blocking my ride, and an officer leapt out.

From her belt, she lifted her Taser.

For fuck's sake. I couldn't do this right now. I had to get back to Mila ahead of the meeting or she'd think I'd abandoned her. In a rush, all my mistakes fell as dominoes in my mind. The fact the police were interested in me. The way I moved like I was invincible. The way I treated my broken body without care.

I reached for my phone.

The cop yelled and ran at me.

The crackle of electricity filled the air, and I ducked to avoid it. But the prongs from the Taser missed their mark of my chest and instead struck my temple. Right over the site of the brain injury that had stolen my thoughts.

I dropped to the ground and my world turned black.

46

Mila

Bright sunshine hurt my eyes, and I shielded them to scan the road outside my apartment block. He wasn't here. Convict hadn't been in the living room when I'd jerked awake, fell off the sofa, knocking a pile of paperwork to the floor, then stumbled blindly to the bedroom. He wasn't there. Nor the bathroom or anywhere. His car was missing, too.

He'd gone. I finally lost faith in him coming back.

Worse was that I'd overslept and had to rush to throw on clothes and get ready. I'd called my brother, and to my relief, he'd shown up.

Kane opened the car door and gestured for me to get in. "Aren't ye—"

I threw myself inside. "I don't want to talk about it."

He shrugged and slammed the door.

We drove across town to the lawyer's office without speaking. I jabbed the radio to try to drown out my thoughts. 'I hope you hate me' by Dead Poet Society blasted out. I stabbed again at the screen to turn it off.

For weeks, we'd been building up to this moment, except it was meant to be me and Convict, side by side. He'd abandoned me. Hadn't I caused that? I'd been angry at him. I'd refused to give him what he wanted. I loved him, and he'd left me despite all the promises that he wouldn't.

My lost boy had done what they always did and returned to his own world.

Tears welled, and I dashed them away.

Thank God my brother didn't comment on that.

We entered the chilly reception of Cochran Family Solicitors and were shown into a meeting room so thick with people, Kane had to carve a path through.

They argued around us, the noise deafening. Complaints, decisions about how the morning would go.

Like they had a say.

Because of the intricacies of the legal situation, everything needed to happen in a sequence. The will reading came first, hence the long queue of relatives who all wanted their slice of the pie, their voices raised and clamouring for attention. After that was done, we could get on with the meeting that finally decided the future of the business.

If my senses weren't muted by a wall of pain, it could've overwhelmed me.

Yet it felt like a dream, and I was a spirit drifting through it.

With low energy, I scanned the room for my grandmother. She wasn't here yet, but the Marchant-Smythes and a dozen other family members sat around the polished conference table or stood with their backs to the wall like the world's greediest peanut gallery.

"Move," Kane snapped to a couple of people taking up seats at the table they weren't entitled to.

They grumbled but left. He settled me in one before taking the other himself. In black leggings and one of Convict's skeleton crew shirts, I was nothing like the woman who used to work so diligently for Marchant Haulage. With all I'd learned and suspected, I couldn't bring myself to be her anymore. I'd stared at the smart blouses and pencil skirts but couldn't choose them.

The version of me who would do anything to save this business no longer existed. I might not have the whole truth, but I was certain of the lies.

A lawyer entered the space, followed by two flunkies. He took a seat directly opposite us. "If we could bring the noise level down, please."

The buzz of angry chatter simmered.

The lawyer peered over his glasses to take in the attendees.

At the end of the table, a woman lurched to her feet. "In light of the unbearable situation after Austin dying on us, I feel—"

"Madam, sit down. I will outline the agenda, and if there is a need for input, I will ask for it." The lawyer shuffled his papers, his annoyance plain.

"You have your agenda, but we are the family who no one thought about for weeks," she griped. "Listen to me—"

"Shut it," Kane intoned.

The woman froze with her mouth open. "Excuse me?"

He didn't look at her. "The lawyer is leading this, not you. Save your breath."

Outrage filled her features, and she planted her hands on her hips.

As small and as cold and as alone as I felt, I was right at the end of my tether. I switched my gaze to her. "Enough. You're in the way. Be quiet."

Never would I have spoken to a member of the family like that in the past, but to my surprise, it did the trick. She plonked back down on her seat with an aggrieved mutter to her neighbours about how rude I'd become.

The lawyer's frown settled on me then swept the room once more. "I ask for silence until the reading is complete."

He switched his gaze to one of his assistants who opened

the door. Wallace entered, followed by my grandmother.

My heart thumped out of time.

With her silver-blonde hair cut in a bob, she was the image of the stylish, poised woman I'd known since I was a young teen. Except her gaze didn't seek me out. Instead, my grandmother took a seat at the table and stared straight ahead.

Wallace slumped in the seat next to her, appearing as bored as he always did in any company meeting.

I couldn't stop staring at his mum. I'd been doing this for her, but I wasn't sure why anymore. The only thing I was certain about was Convict, and he'd done what he'd promised he wouldn't. He'd vanished on me at the moment I needed him most.

And it was all my fault.

The lawyer talked through the preliminaries, noting the exceptional circumstances and significant legal toil to get to this point.

My brother leaned into me. "I have to say it. I'm surprised to see ye here."

"Why?"

"Figured you'd be part of the hunt for your boyfriend, but I guess you're Marchant to the core."

"The hunt? What do you mean? He was gone when I woke. He didn't answer my calls." By now, he'd broken our four-hour rule which had told me our deal was off, just like I'd asked.

"Arran said the cops have him."

I stared, and my world compressed to his words.

"I am able to read the will," the lawyer continued, "but I'm afraid to say the meeting to decide the future of the company will almost certainly not go ahead today."

A chorus of dismayed voices reacted.

Angry relatives demanded to know why.

Cochran spoke over the sound, confirming the document he was reading and that my grandfather had been of sound mind when he wrote it.

I could only stare at my brother.

"Point one. Equal voting rights go to my beloved wife, our remaining son, Wallace, and our three grandchildren."

The room fell silent.

The lawyer continued. "With that said, you will understand that the meeting requires attendance of all eligible voters. However, the fifth named individual has not been in contact or responded to our meeting requests or correspondence."

I barely registered the explanation, but Kane had gone deathly still.

"Fifth voter? Who?" he said.

"Darcy Marchant, child of Able Marchant. Your sibling," the lawyer snipped.

A squabble ensued.

There was another sibling. A secret third child who shared a father with Kane and me. The empty yellow-coded folder screamed at me, mocking with how obvious it had been. Yet none of that mattered in the moment, because at last, I found my feet and made for the door.

What the hell did I care about Marchant Haulage anymore? Convict needed me.

47

Kane

While thirty greedy fuckers spoke at once, Mila sprinted from the room like her arse was on fire. She hadn't known about her lover boy vanishing and counted that as more important than being here. Interesting.

I held my focus on the lawyer. "Darcy Marchant?"

His gaze touched mine, then he reached for the paperwork. "I believe a short break is necessary to restore order to the room. Adjourned, ten minutes."

The arsehole stood and weaved through the throng. I stormed after him, passing the uncle and grandmother Mila claimed we shared but I'd never recognised.

The grandmother's expression was a rigid neutral.

I couldn't tell if she'd known.

In the hall, I grasped the lawyer by the shoulder and spun him around. "Who the fuck is this new sibling?"

He or she couldn't be much younger than Mila because of the age our birth father died. It was possible they were older than me, though Able had knocked up my mother when he was sixteen which made it unlikely.

That meant for over twenty years, another Marchant heir had existed and been entirely unknown. Mila would have told me if she'd had a hint.

More importantly, their vote held all the power.

The lawyer twitched his moustache. "I'm not at liberty

to discuss confidential information—"

I put my forearm up as a bar and drove it into his throat, pushing him against the wall. Then I lifted so his feet kicked. "Male or female?"

"F-female," he spluttered and clutched my arm.

"Age?"

"Twenty-seven."

"Does she use the name Marchant?"

"N-no. We have been unable to find her using her birth name."

Which meant that like me, Darcy wanted nothing to do with this family. My mother had treated them like a den of vipers, teaching me not to trust a word any of them said, particularly their lawyers.

A shocked intake of breath came from a woman down the hall. I didn't stop.

"What does she go by?"

"We don't know."

I put more pressure on his throat, leaning in until I was centimetres from his face. "But ye have an idea. Ye wouldn't have held the meeting at all unless there was a chance she'd come."

His eyes leaked tears. "We employed a private detective to search for her."

"And they found something." I didn't phrase it as a question, because otherwise we wouldn't be here.

The lawyer shook his head jerkily in the negative. "We hoped they would. The family provided a picture. We've done everything we can to track her down."

Fuck them and the horse they rode in on. Mila's grandmother knew Mila had a sister and never said a word. What a bitch. "Show me and I'll let you live."

He reached for his pocket. Found a phone. Then he held up a photo of a young teenager. Even if the picture was over a decade out of date, I recognised her. The set of her jaw was all Mila, though I'd never made the connection when I'd seen her in the flesh only a week or two ago.

She'd had surgery to change her appearance, going from girl next door to bombshell.

I dropped the lawyer to a heap on the floor and strode away.

48

Convict

Someone gripped my jaw, turning my head to the side. "You could've killed him."

"Sorry, sir. It was unintentional. He ducked."

My brain went fuzzy, and I missed the rest of her explanation. I knew the man's voice, though. It was the cop from my hospital room. The man who'd read my chart, laughed, and walked away. He'd told my crew I was dead for his own entertainment.

Cassie had called him Detective Dickhead, but his real name was... I searched my memories. *Kenney.*

Holy shit. The jolt to the brain apparently helped.

I struggled up on my elbows and blinked open my eyes. My hands were cuffed, a chain leading beneath me. I was laid out on a tabletop in what looked like a disused office, the furniture dated and battered, though the place was otherwise clean. Across the room, two police officers raised their heads.

I gazed at Kenney, a lumbering oversized man in his fifties or maybe early sixties, still fit, but with a gut that said he didn't work out so much anymore now he was closing in on retirement.

His face triggered a new recollection.

Instead of seeing a jackass who'd teased my crew, a darker memory surfaced. Of cash and a secret bank account.

A meeting in a dark alley like something out of a police procedural show. At last, I had the whole picture.

Thank *fuck*. I could've laughed.

"You tried turning me into an informant."

His eyes flared wide, and he dismissed the other officer with a snapped word. The door banged at her back.

I held my gaze on him. "That's why I took a cash job for the Four Milers. It was to give you what you'd paid for."

Another piece of information flooded in. Arran knew. He'd suspected that others would dive in on me after he publicly kicked me out of the crew, and he'd been right.

I fell back on the table surface with a gasp of utter relief. I hadn't betrayed my friend after all. Nor had I been paid to traffic women in order to line my own pocket. The burden I'd been carrying lifted.

My happiness quickly died.

"You stood over my hospital bed. Why the fuck didn't you tell my crew where I was?"

He scoffed. "Which crew was that?"

Right, because I was supposed to have left Arran behind. I worked through his thinking. Kenney had sat back and waited to see where I ended up. Had he sent his daughter in to spy, or was she in the dark, too?

The big cop's eyes gleamed. "So Daniels welcomed you back with open arms. Did you remember yet how much you hated him? How his actions put you in that hospital?"

I tightened my jaw and kept my mouth shut. Kenney was trying something. He just had to spit it out.

The cop smiled. "He's playing you, kid. He's relying on that amnesia and you forgetting just how shitty he treated you. You have a chance to make a lot of money, but not at his hands."

Not satisfied with whatever I'd gathered on the Four

Milers, he'd wanted more.

Kenney strolled to the window, hands in his pockets. "Don't get me wrong, I also enjoyed Daniels thinking you were dead. I was hoping he'd feel guilty, but do you know he laughed when he found out? Doesn't that piss you off? Daniels never searched all that hard for you, but I protect my own. You were right that I was recruiting you. Join my payroll. Work for me. He'll never know, and you can have your revenge on him."

There was no way I'd take the deal. I didn't believe him. I couldn't even fake it to offer my crew another chance at being undercover. I was done with lying.

Lying...

My brain rebooted. *Mila. The meeting.*

Fuck! I was going to be late.

Scrambling on the table, I managed to sit up and wrenched at the cuffs. "Get these off me, I need to go."

"You're not going anywhere. You took my money and you owe me information."

"I don't owe you shit."

She'd think I abandoned her. Even if she read the note, there was no way I could get back for the start of the meeting. I didn't even know what the time was. I patted my pockets, moving my chained-up hands from one side to the other. Nothing.

"Where's my phone?"

Purposefully, the cop folded his arms and returned to lean against the door, the only exit from the room. "I'll make this as plain as possible. You're on probation. Daniels has splashed the cash to keep you off the radar in Deadwater. That means you're valuable to him, not as a friend, don't get him wrong, but because he's suspicious of what you'll get up to in your spare time. He already suspects you. So you have a choice. Go back to him, play nice, supply the harmless bits of information I ask for, as I need them, or I'll drive you to prison myself."

Any easiness in him faded to cold, hard truth. "Believe me, I can invent multiple ways for your sentence to be extended once you're there. You'll find yourself in a lot of fights behind bars, Convict. You may never get out."

If he thought I'd accept, he was dreaming. Yet I had no way out of this room apart from through him.

And no one had a clue where I'd gone.

49

The moment we came to a halt, I leapt from the car, my heart constricted in fear. When I'd flown out of the lawyer's office, Tyler had stepped from a shadowy corner and taken control. He'd driven me to Leith in Edinburgh where Arran and Shade were heading with other members of the skeleton crew.

Convict had been seen being put into the back of a police car. His friends had rushed to his aid.

According to updates Tyler received as he drove, Convict hadn't left the port area.

Under the cover of a garage down a narrow street, the leader of the crew watched my approach, his enforcer alongside plus a few others I didn't know.

"Where is he?" My breathing came ragged as if I'd been running, not sitting still for over an hour of agonised travelling.

Arran tipped his head at a window onto another street. "Inside the building at the end of the row."

"What are we waiting for?"

He shrugged as if weighing up a detail. "Leverage."

Shade took over. "That building is used for police surveillance. We've known about it for some time but couldn't get blueprints. Nor do we know how many cops are inside, and it's broad fucking daylight. None of us can walk in there or even past it without risking being made."

"I can," I blurted. "Send me in. Give me a gun."

He rolled his eyes. "Stand down, Annie Oakley. You've been seen around with Convict enough to put ye in the same category. If we fuck this up, we lose our edge."

Frustration had me mangling my fingers together. "So what, we just sit and wait? They could be doing anything to him. They might have moved him elsewhere already." A thought occurred to me. "How do you even know he's in there?"

Arran eyed his enforcer. "Tell her what you did."

Shade didn't flinch. "On the night he came back from hospital, returned to us from the dead, I shot a tracker into him."

From nearer the window where he kept watch on the street, Tyler gave a quiet laugh.

I shook my head. I couldn't be affronted on Convict's behalf. Not when this was the only way we had to find him. "Then what's the plan? Please tell me we aren't going to wait until dark."

An engine purred, and the garage doors cranked open to admit another vehicle.

Driven by Manny, Lovelyn was in the passenger seat. She climbed out and ran a cautious gaze across us, her shoulders going down an inch when she spotted me. "What's going on?"

Arran's single word returned to me. Leverage. Lovelyn was the daughter of a police officer. They were going to use her? New panic washed over me at the thought of the gentle and smart woman turned pawn or even hurt.

"Lovelyn's here to gain access to the police building, correct?" I said.

Lovelyn swung her soft gaze between us. "Manny told me Convict is in the safe house. If you need to get inside, I can walk right in. Is that what you need?"

Tension held the air taut. Arran exchanged a glance with his crew, and at a nod from Shade, it broke. He commenced an explanation, bringing her into the planning, and I withered inside.

I'd potentially just protected my friend at a cost to the man I loved. No, I couldn't think like that. We'd get him back without anyone else getting hurt. We had to.

My phone buzzed with a call from my brother.

"Where are ye?" he said.

"Leith. We're trying to work out how to get him back."

"Good. I just heard where the crew had gone so wanted to make sure you had that information."

I clutched the phone tighter. "Aw, don't do things like that or I might think you care."

He made an off sound and didn't answer.

"What happened after I left the meeting? Did Jacobs show?"

"No. It descended into anarchy, and the lawyer ran away."

I pressed my fingertips to my forehead. "It's all such a mess. I was wrong about the other businesses having trusted company status so getting a vote. What a waste of time, chasing after Jacobs."

"Your grandfather rewrote the will recently. For all we know, that's what he'd intended. Looking back with regret is pointless. It gets us nowhere."

He was right. All I cared about now was saving Convict.

Kane continued. "I grabbed the lawyer for information on the fifth voter."

I released a breath of disbelief, that nugget of information barely featuring against my towering worry for the man I cared about. "You mean our sibling."

"Congratulations, ye have a sister."

A sister. God. "*We* do, and what else did you find out? Do you know where she is?"

"No, but I will."

Lovelyn said something close to me, and Kane paused.

"Is Lovelyn there?"

"She is. Arran thinks she might be able to help us."

He swore and hung up.

Great.

There was nothing else for it but to plot a scheme. It had to work. I couldn't accept another outcome. I needed Convict freed, even if I was the reason he'd walked away.

50

Lovelyn

A daily battle came with the way my mind worked. I was a data girl and a strategist. I saw patterns others missed, and I could produce and assess the best ways to reach a goal.

Such as extracting a criminal from the clutches of the police.

Police that included my father. I knew he was here because his shiny new car was outside the safe house, a fact Arran had apparently already gathered.

And intended to use against me.

On the other hand, my mind rejected logic and belly flopped into emotion. I cried at the smallest thing. At random acts of kindness. At a grandpa walking a child to the park. Send me a good news story about a dog rescue, and I'd be sobbing at the supermarket checkout.

It hurt to see the concern shared by Mila and the crew as they discussed Convict. They all loved him.

I wanted to help. Even if doing so pitted me against my flesh and blood. I was also highly aware of what it would mean if I refused.

Mila might have framed my being here as helpful, sweet girl that she was, but I had no doubt Arran would've used me as hostage if we hadn't come up with another plan.

My father made playing both sides look so easy. For me, it felt the opposite, like I was walking a tightrope in a hurricane.

We were close to agreeing on our course of action when the garage doors rattled open. Kane drove in and parked his car in a mechanic's bay. He climbed out, and his gaze came to me and stayed there.

A chill shot down my spine.

His sister greeted him. "I wondered if you were going to show up."

Kane kicked back against a metal pillar. "Is Lovelyn needed for the extraction?"

I nodded. "I can walk straight in there. Nobody else has that access."

His dark eyes didn't leave me, something in his vision I couldn't get a read on. I held very still, a prey animal in the sights of a predator.

Tyler tilted his head at the man. "You could go with her."

Kane finally blinked that heavy focus off me and regarded the intercept man. "Elaborate."

"Lovelyn's going to walk in, and we have a plan for what happens once she's inside, but it carries risk. She's unprotected, and there's a gap in how we handle whoever's in the way of getting Convict out, if they don't take her bait." Tyler's gaze sharpened. "You can do that handling. My ear to the ground tells me you're unknown as a skeleton crew associate. Congratulations on your temporary promotion to Lovelyn's new boyfriend."

My mouth popped open. "My what now?"

Kane shrugged. "I'm down. Catch me up on who I need to walk through."

Just like that, I'd been paired off.

In minutes, we were prepped and strolling down the street.

"Put your arm in mine, flower girl," Kane ordered.

I pressed my lips together then neutralised my expression and slipped my arm through his. Good God. He towered over me, but I'd had no idea how muscular the man was. Thick, hard biceps curled as I rested my hand in the crook of his arm.

That latent power did something strange to my stomach. I had to battle to keep the reaction off my face. He was just another one of the skeleton crew, dangerous, morally grey, and bad to know.

Ahead, the safe house loomed, a brown-brick, ex-office building. Nothing to set it apart from any other on the street.

I scanned the cars. Though the road was a dead end and therefore without through traffic, it was off a high street and most parking spots were filled. "The gold Mercedes is my father's. At a guess, I'd say the grey Volvo and maybe the dark-blue Polo are police."

"How do ye know?"

"I'm not giving up trade secrets."

"After this is over, don't go anywhere. I need to talk to ye."

I blinked up at Kane. He stared dead ahead.

"What about?"

He didn't answer. It was too late anyway, because we were there, in front of the side access with its discreet number pad. I keyed in the code. The door popped inwards.

Stepping over the welcome mat, I breathed through my nose to calm my racing heart, then walked the hall. The first room had previously been a reception and was often where coats and equipment bags were thrown by the officers who used this building for surveillance. Despite being called a safe house, its purpose was a base of operations for any undercover police action in Leith. Nothing safe about it.

We bypassed that, and I checked the other lower rooms. Nothing.

"No cameras," Kane observed.

"Technically, this place doesn't exist, so nope."

"Meaning anything goes."

I shivered at his implication and took to the stairs. I called out a warning as I climbed. "Julian?"

Kane spoke under his breath: "Who the fuck is Julian?"

"My father."

"You don't call him 'Dad'?"

I shook my head.

"Better than Detective Dickhead," he grouched almost silently.

I couldn't stop an unexpected laugh. Though I knew the nickname used by Arran's crew, seldom did they use it in front of me. "Don't censor yourself on my behalf."

"Never will."

We reached the landing, and I entered another code to access the level. Past the door, Kane slipped into a room with all the blinds closed, vanishing into the shadows.

I called out again, this time adding the first words of our plan. "Julian? What's with the workmen outside?"

A door swung open, and an officer stuck her head out. She squinted at me. "Lovelyn? What's going on?"

I lowered my voice and smiled. "Oh, hi, Jacqueline. Are you parked outside? You might want to move your car. They said they were about to tow vehicles, I think for some work on the street."

Jacqueline heaved a sigh. "There's always something. I'm done here anyway. Thanks for the warning." She packed up a rucksack.

I hovered at the open door to the room she'd been working in. "Anyone else around I need to warn?"

"Only your dad, sweetheart. See you soon."

Jacqueline's footsteps rattled down the stairs, then the street door banged.

She hadn't noticed Kane's presence. Good, as I didn't love the boyfriend alibi. No one would pick him for me.

I stifled a frisson of fear at what I was doing. Adrenaline and I were never friends. Kane appeared from his hiding spot and followed me down the hall. My father had a favourite space he used here, and he was always a creature of habit.

The door was locked, so I rapped on the obscured glass. Kane slid into an opposite room, out of sight once more.

"Busy," my father yelled back.

"It's Lovelyn. There's some kind of work going on outside. There was dust or fumes billowing up when I came in. I thought I should tell you because it's going to set off the—"

An alarm wailed.

"Smoke alarm," I said with a forced laugh.

My father opened the door, using his body to block any glimpse inside. "Fucking Christ. Can't you stop it?"

I pulled a face against the blaring noise. "I don't know how. I think I saw the panel downstairs. Can you help me?"

He bitched and moaned but locked the door, slipping the key into his pocket. Together, we descended the stairs. Smoke billowed through a vent near the door.

That was my part of the plan done, and it had gone like clockwork. Convict had to be in that room, else Julian would've no doubt dragged me in to handle some task he didn't want to do.

All I could hope for now was that the skeleton crew lived up to their reputation. And my father hadn't done anything I couldn't fix.

51

Convict

A thud hit my door. Another, then it burst open, and Kane shoulder-barged through.

I huffed a laugh. "Bad brother."

"You've had weeks to come up with a nickname, and that's all you've got?"

He advanced on my table, and I lifted my chained hands.

"Get me out of here and I'll think up something better." I paused. "That only applies if you're here to rescue and not murder me."

He brought out a dull metal tool from his pocket and didn't meet my eyes. "Shut the fuck up or I'll change my mind and leave ye here."

He worked the cuffs.

I caught up from my surprise at seeing him. Of all the crew members I'd daydreamed breaking down my door while the cop tried every which way to recruit me, I hadn't expected this man. "Why aren't you at the Marchant meeting? Thought the vote was unmissable."

"Long story. Mila can explain it when we get out."

"She's here?"

"Don't ask me why. She seems to like ye."

I swallowed and slumped back on the table, my heart pounding. "I'm going to marry the shit out of your sister. Just saying."

Kane shuddered and released my hands. "Make sure there's an open bar. My 'I object' speech will go down easier with whisky."

The cuffs fell away. Climbing up, I shook out my limbs, winced, and added 'saved by her brother' to the list of things I'd never emotionally recover from.

I moved to the door, but Kane stopped me.

"Can't go downstairs. We gassed it."

"You knocked out Kenney. Wait, and Lovelyn?"

"Lovelyn needs plausible deniability, and I wasn't about to haul your heavy arse through the streets wearing a gas mask."

He approached the tall windows and peered out. I joined him. We were only one storey up, but there was nothing below us but an empty yard. Not a handhold on the plain brick.

"So we're just going to jump?"

Kane shrugged and pulled on a skeleton crew bandanna, handing me another. "Unless ye learned to fly while in police custody?"

Despite myself, I laughed. "Let's do it."

The scramble over the windowsill was oddly reminiscent of how I'd met Mila. Except that was a thousand times more romantic than having her brother's arse loom above me.

Taking care to keep my recently healed leg raised, I lowered to my fingertips then dropped to the concrete below. I hit the ground and rolled, bouncing back up with a quick sense check telling me I'd stuck the landing.

Kane thudded heavily in a crouch beside me, his fingertips touching the ground. He shoved me and flashed a grin. I shoved him back and crept to the wall and the thick metal gate that led on to the road.

A digi-lock secured the gate. I could scramble over it,

but the height of the wall had obscured anything directly behind it from our window view.

Apparently, Kane had eyes on the street, as he listened to an earpiece I hadn't noticed, then paused me. "There's a cop sitting in her car outside, apparently on a phone call. We're going to have to run for it. The crew will pick us up on the move. Keep up, lover boy."

With two strides back for a run-up, Kane vaulted the wall. He was gone in a flash. I sucked in a breath and didn't waste a second more, following him over.

He was already halfway across the road when I landed and ran.

A car door cracked open. "Hey!" a woman yelled.

The static of radio chatter chased us. I didn't give a damn. I was free. I bolted down the streets of Leith as I probably had hundreds of times before, keeping Kane in my sights.

He ducked down an alley, pausing to be sure I saw him hop another wall, then we jumped fences in back gardens. We were taking a cut through in case we were pursued.

The further we ran, the closer we got to the crashing of waves, and I burst out the end of a lane directly into a crowd at the harbour.

Excitement was high, and all eyes were on some kind of operation in the docks. Kane grasped my arm and towed me, but I caught sight of what had drawn everyone's attention. Across the water, a crane lifted the prow of a red-and-white boat.

The *Eden* was being resurrected.

Why that gave me a more sickened feeling than my imprisonment was anyone's business.

We threaded through the throng and out onto Ocean Drive.

Next to where the Glass House used to sit, a vehicle waited, partially blocking the road. Arran's car. I nearly cried. Kane almost threw me inside, slammed the door, and smacked his hand down on the frame with a shout for us to go.

Across the back seat, Mila reached for me, and I fell on her, Arran and Tyler giving relieved greetings while we sped the fuck out of town.

At last, I could breathe again.

Or pass the fuck out. That worked, too.

52

Mila

In a race, we sped down the coastal road, back to Deadwater. Arran might have used subterfuge to get Convict back, but he was giving a clear message to whoever watched us returning home. The four big, black vehicles drove in a tight formation, fast and direct.

No one got in our way.

I cradled Convict's head on my lap. His breathing was steady and his temperature okay, but a red mark stained his temple. God only knew from what. Arran had been on the phone to a medic who'd told us to take him straight to hospital.

It terrified me what they might say.

I stroked his hair and tried to control my spiralling panic.

We rolled into Deadwater's Scottish suburbs and crossed the bridge to the English side, arriving at the hospital's Accident and Emergency drop-off.

Tyler opened the back door, but it was Arran who collected Convict from the seat and carried him to a waiting gurney.

A fifty-something doctor whisked us straight into a consultation room without batting an eye at the crew members who populated the ward after us.

She questioned us, ran tests including a CT scan, then moved us into a private room to await the results.

Still, he didn't wake.

Quietly, I panicked over him being here and not safe in the warehouse. Was he a wanted man? I didn't think he'd been under arrest, at least not officially, but running away from the police while on probation couldn't help that cause.

I twisted my fingers together with anxiety.

Arran held up a sentinel's position next to the door. "He'll be okay. Other than hating being here."

"What if he isn't?"

"He has the hardest skull of anyone I ever met. He took enough hits to it as a kid."

My heart squeezed. "But he wouldn't know if it hurt, would he? What if he missed the warning signs? What if I did? Then the police hurt him somehow."

He'd run with Kane, who'd vanished since, then passed out the moment he got into the car. I didn't know if it was the effort or some other combination of factors, but the fact he still hadn't woken terrified me.

I picked up his hand and held it, a drip in the back keeping him hydrated. "He left this morning before I woke. Why was he in Leith? Do you know?"

The intimidating gang leader twisted his lips. "No. But I know where he was seen being put into the back of the police car. My informant told me he appeared unconscious, then."

He named the road and the building Convict had been outside of.

Our Marchant dockside warehouse.

I couldn't make sense of it. Why not wake me if that's where he intended to go? Realisation crept in. "He didn't want me there because of what he might find. It has to be."

Arran made a sound of gruff agreement. There was pity in his eyes.

My emotions churned all the more. I gently set down his hand then paced to the window and jammed my fingers into my hair. "If he was hurt because of my family, I won't forgive them. I won't forgive myself. I brought him into this mess. If the man I love—"

"Whoa. Now she finally says it?"

I spun around. Convict pushed up onto one elbow, scrubbing his eyes with his free hand.

I rushed to his side. "You're awake."

He reached out and pulled me onto the bed with him, then eyed Arran. "In the nicest possible way, please fuck off for five minutes."

His friend watched for a beat, relief in his smirk alongside a dozen questions. He left us anyway.

The door closed, and Convict palmed my cheek.

"Say it again."

I pressed my lips to his. He took over, holding me to receive his devastating kiss and showing me he felt the same desperation I did. Then he broke away.

"Again, Emilia."

"I love you."

Convict held up his finger and marked the air. A point to him. Yet another game. I burst into tears and hugged him hard.

"One more time," he demanded into my hair.

"I love you. I should've told you."

The wonder in his eyes and his smile of happiness nearly broke me.

"I don't deserve you, but I'm keeping you anyway." He tipped his head to the door. "Pull that curtain around and get naked. We have four minutes left."

I choked on my tears and laughed. "You've been out cold

for two hours. No way am I getting your blood pressure up again. Or anything else for that matter."

"I need you. I've waited all my life for someone to love me."

My heart swelled, and I stroked his cheek, flushed red with warmth. "Then I'll spend the rest of my life showing it to you so you never miss out again."

A knock rattled the door. Arran opened it a few inches without looking in. "The doc's back. If you're given the all clear, I'll get you out of here."

Convict allowed me to hop off the bed, but I kept his hand held tight in mine.

The doctor entered and ran her critical gaze over Convict. "Mr Locke, I'm glad to see you're conscious. Tell me what you remember."

He glanced at me then spoke of getting caught trespassing and tasered by the police. The next thing he knew was waking up in the safe house. The mark on his forehead was from electricity? Nausea churned my belly.

The doctor listened carefully. "I've reviewed the results of your scan. Considering the injury, you were lucky. A Taser incident like that could cause a fracture, haemorrhage, or even seizure-like activity. However, I am glad to say I discovered no new fracture and no bleed. You are concussed, though. That is likely the reason for your loss of consciousness. I recommend remaining here in the hospital where we can keep an eye on you."

Convict shook his head, his lips flattened. "No chance. Tell me what to look out for?"

She sighed though didn't seem surprised. "Headache, confusion, balance issues, and any other instances of loss of consciousness, then you need to be coming straight back in here. Do you understand?"

He blinked. "Perfectly, thanks. Can I go?"

"Against my better judgement, yes."

He punched the air.

Arran's phone buzzed. He read the screen. "What do you know, Detective Dickhead is in the building. Want to say hi?"

Immediately, the doctor stood. "I need to see other patients. Stay out of trouble, Mr Locke."

I stared after her. She'd been paid off. More and more, I understood the sphere of influence the skeleton crew wielded. But I didn't get Arran teasing about Chief Constable Kenney.

"We need to go," I said.

Convict watched his friend. "Or not. Is he here alone or mob-handed?"

"Tyler says alone."

"Let him come in."

I swung my gaze between them. "What are you doing?"

Convict squeezed my hand. He'd never let go. "Showing him that the tables have turned. I won't run scared in my own city."

The door opened, and Tyler ducked under the frame, his expression stony. He and Arran vanished into the private bathroom. Through the gap in the door, Shade guarded the opposite side of the corridor. I knew Manny and others to be around, too, but that didn't settle my rising fear.

I'd only just got him back. I wouldn't let him be taken again.

A stomping came down the hall, then the door burst open. The big police officer entered the room.

On the bed, Convict reclined. "What, no fruit basket? I want my grapes."

Kenney's lip curled. He didn't even glance at me. "We weren't done talking, as I recall."

"Didn't take you for clingy, but I was well over your bad breath in my face."

"You little shit. I should—"

"You should what? Lie to my crew about me? Try to recruit me as a narc? Cover up for trafficking?"

Kenney stalled. Likewise, I'd gone still.

Convict kept hold of my hand. "I mean, on the scale of bad cop to Netflix True Crime documentary, you trying to persuade me that Arran hated me is nothing compared with ignoring my telling you about a trafficked woman."

Kenney's jaw tightened. "I don't know what you're talking about."

"Right, of course. Just a casual threat to have me thrown back in jail for crimes I didn't commit. Classic banter. You were on fire this morning. Real highlight reel stuff. Sorry to piss on your parade by leaving early."

"Like I said, we weren't done talking. Tell your bitch to get out and I'll finish my piece."

"His bitch is going nowhere," I snarked back.

Finally, Kenney glanced my way. Something strange passed over his expression, then he switched his focus back to Convict. "A Marchant? Ironic, considering your shared background. Still want her here if we're exposing exactly what you reported to me? Be a shame to ruin this little love-in when she hears what you colluded with her family on. Do you want to say or should I?"

Convict's gaze darkened. "You knew the Four Milers trafficked women who came in on boats. How many of them did you save?"

Wait, what?

Arran took a single, menacing step into the room, Tyler at his shoulder. "Where the fuck do you get off, Kenney?"

The cop's shoulders rose an inch. "Hiding in dark

corners, Daniels?"

Arran tilted his head, the effect unnerving. "Don't forget, I know where you've buried the bodies. Piss me off any more and watch your career go up in flames. I'll gladly give up your usefulness to see you behind bars for life."

"Don't forget it works both ways. We had a deal," Kenney snarled.

Arran's tone stayed glacier-cold. "And you took my fucking crew member off the street, nearly killing him. Now make your choice. Push this or get the fuck out of this room. I'm dying to see what you pick."

The cop swept his gaze across us all, swore, and stormed out the way he'd come. Tyler and Arran pursued him to the hall, and I gazed down at Convict.

"I'm not going to like what you have to tell me, am I?"

"No. I'm sorry for that."

"Can we at least go home first?"

We left the hospital and travelled the short distance back to my apartment, Arran promising a guard overnight and a full discussion the following day.

We kicked off our shoes, and Convict guided me to the bedroom.

On the rug in front of the silvered mirror, he peeled off my t-shirt. "We have all the time to talk tonight, but if I don't get my hands on you, I'll have a heart attack. Forgive me for breaking our four-hour rule?"

I raised a shoulder, letting my bra slide off that he'd unclipped. The flare of lust in his eyes generated pure need that coasted through me.

"I'm guessing there's some kind of penance you pay in this circumstance?"

He kissed my throat. "I can think of something."

I was certain he could.

This time when I was fully naked, I had no bandanna concealing the view of his hands and inked-up arms roaming my body. His feverish attentions to my flesh.

"On your back, I need to look into your eyes," he ordered.

I obeyed, welcoming him into my arms and the cradle of my hips. I loved this man. Wait, I needed to say it.

I tore my mouth from his. "I love you so much."

"Tell me. Exactly. I need to know."

I stroked his dark hair from his eyes so I didn't miss a single reaction. "I love your carefree spirit and how wild and adventurous you are. I am crazy about the way you're such an open book. You wear your heart on your sleeve, and I'm the luckiest woman in the world that this heart is mine."

Convict shivered.

I wasn't done. "You are loyal, faithful, and you're so giving."

He bucked against me, and I groaned, already wet. Needing him more than I ever thought possible.

"Every time I want anything, you're there. You are the kindest and most thoughtful man I've ever known, and although you say you don't deserve me, it's the other way around. From the very start, you've been all in, and I was the one holding back. All those big statements you made, that I was yours, that you were keeping me, that you loved me, I doubted it all. Except it was true."

He pressed his lips to mine. "I've got one to add to the list: I'm marrying you one day."

Damn. I whimpered. "All my doubt changed the moment I thought I'd lost you. I couldn't bear it. I'm so sorry for not sharing my heart earlier, but it one hundred percent belongs to you."

Convict ran his hand down my leg and picked it up, curling it around his back. He repeated the act with my other leg then fitted his dick to my entrance. He drove inside me and groaned.

Echoing the sound, I closed my eyes against the strength of feeling, so great I never wanted to recover from it.

When I opened them again, he stared down at me, his emotions right there in his tortured expression.

"I changed my mind."

I blinked. "What about?"

"I've decided I do deserve you. In fact, we deserve each other because we fought everything to make this work. I love you. I'm yours, always. Now hold on tight while I fuck that knowledge into you so neither of us ever forget."

He filled me, teased me, then put on a burst of speed that sent me so far over the ledge, I almost lost my mind from the pleasure.

When he came, I held him to me, too aware of his head injury.

"Still alive?" I asked.

"If I'm not, Hell looks nice."

"Then let's stay."

"If you're here? Always, little gangster."

53

Mila

On the sofa, freshly showered and very, very satisfied, I curled up with Convict while the sun set, and he explained what he'd realised in the early hours. The memory of a woman that had been so powerful he'd followed it all the way to my family's warehouse.

It hurt to hear his trafficking suspicion, but I was glad he didn't hide it.

"You told Kenney all this?" I asked.

"I did, though not that I was undercover. He did fuck all about it, suggesting he didn't have the opportunity or more likely that he's been paid not to hear. Tyler gets tip-offs from the police sometimes. No reason not to do it then."

"For Lovelyn's sake, I hope it's the former."

He brushed his thumb over my knuckles in a way that told me not to bet on it. "Do you blame me for taking the job?"

"Of course not. You were acting under orders and gave the information to the police. What else could you have done?"

"Not deliver the woman to the brothel. All I can think is that she probably died in that fire or suffered some other awful fate."

"If you hadn't taken her there, someone else would've. You weren't responsible."

But some other man was.

He watched me carefully. "Do you know if your family ever paid off officials? Maybe customs?"

He meant my grandfather. I swallowed. "Not that I knew of. Call me naïve if you want, but I still can't think that my grandfather would do something like this. If only you knew him. He was the gentlest, kindest man. He was always respectful, and he took care of everyone. Me, his extended family, his employees. I never once heard him make a poor taste comment, even as a joke. No one had a bad word to say about him."

Aside from the anonymous emails, though I had my suspicions.

"I can't explain why Presley was there either. My grandfather didn't like him. He never worked for the business, though his mother asked that my grandfather give him a job."

Convict snapped his fingers. "That's his name. I'd forgot and called him Mini Marchant-Smythe. Pissed him off even more. Feels right that he'd be hating on the business. He said something that might not be nice to hear."

"Tell me anyway."

"That he wanted to know if your grandfather had lined his cabin in gold like his coffin."

I wrinkled my nose. "That doesn't make any sense. He didn't even have a cabin on the *Eden*—"

My words dried up. I reached for my phone.

Ever since getting home, I'd ignored it to get wrapped up in my boyfriend. But Presley's words were too specific.

They were a clue.

When I unlocked my screen, I almost wished I hadn't.

Multiple news articles flooded in from an alert I had on the Marchant Haulage name. The *Eden* had been raised, and with it came a rush of interest in the company's inbox.

Convict busied himself with organising dinner, claiming he was fine and I needed to stop worrying, and I sorted through the messages, forwarding any requests for interview or comment to the caretaker company and not bothering to ask my grandmother if she wanted to make a statement.

Then I shot a message to Lovelyn, asking if she'd seen any police write-up of what they'd found, as the newspaper articles were light on detail of anything other than the salvage operation.

No reply came.

I hoped she was okay after waking from the knockout gas.

Lastly, I hovered over the folder for the hate mail I'd received. Right where the clue had led.

Opening it, I selected the top one and hit reply.

MarchantHaulage: Give it up, Presley. It's all over.

A minute later, and a single-word reply came in.

Anonymous: Bitch.

I laughed and showed it to Convict. "That bitter little asshole, sending messages like that because the gravy train had run dry. Maybe he'll grow up and get a job now."

"You sound like me."

I did. I'd changed a lot in the past month or two. Gone was the woman who believed blindly in the family business, and replacing her was someone stronger. Someone in search of the truth, even if it hurt.

At my throat, I picked up the gold-and-diamond necklace with my initial. "I swore I'd wear this to never forget my grandfather."

But until I knew...

I went to take it off.

Convict stopped me. "We don't know for sure yet. There's an outside chance someone else in the company is doing this."

"Without him knowing?" I huffed a laugh. "I'm becoming cynical, and you're speaking from your heart. We've swapped roles."

"We've swapped a lot of things."

He closed my hand over the pendant. "Keep it on until we're certain. Hold out hope. That's how I won you."

True. I let it fall back into place.

"There's something else I discovered today. I've got a sister."

To Convict's stunned expression, I explained the revelation of Darcy, the missing Marchant grandchild.

At least in that, I didn't need to be the one on the hunt. Kane would find her. I already knew it. He'd seek her out with the hope that when the board meeting was next convened, we could vote three to two and get the money flowing again. Maybe after that, a wind-down programme could be agreed for the business. I didn't much care anymore, so long as it didn't cut beneficiaries off at the knees.

Other questions, such as who killed Esther, were still up in the air.

Our dinner arrived, as did a crew member with Convict's car plus a new phone, Manny giving him a three-strike count for how many he'd now had.

I ate and mused on that other mystery.

With all the drama around my family, I hadn't forgotten

that loss of life. From the first hint that it might be connected, my mind had toyed with the idea, twisting it over and trying to find any more clues.

My phone buzzed, and I nearly dropped my fork at the name on my screen.

"It's my uncle. Finally, texting me after all that silence."

Convict snorted. "Probably pissed off because the will reading never happened and he didn't get his payday."

> **Wallace:** I saw the men you had waiting outside the lawyer's place. One had the markings of the gang that runs that sex club in town.

My shoulders bunched around my ears. Then I loosened the tension. By association, I was skeleton crew now. They were Convict's people. I wouldn't let him talk shit about them.

A follow-up text came in just as fast.

> **Wallace:** So... Can you get me membership?

I shuddered and tossed my phone to the coffee table. Yet my mind remained on the warehouse. More specifically, on the games Convict liked to play there with me.

Next time we were there, I'd bring the fun. When I was sure he'd healed, I'd have him chase me around the basement, or maybe blindfold me in the sex club. One thing was certain, aside from my brother, no Marchant relative of mine would ever be allowed in the building.

Convict touched my knee. "You have an interesting expression."

I slid him a look then batted my lashes.

His eyes darkened. "Mila, arms over your head and hold the sofa back. Don't let go unless I say so."

Fine, maybe this time, the game could be all his.

Epilogue

Lovelyn *– a few hours earlier*

In the yard at the back of the safe house, hidden from the street, a medic fussed over my father. We'd been moved outside for fresh air once the short-acting knockout gas had worn off.

He slapped her hand away. "Get to fuck. My blood pressure is fine, and if you attempt to put that mask on me again, I'll arrest you and use it as handcuffs."

The medic recoiled and came to me.

More politely, I refused further treatment. "My head has cleared, thank you."

Jacqueline appeared in the doorway to the building, her expression grim. "It looks like his accomplice picked the cuffs and they went out the window. Sorry, sir."

My father's cheeks reddened. "You let them go, you mean. Two men jump the wall and ran, and all you do is sit in your fucking car and watch them?"

"It happened so fast. I gave chase—"

"While the rest of their gang gassed me. Didn't see them either. Convenient." Fury raged in his eyes.

Jacqueline darted her gaze at me.

I smoothed out a wrinkle in my skirt and set my tone to reasonable. "It's hardly fair to expect her to both chase them and intercept the men who attacked us. She had no warning, and neither did we. If you can tell me who you had up there,

I can help work out what happened."

My father swore. "Police business."

Yeah, right. Anything routine, I knew about. He only hid his under-the-table dealings.

But I knew. I was glad Convict had gotten away.

With a muttered apology, Jacqueline beat a hasty retreat.

"Can you tell me now she's gone?" I asked.

His focus snapped to me. "No. It's also convenient that you walk in and two minutes later I'm unconscious and my mark has gone."

"What mark? You're keeping me in the dark, and that's hardly helpful."

His eyes held mine, thoughts ticking away behind them.

I hated this. I took care not to lie directly as the nerves would consume me, so I placed my words carefully.

"I'm not in the habit of looking too closely at workmen, which you wouldn't either if you were a woman. If I'm walking past a dust storm, I run. I had no idea it was a decoy. Then they gassed me, too. Or did you forget that?"

He didn't acknowledge the explanation I'd already given once we'd woken from a heap in the hallway. "Why are you here, Lovelyn?"

"They're raising the *Eden* today. Wait, did I miss it? I need to go."

Again, not a lie. I was highly curious over what they'd find once that ship was brought out of its watery grave.

There was a reason it had been sunk, and it couldn't be good.

Finally, the weight lifted from Julian's scrutiny, and he scrubbed his bloodshot eyes. "It's already up, according to my messages. If you walk to the dock, you'll see it."

I leapt to my feet with a quick thanks, my head swimming

with the after-effects of the gas.

He paused me. "Not so hasty. I had a piece of intel land on my desk a few days ago. A warning."

My stomach tightened, and I spun back from the gate. "Oh? About what?"

"You. A threat. Maybe don't go out at night for a while."

"A threat to me? What did it say? How did it reach you?"

Without further answer, he strode back inside the building, leaving me to white-knuckle the gate handle. A direct threat to me was new. What was old was how my father gave the information like he didn't care.

I'd find out through other channels, but it hurt how he'd known about this for *days* and said nothing. I pondered if I'd truly damaged a relationship that was important to me, but what had been my alternative? A small voice inside me whispered that if Arran had tried to use me as a hostage, my father wouldn't have taken the bait.

The voice needed to shut the heck up.

Right now, I needed to get over to the harbour.

In a hurry, I fled the safe house and crossed Bernard Street, taking a shortcut through a warren of new-build flats and older buildings, the narrow streets and lanes giving me a quick route up to the area of the harbour where the *Eden* had been moored.

My urgency made me careless.

Hadn't I just heard a warning? It was the lack of detail that made me sloppy. Or perhaps the underlying thought that Julian could've made up a story to scare me because he was pissed off that I'd been around when he'd been bested.

That was my excuse for not looking twice.

On Timber Bush Lane, a dark-coloured van purred along the pavement behind me. I barely gave it a glance, ducking into an archway under a building and pretty certain

I could get all the way to the front this way.

As I walked, I checked the police messaging group my father was a member of that gave CliffsNotes on active operations. An illegal chat, obviously, but always buzzing with gossip and corpse humour that made awful situations bearable, or so I gathered.

Scrolling back, I scanned the pictures of the *Eden* rising from the water then read through the flurry of comments. From the amount, every officer in a hundred-mile radius was intrigued by this boat.

If I had a pound for every dirty secret in that hull, I'd retire and buy a nicer mistress.

Lifted her faster than my ex ever lifted my dick.

Someone crack it open. If there's no coke or corpses, I want my taxpayer money back.

A door clunked open, and something slid on rails.

I kept scrolling, fighting the urge to roll my eyes at how the remarks got cruder the longer they waited for an update from the first camera views inside.

Then I stopped breathing.

A breaking-news style comment gave an update. One that had my heart restarting and the chatter whooping and hollering. *Bodies found inside.* Holy hell. Poor Mila would be devastated. I had to call her. Better to hear it from me and not when the police gifted the media with their field day.

I went to place the call.

A black cloth descended over my head.

I squeaked in shock and lashed out, but a hand clamped over my mouth, smothering me with the material and cutting off my ability to scream. Thick arms picked me up like I weighed nothing and carried me to a vehicle.

It had to be the van I'd ignored, which meant my abductor had followed me here.

I kicked out. Struggled. It made no difference when the door slid closed.

Unlike earlier, I had no idea of who'd attacked me, only of the terror at becoming their prey.

Thank you for reading the first in the *Skeleton Crew* trilogy! We're not done yet. For more clues on the murder mystery and to wander deeper into the twisted world of the missing Marchant, Order *Kane's Prey* now!

Want a bonus scene where Mila designs her own game for Convict? Grab that here:

https://dl.bookfunnel.com/olwyszhoka

(I write free bonus scenes for many of my books. Please note that downloading any adds you to my email reader list. You can unsubscribe at any time with no hard feelings. I keep the list so I can give you publishing updates.)

You can also read along and discuss theories with my very active Facebook reader group. Add yourself here:

https://www.facebook.com/groups/JoliesFallHardFans

ACKNOWLEDGMENTS

Dear reader,

So, you've fallen for Convict.

Was it the scars, the growl, the knives, or the soul-deep ache that did it for you? I know it was all of it. You cracked open Convict's Game and tripped into the arms (and chains) of a broken, brutal man with no memory and no business falling for anyone.

But fall he did. Hard, messy, desperate, and in an instant.

And so did we.

This book took me to some gritty places. Convict's story has haunted the corners of my mind since I first introduced him in Arran's Obsession. From the moment he clawed his way back from the dead with nothing but a name, I knew he'd put me through my paces. His journey is raw, dangerous, and deliciously dark.

And Mila? Our corporate princess with a spine of steel and a soft heart never stood a chance. Not with our man. Not when he's obsessed at first sight and not when he puts her in that gilded cage for his game.

Speaking of games, who do you think the killer is? The breadcrumbs are there (along with a code that you can't crack until book three, so keep hold of that pen and paper), and the bodies aren't done dropping yet. Come join my Facebook reader group and give me your guesses. I love hearing your theories, and also love watching them get blown to pieces as the series unravels. Rather like the Eden.

To my incredible readers. Yes, you. Thank you for riding this morally grey rollercoaster with me. You pick up my books knowing full well there will be sex, sin, blood, and chaos, and still you come back. You're the best kind of unhinged.

To Liz, my powerhouse PA, thank you for being the glue that keeps my author world together. I don't know what I'd do without you. To my beta squad: Elle, Shellie, and Lori—you helped carve Convict into the chaos king he needed to be. (Especially the comments that had me lean harder into the depravity. You're the devils on my shoulder.)

To the incredible narrators, Zara Hampton-Brown, Lucas Webley, Ella Lynch, Shane East, and to Denise and Marnye at Audio Sorceress: you made these characters sound as filthy and feral as they feel. To Amanda for the artwork that made me SO happy to see.

Huge love to my editorial and design dream team: Emmy Ellis, Lori Parks, Erika Levesque, Cleo Moran, Natasha Snow, and Najla Qamber. Your work makes my words shine and my graphics so utterly perfect.

To my ARC and Street Team: your hype and mad love for this story gave me life. Your excitement for this world and the way you share the love with new readers fills my heart. I write in the dark for readers like you.

And to N&M, my sounding boards and reality checks, I love you more than Convict loves surveillance footage.

Now breathe, hydrate, and prepare. Kane and Lovelyn are next, and they're about to rewrite the rules of the game.

Love, Jolie

P.S. You didn't just swoon for a broken bad boy. You fell hard. Welcome to the game, little gangster.

ALSO BY JOLIE VINES

Marry the Scot series
1) Storm the Castle
2) Love Most, Say Least
3) Hero
4) Picture This
5) Oh Baby

Wild Scots series
1) Hard Nox
2) Perfect Storm
3) Lion Heart
4) Fallen Snow
5) Stubborn Spark

Wild Mountain Scots series
1) Obsessed
2) Hunted
3) Stolen
4) Betrayed
5) Tormented

Dark Island Scots series
1) Ruin
2) Sin
3) Scar
4) Burn

McRae Bodyguards

1) Touch Her and Die

2) Save Her from Me

3) Take Her from You

4) Keep Her from Them

Body Count

1) Arran's Obsession

2) Connor's Claim

3) Riordan's Revenge

Body Count novella

1) The Game: the Surgeon and the MMA Fighter

2) The Game: the Billionaire and the Spiked Heel

Standalones

Cocky Kilt:

a Cocky Hero Club Novel

Race You:

An Office-Based Enemies-to-Lovers Romance

Fight For Us:

a Second-Chance Military Romantic Suspense

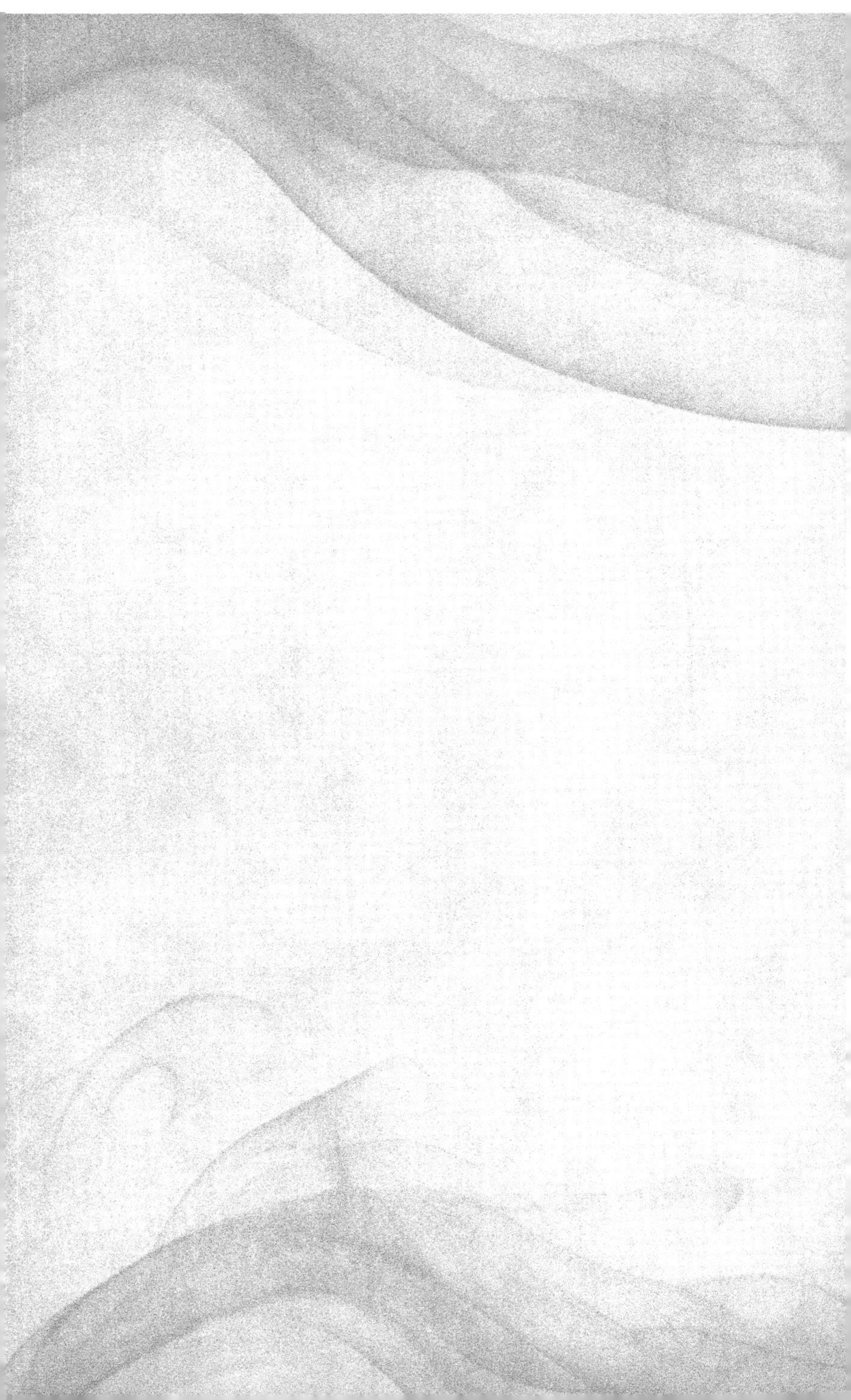

ABOUT THE AUTHOR

JOLIE VINES is a romance author who lives in the UK with her husband and son.

Jolie loves her heroes to be one-woman guys.

Whether they are a brooding pilot (Gordain in Hero), a wrongfully imprisoned rich boy (Sebastian in Lion Heart), or a tormented twin (Max in Betrayed), they will adore their heroine until the end of time.

Her favourite pastime is wrecking emotions, then making up for it by giving her imaginary friends deep and meaningful happily ever afters.

Have you found all of Jolie's Scots?

Visit her page on Amazon

http://amazon.com/Jolie-Vines/e/B07MKS5JSC

and join her ever active Fall Hard Facebook group.

https://www.facebook.com/groups/JoliesFallHardFans